Pesto & Potions

Pesto & Potions

....

Kat Blakely

R.A. Gates

Kelly Haworth

Cheryl Mahoney

....

Stonehenge Circle Press

PESTO & POTIONS

First edition. April 25, 2025

Copyright © 2025 Kat Blakely, R. A. Gates, Kelly Haworth, Cherly Mahoney

ISBN: 978-168 0124538

WRITTEN BY Kat Blakely, R. A. Gates, Kelly Haworth, Cheryl Mahoney

Chapter One: Charlie

Charlie held her breath, and steadied her hand. Carefully, she let one drop of oil fall from a tiny bottle into the shining liquid waiting in the cauldron below. The next drop of St. John's Wort-infused oil glistened on the lip of the bottle. It had taken hours to reach this most delicate and most uncertain point in mixing her healing salve. She'd been making the same salve practically since she was a child, but today she was experimenting. Just a few tweaks to the recipe, a few additions and a few changes to amounts, and if she had calculated correctly the new version should be much more powerful than the traditional one.

As one more drop splashed down, she could almost hear the ping of a distant bell as her magic permeated the salve. Then she leaned closer, watching – the salve had just the right glossy sheen to it, a lovely soft green color, so now all she had to do was let it cool...wait, was that a bubble?

The salve was still warm, but it shouldn't be *bubbling* – unless she had calculated very wrong after all.

A second bubble followed, and a third, and there was no denying this wasn't going to plan.

"No, no, no!" Heart leaping into her throat, she reached for something, anything to cover the bowl, but she was too late. With a massive bubble and a belch, a cloud of smoke rose and warm salve splattered everywhere – across the table, spattering her shelves of jars with their supplies and completed potions, even reaching as far as the bundles of herbs hanging from her ceiling to dry. Not to mention all over her tanktop and bare arms, and even onto her terrier Sammy, who had come trotting in to see what she was yelling about. Sammy circled around her feet, yapping at all the excitement, looking adorable but not making the scene any calmer.

So much for all the work she'd woken up early to do. Charlie groaned, setting down the bottle of oil and feeling guilt clench her stomach as she looked around. Her grandmother had always taken such meticulous care of the workroom. She could almost hear her voice, reminding Charlie that such care was an honoring of their craft.

She had just wanted to try something new, something that wasn't merely going through the motions. The way she had been doing for months.

A discordant jangle broke through Sammy's barks, and for a fleeting moment Charlie was afraid the salve was going to somehow do something even worse – but no, that wasn't a magical sound. It was just her doorbell.

Exactly what she didn't need in the middle of this chaos. She thought of ignoring the bell, but a brisk rapping noise followed. Apparently whoever was at the door was determined. Charlie snatched up a spare cloth and hurried towards her front door, wiping off the worst of the salve on her arms and shirt as she went. Rubbing a stubborn spot and not watching her path, she nearly tripped over Sammy as he wove around her feet, heading to the door too.

"Oh, Sammy, be careful!" she said, catching herself on the lintel of the doorway they were passing through. He just grinned at her, tongue lolling, as though he knew perfectly well *she* should have been watching where she was going.

Her friends in her ballet company would laugh at her if they knew she was being so clumsy this morning. But experimenting with a new recipe and having it literally blow up all over you could throw off even the most graceful person. Not that she was going to tell her friends she'd exploded a magic salve today. Her identity as a witch was firmly removed from her career as a ballerina. Too many people wouldn't understand.

She dropped the cloth on an end table and followed Sammy, who had gone to bark at the door. Almost eleven years old, he didn't move as fast as he used to, but he still always went to greet visitors. She tried not to think that he was still waiting for her grandparents to come home. It had been six months since her grandmother died, nearly five since her grandfather followed. Was that long enough for Sammy to believe they were gone?

She wasn't sure *she* believed that all the time either.

Pushing those thoughts down, an all too familiar effort, Charlie checked through the door's peephole. Two people were standing on her porch – people she didn't want to see but couldn't ignore. You can't just ignore the leader of your coven.

She could tell *them* that she'd exploded a magical salve – if it wasn't all ridiculously embarrassing too. She had even been telling herself, in the early stages of the experiment, that it was so liberating to be working on her own, so freeing to come up with her own ideas. Now it felt like she should have asked for some advice after all.

Charlie wrenched the door open and plastered a smile on her face. "Betty, Esther – how nice to see you!" That sounded mostly sincere.

Sammy pushed past Charlie's legs to dance up to Betty, receiving a pat on the head. His dance was slower than it used to be, but still as enthusiastic as ever. He moved onto Esther, flopping over to present his tummy for a scratch. His feelings about these visitors were clearly less complicated than Charlie's.

The two older women smiled back at Charlie, the sunlight picking up the gray in Betty's hair and the turquoise sheen in Esther's dangling feather earrings. "Good morning, Charlie," Betty said, as Esther nodded a greeting. A leader in all areas of life, it wasn't surprising that Betty was taking charge of this conversation. "I do hope we haven't interrupted you – we wondered if you had any dried arnica that we might borrow?"

Charlie's thoughts flew back to her salve-strewn workroom. "I think I'm all out," she said quickly, not bothering to calculate what she actually had. She rarely had arnica in any great quantities, so she doubted she had any left if the other women didn't.

"Oh, what a pity!" Betty said. "But perhaps we could take a look and make sure?"

And see her disaster of a workroom? It was bad enough that she'd been distant from the Singing River Coven these last few months. What would they think of her if they saw the mess she'd made? It would be too humiliating. "No, I'm sure I'm out," she said. "In fact, I was about to go cut some new herbs from the garden, my supplies are all so low."

"Ah, now that's a good suggestion!" Betty said. "We could select some fresh eucalyptus as a substitute. We'll walk with you."

"Oh. Great," Charlie said flatly. That was what she got for lying. Now she had to pick up the basket and shears she always kept by the door and actually go out to the garden.

It wasn't all bad, though. She breathed in the fresh morning air as they walked through her small backyard towards the community garden beside the house. It was still cool, but with that summer quality that promised hot weather by afternoon. Sammy ambled along happily beside her, and she could hear birdsong in the nearby branches and a distant sound of bells on the breeze, a sign of the magic permeating the garden.

"I'm glad we're doing this," Betty remarked as she lifted the latch on the small side gate into the garden. "We haven't seen enough of you these past few months."

"We've all missed seeing you at our gatherings," Esther said, smiling as warm as the red of her hair – though Charlie was sure the smile was the more genuine of the two.

"I've missed you too," Charlie said, mostly on automatic, realizing only as the words were out that they were true. She *had* missed these women, and the coven they all belonged to. She had not been successful at entirely avoiding Betty in the past few months – Betty was unavoidable – but she had not been involved the way she had before. Because it had been so hard seeing them. Ever since her grandmother died.

Esther moved to a eucalyptus tree and reached up for the nearest branch. Sammy sat down near her, head cocked to one side as he watched her drop leaves into her basket. "Will we see you at our next gathering then?" Esther asked. "You know we'd love to have you there."

Charlie's shoulders stiffened, her mellowed feelings from the garden evaporating. It had taken them, what, two minutes to get to the most fraught issue of all? "I'll have to think about it," she said, and gestured vaguely with her basket and gardening shears. "I was planning to get some – holy basil, so if you'll just excuse me..." She could use holy basil, but she had mostly chosen that herb because she knew it was planted several rows away.

"Marvelous, my supplies of holy basil are low too," Betty said, and fell into step with Charlie. Of course she did. She probably had *plenty* of holy basil. "We *do* hope you'll join us at our next meeting. The coven needs you."

How much could a group of eleven witches need her? They were fine. They had each other.

If they needed anyone, they needed her grandmother. Well, so did Charlie. But that wasn't an option.

"I'll think about it," Charlie repeated, gaze on her feet as they walked.

Betty put one hand on Charlie's arm, a warm and kind gesture that untied some knot inside of Charlie, making her feel simultaneously loved and too vulnerable. "You know we don't want to push you, Charlie, and we don't want to force more sympathy on you than you want. But maybe it's time to come back. We're all here for you, my dear. We'd never try to replace your grandparents, but you don't ever need to think of yourself as alone." Her hand tightened gently, so Charlie could feel the press of her fingers and the silver rings she wore, then fell away. "And if you want to keep the next few meetings at my house, I'd be happy to continue hosting for now."

That would make it a little easier. The thought of the women gathering in her own home, sitting in the same room, the same chairs, everything the same as always but without her grandmother in the circle, without her grandfather puttering about in the kitchen to pour lemonade...it had to be easier in a different setting. "Thank you, I'd prefer that."

"So you will consider joining us? It's been hard enough to continue without your grandmother. With you gone as well, everything has felt so unbalanced. We miss the youthful spirit you bring to our group, and your unique perspective. We have important work to do, work we need you for. In fact, we're not the only ones who need you. There have been some – troubling developments in these last few months."

Charlie set her basket down, reached for the holy basil. "I said I'd think about it." She wanted to ignore that last sentence, the bait that she knew Betty had deliberately dangled for her – just as she'd probably come to the door to deliberately inveigle her into this conversation. She snipped a few leaves, added them to her basket, kept up a studied silence for a solid minute. Then she gave up. "What troubling developments?"

Betty could talk around a topic for fifteen minutes without coming to the point if she felt like chatting, but this time she didn't mince words. "Vampire activity has increased locally. They're going beyond willing volunteers, started going far enough to kill or turn their victims. You know how serious that is."

"*Vampires*?" Charlie echoed. The existence of vampires was well-known to the witch community, and vice versa, though both had their reasons for staying under the radar of the larger population. Vampires were fortunately small in number and usually selective in their feeding, careful to avoid attracting attention.

"Vampires," Esther repeated grimly, coming up with her basketful of eucalyptus leaves. Sammy trotted next to her, then hared off down the row of herbs to chase imaginary squirrels. Esther moved to the stand of *Hypericum Perforatum* beyond the holy basil and began taking cuttings. "There's been vampire activity for years, of course, but lately it's escalating. Over the past few months, there have been a growing number of strange disappearances."

"Are we sure it's vampires?" Charlie asked, only noticing she'd slipped that *we* in after the words were spoken. Never mind, it didn't commit her to anything. She had enough to deal with. And maybe the coven was being alarmist. When you dealt in magic, it was easy to see the supernatural in every shadow.

"All the whispers from our special sources around town suggest vampires," Betty said, picking up the story again. "They're too careful to leave a lot of drained bodies with bite marks, but the pattern of the disappearances points to vampiric activity. Most disappearances have been among the homeless, and there wasn't a great deal of notice from the non-magical population before this. But did you see today's headline in *The Sacramento Bee*?"

"No, I haven't checked my news app yet," Charlie admitted.

"It's all about the missing persons. They've done a very thorough investigation, putting together a number of pieces no one had connected before. They're calling the missing the Disappeared – rather sensational, but it does capture the idea. Several of the homeless interviewed for the article mentioned their fears. They've begged for someone to pay attention, and now people are beginning to." Betty's mouth twisted. "That may be because the vampires are starting to expand their feeding beyond the unhoused."

Charlie slowly resumed clipping from the holy basil, absent-mindedly moved on to the next plant over, *Symphytum Officinale*, and clipped a few sprigs there as well. Betty wasn't actually clipping anything, just standing beside the plants – what a surprise. Charlie tried to tell herself none of this was her concern. She didn't want people disappearing, obviously, but she had enough responsibilities with Sammy and handling her grandparents' estate, not to mention her actual *job*. Professional ballet was a demanding career, especially if you wanted to have any success.

And everything had just felt *harder* since her grandparents had died.

"I assume the article doesn't say it's vampires?" Charlie said, tone caustic from her guilt about trying to avoid responsibility, and her resentment that they were making her feel guilty. If it wasn't vampires, it definitely wasn't her problem to deal with. Not that it would be even if it *was* vampires. There were a lot of problems in the world, and she couldn't take on all of them.

Betty cast her eyes heavenward expressively. "Fortunately, no – no one is suggesting vampires. That would create a whole different kind of crisis, both for the panic it would cause and the attention it would bring to all magic users. Right now there's only wild speculation; that this might be the work of a serial killer, or a group trying to force homeless people to leave the city, although the recent expansion of victims makes that last look less plausible. But as I said, our contacts make it clear what we're really dealing with."

Betty and the other women of the Singing River Coven formed the center of a complicated web that stretched across the Sacramento area: extended family and friends of friends and former colleagues and all the contacts that could be made in a lifetime in one place that, despite its population of millions, still sometimes felt like a small town. Charlie had to reluctantly admit that if the coven said it was vampires, it was almost definitely vampires.

Esther's strong voice cut in again, her long feather earrings swaying as she looked back and forth between Betty and Charlie. "We *know* it's vampires. And they're getting bold enough that people are getting interested. It was inevitable this day would come. The way things have escalated over the past few months, I'm surprised people didn't notice sooner."

"We need to start making plans," Betty resumed. "With the number of vampires growing, and the number of those missing and presumed dead escalating, it's time for us to do something. Before the vampires become too powerful to fight."

Charlie tried to picture the women of her coven wielding weapons against a horde of vampires. The image was as preposterous as it was disturbing. "What are you going to do, go out and stab a bunch of vampires with wooden stakes?"

Esther's eyes twinkled. "Most of us *do* carry wooden knitting needles, you know."

Betty pursed her lips. "Our philosophy has always been to avoid violence. The only reasons to fight are to protect yourself or others. At our next meeting, we plan to consider what non-violent activities we can initiate to prevent further disappearances. We don't want this to come to a war between witches and vampires."

A war? They *were* taking this seriously. Did that make Charlie a draft-dodger if she bowed out? No, of course not – this wasn't really a war. It was just a – situation.

"Will you come to our next meeting?" Betty asked. "It would mean a great deal to us all if you were there."

Charlie hesitated, torn. "I...need to think about it," she muttered for what felt like the thousandth time. She gave up the pretense of gathering herbs, and stowed her shears in her basket with the few cuttings she'd already made. "I'll let you know, all right? But I have to get to the ballet studio." She suddenly remembered the mess in her workroom, and fought not to grimace. "Sammy – let's go home!"

"You might like to see the article in *The Bee*," Betty said, lifting the folded paper out of her basket and deftly slipping it into Charlie's.

Charlie had suspected it, but now she was positive that Betty had not really come to her door looking for arnica. She *knew* it was out of season. This had all been nothing but a set-up. Her annoyance about that made it a little easier to walk away, Sammy by her feet.

She let herself in at the side door of her grandparents' house – *her* house now, she had to start thinking of it that way, and took a breath. She wasn't actually due at the studio for a little while. Maybe she could make more headway with cleaning up the mess in her workroom; if she left the spilled potion too long, and if any of it had landed on other herbs that it could interact with...better to clean up before she found herself opening the door on clouds of smoke or a melted workbench or worse. She carried her basket of herbs with her. It would dishonor her craft and the plants of the garden to waste the herbs she'd cut.

Charlie set the basket on the table in her workroom, lifting out the bundled newspaper. She couldn't help glancing at it, and saw that Betty had, of course, folded it to show the recent news story, with its blaring black headline. What caught her eye, however, was the photo of one of the Disappeared. An older man with a white beard and a bald head. Charlie swallowed.

He looked a lot like her grandfather. Not so much of resemblance for it to be a strange coincidence, but enough that she couldn't help making the connection. Was he someone's grandfather too?

All those people who had disappeared, they had family and friends and people to leave behind who would mourn them, just like Charlie was mourning her grandparents. She didn't want anyone to have to feel like that. Not if she could do something to help it.

"Well, now we know why Betty wanted me to look at the article," Charlie remarked to Sammy, and shook her head. She had clearly been manipulated this morning. But recognizing it was manipulation didn't make it less effective. She dug into her pocket and pulled out her phone. She tapped out a quick text to Betty.

I'll be at the next meeting. Thanks for hosting.

In less than a minute her phone buzzed with a response: **Wonderful! We'll be so glad to see you.**

Charlie straightened her shoulders, lifted her head a little higher. Part of her did resent how neatly she'd been dragged into this. But maybe it was time. Time to work past her grief and become a useful member of her coven again.

Chapter Two: Lola

I prayed the hinges didn't squeak as I slipped out of my bedroom. What kind of host would I be if I woke my sleeping guest? After the evening we'd had, the woman would be exhausted. I was too, but also thirsty. I stretched the kinks out of my back and arms as I padded down the dark hallway to the kitchen. My favorite water bottle lay right where I'd left it on the draining board. As I passed the refrigerator, I fist bumped the picture of Robbie Day stuck to the door of the fridge. It had become a habit, a way to motivate myself to become as good a chef as the inspirational cooking show host.

The light from inside the refrigerator nearly blinded me as I reached in for the water... in the empty pitcher. "Mario..." I cursed through clenched teeth as I stomped to the sink. What was the purpose of putting an empty pitcher in the refrigerator?

"You called?" Mario asked softly as he strolled bare-chested into the kitchen. His smile lit up his face in an all too familiar way. "Hey, Lola. Fill a glass for me too, will ya? I'm parched."

I rolled my eyes as I pulled out a glass from the cabinet. I knew what he meant by 'parched.' "Where did you find this one?" When I shut the fridge after putting the water inside, the apartment was once again doused in darkness, with only the moonbeams peeking through the blinds and stretching out over the floor to light our way.

Mario leaned against the counter, arms crossed over his chest. "I tried out the new club on K Street. It was wild! I met this chick, Ashley...No. Ashlyn. Ashanti?" He shrugged. "Ash-something. Anyway, she was a dainty little Irish tiger on the dance floor, so I brought her home to do the horizontal cha-cha." He swayed his hips suggestively, as if I couldn't break that code. "Needless to say, she's fast asleep as we speak."

I handed him the glass. "If you don't keep your voice down, she won't be. Is she a lovely ginger with a bleeding-heart tattoo on her right hip?"

He frowned as he took a sip. "Yeah. How did you...? Please don't tell me you know her."

I smirked as I strolled to the living room, remembering how much I admired that tattoo. "Intimately."

Mario followed, tripping over a pair of shoes left on the floor and then plopped down on the sofa next to me. "No way. That woman is not gay. She definitely knew her way around my equipment, if you know what I mean."

I reached over and turned on the lamp next to him, bathing the room in a warm glow. "I always know what you mean." I loved him, but he wasn't the deepest pothole in the street. "I think she's pan."

"Like Peter?"

My knuckles popped when I punched him in the arm. He was either being dense or sarcastic. Either way, he was annoying. "Pansexual, dumb ass."

He rubbed his bicep. "Don't take it out on me if you're spending Friday night alone."

"I'm not alone."

"*I* don't count."

"That's not what I meant."

"Oh, really? Do tell." He propped his bare feet on the coffee table, getting comfortable to hear my story.

I got comfortable as well. "I met a very fit firefighter at Gallagher's tonight. Rebecca. She challenged me to pull ups."

He laughed under his breath, doing his best not to disturb our guests. "What did you win?"

I smiled, loving that he automatically assumed I had won the bet. I didn't have the biggest guns in town just by hefting cast iron pans at work. Our parkour workouts had done wonders for my physique. Although I had always been the buffest girl in school, and out of most of the boys too, the intense training sessions had really made me ripped. "Well, my bed isn't empty, so you tell me."

"Another firefighter, huh? How did you ever hook up with my Ashley? I think she's a psychologist or something."

"First of all, her name is Ashden. And secondly, she's a teacher. I met her in the park after a workout." I took a sip of my water to hide my smile as the image of the redhead filled my mind. "She has very sensitive toes."

"Yes, she does," Mario said, clinking my glass in celebration. "Too bad you refuse to try a threesome. She'd be a good third."

"Mario," I said in warning. "That's repulsive. You're like one of my brothers." I shuddered.

"I know," he chuckled. "I like watching you get grossed out."

My phone vibrated, alerting me to an incoming message. Speaking of brothers, Gino was texting to ask if I was awake. I typed **No**, not wanting to discuss family business at this late hour. He was always pestering me about spending more time with the family. He just didn't understand how draining being around everyone was for me. No matter how many times I tried to explain it to him.

Mario's phone rang. Gino's name popped up on the screen. Man, he was being relentless. "Oh, hey bro," Mario answered. "Yeah, she's..." Mario glanced at me and noticed my hard glare before finishing that sentence. "She's, uh, fast asleep in bed right now. What's up?"

I sat quietly, watching a wipeout video my friend Jackie sent me while listening to Mario, *mhmm*, and *yeah* through the one-sided conversation before ending it with an *I'll tell her*.

He turned off his phone. "You'll never guess who that was."

"Lady Gaga?" I asked in mock excitement.

"Close. Gino wanted to let us know tomorrow's practice time has been changed to noon."

"Anything else?" There had to be more; otherwise Gino could've just texted the time change.

"He also mentioned that your momma is making your favorite lasagna for dinner this Sunday and the new baby will be there."

I groaned, rubbing my free hand through my short, stubby hair. Why did they have to use momma's lasagna as a weapon? It was almost worth enduring the barrage of questions my family would lob at me about when I was going to settle down, wasn't it time I found a better job, and didn't I want to hold the baby? My skin itched just thinking about the nightmare. Great, my family was giving me hives. At least I had an out. "Well, I can't do dinner this weekend. I have to work a double shift that day. One of the other Senior Chefs is getting married, so I'm stuck taking over most of his shifts next week. Damn." I tried to sound disappointed but I didn't think Mario was buying it.

"You weren't invited to the ceremony? That's harsh." Mario stretched out his toes, scrutinizing them in the moonbeam. I cringed as he picked something off his pinky toe and flicked it across the room.

"It's okay," I shrugged. "I don't know him all that well. And this way, I don't have to buy him a wedding gift." We clinked our cups together again. Some people called us cheap, but I preferred the term 'frugal.' That was one of the reasons we were able to live together so well. That, and he was one of the few people I completely trusted.

We sat in a comfortable silence for a few more moments, enjoying the quiet that was only interrupted by the sounds of the occasional drunk stumbling down the street to the next bar. My musings wandered back to the woman lying in my bed. She was hot and nice and came pretty close to beating me in our pull ups competition. I enjoyed our little escapade tonight. But what I couldn't wait for at this moment was for her to leave. I really hoped she wouldn't be the clingy type and want to schedule an actual date. My heart still hadn't totally recovered from Darlene. If it ever would.

Mario reached over and picked up yesterday's newspaper off the coffee table. Our elderly neighbor, Murray, always left his copy for us after he finished the crossword so Mario could cheat on the app. He gazed at the headlines, shaking his head. "I can't believe someone else went missing. What are the cops doing all night? Why haven't they caught this guy?"

"Why are you assuming it's one man taking these people? It could be a woman, or a group of women. Or a group of men." Sometimes his assumptions hit my feminist nerve wrong.

"Remember Son of Sam? He was one guy?" Mario said.

"He also killed people, not take them. It's totally different."

"We don't know that the Disappeared are still alive. They could be dead, too."

I squeezed my eyes shut, not wanting the image of all the people that had gone missing over the summer being found dead. "This conversation has gone really dark."

"You're right. I'm sure all those people are fine and living on a nice farm with their new cult leader. Just...be careful out there, okay."

I was touched at Mario's concern. "You too. And don't drink the Kool-Aid if you're right about the cult thing."

"I make no promises if it's fruit punch. That's my kryptonite." Mario yawned, which involved his entire body. "I'm gonna try and get a few hours of sleep." He stood and headed back to his room at the opposite end of the apartment. He stopped before going down the hallway. "Are we making Out-the-Door-Oatmeal tomorrow?" In other words, helping each other get our overnight guests out the door in the morning with as little fuss as possible. We weren't in the market for relationships right now. Maybe not ever.

"As always," I said as I watched him disappear into the darkness. I may not have found the love of my life, and probably never would, but I was content with the awesome friends I had.

Chapter Three: Charlie

Charlie smoothed her hands over her black leotard as she waited in the wings for her cue. Just a few more steps to carry her out to the center stage for her bow, and then she was done dancing for the night. Her muscles ached, but it was the good kind of ache, the kind left behind by stretching and reaching and creating something incredible onstage.

Most of the company was already out, formed into their twin lines at opposite sides of the stage. Charlie looked across to the far wing to meet Nathan's gaze, and they both started forward on exactly the same beat, meeting in centerstage and moving together towards the clapping audience. Nathan made a bow with the extra flourish he always added, then extended an arm towards Charlie. She did a quick *chassé* forward and dipped into a curtsy, letting the sound of applause wash over her.

As she rose from her curtsy, she automatically glanced towards the third row, just left of center. Her grandparents had always sat there to watch her performances, showing up for every important moment of her career. She hadn't managed to stop herself from looking for them yet.

Tonight it took her by surprise to see familiar faces there: Betty and her husband Herbert, clapping hard and beaming right at her. She made herself smile at them as she retreated back into the line of dancers. It was sweet of them to come, and it wasn't their fault that seeing familiar faces in those seats was somehow harder than seeing strange ones.

Charlie swallowed against the ridiculous lump in her throat, extending her arm in perfect unison with all the other dancers to welcome forward Victoria, the principal ballerina, to take the final bow of the night.

The bows and the applause went on long enough that Charlie had plenty of time to get herself under control again, to let the ache of missing her grandparents, so different from the ache of tired muscles, throb and dissipate through her. She had learned that it was no good fighting it; all she could do was breathe and let it flow by, and ballet had taught her nothing if not how to breathe.

She tried to focus on practical matters. She hadn't seen Betty since the previous morning, since she'd agreed to come to the next coven meeting.

She'd try not to interpret the attendance at her performance as Betty keeping an eye on her.

Actually, that was silly. *Of course* Betty was keeping an eye on her, but that was easily explained by her role as Charlie's grandmother's best friend, with no need for her role as coven leader to be involved at all. Still, Charlie had better text her later to thank her for coming and maybe reaffirm that she'd be at the next meeting. That might reassure the older woman.

The curtains whisked closed at last and the dancers broke formation, ready to scatter off to change clothes and head out for the night. Charlie had just started towards the back hallway and her dressing room when Nathan ambled up and fell into step with her.

"Hey, Charlie, some of us are going out for drinks tonight," he said with a grin. "Care to come?"

"Sounds fun, but it's pretty late," she said, trying to decide if she wanted company more than she wanted to go home for a hot bath and sleep.

"Sure, but it's Saturday night and tomorrow's our day off. It'll be a good time – Victoria already turned us down because she's planning an extra practice session tomorrow, so that guarantees to improve the quality of the conversation."

Charlie laughed in spite of herself. Nathan's ongoing feud with the principal ballerina was legendary. She was sure Victoria had been invited only to be polite. "You do make it sound appealing."

"We thought we'd hit that new bar over on K Street." Nathan waggled his eyebrows and his voice went into his wheedling tone. "They have vegan appetizers. You know you want to try them."

She did, actually, and a night on the town with her ballet friends sounded like a good way to spend an evening – but just before she agreed, her gaze drifted to another cluster of dancers. Jacob was talking to Kayla while gesturing toward Nathan, both nodding like something had been agreed on. Charlie sighed. "Kayla's coming, isn't she?"

Nathan followed her glance, and frowned. "Hey, that doesn't mean anything. You can still join us. It's a group thing, it'll be fun."

"I better not." Maybe she was being silly about this. Nathan had already told her she was. After all, she and Kayla had only gone out three times before Charlie had broken things off.

It had only taken three dates to realize that, while she still thought Kayla was pretty and interesting and fun to be around, while she still wanted some new person to fill the suddenly empty-feeling landscape of her life, she just hadn't felt any real interest in kissing Kayla goodnight. She'd already learned the hard way that it was no good trying to force things with that kind of non-chemistry. She didn't need to spend another five months of her life relearning that lesson, and it wouldn't be fair to Kayla either. So she seemed doomed to spend that time trying not to make things any more awkward than it inevitably was when you had to tell someone you worked with, someone who clearly really, really liked you, that it wasn't going to happen.

"You don't have to go into hiding just because the two of you didn't end up getting together," Nathan protested. "Maybe you'll even meet someone new if you come along with us and–"

"Another time," Charlie said firmly. "It's only been a couple weeks. I want to give her space. You all have fun." She turned to head for her dressing room, but stopped after a step, remembering everything Betty had told her. All about vampires and mysterious disappearances, especially downtown. "Hey, Nathan?" she said, and tried to sound casual. "You guys be careful out there, okay?"

He shrugged. "What could happen?"

"I don't know..." She did know, all too clearly. A vampire could loom up out of a dark alley and drag someone away, never to be seen again. "It's just, there's been all those news stories lately about people disappearing. You'll all stick together, right?"

"Yeah, sure, we'll make sure nobody walks back to their car alone. Or you could come along to keep an eye on us."

Part of her felt like she should – but she snuck another glance towards Kayla and thought better of it. The other dancers were good about watching out for each other. She shook her head. "Sammy will be waiting for me at home."

"That's an excuse and you know it," Nathan called after her, but this time Charlie walked the last few steps to her dressing room without stopping and slipped inside, closing the door on Nathan and the chatter of the other dancers. It *wasn't* an excuse; Sammy was an older dog now, and it was perfectly reasonable to be concerned about him.

She sat down at her small dressing table, smiling at the photo of herself with her grandparents from a year ago, and the faded one of herself at five with her parents. She reached up to pull off the elastic band holding her hair in its tight bun and shook her head, letting her blond curls fall in a crinkled mass down to her shoulders.

She had finished removing her stage make-up and was about to change clothes when a knock sounded at her door. She might have guessed it was Nathan, back to try to get her to change her mind, but the brisk little tap didn't sound like him.

"Come on in," she called, and the door opened on Betty and Herbert.

"My dear, you were so lovely tonight!" Betty gushed, darting forward to envelop Charlie in a quick, lavender-scented hug. Herbert beamed from the doorway, holding a bouquet of roses.

"And who did you bribe to get back here?" Charlie laughed, getting up to take the flowers. Looked like she wouldn't need to text Betty later after all. Maybe this was pushy, but it was hard to be upset when they were making such a nice gesture.

"Oh, we met a very pleasant young man at the stage door. I told him all about how we knew you and were waiting for you, and could he maybe find us a chair for Herbert, on account of his hip. He said we could come back this way."

"Is your hip bothering you again?" Charlie asked Herbert, with a guilty feeling that she really had been too much out of touch.

"Eh, it's fine," Herbert said, waving one hand dismissively. "She worries too much."

That was true about Betty, but Charlie made a mental note to increase the strength of the healing salve they usually prepared for Herbert. The coven had surely been taking care of it, but that didn't mean Charlie couldn't keep it in mind too. Her thoughts flitted to the healing salve that had burst all over her workroom. She'd have to make up a new batch soon. Good thing they'd had a good crop of lavender in the garden this summer.

"Your hip would be better if you came to Charlie's yoga classes," Betty scolded, "like we keep telling you. You know they do wonders for my balance and flexibility."

Charlie had never been entirely out of touch with the Singing River Coven – but they had all been 'undercover' in a sense when attending Charlie's classes, making it easy to avoid discussing anything witchcraft-related. She'd been carefully ignoring any pointed looks or attempts for a private word. It might actually be a relief in some ways to re-engage more fully with the coven, and drop the effort it took to avoid all that.

"That reminds me," Charlie said, "I have some new ideas for our senior ballet class that I think you'll like. This new performance we're doing has been giving me all kinds of inspiration."

Betty's smile went a little strained. "Oh? Because, while I'm sure it was all very, um, impressive and artistic dancing, this wasn't *exactly* classical ballet, and I'm not sure our class is quite, ah, ready for–"

Charlie knew her own grin was growing wicked. It was fun to tease her friends. She'd been right to say she'd come to the next coven meeting. The atmosphere already felt lighter with Betty tonight than it had in months. "But wouldn't you enjoy doing ballet to the Rolling Stones?"

Betty's mouth settled into a prim line. "You know I was always a Beatles girl myself."

"She'd throw me over in a heartbeat today if Paul McCartney came calling," Herbert said with a cackle.

"It's not a matter of the music anyway, but some of that rolling about on the floor, I just don't know if..."

"Have an open mind, Betty," Herbert chided. "You know the kids are always trying new things these days. It can't all be *Swan Lake*."

"You know I wouldn't ask you to do something you weren't comfortable with," Charlie assured Betty. "And if you want to see classical ballet, don't forget we do *The Nutcracker* every Christmas." It was the perennial show in ballet circles, as reliable every December as Christmas trees and Santa Claus.

"Ooh, yes, that's right!" Betty said, eyes sparkling. "And is this the year they finally do the smart thing and cast you as the Sugar Plum Fairy?"

"Here's hoping!" Charlie said, and knocked her knuckles against the wood of her dressing table.

She had seen or danced in *The Nutcracker* every year for as long as she could remember, starting as a tiny Polichinelle hiding in Mother Ginger's skirts, working up to better and better roles. And even though it wasn't modern and innovative and the kind of ballet she loved best, she wanted to achieve that lead role more than she liked to admit. It would prove something, to be cast as the Sugar Plum Fairy. To herself, which ought to be the most important thing, and to all her friends who wanted so much to support her dancing, but who didn't understand performances like tonight's at all. They'd understand the Sugar Plum Fairy.

Her grandparents would have understood too.

"We should be going," Betty remarked, "and let you finish getting ready and go home. But we'll see you at the next coven meeting, of course?"

Charlie smiled. All right, this was *definitely* pushy. But she realized that part of her had missed having someone be so involved in her life too. "Yes, I'll be at the next meeting. And let's go for brunch tomorrow too. There's a restaurant near here I've been wanting to try. It's called *Sorelle*, and I just love the name – sisters, you know."

Betty ushered herself and Herbert out soon after that, with more remarks about how Charlie surely needed to get home to rest. After they'd gone, Charlie changed back into her street clothes, carefully easing her shoes on over her sore toes. Definitely a night for a good hot soak.

She was just unlocking her car when she heard footsteps behind her. She glanced back, half expecting Nathan with another argument in favor of going out. But as she looked around the empty parking lot, she didn't see anyone.

Charlie frowned, then shook her head. She'd probably imagined it – or the sound had carried from somewhere outside the lot – or...well, there had to be lots of explanations. Even if none of the ones she could think of were quite convincing enough for the prickle of unease on the back of her neck.

She slid into the driver's seat, and hit the button to lock the doors before she even started the car. She had made sure Nathan wouldn't let anyone go to their cars alone – maybe she should have made sure she had an escort herself!

Or she was tired from dancing and she had vampires on her mind and this was nothing but simple paranoia.

It was a long drive home, out of the brightly lit downtown, then east on 50. And the whole way she couldn't quite shake her uneasy feelings. She kept watching the headlights on the road behind her, changing lanes unnecessarily, just in case... She gripped her steering wheel tightly, impatient with herself. Why would anyone be following her? Even if there *had* been a vampire in the parking lot – a huge if – they didn't usually follow people. Vampires were opportunists, picking off easy victims.

Finally she exited the freeway and entered her own sleepier part of town, full of winding streets, tangled trees and open lots, unlike the packed grid of downtown. She felt a little better when no cars followed behind her.

Even though it was Saturday evening, here the houses were already dark, perhaps just a porchlight left burning through the night. Charlie smiled, turning the corner into her neighborhood. She counted off houses as she drove past them. There was Elaine and Bob's house, then Rachel's, then Emily and Ted's, and so on and so on. She had lived here since she was five, and her grandparents had lived here for fifty years. Most of the residents were connected to the coven, and had chosen to move in at the same time in the '70s. Charlie had spent her childhood running in and out of most of these houses.

She reached the end of the road, the wide curve of the cul-de-sac. There was Herbert and Betty's house, one light still on at the back, and then Esther and Douglas' house, and finally her own home right at the center of the curve. A single lamp in the living room shone through the rainbow flag pinned in the front window, the light Charlie had left on so she wouldn't have to come back to a dark house.

Charlie turned into her driveway, running parallel to the path to the community garden, and squeezed her car into the cluttered garage. She opened the door to the kitchen, the light from the adjoining room casting a glow on the linoleum. A furry bundle collided with her ankles when she was barely across the threshold.

Charlie laughed, kneeling down to greet Sammy, rubbing between the terrier's ears, feeling the last of her tension drain away.

"Hey there, buddy," Charlie said, as the dog flopped over to present his stomach for scratches. "I missed you too."

Sammy circled around her as she creaked back up to her feet, sore muscles protesting. She let him out into the backyard to do his evening business, and when he was done she headed straight to the bathroom to run a hot bath. This was a night for a double dose of her special home-brewed bath salts. She loved the smell of the peppermint, and the chamomile gave it extra potency. She could feel her muscles unknotting and soothing from the moment she slid into the fizzing, steaming water.

She felt relaxed and sleepy by the time she crawled into her big bed, pulled up the sheet and closed her eyes to sleep. And then of course her brain decided to wake up and poke her.

Had she locked the doors, and were the little stairs by the bed in place for Sammy, and how soon would the management decide *Nutcracker* roles, and was it really true vampire activity was on the rise in Sacramento? She tried to tick through the items and dismiss them – she had locked the doors, Sammy had his stairs, *Nutcracker* try-outs would be held soon, and...she had no answer about the vampires. Or whether someone had been in the parking lot tonight.

Charlie flopped onto her back. Every muscle was tired, but her mind didn't want to quiet down.

She glanced at the empty half of the bed. She wished things could have worked out with Kayla. The other half of the bed had been empty for a while now, and the larger emptiness in the house only made it feel worse. Dating would be easier in some ways if love potions actually worked. And weren't totally contrary to all moral standards about consent, of course.

After her mind went around all the same circles two or three times, and she tried every possible position at least once, she gave up and turned the light back on. Some nights were going to be restless and blue, and there was no use fighting it.

She reached down to the bottom shelf of her bedside table and came up with her worn old paperback of *The Two Towers*. She opened at random, landing near the beginning of Chapter Four. She knew the story backwards and forwards, so she started reading where she was.

Only a few pages in, she heard a thump as the mattress shifted, and then Sammy's cold nose was pressing against her shoulder.

Charlie rolled over to rub Sammy's favorite spot between his ears. "At least I have you, right, Samwise? That was enough for Frodo." He'd *had* an entire Fellowship, but Sam was really the only one he'd needed, to get all the way through Mordor.

Sammy snuffled, turned around twice, and curled up against her. Charlie went back to her book, the little terrier a warm lump at the small of her back, and read about Merry, Pippin and Treebeard until the book slipped from her fingers and she fell asleep.

Chapter Four: Lola

Saturday had slipped by, parkour and work and not enough sleep passing in the blink of an eye, and now here I was prepping for the Sunday morning brunch at *Sorelle*. Almost a dozen chefs and cooks buzzed around the kitchen. Stacks of pots and pans waited to be used on that counter, various meats ready for prep rested on the other counter, and piles of vegetables ready for chopping sat closer my way. Bouncing between everyone like an arcade ball was the manager, Madeline, her ridiculously long bleach blond hair pulled up into a tight bun, and the pale skin of her face pulled even tighter. She was cheerily yelling about our new menu items, and making sure we performed beyond perfection – yadda yadda. I wasn't really listening.

Instead, I was focusing on me. My knife sliced through cucumber, shallot, carrot, and lime in quick succession, years of practice allowing expertise to fly through my fingertips, and allowing my mind to dwell on my slip-up on Gino's circuit yesterday. I shifted my weight from one foot to the other, winced, and shifted it back. That ankle was still tender and I was still mad. I let a couple of chops really thwack the cutting board, but that didn't do much to ease the annoyance gripping me.

I shouldn't have messed up such a beginner's move. How many times had I leapt down a staircase? Thousands? But being just a centimeter off on the landing meant a pop of pain, and me sitting out the rest of the run to make sure my ankle was okay. Disappointment didn't cover what I had felt – it was deeper, and far more personal than that. I wasn't supposed to miss something *easy*. And to make matters worse, I had playfully bet on finishing in record time, so my punishment for failure was to attend a Pilates class at the ballet company near my work. Which had been the most suitable punishment Gino could think of, given my injury. "You can work on your strength and balance," I think he had said. I'd have to come up with an excuse not to go – or a way to seek revenge.

With the fruits and veggies done and on ice, I started on the protein of this dish – tofu. I sliced and pressed each block, tossing the tofu cubes into a marinade prepared by a colleague – soy sauce, sesame oil, and garlic. The absolutely delightful mix of smells attempted to calm me, but unfortunately this onion had *layers*. And within the layer mad about my parkour ability, was the layer guilty as hell about ditching Momma's big Sunday dinner with the Whole Family including Aunt Elena and the cousins. Again. I started up three pans for sautéing the tofu at once, echoes of our phone conversation filtering through me.

"Lola, my oldest daughter, how can you abandon us again?" Mom had said, loudly. "How much longer will your grandparents be around for you to spend time with? Your brother joins us every Sunday, you know!"

"I know, Momma!" I'd said, not hiding the exasperation from my voice. "But I'm working a long shift that day, starting early!"

"Perfect, you know we meet at three!"

"I don't get off until five o'clock, and I just gotta *crash* for a while. By the time I could get there most of the family will have gone home anyway."

"Then say you can't work."

"Momma, I can't do that. You want me making money, don't you?"

That was usually the way to get Momma off my back, to remind her I was working my ass off to live my dream.

Sometimes it worked too well.

"Oh, Lola. You owe me. Next time, you'll be there." And then she had hung up. It was the lack of "I love you," of saying goodbye, that proved I'd cut a little too deep. But it was so hard being the daughter focusing on career instead of family. If I was berated one more time just because I wasn't carrying an infant to dinner like my sister Stella... Or because this wasn't a job with regular hours and free weekends like corporate star Leo...

I sighed, flipping the tofu in each pan, listening to the satisfying sizzle. Even if it wasn't meat, it still gave off that same sound, and with this bomb marinade, it was damn good. I'd expect no less from one of my dishes – hell, I bet even Robbie Day would be impressed... if I could cook it on his show.

"Lola, are you okay? You're not as far in prepping as usual by now. We open in fifteen." Madeline had come to a sudden stop beside me, and gestured at the marinade bowl full of tofu still to be cooked.

"I'm fine. I'm taking my time," I assured her, even though she was definitely right. I flipped the tofu in the pans again, confirmed that the sides were done, and laid the cubes out on racks to cool. In one fluid motion,

I scooped new helpings of tofu into each pan. "It'll all be done and ready before you can crack an egg."

Madeline gave me a big "Hummm" before bouncing away, which started my grumbles back up where I'd left off, being mad that I messed up my body and mad that I messed up my family relations and here I was stuck making this vegan dish because the manager wanted a more diverse menu. At least he'd let me design it. People could be vegan however they wanted, but if they were going to eat *my* food, they'd be eating plenty of protein.

The rest of the tofu sautéed up quickly enough, and as the bustle about the kitchen tilted into the nervous energy of a day about to start, I finished up my prep by chopping my way through several bunches of cilantro and slicing half a dozen avocados.

The first set of waiters filling drink orders rushed through the front of the kitchen, and I let out a breath. Yeah, I was nervous.

I liked this dish, but I wasn't vegan. What if vegetarian or vegan customers didn't like it?

"Girl, you made it," I muttered to myself. "It's going to be bomb. Hear me? Bomb." A twang of discomfort shot up my leg from my ankle, and I winced. Maybe it was time to sit for a minute before the food orders started coming in.

After grabbing a stool from one of the back counters, I sat in front of my station, admiring my prep work. The greens of the vegetables and browns of the tofu and orzo would give the dish that lovely earth pallet I wanted – and the red pepper flakes on top would be that splash of color and spice that I knew would bring it all together.

There was a buzz from my pants pocket, and I winced. I'd forgotten to put my phone away, which was a big no-no, and I knew the text was from Mom. I regrettably hopped off the stool and out of the kitchen, and my shoulders scrunched up in anticipation of a wave of guilt as I pulled my phone out of my pocket.

Sure enough, there was a picture of my baby nephew being held by my dad. Mom had added a caption: "Baby Gregory misses you!"

I missed him too, but it almost felt like salt in the wound for Mom to remind me after the fight we'd had. What, had they all been talking about me today? Saying how much I didn't care enough about my family? With a pang of regret, I shoved my phone into my locker, and reentered the busy kitchen.

"Orders up, come on, team, we got this!" Madeline cheered, as she started in on some of the more delicate appetizers. Those always had the most elaborate plating. As I waited for an order of my dish to come in, I helped one of my fellow chefs get some of the entrées started.

What if no one ordered my dish? This was one of my first opportunities to express my style as a chef, after over a year of working at *Sorelle*. If I missed the mark, I'd be back to just making what I was told, for heaven knew how long. Could I keep doing that? For how many years? What if –

"One tofu bowl, Lola!" Madeline called, and I jumped back to my station and got to work.

Orzo bed. Fan of cucumber slices. Fan of shallot slices. Half a cup of the tofu mixture right here. Shower of carrot shreds and cilantro. Side of fresh spinach, with more of the veggies pickled in the lime and vinegar. Avocado slices. Drizzle of marinade. Squeeze of lime. Aaaaand red pepper flakes.

I whistled. It was beautiful, just like my practice bowls had been last week. How would anyone not like this? I was awesome!

With the dish safely escorted to the front of the kitchen, I returned to the grills. I'd probably only get to make a dozen or so of the tofu bowls today, but I still had more than enough to do to help keep this kitchen running smoothly. I soon had a crab cake frying in herbs and butter in one pan and snow peas sautéing in olive oil and garlic in another pan, with both hands working to keep everything cooking evenly. I loved moments like this, where my whole body was in tune with the kitchen and I could just get lost in it.

"Lola, did you hear me? Three bowls just got ordered!"

Shit. Got a little too lost.

I hopped back to my station, whipped the bowls into existence and sent them on their merry way.

About an hour into the brunch time, I'd prepared more bowls than I had anticipated, and had to switch from helping with other entrees to prepping more ingredients. Well, maybe everyone had been right about expanding the options in our menu. No criticisms had made their way back to me yet, but my first bowls had only barely been finished by this point, so the verdict was still out.

I told the damn butterflies in my stomach that I wasn't going to give in to them. I'd never been the kind of girl who was into butterflies anyway. And I definitely wasn't into this whole self-doubt thing. It wasn't the me I wanted to be.

Not even a few minutes later, one of the waiters, a dude barely out of high school named Keegan, approached me. "Hey, Lola, will you have a moment to step away from your station soon?"

Oh no, here it was. "What's wrong?"

"Ah, sorry, nothing! I don't think anything is wrong. A customer wanted to speak to the chef who did the tofu bowl. She had a big smile on her face."

A smile didn't necessarily mean the customer was happy; they may have just been very polite, or didn't want to take it out on the waiter. I brushed piles of chopped cucumber into their designated bin and followed Keegan toward the front of the kitchen. Several eyes darted our way. This was rare, and we all knew it was usually good, but you never knew when it was going to be really, really bad.

I hung up my apron before stepping into the dining hall, mostly because it was covered in bits of cilantro and stains of marinade, and stepped out onto cream-colored tile with my black slacks and trim, white chef's shirt. The soft clink of silverware on plates tinkled through the air above the melody of some orchestral music track and the murmur of quiet voices. What a shift from the bustle of the kitchen. A laugh pierced through the polite atmosphere, and I flinched.

Keegan approached a table where three people sat – an older man and woman, their hair gray and their hands clasped gently on the table, and a young woman who watched our approach with a million dollar smile. She was thin and porcelain, with blonde hair that lay in waves around her shoulders. She wore a light gray sweater over a form-fitting emerald dress. The outfit looked expensive. Who did she think she *was*? The sheer perfection of her made my stomach churn. And the older couple... her grandparents? Or older parents? Well, *someone* was hanging out with family today. Someone who probably worked a nine to five and had grandparents with the extra cash to come to *Sorelle*.

"Miss, this is Lola Morelli, one of our top chefs," Keegan said, giving a little bow in my direction. Man, it was like him to talk me up that way. I wished it helped my confidence instead of bruising it.

Still, I gave the woman a big smile. "Good afternoon, Miss. I hope your meal has been prepared to your satisfaction."

"Oh, it has been more than satisfactory, it's fantastic!" She waved her hands excitedly over her plate. "I've been vegan for years, and it's rare to be able to go to an establishment like this and see a vegan option that isn't just a salad. I appreciate it so much."

My eyes widened. I had not been expecting a compliment like that, even if that was exactly what I had wanted to hear about this dish.

"Charlie has been raving about this dish ever since it was brought over," the older woman next to the blonde jumped in. Did she mean her husband? But he had the French toast with citrus in front of him – oh, maybe Charlie was the blonde? Huh, okay. "There are so many restaurants we don't even go to together because there's nothing vegan available. I applaud you for having such a progressive option on the menu."

Oh good, this old lady with her totally Norman Rockwell family was going to congratulate me on being progressive. Could this get weirder?

"I really loved the flavors," the blonde spoke up again. "It was spicy, but not too spicy!" She laughed, and I smiled politely to hide the inner rolling of my eyes.

"I am so glad you've enjoyed it! It is our mission here at *Sorelle* to have variety in our dishes for all our patrons to enjoy." Here, have some corporate language.

"That's wonderful. The meal was just fabulous. Thank you so much."

I thanked the woman again, and got the hell outta Dodge, my cheeks on fire from her compliments and my anxiety at being in the middle of the dining hall. Back in the kitchen, Madeline clasped me on the shoulder.

"Good job, chef."

"Thank you."

I returned to my work station. I tried to feel proud, but it didn't sit right in my chest. I hadn't even wanted to make this dish. Yeah, I'd made it the best I could, and now I had a walking personification of feminine veganism saying she liked it, but that hadn't done anything inside me. They were just words. The bowl was just pasta and vegetables.

Why couldn't I just take a compliment and be happy?

I picked up my knife, pushed my breath out between clenched teeth, and resumed chopping.

Chapter Five: Charlie

Precisely at 10:00 on Tuesday morning, Charlie hesitated on Betty's porch, preparing herself to cross the threshold. It felt like one of the hardest things she had ever done. One of them, but not *the* hardest. Standing in the cemetery as each of her grandparents had been laid to rest had been much worse.

Charlie squared her shoulders. She could do this. Yes, seeing these women sitting in circle might be like grinding salt into the not yet healed wound of her grandmother's death. But if it got to be too much, she'd leave. After all, it wasn't like they'd try to stop her.

She eased the door open and stepped into the house, causing a momentary lull in the various conversations filling the room. She took a deep breath and felt more of her tension drain away. She'd been in this house hundreds of times. She knew the purpose of each candle on the bookcase, each with their varying colors and scents. She knew the meaning of the pale amethyst paint on the walls. The use of the various bowls of herbs, salt, and tumbled stones sitting on Betty's spiritual altar. And above all, she knew the relaxing scent of lavender oil that permeated the living room.

Betty always smelled of lavender.

Eleven women, not the twelve that *should* be there, filled the couch and all but one chair crammed around Betty's living room. Proof of her grandmother's absence made her ache all over. They'd need to find another member eventually. Thirteen was the optimal number for a coven, but Charlie was thankful they hadn't done it yet. It would have made this meeting impossible.

"Charlie, you made it. I'm so glad." Betty smiled and motioned to the only empty chair, on the other side of the room.

"Thank you, Betty." Charlie smiled back, then awkwardly made her way to her seat while a few other quiet welcomes came her way. Thankfully, none of the coven members, sitting so close their knees nearly touched, made a big deal of her being there. They showed their solicitude in gentle smiles, without a hint of reproach for how long she'd been gone.

Charlie's toe caught on a chair, causing her to stumble. This room really was too small for twelve grown women and their flashing knitting needles to fit comfortably. There was hardly a square foot of unused space with the full coven there. Her grandparent's house – Charlie's house now – would be far more comfortable for a full meeting.

Someday.

Maybe.

Her eyes swept over the circle of women again, afraid she would notice changes on the familiar faces of the coven members. But though age was softening their skin and had been adding a few new wrinkles to some cheeks, their eyes remained clear and intent. These were women who understood their purpose.

Charlie had put off coming here for the past six months, afraid seeing them would make her grandparents' loss that much worse. But maybe she'd been wrong. Maybe, Charlie thought, this was exactly what she needed.

Betty clapped her hands, filled with silver rings on most of her fingers, as Charlie took her seat. Her numerous bracelets and bangles chimed together softly. "Blessed be, all who gather here."

The other women in the room echoed those words back to her.

"Since we're all here now," Betty continued, "it's time to review our efforts to discourage the vampires living in Sacramento, and to see if anyone has thought of new ideas. Frances, why don't you go first?"

Charlie leaned forward, interested to learn what they had been doing. Hopefully they'd been careful, because vampires could be dangerous if they ever decided to move against the coven.

Frances ran her fingers through her fluffy cap of brown hair, highlighted here and there with gray, before answering. "I asked the priest at Our Lady of Perpetual Help if he could bless a rather large number of water bottles. I didn't get a chance to explain that we wanted *all* the water bottles in the grocery stores and gas stations near downtown blessed. Apparently, blessing water through plastic bottles is considered disrespectful." She blew out a sigh that fluttered the short bangs on her forehead. "Of course, I couldn't tell him *why* I wanted him to do it."

A murmur of disappointment ran through the room. Charlie barely suppressed an amused grin, then wondered if she could think of anything more credible.

Betty turned and said, "Esther, why don't you go next."

Esther shifted in her seat, her hair creating a flaming scarlet nimbus around her head. "I've been studying ancient methods of...um...discouraging the undead," she said primly. "I've shared them with a few of you, and I've been trying to research recipes we could use that would cause the vampires to decide that Sacramento isn't a...healthy...place for them."

How could they use a recipe on vampires? Charlie found herself intrigued by that possibility.

Esther continued, "So far, I've found eight herbal possibilities." She began ticking them off on her fingers. "Garlic. Salt. *Hypericum Perforatum,* also known as St. John's Wort. In addition to repelling vampires, it alleviates depression. *Verbena Officinalis.* It's also good for headaches, inflammation, depression, and anxiety."

"Maybe," Charlie said – only half joking, "scaring away vampires acts as an antidepressant."

"Well, it would certainly make me feel better." Esther grinned briefly, then continued, "There's also Holy basil, *Rosa Acicularis*, coriander, and cilantro listed in some texts. I haven't found a recipe that combines most, let alone all of these. Yet."

Still unsure what they were planning, Charlie began calculating how much of each herb was available in the garden. Actually, it would help to know how much of each herb Esther would need.

Elaine leaned forward in her chair, tea cup cradled in her hands. "As you all know–" She stopped abruptly and cut her eyes toward Charlie, then took a quick sip before continuing, "As most of you know, we started a Facebook group on gardening in the Sacramento area encouraging residents to plant, among other things, those very plants. We're hoping if enough gardens are filled with plants known for anti-vampire qualities, the vampires will decide to leave. We've received some good feedback, but it has been a slower process than we'd hoped."

A Facebook group to encourage planting herbs? Now Charlie really did wonder how much of each herb Esther thought they would need. And did they plan to raid all those residential gardens? She pictured a story in *The Sacramento Bee* about geriatric garden thieves and winced. She had to check their community garden for those plants as soon as possible!

"Thank you, Elaine." Betty gave her a wide smile, then raised her hand, rings sparkling in the light, and pointed to Charlie's side of the circle. She tensed. Could Betty really expect her to have ideas already? Then Betty asked, "How about you, Samantha?"

Charlie barely had time to relax before Samantha said, "Before we talk about me, could we ask Charlie if she has any clever ideas? She has such a flexible, youthful mind."

Charlie shifted awkwardly. She had no idea what to suggest at this point. "Um, I'm really interested to know what all of you have been doing." Samantha looked disappointed, so Charlie added hastily, "I'll let you know if I think of anything useful."

Samantha leaned over and patted Charlie's hand. "Don't worry, dear." And for just a moment, Charlie let herself begin to slide back into their old, familiar dynamic. There was something so comfortable about it. Something undemanding and safe. The members of the Singing River Coven had always treated her like an apprentice rather than a full-fledged member. Well, she'd joined them when she was just a kid, and none of them had seemed to notice when she finally grew up. She hadn't minded while her grandmother was alive, but now?

Now, it was no longer enough.

Charlie patted Samantha's arm, then cleared her throat. "I do like the idea of using the garden against the vampires. But can herbs possibly be enough to stop them?"

Esther must not have heard the doubt in Charlie's voice, or chose not to react. She nodded, hair glowing in the sunlight from the front window. "Herbs have traditionally been used against vampires. Most won't cause permanent damage, but they do cause reactions in vampires, ranging from irritating to severe. I doubt miserable vampires will want to keep inhabiting Sacramento."

Charlie frowned, uncomfortable with her implication. "We're just going to drive them off somewhere else?"

"Vampires have existed in Sacramento for years," Betty reminded her. "When they have small numbers, they hunt carefully, never causing death. But with so many now, they have exceeded their willing donors. Some have begun resorting to murder. If we can drive most of them off, they will have to start over in other places in smaller numbers, forcing them to be careful to cause no real harm."

Charlie felt her shoulders relax. That made sense. After all, she'd always known that vampires...well, not lived exactly – perhaps existed *was* more accurate...in the Sacramento area. And they'd never posed a real threat in the past.

Frances spoke up quickly. "It's all very well to try to help everyone, but the homeless are most at risk right now of joining the Disappeared. We must protect them."

Shy Amelia spoke up hesitantly. "I agree about the homeless. In fact, Helen, Margaret and I have been knitting bracelets." She raised her needles, showing her current project. "We infuse them with several of the herbs Esther mentioned. Even though the potency doesn't last long, the bracelets retain the scent of the herbs. We're hoping the scent itself may act as a sort of deterrent."

The rapid clicking of wooden needles filled the momentary silence. Charlie was sure they were knitting protection spells of one type or another into their work. She'd grown up watching these women knitting magic into scarves and sweaters, though this was the first time she'd seen them knit bracelets. Then she stared as Amelia's fingers rapidly moved the yarn on those long wooden needles. Their tips looked a lot sharper than she remembered. In fact, they could really make a good defensive weapon if necessary.

Maybe she should consider taking up knitting.

Betty cleared her throat and repeated what she'd told Charlie two days before. "With the number of vampires growing, and the escalating number of those missing and presumed dead, we need to step up our efforts. Before the vampires become too numerous and powerful to fight."

Esther added, "We have two possibilities. First, find ways to protect those who might be victims. Second, determine ways to deter the vampires. If we can cause them adverse reactions, even pain or illness, it should convince them to leave the area."

"Adverse reactions," Charlie repeated. What if it wasn't enough? Was there something else could they do? What if it came to a fight? How far would the coven – would she – be willing to go? "Has anyone considered just asking the vampires to move?"

"We'd have to ask the vampire leader for permission to speak to the members of the nest, and we don't know who that leader is. They've been very secretive." Esther's stiff shoulders telegraphed her frustration.

"Should we consider anything else today?" Betty asked patiently.

"We haven't discussed patrolling downtown," Dorothy said. "We could all take shifts."

"I'm sorry, Dorothy," Elaine said. "I can't walk that much anymore. Bunions, you know."

Several others spoke up with reasons patrolling wouldn't work. Then someone suggested putting Esther's herb list in the water supply. Esther interrupted quickly. "I don't think most people would drink water that tastes strongly of garlic..."

Garlic water? Charlie shuddered. Not something she'd want to drink.

Dorothy was tapping on her cell phone. "I found several websites about fighting vampires. Oh, goddess. This one says 'Traditional methods of killing vampires include decapitation and stuffing the severed head's mouth with garlic.' I'm sorry, I'm not comfortable with doing that!"

Betty spoke briskly, voice pitched louder than usual. More resolute. "This is our town. Our people. We each must do everything in our power to fix this. Look for every possible *non-violent* method."

Charlie realized she was on the edge of her seat. The coven clearly needed help, and she began considering how those herbs could be combined. Something, she thought wryly, that would drive the vampires away without filling the town's water supply with garlic.

Could she create something that could be spilled onto vampires? Something that would make them extremely uncomfortable. She shuddered, hard enough that her chair rattled against the floor. Bad idea. They'd need to get far too close. That could only be a last ditch, desperation measure.

Betty spoke again. "Using our herbs would be my preference. The idea of vampires trying to feed on unsuspecting humans protected by our herbs is extremely satisfying."

Charlie thought of the garden, which had been her grandmother's passion project for over fifty years. Betty was right. Using their own herbs to make the vampires leave would be extremely satisfying. When she got home today, she'd go into the garden and encourage each of the plants Esther had mentioned. She'd treat them with water infused by the full moon, and touch each with prayers to the goddess. And she'd been aching to try one of the ritual dances she'd been working on. Dances that should bring down the blessings of the goddess.

Esther clapped her hands. "We're in agreement. We should all pursue herbal remedies as our first defense. Review your family's receipt books and grimoires. Someone, somewhere, must have a recipe that will work."

Elaine leaned back in her seat, her long peasant skirt giving off a sound like a sigh. "If only we had Maria Teresa's book."

There was a brief, respectful silence for the most famous witch on the west coast. Though Charlie was too young to have met her, even she knew all about Maria Teresa. The witch who convinced several covens in Sacramento to work together on a regular basis, using their magic to support the entire community. When Maria Theresa died, over twenty years ago now, her receipt book had gone missing which led to accusations and misunderstandings, and finally broke the long cooperation between those covens.

Now, only two covens remained in the Sacramento area – Singing River and Mystic Oak. And the only time they gathered together was the Summer Solstice.

"Has anyone tried to find Maria Teresa's book?" Samantha asked. "I moved here a few years after she died and no one would ever talk about what happened."

Disquiet rustled around the room before Betty said, "It was an uncomfortable time for all of us, and no one wanted to speak of it. Many witches spent years trying to find her book. Unfortunately, Maria Teresa's family rejected magic years before her death, and her family gave away or destroyed all of her belongings. No one knows what happened to her book, or even if it still exists."

Charlie looked around at the faces she knew so well, each filled with emotions ranging from regret to sorrow to frustration as silence fell again and stretched uncomfortably between them.

Dorothy cleared her throat. "There's plenty of receipt books available to us. I don't remember seeing anything we can use in my grannie's book, but I haven't looked through all those old boxes in my attic in years. I'll start there."

That started everyone talking, chiming in about family records. Then Elaine volunteered, "I'll check the magical wing underneath the library. I work at the regular library two days a week. I'm sure I can sneak down there without anyone noticing."

Betty clapped her hands, bracelets jingling. "If you find recipes that use some or all of those herbs, let us know. If *any* opportunity presents itself, we need to be ready." Betty's gaze rested on each of them. Charlie could swear she felt Betty's concern through that gaze, and it ignited an answering urgency in her.

Betty continued, "Promise me, sisters – give me your binding vow. We will take whatever actions we can to stop the evil spreading through our town. We do have the ability to stop them. Please, I need your word."

From somewhere a bell tinkled, underlining the importance of Betty's request. Charlie wasn't the only one whose head came up at the sound. All around her, shoulders and backs straightened. An urgency similar to Charlie's filled that crowded space before the room rang with each woman's unhesitating vow.

Charlie's blended into the others, but she felt the weight of it, as if it were written on her heart. She'd willingly bound herself to do whatever it took to help stop people dying in her town.

Chapter Six: Lola

By Tuesday morning, Momma still hadn't called, and I knew it was going to be a disaster the next time we talked. Monday had included a morning workout – a light one due to my still-tender ankle – and an evening shift at *Sorelle* anticipating the missed calls or wall of texts I'd find on my phone.

But nothing had been there but a few texted memes from my friend Jackie.

I spent far too long worrying that I'd disappointed my mom. But I had to work. She must have known how hard it was to get around a restaurant schedule by now, after years of me working in this biz. I couldn't skip the shift for anything but incapacitation. It wasn't fair for her to guilt me for something that was out of my control.

Not that I'd ever be able to say that to her face.

I sat at my small kitchen table, an empty cup of coffee in my hands. The soap operas Momma loved weren't on yet, and I had a closing shift at *Sorelle* again. So I decided to make the first move, and call her.

"Oh, Lola, darling, I've been meaning to call you!" Momma started, her voice high and sweet, yet somehow making me shudder. "I need to tell you all about Sunday. You will not believe how much your nieces and nephews have grown since the last time you were here. Everyone missed you. And Stella brought the best wine, Bruno got it from his family in Italy, isn't that fancy?"

"Yeah, it is!" I blurted out, trying to figure out if this explosion of words was sincere or as veiled with venom as I imagined it was, even if she was *right* that Bruno always brought the best Italian wine.

"It was so good, Lola. I hope I can go on a trip to Italy one day. See the villas and the water, who knows? Maybe Leo will surprise Dad and me with a trip so I can see the land where Nonna grew up before I die."

"Momma!" I groaned, which was a common reaction whenever she purposely mentioned death, and even more purposely tried to get me on her side by mentioning my great-grandmother Nonna.

"What? I'm going to die one day. And to think, you missed another one of my fantastic meals, how many of those are even left in me? I'm going to get too old to make the marinara from scratch, you know. Not without your help anyway."

There was the venom out in plain sight. "Momma, please. You're not even sixty yet."

"Heart disease runs in our family!"

I pinched the bridge of my nose and repressed a groan while I limped back and forth in my apartment's tiny kitchen. Guilting was her love language, but damn if it didn't still hurt.

"Can we just have a normal conversation, please?" I asked.

"Of course we can. You called me. What do you want to talk about? Do you still do that dangerous street jumping? Throwing yourself down staircases? I don't know how you and Gino don't end up in the hospital. And how could Mario do it too? I thought he was more responsible. I lie awake at night worried about all of you."

During this new angle of attack, my front door jittered and Mario burst in, grinning ear to ear, at least until he saw me. The smile vanished as he looked from my surely panicked eyes to my phone.

Momma, I mouthed, and he nodded, smirked, and sat down on the couch to watch. I could bloody kill him, but I forced myself to re-engage with the conversation.

"It's called parkour, I don't know how many times I've told you that. And it's a sport. Just like any other."

"But what if you get hurt?" Momma asked. And I was about to yell that I don't, except I had. I was definitely not going to tell her about my ankle. Ugh. That reminded me about Pilates tomorrow morning.

Momma continued. "Do you have health insurance?"

Had I been working full time for years? Yes. Had she asked me that question before? Also yes.

"You know I do." It wasn't the best, but I had it.

"Heaven forbid you ever had to use it. I'll say it again. Don't you dare get hurt doing that dangerous sport Lola. There's no way you'd stop doing it, is there? For me?"

My teeth were bared in a snarl and I was seeing red before I knew what had hit me. I only partially came out of it when Mario snickered. I muted the phone. "Don't you start, Mario!"

"You're struggling!" he laughed.

"Stop it!" and I brought the phone back to my ear. "Momma, I am strong, and careful, and know what I'm doing. I will not stop doing something that I love."

It was hard to keep my voice calm through a clenched jaw.

"Oh, alright, I understand," Momma said, her tone clear that she didn't. "Anyway, Lola. Sunday. I can't believe you missed it again."

Here we go. "I'm sorry, Momma, I really am. You understand I have to do the shifts I'm assigned, right?"

"Then ask for them off. You're allowed vacation!"

I groaned. "I gotta submit time off requests weeks in advance. And in this case even that wouldn't have worked cause my coworker got married and was out. So I was needed at *Sorelle*."

"Why do you always choose your job over coming to see me?"

And then I lost it. "You are impossible! I couldn't abandon my shift. I didn't *want* to abandon my shift! My coworkers needed me and you need to respect that!"

"I needed you, Lola. Your sisters need you too, you know. It's called work/life balance."

I palmed my phone again and screeched. Mario fell over onto the couch pillows, laughing.

Back to mommy dearest. "I gotta go, Momma. Can we talk more later this week?"

I barely let her get an "of course" out before I said bye and ended the call, resisting the urge to throw my phone across the room. Maybe at Mario. I motioned the throw, my phone in a vice grip, and threw a couple choice words at the wall instead.

"At least she wants to talk to you," Mario said, his giggles fading. With his mother passed on and his father remarried with young kids, I understood why he said that. But...

"Now you're going to guilt me too?"

He shook his head, smiling. "She's still asking you to quit parkour?"

I nodded, rolling my eyes.

He whistled, hopping up from the couch. "How many years has it been now?"

"At least five?" I leaned forward over the kitchen counter. "And then at the last second she asks me why I didn't ditch my shift to come see her. I need a damn drink after that, but I'm not gonna drink before work."

"Smart thinking." Mario grabbed sandwich fixings out of the fridge, and I stepped back from the counter to make room for him.

"So instead...why don't you meet me downtown at eleven?"

Mario's disposition shifted, from his usual jokester self to someone more serious than I recognised. "Oh, um, I'm not sure I want to go out drinking tonight. It's Tuesday, after all."

I frowned at him. "When has that ever stopped you before?" Momma might think he was the responsible one, but obviously she was deluded.

He shrugged, keeping his eyes down on the counter. "I've got some clients at the gym in the morning."

Right, he was becoming a more popular personal trainer lately. "Oh, sure. I'll go by myself. I'm going to need it."

He scrunched up his face, as he washed off some pieces of romaine for his sandwich. I had drilled him for years on proper food hygiene. "How about I make you a drink here instead?"

That was really unusual. I looked him up and down, as he threw everything but the kitchen sink into this sandwich and wouldn't meet my eyes. I decided to prod. "What's up?"

"Nothing, you know, it's just that... have you watched the news at all lately? The Disappeared. I'm just..."

Aww, my mother away from mother. "Now I get it, you're worried about me."

"Well, yeah, I am. How many have disappeared now? I don't want anything to happen to you – you could get, like, bit by a vampire."

I let out a high pitched laugh. "Vampires? What the hell are you talking about? That's ridiculous."

Mario blinked, and shook his head. "Uh, yes. Yes, it is. But you still could disappear."

"Look, dude, I appreciate that you care. But no one's going to mess with this gun show." I flexed for him. "If you want to be my bodyguard, or more accurately if you want me to be yours, you can come along."

A cloud seemed to linger over him for a moment, his dark expression unusual and making me more than a little freaked out. But then he put on a smile, and put the top piece of bread on his towering sandwich. "Alright, alright. You've convinced me. I like the idea of having a bodyguard. Makes me feel special."

"Don't let it go to your head," I snapped. "Want to throw together some Out-the-Door-Oatmeals before meeting me downtown?"

"You think you're that good?" He quipped, and I smiled. The darkness around him was gone.

"Can't a girl be prepared for anything? Who knows, maybe I'll find some hot vampire to take home."

We laughed, though I had to admit to myself his laugh sounded forced.

Chapter Seven: Charlie

C harlie was running late when she left her house Wednesday morning. With yesterday's coven meeting on her mind, she'd stopped to watch the news before leaving. She suspected it would become something of a compulsion until they'd found a way to make the vampires leave.

The increasing number of missing persons had made it onto every news program. No wonder everyone in the coven was feeling the pressure to stop this. Every one of the Disappeared felt like a weight on Charlie's heart.

She intended to put herself through one heck of a workout today while Sammy was at the groomer's. Maybe good physical action would help her think of something they could do. Or if nothing else, maybe it could do the opposite and stop her churning thoughts. Maybe she'd even reward herself with something good for lunch. She wondered if *Sorelle* would be open. Sunday's brunch had been excellent, and something about the chef who'd visited their table had caught her attention in a way no one else had lately. Charlie might have laid on her compliments a bit thick, but she'd enjoyed watching the slight flush they brought to the woman's face.

She wouldn't mind seeing her again. She could always ask Sammy's groomer to keep him there for an extra half hour.

She hurried up the steps to the studio, watching her feet. It would be stupid to trip on the stairs; she might never live it down. She reached for the door handle just as a strong hand with short, well-shaped nails grabbed for it. She pulled her hand back quickly. She hadn't noticed anyone next to her – probably her own fault; she'd been too busy thinking about brunch and vampires.

She glanced over to see who was there, then had to shift her gaze down a few inches. Her breath caught as she stared into the same rich brown eyes she'd seen at *Sorelle*.

It was *her*. The chef. Lola. It felt like a mirage, to see her appear just when Charlie had been thinking about her.

Lola's smile had been beautiful the other day, but it was missing now. She looked frazzled and irritated. And a bit lost. "Sorry," she muttered, belatedly jerking her hand off the door.

"Hi," Charlie said, wondering if the other woman would remember her or just brush her off. "Lola Morelli, right?"

She looked blank. Charlie tried a quick smile, hoping Lola wouldn't think she was stalking her. "I met you at the restaurant Sunday. I loved your vegan dish." She watched as comprehension relaxed her features. "My name is Charlie. Charlie Ryan."

"Nice to meet you," Lola said, then gave a crooked smile that made something inside Charlie jitter. "Again." Lola glanced at Charlie, giving her a quick once-over. "Most people don't recognize me outside the restaurant without my chef's coat."

Charlie felt her cheeks heat. "I guess I just have a good eye for faces."

Lola glanced above the door at the large sign reading *River City Dance Studio & Ballet Company* with a distinct lack of enthusiasm. Charlie couldn't tell if that lack was directed at being here, or at her. Lola brought her eyes back to Charlie's face. "So, what are you here for?"

Hopefully it was just the location that bothered her. "I work here. I'm in the ballet. I'm just here to get some practice in today." With *Nutcracker* try-outs coming up, she'd been trying to fit in some extra sessions where she could. She and Nathan planned to dance together at try-outs, and she wanted to work on some parts of the choreography.

"That's cool," Lola said, in a noncommittal tone. Then she cleared her throat and said with more warmth, "Hey, thanks again for the compliment to my dish. My boss loves it when customers are happy enough to thank the chef, especially about a new menu option."

Fresh proof that if you put good things into the universe, they'd come back to you. "I really loved it!" Charlie said, beaming. She decided impulsively that another practice session could wait. It wasn't like she was meeting Nathan for this one. "I'd like to find out more about how you created the recipe. Maybe we could, um... get some coffee?" Oh goddess, did that sound as transparent as it felt?

Lola gave that same crooked smile. "I can't right now." She heaved a sigh and rolled her eyes, then yanked open the door. "I have to take the Pilates class." Her tone, when she said *Pilates class*, made her sound like a kid who'd been ordered to eat brussel sprouts.

That image made Charlie grin back. She not only liked brussel sprouts, she liked the Pilates classes here. She tried to go several times a month; sometimes it gave her ideas for teaching her own Senior Ballet class. She couldn't imagine feeling like it was a fate nearly worse than death. "Why do you *have* to take it?"

Lola's lips tightened and she started, slowly, down the hall. Charlie nearly allowed herself to be distracted by the cute little freckle at the corner of Lola's mouth. Then Lola heaved a sigh. "I lost a bet."

"And that means you have to go to pilates?" Charlie gave her a quick, hopefully unobtrusive glance. She looked athletic and buff. Someone who shouldn't have any trouble with pilates.

"I'm into parkour." Lola's lips twisted and she slowed her steps even further, clearly in no hurry to reach the classroom.

Parkour. Charlie had seen video clips of people doing parkour. Throwing themselves with abandon down stairwells and up the sides of walls. Bouncing enthusiastically from one obstacle to another. Her estimation of Lola went up. Parkour had always reminded her a bit of modern ballet, her favorite to perform.

"I made a bet I could finish a new circuit in record time," Lola continued, and shook her head. "I should have had it! And losing the stupid bet means I have to take this Pilates class now that the ankle I twisted is better."

Clearly Lola wasn't happy, but Charlie thought she might enjoy the class more than she expected to. "Have you tried Pilates before?"

"*Not* my style."

Charlie smiled at her. "I love Pilates. I'll go with you, if you'd like." Hopefully that didn't sound too pushy. Offer to help her, Charlie! "I could help you with your form." It was such a lovely form.

"Not necessary," Lola said stiffly. "It's Pilates, not ballet."

Charlie knew she'd managed to insult her, which hadn't been her intention, damn it. "Well, I'll just get to my workout, then. I hope you enjoy the Pilates class."

Lola sighed, mouth twisting. "Look, I didn't mean to run you off if you love Pilates so much. I mean, it's not like I own it or something. It's a public class."

Not exactly an eager invitation, but permission, at least. Charlie could still walk away though she'd rather not.

They stepped into class together. Charlie grabbed two mats from the pile and staked out places in the second row. Lola glanced mournfully at the back of the room, but took the place next to Charlie.

"Near the front is better if you haven't done this before," Charlie said, trying to sound casual. As if she hadn't noticed that backward glance. "That way you can see how the teacher performs each of the positions."

"Fine," Lola said, and shrugged. She shoved her hands in her pockets and stared around the room at the rows of women in capri leggings and tank tops.

"You can use the changing room," Charlie said, pointing to a door on the left.

Lola pulled off her hoodie and looked down at her loose t-shirt, with its Girl Power message under a bold rainbow, and her olive-green cargo pants. She shook her head. "I'm wearing this."

"Okay," Charlie told her easily, fighting off a pleased grin; she had a similar shirt at home. She pulled off her oversized t-shirt, careful not to let her pride button get caught in her hair. She felt Lola's eyes on her and fought off the crazy desire to stick out her chest, trying to make her small breasts more noticeable. Normally she didn't worry about her lack of cup size; most women in the ballet weren't particularly well-endowed, and she knew her body looked good in her leotard. She was slender and sleekly muscled.

She straightened her shoulders with a small smile. She refused to start second guessing how she looked, even if she did hope Lola found her attractive. Charlie wanted to sneak a glance at her, but forced herself not to, not quite ready to meet that intense gaze.

Julie came in and took her place at the front of the class, and Charlie let out a satisfied sigh. Julie was a great instructor. She always gave a bit of extra explanation about proper form, unlike some of the others. Lola's gaze finally shifted to Julie, and Charlie let her breath out in a rush, feeling her shoulders relax.

She snuck a quick glance at Lola, who looked pretty uncomfortable. She kept fidgeting, shaking out her hands and shoulders. Rocking from one foot to another. And Charlie couldn't think of a thing to say to her.

Goddess, why was this so hard?

Finally, class started. Charlie and Lola kept glancing at each other, watching each other. As far as Charlie could tell, Lola had no trouble following the instructor's directions. Both of them were able to reach the positions with ease.

Charlie was extremely aware of Lola only three feet away, lying on her back on the mat. It made her mouth go dry, and she nearly stopped to get a drink of water. But as the class continued, an unspoken competition began. Each of them striving to have the most perfect form in the Pelvic Curl. To hold their legs up longer in The Hundred. To lift themselves highest in the Teaser. Fighting to be the best. Charlie couldn't take a break now. She definitely held an advantage, having done this before, but she was surprised how much effort she had to expend. Lola was better than she'd expected.

By the time they got to arm balances, Charlie was having trouble with her breathing. Normally, she found Pilates relaxing. Today, it was invigorating. She glanced at Lola next to her. Close enough to touch. Arms glistening with perspiration. Muscles quivering. Make that intoxicating.

Then, near the end of class, Lola began to struggle with one of the positions; she was lifting her leg too high, causing strain in her gluteus muscles and abductors. Charlie reached over and gently pushed Lola's thigh into the correct position.

Lola froze for a moment. Charlie could feel the firm, muscled thigh flex beneath her hand, and a current of warmth seemed to pulse between them. Charlie had to clear her throat, twice, before she managed to get out, "You should try to keep your leg in this position, during this...position." Oh goddess, that was awkward. She'd forgotten the name of it. Total Side Shaper or something. How could she forget something so simple? The instructor had said it less than a minute before.

Lola muttered, "Okay. Um...thanks."

And Charlie realized with horror that her hand was still resting on Lola's thigh. She jerked her hand back and muttered, "No problem."

The last few minutes of class passed in silence.

The instructor thanked everyone for participating, and Charlie picked up her t-shirt. She raised it above her head and began to pull it on. She paused for a moment, t-shirt still covering her face, convinced she could feel the warmth of Lola's eyes tracing over her body. Touching on her breasts –

did she think they were too small? As the shirt dropped down her body, she imagined those eyes move to her waist, then to the swell of Charlie's hip. Then the shirt dropped over her thighs, and the feeling of those eyes, whether real or imagined, stopped.

When Charlie looked up, Lola was staring at the mat at her feet.

"We wipe those down," Charlie told her, voice too high and a bit breathy. She hoped Lola would put it down to their work-out. She picked up her mat and carried it to the front, grabbed the sanitizer spray and cleaned it quickly. She turned to hand the spray to Lola and caught her staring. Was Lola checking her out? Or was that just wishful thinking?

They made their way slowly out of the building, not talking, but walking close together. As they emerged into the sunshine, Charlie said impulsively, "That offer to join me for coffee still stands. If you'd like." It would seem odd to mention *Sorelle* now, right? Besides, Lola probably wouldn't enjoy relaxing where she worked. Charlie quickly changed what she'd been about to say. "We could hit this little cafe I love."

Lola hesitated, her gaze intent as if searching Charlie's face for...something. Then she muttered, "Coffee? No, I need to eat something before my shift starts. I–"

"That's perfect, the cafe serves great sandwiches too! It's just half a block from here." Charlie pointed down the street.

Lola stared at her for a moment, face completely without expression. Like she was trying to hide her real reaction. "Sure," she said. "I guess."

Charlie realized Lola hadn't actually said she wanted to eat *with her*. Just that she needed to eat. There was a distinct difference. And she was suddenly sure Lola had never meant to eat with her but was too polite to say so. She could try to retract the offer now – but that would just be even more awkward, wouldn't it?

Charlie's phone pinged with the alarm she'd set. Sammy was ready to be picked up. She sent a quick text to the groomer, asking if she could bring Sammy to the cafe; it was only a block away. At least Sammy would want to be with her.

They turned and walked down the block, further apart than they had been earlier. And Charlie promised herself she'd ask Lola before assuming something in the future.

If they had a future.

Chapter Eight: Lola

The line at the downtown café was nearly out the door with patient people scrolling through their smartphones. Business suits took over every table, State workers maybe, conversing about work while eating their artful salads and sipping their dose of caffeine just to get them through the rest of their day. I wished this place served something stronger to get me through this...whatever this was with the dancer chick. Why did I agree to this? A waitress walked by with a giant sandwich on a plate, and I remembered. Because I was hungry.

"Do you live around here?" Charlie asked as we took a step closer to the order counter. She had a nice smile and very white, straight teeth. She must've had braces when she was younger.

"Kinda. I live in Midtown. I share an older apartment with my roommate, Mario." It was only a ten-minute Light rail ride away from here. Charlie's eyes widened slightly at the mention of the hipper, trendier part of the city. Had she never set foot in that part of town?

"Oh. Did you grow up there?"

"No, but it fits our needs and budget." It was close to work and fairly affordable. "Do you live Downtown?"

"No. I live in my grandparents' old house in Orangevale."

I slowly nodded as I searched my brain for where Orangevale was again. Images of driving by the Nimbus Dam which stood east of Sacramento on the American River came to mind. "Nice."

The line moved again, and we both took another step forward in silence. Charlie glanced toward the door again. Had she decided this was a bad idea and wanted to bail? I wouldn't have minded, but it was pretty rude since she was the one who had invited me to join her. Whatever, I'd order a sandwich and be on my way.

"What can I get for you?" the guy at the counter asked, fingers poised over the tablet. His gaze darted between me and Charlie. She motioned for me to order first, a smile on her face.

It was reassuring to see that each employee had clean workspaces and proper hairnets. I'd hate to have waited all this time only to go to work hungry because I didn't want to risk food poisoning. "I'll have a ham and cheddar on whole wheat and an iced tea."

I quickly pulled my wallet from my back pocket to pay. Charlie seemed the type to want to pay but I wasn't going to give her that power. I didn't need the obligation to pay 'next time' hanging over me. I seriously doubted there would be anything in common between us to allow for any future lunch dates. The pretty Ballerina Barbie was just slumming. Attraction wasn't enough, though that was a bonus. My heart thudded at the memory of her hand on my thigh. The sudden rush of heat had me fanning the front of my shirt for relief. If I kept thinking about that Pilates class, I'd die of heat stroke.

I waited for her to order her veggie sandwich and lemon water before searching for an empty table. The only one available was outside on the terrace. At least it was under a tree, giving us some shade. As it was, I thought I might melt in the summer heat.

My back pocket buzzed. I pulled my phone out to see that my mom was texting me. Again. Not wanting to be rude, and not really in the mood to talk to the Guilt Master, I turned my phone off before slipping it back into my pocket.

We had just sat down at the cozy wrought-iron table when someone shouted Charlie's name from down the street. Charlie walked over to the side gate and hugged the too cheerful woman. "Sorry I'm late," the woman said. "But he's all groomed and smelling pretty again."

"Thanks for getting him in on such short notice and bringing him here," Charlie said as she took a leash from her.

At the end of the leash was a tiny black mess of fur. When she walked back over to the table, she lifted her chair and slipped the handle onto one of the legs before sitting back down. "This is Samwise. He was my grandpa's dog. I will apologize now if he seems standoffish. He isn't comfortable with strangers."

The little dog studied me, his tail wagging. He was cute in a mutt kind of way. I liked dogs. Well, other people's dogs. I didn't have much experience with them since my dad was allergic, so we couldn't have one when I was little. Gino had a Golden Retriever now that he routinely ran with through the park. I doubted little Samwise here could keep up for more than a few blocks before needing to be carried back home.

I leaned over, holding out my hand to let the dog sniff me. "Hey, Samwise. Are you a Hobbit?" He eagerly licked my fingers. Seemed friendly enough to me.

"Are you a Lord of the Rings fan?" Charlie asked, as she also reached down to pat the dog's head.

I shrugged as I leaned back into my uncomfortable bistro chair. "I've seen the movies." Liv Tyler. Duh. "I couldn't get into the books, though. I was more into Narnia."

"I love those, too. I have the whole collection at home." Charlie crossed one long, slender leg over the other in one smooth move. Was that a ballerina thing or did she have to practice to move so gracefully?

"Which book is your favorite?" I asked, not really paying attention to what I was saying.

Her arms were long and slender like her legs, moving with the same flowing motion. Even her hands and fingers were long and slim, slipping a golden lock behind her ear. I couldn't have felt more like a Dwarf if I were sitting next to Galadriel herself.

Charlie cleared her throat, a bright smile showcasing her perfect teeth. "I liked the first one best."

First what? What was she talking about? We were discussing the dog and then Liv Tyler, and then... "Oh, yeah. *The Magician's Nephew* is definitely the best. I used to read the books in my closet, wishing it would turn into the wardrobe and take me to Narnia." Okay, that was a close save.

Charlie frowned. "I thought *The Lion, the Witch, and the Wardrobe* was the first one."

"It is," I said. "I was referring to the books' timeline."

"Here you go," a server said as she placed our lunch plates in front of us.

I was relieved to have a distraction to change the subject. I scooped up that sandwich and immediately took a bite to occupy my mouth before I stuck my foot in it. It was pretty tasty. A little heavy on the mustard but I wasn't going to complain about it in front of Charlie.

"I'm so hungry," Charlie said before taking a huge bite. Her eyes practically rolled back as she savored that first taste. She even chewed gracefully. Meanwhile, I dripped mustard all over my cargo pants.

Samwise brushed against my leg as he stared at my sandwich, his tongue licking his chops. "Are you hungry?" I asked him while I tried to scrub my pants clean with a paper napkin before a stain set in. A little piece of ham hung over the bread that I could live without. I picked it off to give it to my new furry friend when Charlie cleared her throat, napkin over her mouth full of food while she spoke.

"No meat," she said around a mouthful before she swallowed. "He's a vegetarian. I get this great vegetarian dog food online that he absolutely loves. It's formulated especially for senior dogs."

"Oh," I said, dropping the bit of ham back on the plate. "I didn't realize that was a thing." The poor dog looked desperate, though. His tail wagged furiously as his ears perked up and he pawed my leg like a tweaker looking for his next hit of meth. Sorry, buddy.

"So," Charlie said, taking a sip of her lemon water. "How did you get into cooking? Did you go to culinary school?"

"No, I don't have any formal training or anything. I met a chef from a local restaurant who saw something in me and offered me an apprenticeship." And other things much too personal to go into with Charlie. "I didn't have any other plans for my future at the time, and I'd always enjoyed cooking with my Nonna as a kid, so I took it. She taught me a lot about cooking and working in the food service world." Both the good and the bad. Some of those lessons were tough to learn, especially the ones that affected my heart. Kitchen politics was the biggest thing to master, one I was still working on.

"What do you like best about cooking?" Charlie asked.

I thought about that question as I finished chewing that last bite, wiping mustard off my bottom lip with my napkin. "Well, I'm good at it."

Charlie chuckled, nodding her head. Little streams of sunlight broke through the tree branches above us and cast a golden glow on her blonde hair. It reminded me of that old fairy tale about the girl spinning straw into gold. "I agree with that," she said. "I really did love that dish you made on Sunday. And my friends had nothing but good things to say about their meals, too."

"Your friends? They weren't your grandparents?" I glanced down at her dog who was laying by my foot. Didn't she say Sammy was her grandpa's dog?

Her smile deflated a bit as she dabbed the corners of her mouth with her napkin. "Not quite. Betty and Herbert were good friends of my grandparents and in a way helped raise me, but my grandparents both passed away recently."

Good going, Lola. Way to put a damper on lunch. "Sorry to hear that," I mumbled, not knowing what else to say. I knew how painful it was to lose a grandparent. I missed my Nonna. At least I had her old recipe book to keep her close to me. Some of my best memories are of cooking with her when I was little.

I needed to change the subject, chase away the depressing cloud that hung over our table. "So, have you been a ballerina since you were like, three?"

Charlie laughed, a light and sparkly noise that wasn't unpleasant. "Actually, I didn't start dancing until I was eight. My grandparents took me to *The Nutcracker* for Christmas, and I fell in love. It was so magical the way those dancers practically floated across the stage like real fairies. They were so beautiful and graceful that I knew right then that I wanted to be just like them." Her entire face lit up as she spoke of that memory. I couldn't look away.

"I bet you took to ballet pretty easily." The way her body seemed to flow when she moved had to be a natural gift. Not just anybody could dance like that. I couldn't picture myself pirouetting across the stage. My strength lay in my speed and power.

"Not really. I was always coming home crying with scraped up knees and elbows from falling off fences or tripping over my own feet. Ballet taught me how to control my body and move through the world with a little more grace." She leaned over the table as if she were about to divulge a huge secret. I leaned in closer, too. "I was a tomboy when I was a kid. Always running around the neighborhood and playing in the mud. I used to collect bugs and leaves to make pretend potions."

"Pretend potions, huh? Did you want to be a witch when you grew up?"

"Something like that," she said with a grin.

I liked seeing her smile at me.

What was I doing here, again? Charlie was in a whole other world than me. So, we had a few things in common like fantasy books and athleticism.

She was good at Pilates. Really good. Just being friends with someone like her was dangerous. Eventually, she'd get bored and leave. And if I got to know her any better, that would be painful for me. I had promised myself I wouldn't let that happen again.

Sammy barked, making me jump. He stood up on his hind legs, leaning against my thigh. "Sammy!" Charlie said and reached over to pet him.

I did the same and our hands touched on the little dog's head. She didn't pull away but let her fingers linger on the back of my hand. Her gaze locked onto mine.

My foolhardy heart leapt at the intensity burning in her eyes. I pulled away and stood. "It was nice meeting you, Charlie," I said, trying not to react to the frown taking over her face. "But I need to get ready for work."

"Oh, okay," she said as she took up Sammy's leash. "I hope you'll come back to the dance studio. There's a challenging lower body class we could take together."

"Oh yeah, definitely." Not. I patted Sammy on the head and smiled my goodbye to Charlie before making a beeline for the exit gate. She was too beautiful and nice to get to know any more than I had already. It was best to stop before I found out she wasn't what she seemed. And that I wasn't what she wanted.

Besides, I had a very angry little Italian woman I needed to get back to.

Chapter Nine: Charlie

Charlie kicked herself the rest of the week for not getting Lola's number. How hard would that have been? It was just dumb to say "hope to see you again" without establishing any way to make that happen. She knew she should probably accept this as a ships passing in the night thing and let it go...but how often was she going to meet a totally buff, totally cute woman who liked *Lord of the Rings* and *Narnia*, and who even knew how to make amazing vegan food? Well, one recipe, anyway – somehow they'd never actually talked more about Lola's vegan cooking techniques, but Charlie would be more than happy to sample many, many vegan meals cooked by Lola.

If she could actually *find* her again, without being super pushy and invading her workplace. She looked out for her around the dance studio but, surprise, surprise, Lola didn't show up for another Pilates class.

Was that because she hated Pilates, or did she not want to deal with this crazy ballerina who was so awkwardly into her? But they'd had such a great conversation – until Lola rushed off. Maybe she'd just been late for work though.

Charlie read a lot of *Lord of the Rings* late in the night, trying not to think about her hand brushing up against Lola's, just before Lola had walked out, maybe for good. If only she could cast a summoning spell, or use a scrying spell. *Mirror, mirror, search right and left, help me find the cutest chef.*

The witchcraft she *was* doing focused on tending her garden, gathering herbs, and trying different combinations that might fight vampires. The coven had been searching everywhere they could for new recipes, new potions. The trouble was that, even if they came up with something powerful and effective, what were they going to *do* with it? They couldn't force feed the concoctions to vampires, *or* to the people the vampires might feed on.

That, she knew, was what she ought to be thinking about: preventing any more people from joining the Disappeared, finding ways to use the herbs against vampires, not about a woman she barely knew. But somehow, even knowing that, she couldn't stop thinking about Lola.

By Saturday, she'd decided she had to do something, if only to finally get this distraction out of her mind. Which still left her trying to decide if it was weird and stalkerish to show up at Lola's restaurant for Sunday brunch again.

First she asked herself if she should do it, with no good answer; then she asked Sammy, who just thumped his tail happily at her, which was an unclear answer; and then she finally asked Nathan, who immediately insisted on going to brunch with her the next day.

And so somehow she ended up hanging out on the patio outside *Sorelle* with Nathan, waiting for a table for two to open up. It gave her too much time for second thoughts.

"I don't know," she said, chewing on her nail. "Maybe this was a mistake. Maybe we should take the wait as a sign and leave before–"

"So you can mope around for another week and then come back again next Sunday anyway?" Nathan shook his head. "We're here. Let's *do* this thing. It's not like she told you she never wanted to see you again."

"But showing up at her work..."

"Yeah, it would be creepy if she worked in an office or something. But a restaurant is public. We're part of the public." Nathan slung a comradely arm around Charlie's shoulders. "We are two dancers, out enjoying brunch and fortifying ourselves for all that dancing we're doing getting ready for *Nutcracker* try-outs."

The reference to the upcoming production distracted Charlie, as Nathan had probably known it would. Nothing like substituting a new worry to interrupt the anxiety spin of another. "We should go over the choreography we planned again. I'm still not sure about that last lift – maybe it's too ambitious?"

"Ridiculous," Nathan scoffed. "We'll keep practicing it, and when we dance together at the try-out it'll be the perfect finish to really wow them. They already know we can dance; we have to show them we can go to the next level. And then, the Sugar Plum Fairy and her Cavalier, here we come!"

Charlie had a bad feeling she wanted this role too much. She usually tried not to set her heart on any particular role. Just being part of the company, contributing to the overall production – usually that was enough. But the Sugar Plum Fairy was special. "Yeah, I hope you're right." She sighed. "And I hope you're right to try-out with me. Victoria probably would have partnered with you." The lead ballerina always exuded an effortless quality in her dancing that Charlie envied even while knowing it was complete illusion. Victoria and Nathan didn't get on personally, but they danced together beautifully.

Nathan snorted. "Don't count on it. Victoria has an itemized list of every single time she's convinced I messed up a lift for her. Not every time I *did* – every time she *thinks* I did."

"Come on, she knows you're great." The lead ballerina was stingy with compliments, but she was a good judge of dancing too – and Nathan really was great.

"No one is great enough for Victoria," Nathan said darkly. "Don't talk about her, you'll ruin my appetite. Let's go back to strategy talk."

"For the try-outs?"

"No, for *today*. After we eat that fine vegan dish you're so excited about, how do we get that fine vegan chef you're so excited about out of her kitchen?"

Charlie's cheeks went hot. "She's not vegan," she mumbled. "And I'll just...tell the waiter I know her and want to say hi?" It sounded so dumb and pathetic said out loud. "Or I could want to compliment the chef...again?" Not much better.

"Could work," Nathan said, nodding. "*Or* we play this good cop/bad cop. I'll raise a big ruckus complaining about the food, and then you can rescue your cute chef from me! I'll probably get arrested for creating a disturbance, but anything for you, Charlie."

She laughed in spite of herself. "I think that would be going too far." The words, light as she'd intended them to be, hit close enough to home to make her laugh fade and bring all her original worries back. Was this whole business, stalking the Pilates classes, showing up at brunch, going too far? Was she building way too much on one charged exercise class, and one not-quite-a-date?

But it had been such a *good* sort of date. It had been a long time since she'd felt a connection like that. And Sammy had liked Lola – who had understood his name. Charlie only introduced him as Samwise when she wanted to see if someone would catch the reference, pick up the semi-secret code she was sending out. And Lola hadn't just asked about *Lord of the Rings*, she had asked Sammy if he was a Hobbit. *So* adorable.

Oh goddess, she had it bad.

Nathan, mercifully, appeared to have missed her drift off into ruminative crush-land, and was cheerfully saying, "I guess we could save the table-flipping for a last resort."

Charlie didn't think he was serious, but she gave an emphatic nod. "Before we try that, we should definitely–" She cut herself off, instinctively grabbing Nathan's arm.

A side door of the restaurant had opened, and Lola was walking out, talking animatedly to a man a foot taller than she was. Her chef's coat was slung over one arm, while she wore a tight t-shirt that showed every ripple of muscles in her arms. Her eyes were shining, hands waving as she discussed something with her – friend? Not a boyfriend, right? Unless Charlie had read *that* semi-secret code wrong. Lola's t-shirt had seemed pretty clear though.

"I wasn't about to flip any tables," Nathan protested, looking down at Charlie's hand on his arm.

"No, no, it's not that," Charlie whispered, hastily snatching her hand back again. "It's *her*. Over there. No, don't *look*!"

"Muscled with short hair?" Nathan said out of the side of his mouth. "Didn't know that was your type."

"I like lots of types and she's really cute and..."

And she was walking this way, and in another second she couldn't help noticing – yeah, there it was, Lola's gaze landing on her and Nathan. Her eyes widened, and then she smiled that crooked smile Charlie suspected she could really, really start to like.

"Hi!" Charlie said quickly, because Lola was staring at her so she had to say something, and fought an urge to wave. "Lola – nice to see you again! I was telling Nathan – this is Nathan – about your food, and we just had to come and...and it's nice to see you again."

Damn, she had just said that twice.

Lola grinned, so she'd probably noticed. "Always good to hear that someone appreciates the food." Which was not the same as saying it was good to see her. Gah.

Lola's friend seemed to think it was good to see her though, based on the way he smiled big, stepped closer and extended a hand. "Hello there. I'm Mario, and it is so good to meet a friend of Lola's."

Charlie shook his hand and gave him a genuine smile back – because hadn't Lola said something about her roommate Mario? Pretty sure that was a platonic relationship.

Mario gave a little tilt to his head and kept smiling at her, gaze intense. Oh goddess, was he flirting with her? "So have you been waiting long for a table? You and your...boyfriend?"

"Oh no," Nathan said quickly, glancing at Lola, in case it wasn't obvious enough to the entire world minus Mario who Charlie was interested in. "We're just friends. We work together, actually, dancing."

"Oh?" Mario said, his gaze still on Charlie, and his smile got bigger. "You're a professional dancer?"

She knew *that* tone – any minute now, he was going to ask her how flexible she was, and if she did any tricks that involved removing her clothing.

Before Charlie could try to deflect this, Lola elbowed Mario and said, "Cut that out. She's a ballerina. It's very artistic."

"Oh," Mario said, but only looked slightly disappointed. "That must be...interesting." Then he frowned, looking at Nathan. "Wait, you work together?"

"We do," Nathan jumped in, beaming. "I adore the ballet. And may I say, you have a beautiful smile."

Mario's expression suddenly turned a little glassy. "Uh. Thank you?"

Charlie rolled her eyes. Nathan was about as straight as they came, but he took an unholy pleasure in teasing a certain type of het guy who had assumptions about men in the ballet. "Right, so," she said quickly, because this was all super embarrassing, "you were probably on your way somewhere; we didn't mean to hold you up..."

Phone number – how could she work this around to getting a phone number? Or maybe she should let that go because after this fresh awkwardness, what chance did she have?

"We were on our way to try a new parkour course this afternoon," Lola said. "It looks like a really cool one."

"Will I see you at the Pilates class if you lose another bet?" Charlie asked impulsively, then realized that was rife with the possibility of being taken the wrong way. "I mean – not that I think you'd lose!"

Fortunately, Lola laughed. "Nah, Gino thinks I didn't hate the class enough, based on my description. He'll come up with something else for our next bet. Which I definitely won't lose."

So she didn't hate the class – was that a good sign, or was Charlie *really* reading too much into it?

"Hey, you should come with us!" Mario said, smile and cockiness back, attention focused on Charlie again. "You could watch us run the course."

Watch Lola perform awesome physical feats in a tight t-shirt that was going to show everything? Um, yes, please. Except Mario wasn't the one she wanted an invitation from, and Charlie didn't want to force her presence on Lola. That was just rude and bound to end badly. "I don't know, we really shouldn't intrude."

"Aw, come on," Mario urged. "It's an awesome sight to see. We do jumps that make you ballerinas look like you never left the ground."

Oh, he did *not* just say that. Charlie found herself smiling; Nathan could have told Mario that it was not a safe smile. "Maybe we shouldn't come *watch*. Maybe we should drop by our studio to change clothes, then we could come try out your little course with you." That's right. It was on now.

"Actually," Lola interjected, "parkour can be really dangerous if you don't know what you're doing."

"I think we'd be up for it," Charlie said firmly. "Right, Nathan?" A pause. "Nathan?"

He rubbed the back of his neck. "Yeah...I kind of have a fear of heights – I don't think I'm going to go jump off of anything, but *you* definitely should–"

"You have a fear of heights?" Charlie repeated, because was he seriously trying to make up a lame excuse to get out of this when they had been *challenged*?

"I do! I lift people – I don't *get lifted* – there's a reason for that–"

"Yeah," Charlie said, "the relative strength and size of the average man and the average woman, not to mention conventions of ballet that date back into a sexist past and–"

"So, you're coming, yeah?" Mario interrupted. "We're meeting the group in an hour, over at this empty warehouse on E. 25th. How about I text you the address?"

Now *he* was asking for her number. That was so not the goal of this morning. "Right," Charlie said faintly. And with a few seconds' reflection, what had she just got herself into anyway? "That sounds..."

"You're still waiting for a table," Lola pointed out. "They're slammed in there; you'll never be done in an hour."

"It's okay, we could just grab Taco Bell or something instead," Charlie said, words spoken before her brain caught up that Lola was trying to give her an out. Or was she trying to get rid of her?

And then Lola winced, and for a moment Charlie thought this was all a lot worse than she'd feared – until she said, "Please tell me you did not propose abandoning my restaurant in favor of – fine, come with me. If we go back into the kitchen, I can get them to give you a plate. If you're sure about this."

"Yeah, that...sounds good?" Charlie offered. Had Lola kind of just invited her for brunch?

"You go meet the group," Lola said to Mario, as she started back towards the door to the kitchen. "*I'll* text Charlie the location."

Well. *That* seemed promising.

I was going to kill Mario. And not just for the heart eyes he was shooting Charlie the whole time we talked, either, but for *inviting a porcelain doll to parkour.* Obviously the girl was strong, but if she broke a leg it was not going to be on *my* conscience. It was going to be on Mario's.

When I ducked back inside, all I was able to grab Charlie to not disrupt the flow of the kitchen was an Impossible Burger on a sprouted wheat bun – one of our few vegan lunch items – and a beef burger for her friend. But the way her eyes lit up when she saw the plate did all sorts of weird things to my insides, so I got out of there fast.

After texting the warehouse's address to her, that is.

As I drove there myself, I kept thinking about Charlie having my phone number. Even my best weekends with a girl wouldn't involve getting her number. But after the Pilates class and our kinda-date, I was as uncertain as ever that I wanted us to go down that road.

At any rate, I still didn't know if she was into women. A few tension-filled touches didn't necessarily mean much, and the pride pin she had had on her sweatshirt could have meant many other things besides just "into women."

Though, with Mario inevitably making his move within the next hour, I'd probably find out.

Damn him to hell, I was going to kill him. And I tried not to think too hard about what my protectiveness for Charlie already meant.

I pulled into a cracked, mostly-vacant parking lot beside the sun-bleached cement walls of a warehouse almost the size of a football field. It looked abandoned, like this would be the perfect place to get snatched by one of those serial killers the news – and Mario – had been ranting about. But gauging by the handful of cars next to mine and the sounds of yelling and laughter coming from within, this was the right place. We'd been told a parkour course had been set up inside for an upcoming competition, and for now, it was free to use.

I stepped into the relatively dim room – at least compared to the blinding sun outside – and could only make out the first few hulking walls and ledges in front of me. After I wandered around the first wall, the fluorescent lights on the ceiling let my eyes catch up enough to make out the absolute killer maze of platforms, walls, rails, and slopes.

"Hoooooly shiiiiiiiiiiiit," I called out, and my friends yelled back. From around the side of a platform, Andrea jogged up to me and gave me a tight hug. I hugged back, releasing her with a pat on the back.

"You ready to tear up this place?" she said, her dark eyes glittering. I nodded, smiling wide.

"This course is sick!" Jackie whooped from atop the platform we stood beside. I waved up at her. Somewhere across the warehouse, Allen hollered, and then I heard the rough scuffing of his shoes.

"It's perfect," Mario agreed.

"Do we know what any of the tournament's routes are going to be?" I asked, and I got mostly shrugs back from them. "Perfect, let's figure out our own."

Gino greeted me with a firm grip of his hand around mine, and we shared a little chest-bump. It always made me giggle the way my brother puffed out his chest as though it made his five-foot-six stature appear taller. But those who knew him understood his slightly-smaller build was a wound spring. He could jump higher than any of us.

We spent the next half hour walking the place, discussing gaps and angles, identifying some harrowing jumps that would definitely require the gymnastics foam mats Jackie had rolled up in the back of her truck.

"Okay, enough chit chat," I declared. "I want to fly."

Then a distinctly feminine voice echoed through the warehouse. "Hi! Are you getting started?"

The group did double takes as lithe, tall Charlie walked up to us, with her fellow dancer in tow. Charlie had changed into leggings and a t-shirt. Her hair had even already been pulled into a ponytail.

"Everyone, this is Charlie, she's a ballet dancer and wants to dance with us today," I said. Then I gestured at the group. "Charlie, you've already met that asshole, my roommate Mario. This gunshow that *almost* rivals mine belongs to my brother Gino. Unstoppable female strength right here is Jackie, the woman to never let your guard down around here is Andrea, and Mister tall-dark-and-handsome is Allen. Charlie, I hope you don't mind reminding us your friend's name…"

"Oh, I'm Nathan," he chirped. "I'm just here to watch."

"You sure you don't want to try?" Allen said, sweeping his long, braided hair over his shoulder. Nathan smiled and nodded.

"But you're going to jump with us?" Jackie asked Charlie directly, and she stood tall, and nodded back with a shockingly confident smile. I couldn't help but chuckle. She wouldn't be smiling the first time she hit the ground.

We all warmed up by making our way across a series of sloped platforms. I had to hop a bit between each one. But after seeing the taller Allen leap directly from one to the next like a goddamned gazelle, Charlie perfectly mimicked his movements, landing on the last one with her arms outstretched and expertly curved.

I'm not sure whose jaw hit the floor louder – mine or Mario's.

"Charlie," Nathan stage-whispered, as she came back over to him after that performance, "Are you sure this is a good idea? With try-outs coming up and all?"

Charlie waved a hand at him. "Don't worry about me. I can do this."

Well. We'd see.

We spent a few minutes scrambling over increasingly high walls, and I was relieved to find Charlie was terrible when they were above her shoulders. There was something I could do that she couldn't! Finally, we started attempting the longer course we had mapped. As Allen took a stab at it, I explained the route to Charlie.

"So you're going to start up there," I said, pointing to a fifteen foot platform made of plywood painted black, with grooves cut into one side to act as a ladder. "You're going to jump across this gap to that lower, wide open platform – try to do a rolling landing if you want to show off. Then over that first railing, up onto the second, and then jump across that gap onto those two pillars. If you make it that far, you can try scrambling up onto the next platform beyond them."

As I explained, we watched Allen make the first jump, side-leap over the railing, and then skid to a stop in front of the second railing.

"Not enough speed," he called out.

Before he tried again, Gino got ready to go, and I flashed Charlie a wide-toothed smile, knowing I probably had that wild look in my eyes that I got before doing something daring. "I'm going up; you're welcome to watch for now until you'd like to try it."

Charlie smiled back. "You're going to crush it. I mean, the course, not you!" And she laughed, and it was just silly and cute enough for me to genuinely laugh with her, and then rush up the stairs before she could notice I was blushing.

And as soon as Gino landed safely on the other side of the far railing, I took a deep breath, ran a few steps, and flew.

Drop roll, hitting my shoulder hard but not too hard.

Up.

Over the railing. The second railing was coming up fast, so I pumped my arms and pulled up my legs, hopping onto it. Pushing off of it.

Feet made contact with the pillar on the other side. Then the second. I leapt for the far wall, caught the edge with too little of my fingertips.

With a barked laugh and a gasp of breath, I let myself fall the few feet to the ground, and shook out my adrenaline-soaked limbs.

"That was a fucking *trip*!" I exclaimed, and my friends yelled back their agreement.

As I rejoined the others, Andrea was already tackling the course, and with only a wobbly slide after the first jump, she skidded to a stop at the pillars.

Andrea leapt down, and together we watched Jackie take her first attempt which, surprising none of us, went quite well until she almost took the second railing in the gut. As we gave her some friendly jeers, I realized Charlie had left my side.

I panicked only for a moment, thinking that she had already given up on us, only to find Charlie at the top of the platform. Despite myself, I let out a sigh of relief, which Mario took as an opportunity to elbow me in the ribs. I flipped him off, and brought my gaze back up to Charlie, her brow furrowed as she studied the first jump, and the two foam mats stacked in between, just in case.

"You got this, Charlie!" Nathan cheered.

For a moment, Charlie kept standing there.

"You can just jump across really easy to get a feel for it," Jackie suggested.

She nodded, and barely had to exert herself to fully leap across and land gracefully on one foot and then the other on the other side.

"That was really good," I told her, and Charlie hummed.

"Just like a *grand jeté*." As she eased herself under the railing and hopped down a few platforms off to the side, back to the warehouse floor, Mario took his turn on the course.

We cheered Mario on until he slipped off the first pillar, landing on one of the mats Jackie had put down. About a five foot fall.

"I'm fine!" he called.

"Prove it," we all called back. Our group motto, in a way.

Everyone started second turns. Before I knew it, Charlie was back up there, trying again. She didn't stop with the first leap this time, instead making a spectacular splits-leap over the first railing, and then splaying her arms and digging the heels of her sneakers into the plywood before she could be hit by the second railing.

We were all whooping and hollering after that one. When she rejoined us, absolutely beaming at me, Mario clapped her on the shoulder and said something about how impressed he was. She almost startled from him, with a rushed thank you, before smiling again at me.

"I can't believe you do this," she said breathlessly. "I feel like one wrong move is going to kill me – but it's so exhilarating!"

"You're killing *me*, Charlie!" Nathan yelled, and she just rolled her eyes at him.

I chuckled. "That's why it's fun, and why I love it. I laugh in the face of danger, ha ha ha ha!"

She snorted. "*Lion King*."

"You know it," I said.

We all took another stab at the course. Gino and Allen made it all the way to the end. Andrea lost her grip on the final platform, and Jackie needed to bail at the same spot I had. Mario nicked his foot on the first railing and stopped before the second rail, which he handled well this time with a nice roll and smooth stop.

Then it was my turn again, and I nailed the roll and railings. Though I lost my balance and had to jump off the first pillar to keep myself from falling, I still felt good about the run.

Charlie ascended the starting platform, and gave us all a little wave before running and leaping like she had wings. Across, over, up, and then right where I'd lost my balance on the last round, her foot slipped, and she let out a yelp and went down.

I muttered a swear as I heard a scrape and a thud. I jogged over there, Nathan keeping pace with me.

"I'm, uh, okay!" she said in a pathetic, wind-knocked-out voice.

"Prove it!" the others called.

"Charlie..." I practically whimpered, holding out my hand. She grabbed it and I pulled her to her feet. Her leggings were ripped on her left side, exposing parallel lines of raw, pink scrapes running down her calf, blood starting to bubble up in several places. I sucked in a sharp breath, ordered myself to keep it together. Not like I hadn't seen injuries before. Nathan was inspecting it thoroughly, as I looked back up at Charlie.

"We have a med kit," I said quickly. "I can't tell yet if you need stitches."

"Oh, no, no. It's fine!" she managed, though her voice was shaking. "I'll be fine. That was so fun." The others approached, and I gave them a nod to mean everything was cool. At least, I hoped everything was cool.

"I'm so sorry about your leg. Have I ruined your career?" I mumbled, while Gino squatted beside her to get a better look at it.

She laughed, shaking her head, and showed off the scrape, which now had a few streams of blood running down to her shoe. "Dancers get hurt."

"Yeah," Nathan said hesitantly. "This is mostly just a surface scrape, which Charlie has always healed from incredibly fast."

"You get hurt like this a lot?" I asked.

She gave me a sheepish grin. "Honestly, yeah. It's just a scrape, and probably a bruise on my ass. I'll be fine."

"Not that ass," Mario said in joking horror. Allen snorted, and I repressed a growl.

There I was, feeling protective again. Huh.

Jackie jogged up to us after having ducked outside, a med kit under her arm. "That's a pretty nasty scrape. But I'm glad it's not something worse," she said, taking out a bottle of disinfectant and some gauze. Charlie offered her a smile, and held out her hands.

"I can clean myself up," she said, and Jackie nodded and handed over the supplies.

"One more round," Gino declared. He and Andrea headed back to the start, and a moment later Jackie jogged to catch up. But Charlie still stood there, so I hung back. Charlie got her leg cleaned off quickly, as she and Nathan talked to each other quietly. I felt awkward watching them, but I didn't want to leave her yet.

Finally, Charlie looked up at me. "I should probably call it with this," she said, gesturing at her leg.

"Hey, thanks so much for joining us out here," Mario said, sliding just a little too close to her. "I'd love to hang out again, if you'd like. You're really good. Maybe I could come see you dance sometime."

Charlie's eyes widened, and she stole a glance at me, before regarding Mario again. "Oh! Uh, that's really sweet of you. Though I totally understand if you're not into watching ballet."

He nodded, thankfully taking the hint, and strode off to join the others.

Nathan scrunched his nose, then pulled car keys out of his pocket. "Hey, why don't I bring my car right to the front door so you don't have to walk as far?"

"That'd be great," Charlie said softly. And off he went.

Which left the two of us standing there. Heat returned to my cheeks and I found myself inexplicably tongue-tied.

"This was definitely the most fun I've had in a while," she said, holding out her arms in a wide gesture.

I smiled at my shoes. "It was! Thank you. For coming. Sorry again about your leg."

"It's fine, I promise. Maybe next time you can come. At my place. I mean *to* my place!"

I gasped, and when our gazes met we both burst into laughter, Charlie hiding her open mouth with a delicate hand.

"Are you inviting me over?" I asked, the laughter giving me back my ability to form sentences.

"I have a garden!" Her eyes twinkled, and she clasped her hands together in front of her chest. "It's a really nice garden, really big! A whole acre! And... I thought you'd like to come see it and take home some rare herbs."

She was so genuinely *excited*. I ran my hand through my short hair, still not completely sure I had this girl figured out. But I found myself wanting to spend more time with her now.

"I'd love to. When?"

"Wednesday, say around noon?"

I smiled. "Sounds great."

"I'll get going. I should rest before practice first thing tomorrow, and *Nutcracker* try-outs are coming soon. But, Lola? Thanks for letting me come along."

The way she softly said my name sent shivers down my spine. "No problem. Catch you soon... Charlie."

She twiddled her fingers in a wave, and hopped into a gentle jog – albeit with a limp – over to the warehouse door. I watched her go, still in awe.

Behind me, Andrea had completed the course and was whooping from the end platform. I heard the thud of someone hitting the mat, and turned to find Mario looking up at the ceiling. I helped him up just like I had with Charlie.

"That dancer's into you, huh?" he asked, sounding defeated as he brushed himself off. "And to think I thought I had a chance."

I elbowed his gut. "There's a million beautiful girls – just let me have a few."

He shoved me back with a smile. "I don't need a million girls. But she does seem pretty special. "

I laughed. ' "At any rate, I think we're just friends."

"With the way she was watching you do the course? And blew off all my awesomeness? No way."

My cheeks grew hot as I let out a smile. And that little push toward a positive mood made the rest of our parkour that much more enjoyable.

I was already looking forward to Wednesday.

Chapter Eleven: Charlie

C harlie had Nathan take her straight home, after assuring him repeatedly that she wasn't badly hurt, no matter what it looked like. And she had to admit it did look bad. She climbed carefully out of the car, and waved to Nathan after opening the front door. Ignoring the now familiar feeling of emptiness in the large house, she limped directly to the potions room at the back and reached into the herb cupboard for her favorite healing salve. Dozens of jars lined the shelves, but none with the salve she needed. She smacked her forehead with her palm and groaned. Because the main ingredient had exploded last week. With everything going on since, she had never made it up again. "Damn, damn, double damn!"

Sammy hurried in at the sound of her voice, and Charlie took a moment to scratch behind his ears as she muttered, "I definitely should have made time for this."

She had to push Sammy's inquisitive nose away from the scrape on her leg. "Stay down, Sammy. In fact, have one of your treats." Her hand brushed against some of the drying herbs that hung from hooks above the cupboards, causing the scent of peppermint and rosemary to fill the room. She reached up to a higher shelf for his tin of treats, and held up a dog biscuit. He wriggled and wagged his tail madly until she dropped the treat where he could crunch on it. She laughed and patted him again before turning back to the cupboard. She'd have to make a new batch before she could deal with her leg, which was annoying. At least in the meantime she could use some Achillea Millefolium to help stop the last bit of bleeding.

She'd really been afraid for a few minutes that the others would try to make her go to Urgent Care. They'd all been so sweetly concerned, which was nice. But her magic meant she could take care of this far better than any standard medical practitioner could.

Herbs themselves were powerful when used in the right combination. The problem was people sometimes swallowed herbs like candy. *It's natural so it must be safe.* They didn't understand that plants had medicinal properties that could be harmful when not used properly. Some of the information on the internet these days was horrifying.

Of course, her herbs had the added benefit of being enhanced by her own special skills. Gathered at sunrise or moonrise, some suffused with the smoke of bay and sage under the full moon, others infused into spelled coconut or sweet almond oils. There were dozens of different treatments, each designed for a specific effect. And when performed properly, by a trained witch like her, they could create some very potent healing.

After rubbing the Achillea Millefolium oil on her aching leg and chanting the appropriate healing spell, Charlie began pulling the necessary ingredients from the cupboard, her fingers automatically reaching for the correct jars. There were rows of them, all carefully labeled, filled with dried herbs from her garden, sorted by their various medicinal and magical effects.

She pulled her marble mortar and pestle toward her, and hand ground Calendula, *Lavender Officinalis*, and *Symphytum Officinale*, along with a few others in the proper proportions before placing them into a tea bag. Next, she heated coconut oil, honey and beeswax over a low flame in her cauldron. Once the ingredients liquified, she added the full tea bag and turned off the heat. After steeping, the mixture was still liquid but cooling rapidly. She quickly removed the now useless tea bag and stirred in healing essential oils, including Eucalyptus, Cypress and Roman Chamomile. Then, lastly, she placed two careful drops of St. John's Wort-infused oil into the mix.

With a grunt of effort, she set the heavy cast iron cauldron on her worktable and spoke the proper spells as she stirred it slowly three times with her left hand.

As she finished, she closed her eyes and intoned, "Thank you for dyes and fragrances for our enjoyment, food for our bodies, and herbs for our ills. Thank you for cradling them, nurturing them, and filling them with nourishment."

Her potions room seemed to brighten once she opened her eyes, and she thought for a moment that she heard the tinkling of a bell. Good. Both the herbs and the magic were ready. She poured the thickening fluid into salve jars and set them aside to solidify.

Only then did she allow herself to take out a clean cloth and scrub the inside of the cauldron. Once the cloth was liberally coated in the leftover salve, she rubbed it over her leg and instantly felt a surge of relief.

Oh goddess, that was good.

The stinging pain of the scrape was already easing. She looked down in satisfaction, watching her flesh knit together until most traces of her carelessness were gone. Her skin darkened as bruising formed, yellowed, then slowly lightened. She'd have a few lingering bruises; the deeper ones would take a bit longer to heal. But at least she wouldn't have to worry about her ability to dance tomorrow.

Charlie looked around her potions room, what used to be her grandmother's potions room, at all the pretty jars and bottles, each clearly labeled by her grandmother. She had to blink back a few tears, knowing that all her magic – all the coven's magic – hadn't been enough to keep her grandmother alive. The cancer had been too far advanced when they realized it was there. The doctors had only given her a few months, but the coven had kept her relatively pain free for far longer. Even so, with all their magic, they hadn't been able to save her. And just six weeks later, she had watched helplessly as her grandfather seemed to fade away before her eyes. He hadn't wanted to build a new life without her grandmother. And, with his passing, she'd been truly orphaned. She'd never felt so alone.

At least she had the ballet, and was back with the coven again. And she'd be able to dance tomorrow, thanks to her magic. Everyone in her coven knew the importance of counting the blessings they were given, so she offered up a quick prayer of thanks.

But with those thoughts gone, she had time to fret about next Wednesday. What had possessed her to make that crazy invitation? How could she have invited Lola here, into her home? Into her garden?

Although it wasn't just *her* garden.

She glanced over the small garden fence at the profusion of plants growing outside, wondering what Lola would make of them; a mix of culinary, medicinal, and flowering shrubs. That was the public part of the garden, the part Lola would see. Further back, hidden by magic, were the plants with magical properties, the area where she'd gone with Betty and Esther. No one, outside the Singing River Coven she'd belonged to since birth, had ever seen that part.

She walked outside, crossing her small yard and opening the hidden gate into the garden. She hurried through the public front half, and made her way toward the back. Her grandmother had planted it over fifty years before, labeling each of the herbs in her beautiful flowing script, making sure the coven had everything they needed for their earth based magics. Some of these plants weren't available any more, while others had been infused with the coven's magic for over fifty years.

This garden would be the source of the magical plants they could hopefully use to fight the vampires who had been feasting, unseen and unknown, on the defenseless residents of Sacramento. She stroked her hands over those Esther had mentioned, encouraging them to grow quickly. To multiply their healing properties.

She began checking for weeds and pests, though she didn't expect to find any. The garden had long ago been charmed to accept only useful volunteers. This part of the garden, hidden by enchantments, was a labyrinth of sorts, edged with tall elderberry and yew trees. And in the labyrinth's center, she kept an altar and tended her most cherished magical herbs.

She inhaled deeply as she made her way along the winding paths bordered by boxes of culinary and medicinal herbs. She brushed past rows of lavender and rosemary and lemon verbena, the mingled scents nearly intoxicating.

This part of the garden was not only beautiful, it was a place of power. Her coven understood how these herbs could be used for potent magics. Lola would no doubt find these plants interesting if Charlie ever brought her back here, but she wouldn't understand how they could actually be used.

The members of her coven had pledged to protect the inhabitants of this city and this sacred place to the best of their ability. All they needed was to figure out how to make that happen. Charlie whispered, "Goddess, help us protect those who need our assistance. Help us stop those who hunt the innocent. Give us the ability to use our powers to save them. As I will, so mote it be."

As soon as she stopped speaking, she heard the faint tinkle of a bell. She looked around and sighed. She could sense the garden's power prickling against her skin now that she was standing still. What on the goddess-loved green earth was she going to say to Lola if she noticed?

She compulsively checked the wards on the house and garden, only relaxing when they all flared a bright, warm turquoise, indicating they were at full strength. For now, at least, no vampire could attack her home or break in to steal her coven's magic.

Chapter Twelve: Lola

"**I** can't do this," I muttered, standing outside my parents' older ranch-style home. Beside me, Mario shrugged.

"I think you can," he said. "It's just dinner."

I shot him a look. "It's the first dinner I've attended in months. My sister is here with her three screaming kids," I argued, gesturing at her minivan, "Momma is going to oscillate between praising Leo on his success in corporate America, Orlando working toward a doctorate, the grandkids, and complaining that *I'm* not like my other siblings."

"Lola. Darling. Honey," Mario cooed, holding my face in his hands. "You are being too hard on yourself. It will not be that bad."

I swatted his hands away. "Stop acting like my mom, you fool. And at any rate, we'll see." I left his side and stepped up to the front door.

I'd hardly rung the bell before Momma flung the door open, squealing and giving me a tight hug.

"Lola! Darling! I thought you'd never make it! And Mario – it's been too long!"

I met eyes with Mario briefly – and he winked at me.

"Watching me from the window again?" I asked, but I was dragged into the house, my words lost in the commotion.

My parents' home, with its open floorplan and outdated decor, did give me a temporary pang of nostalgia. The dining table where I did homework and put together puzzles, the bright orange tile of the kitchen counters, way too many photos and paintings on the walls. It was all familiar and comforting. The newer couch and 4K television, gifts from brother Leo over the past few years, were an ugly modern intrusion in the otherwise pleasant time capsule. But such was life, and time, changing bit by bit until everything was different.

My sister Stella sat on the couch with a five-year-old clinging to her – my niece Isabel – and a toddler – my nephew Tony – at her feet with a wooden train set. Stella chatted away with my sister Bianca, who must have recently touched up her bleached hair because it shone perfectly. Their husbands and my brother Leo all mingled in the dining room beyond the couch, laughing and holding bottles of some IPA.

Momma dragged me to Dad, who sat on his leather armchair with Stella's youngest, plump-cheeked six month old Gregory.

"Lola! Say hi to your father and nephew," Momma said quickly, "And then come help me in the kitchen."

She was gone before I could respond, and Dad smiled at me. "It's so good to see you, honey. I'd hug you but my arms are a little full."

"It's alright, Dad," I said. Gregory had turned his head and buried it in Dad's shoulder. "Hey, buddy," I tried. "Wanna say hi to Auntie Lola?"

Gregory kept his head hidden and whined, the noise getting his mom's attention.

"Oh, Lola, he's got the worst stranger danger right now, I'm so sorry! It's not you, I promise."

"You just gotta come around more often, sis!" Bianca added.

Yeah. Sure.

"Marioooooo!" a voice yelled out from down the hall, and Mario yelled back in turn, "Ginooooo!" before bounding toward my brother and clasping him on the shoulder.

Well, at least he would have a good time. He usually did with the guys.

"It is good to see you, Lola," Stella added, slipping Isabel off of her lap to pull me into a hug. I tapped her back lightly. She squeezed my bicep and giggled. "Every time I see you it's like you're more buff."

"Of course she is, you should see her tearing up a parkour course," Gino boasted.

"Me? How about you, Mister I-can-jump-five-feet-straight-up?" I shot back at him, but he just rolled his eyes.

"Don't let Mom catch you talking about that stuff," Bianca whispered, laughing. The whole family knew about Momma not approving of Gino and me doing parkour, and I was certain any indication we were still "leaping off of buildings" would stir up that whole pot again. After it coming up in our fight last week, I definitely wanted to avoid the topic.

"Yeah, don't tell Momma," I added to my dad, punching his arm lightly. He held up his palms in clear innocence.

Okay, okay, I was smiling. This banter was okay so far. Maybe this evening wouldn't be so bad after –

"Lola!"

– all.

"Coming, Momma!" I called, jumping to my feet and sliding into the kitchen.

Momma had tied her golden brown waves back into a bun, and stood in front of a large pot on the stove, steam billowing toward the ceiling and the smell of garlic and tomato hitting me in the face with another wave of nostalgia. On the counter to her side were all the ingredients for meatballs.

She didn't have to tell this chef what to do. I had washed my hands and was chopping onion and more garlic within the minute, content to zone out and cook. I was brought back to my teenage years when we cooked together. Those, at least, were good moments. But my daydreaming was interrupted when she unsurprisingly went for the jugular.

"So nice to see your niece and nephews, huh, Lola? They're getting so big. I told you they'd grown since the last time you saw them. How long has it been now?"

"It is nice, Momma," I said, finishing up the aromatics and brushing them into a big bowl. "You know, I have my own dish at the restaurant. I told you about that, yeah? It's been a busy month preparing that dish and making sure it's rolled out right."

"Now that's my girl," she said, pulling a frying pan out of a cabinet and pouring in a good helping of olive oil. "Maybe you can own your own restaurant one day. I know you'd be just as good at the business side of things as Leo."

Ugh, did she always have to compare us? "I'm sure I would." With the ground beef and pork and all the ingredients in the bowl, I started mixing it together with my hands, the way any Italian mother would expect. "But nothing beats being in the kitchen," I added, punching into the bowl for emphasis, "making a masterpiece."

"Ah, you're right about that," Momma said. "I just wonder when you'll move up, Lola. If you were your own boss you could take off any time you need."

Momma joined me by the bowl, and together we formed meatballs in our palms, throwing them quickly into the heated pan. The sizzle was pleasant, and I focused on the sounds and smells of the kitchen so I wouldn't have to respond to this critique of my ambition.

Because no, I didn't need to do more, when I was happy where I was and made good enough money doing it, and why couldn't that be enough?

For a while, our conversation focused on the meal, and what else needed to be prepared, and together we did that dance around the kitchen of two experienced cooks, getting things done on time, straightening as we went.

"Oh my god, it smells amazing in here!" Bianca cried as she walked in, peeking over my shoulder at the last of the meatballs finishing in the pan. I tossed them into the large pot of sauce with the rest.

"Almost as good as Nonna's," Momma said, leaning her head on my shoulder. "Though Lola does bring something special and modern to our tradition."

I recalled my great-grandmother's cooking, me watching her as a wide-eyed little girl. That was quite a compliment from Mom that I hadn't expected and couldn't figure out how to react to.

"Of course she does, our very own Robbie Day!" Bianca laughed. Momma giggled too, preparing a second large pot for the pasta, as I pulled the now-empty pan off the stove.

I smiled. "No one he's had on *Outcook Me* could make a sauce like this one," I declared, and Bianca nodded, still chuckling.

"Bianca, go tell the boys it'll be about half an hour to dinner," Momma said, and my sister whirled out of the kitchen.

Then, Momma leaned toward me. "She and Jeremy have been married for almost an entire year, can you believe the time's flown that fast? I hope to see a baby announcement before their first anniversary!"

"Oh my god," I almost yelled. "Let them take their time!"

"I'm not getting any younger and want to be able to play with my grandkids!" she said, and I tensed up for the inevitable next line. "And at any rate, I don't know if any of the rest of you are even going to have kids!"

There it was. I gritted my teeth, and focused on cleaning some of the dishes. When Momma must have realized I wasn't taking the bait, she turned from me and started slicing french bread.

"You and Gino aren't getting any younger either," she said quietly.

"I'm only twenty-six!" I practically shouted.

"Lola, you don't have to yell."

I huffed with frustration. "Do I need to remind you I'm gay? *And* single?"

"Oh, you'll find someone. Plus, gay couples adopt all the time. And there's modern options! Test tube babies!"

That was it. "This conversation is *over*."

I didn't mean for it to come out as a growl, but it did. Momma flinched, and went on slicing, without saying another word.

And for the rest of our prep, then as everyone sat down for the big meal, I felt terrible.

Around me, my family was laughing and talking and passing around food and wine bottles and I kept a smile on my face but didn't feel like I was really there at all.

Children squealed and ran around the table. Momma and Stella talked loudly, clinking their wine glasses together. Leo asked how things were going at the restaurant, and I answered quickly and smiled. Mario, the traitor, was tousling kids' heads and laughing with my dad.

Mario shot me a look, like he saw right through my fake expression. Okay, maybe he wasn't a total traitor. I gave him the sublest head shake I could.

After the meal, which of course was amazing, Stella and Bianca insisted on handling clean up so I stepped outside.

My parents' backyard hadn't changed much since I was a kid either, though the small raised garden beds had multiplied in recent years and there must have been twice as many potted plants on the porch as there used to be, a little bit worse for wear now that we were in the middle of another long, hot summer.

Bright orange sunlight filtered through the tall scrub oaks in the surrounding yards, and I leaned onto the porch railing and let out a breath.

"She just wants what she thinks is best for us."

I looked up at Gino approaching, and he leaned on the railing beside me and crossed his arms. Apparently someone else had seen through my fake expression too. "I know, but does it need to hurt this much?"

He shrugged. "Probably not, but I'm not sure she knows how to say these things any other way."

I stared out at the yard, at little bugs catching the light as they darted to and fro. "I don't know how to tell her that our priorities are different than what hers had been."

Gino nodded, his expression solemn. "If you figure it out, let me know."

"At least we're failures together," I said, and Gino laughed and punched me in the arm.

"Yeah. Unless you're hiding a girlfriend or something."

I thought of Charlie, and my hesitance made him punch me again. "No! No, I'm not. I don't think I am anyway."

What would Charlie think of this big, messy family? Of course, even if we did start going out, we had a long way to go before such a milestone as her coming to a family dinner.

But, as much as the thought of her meeting my family made me shudder, there was still a small part of me that liked the idea of it happening one day.

Chapter Thirteen: Charlie

Charlie woke early on Wednesday, amazed to feel her fingers tremble – ever so slightly – when she thought of Lola coming here today. She couldn't have said if it was excitement or nerves; probably both. She dressed, amused at the care she was taking; leaving her hair down loose around her shoulders instead of in a bun or ponytail, adding a quick dash of blush to her cheeks, coating her lips with lightly tinted gloss, and stroking a trace of soft shadow on her eyelids.

Nathan would no doubt tease her about it when she met him for practice that afternoon. But it would – hopefully – be worth it.

She hurried through each of the rooms, twitching unnecessarily at curtains and pillows, straightening already straight pictures frames, rubbing at a spot on the sliding glass door.

She opened the coat closet, grateful to see there was space, just in case Lola had something she needed Charlie to hang up. Which showed just how keyed up she was about Lola's visit. It was the middle of summer; Lola wouldn't need anything hung up.

She stepped back and placed her hand on the door, but before she could close it one of the thirteen folding chairs all but leapt out of the closet, barely missing her foot. Charlie stared at the chair, momentarily stunned. There was absolutely no reason for it to have fallen like that. A shiver ran down her spine as she slowly bent to pick it up. There was a feeling in the air; something charged. Almost like pressure. The hair on the back of her neck prickled. This particular chair had been her grandmother's. There was a distinctive scratch in the shape of a crescent moon on the back.

The image of her grandmother sitting in that room kept intruding. If it wasn't for the coven and the garden, she might think about selling this place; it felt too large, and seemed to echo with emptiness.

Charlie cleared her throat as she lifted the fallen chair. "I'm not ready to take you out. Not yet. Maybe not ever. I know it's been months, but you need to stay in there." For a moment the pressure increased, then the air went flat. Charlie shoved the chair back into the closet and hurriedly shut the door. Maybe she wouldn't offer to hang anything in the closet after all.

She glanced out the back window, and her fingers clamped on the windowsill as an errant thought itched in the back of her mind. The entire Singing River Coven regularly came to the garden to cut herbs they needed. What if someone showed up today while Lola was there? They all treated her like a young, beloved grandchild. That could end up...embarrassing.

The doorbell rang, startling her, and Charlie's heart began to pound. She tried to tell herself she was just nervous about one of the coven coming over, but knew it was more than that. Lola was there, at her house. Waiting for her.

The truth was, Charlie hadn't felt this way about someone for a very long time.

She glanced at her phone as she crossed to the door. Noon straight up. At least Lola was on time. Charlie hated waiting – especially when she was so full of nervous excitement. She rubbed her hands on her skirt before reaching for the doorknob – she didn't want to gross Lola out with sweaty palms. She pulled the door open and smiled, hoping her feelings weren't written all over her face. What was it about this woman that made Charlie's mouth water?

"Hi," Lola said, and tugged at the neck of her snug blue tank-top, drawing Charlie's eyes along her well defined collarbones. Charlie forced her eyes back to her face. To her soft, moist lips. Her-

Charlie gave herself a quick mental shake. "Welcome," she said with a smile, and stepped back, enjoying the sight of Lola entering her home.

Lola shrugged off her backpack and gazed around the foyer. Samwise trotted in and danced around her feet.

Charlie gazed down at Sammy in amazement. "I don't remember seeing Sammy take such a liking to someone outside the family before." He was acting like Lola was his long-lost best friend.

Lola bent down and awkwardly patted Sammy on the head. Sammy didn't seem to mind the awkwardness, based on his pleased bark. "You still haven't told me if you're a hobbit," Lola told the happy dog, who merely plopped his butt on the floor and panted contentedly.

Charlie realized they were just standing there, and nearly blushed in mortification. What kind of hostess kept her guest waiting by the front door? "Would you like a quick tour of the house before I show you the garden?" There, that sounded polite enough.

"Uh, sure." Lola shrugged like she didn't really care. But she was acting as uncertain as Charlie felt. She put her hands in her pockets, then pulled them out and let them hang by her sides. Then she bounced them against her shapely, muscular thighs, then returned them to her pockets. Although Charlie appreciated not being the only one who felt unsure of herself, she had to wonder – would they ever feel comfortable around each other?

Charlie led the way through the living room. Lola glanced around, eyebrows drawing together in puzzlement. "Wow, this room is huge!"

Charlie looked around, trying to see her home as if she hadn't seen it before, and her breath backed up in her lungs. This part of the house was wide open. Large enough for thirteen women to sit comfortably on those thirteen chairs tucked into the closet. It had just been a large, barren space since her grandmother died.

Charlie realized she'd gotten really good at not seeing that space; it was painful. A brief touch of remembered guilt pushed at her; Betty's living room was so small in comparison. Should she – could she – start holding coven meetings here? She glanced over at Lola, here, in her home, and smiled. That decision, thank the goddess, wasn't something she had to make today.

"My grandmother used to have some friends meet here," she said quickly, dismissively, and motioned toward the kitchen. She'd started to turn, but noticed Lola's eyes sweep up and down her body.

A warm flush started to creep up her cheeks, then Lola's eyes focused on her calf. "What did you do to your leg?"

"My leg?" Charlie asked, unsure what Lola meant.

"Yes. Your leg." Lola frowned in confusion. "The one you scraped so badly during parkour. It looks like it's already healed."

Oh, damn. Why had she worn a skirt that left her legs bare? Oh yeah, she liked showing off her legs. They were one of her best features; she was a ballerina, after all. But she should have remembered this would lead to questions. "I told you it wasn't that bad," she said, and turned away quickly. When in doubt, change the subject. "Come and see my kitchen."

Behind her, Lola muttered something about unnaturally fast healing and Charlie grimaced. She'd have to explain it to Lola at some point. If they kept seeing each other. But this was probably too early to mention the whole "guess what, I'm a hereditary witch." She had no idea how Lola would react, and wasn't ready to find out. Besides, the coven preferred to keep its existence a secret to all but the most trusted people.

She led the way to her kitchen, conscious of Lola behind her, and the grinning Samwise, who trotted along behind Lola. It felt ridiculously like she was leading a parade. She shook some of the tension from her shoulders as they reached the kitchen and stood aside to let Lola enter.

This room was large and bright, and felt like it was wrapping around you in a hug. Her grandmother had chosen the colors, and Charlie wouldn't change any of it. Bright yellow walls, for wisdom, inspiration, and concentration. Cupboards painted white, for enlightenment, clarity, and protection on three of those walls. Curtains and other accents in shades of green, for abundance, success, and health.

But it wasn't the colors that held Lola's attention.

"Wow. I love your countertops! And a double wide refrigerator and oven? This place looks like it would meet commercial kitchen requirements." Lola was taking in everything, her eyes gleaming with desire. Charlie's breath caught. She wanted Lola to look at her just like she was looking at this kitchen someday. Soon.

She shoved down that thought and managed an easy grin. The granite countertop that Lola had mentioned swirled with tones of green and brown. It wasn't just beautiful – her grandmother had chosen it to enhance the ability to see the big picture, assist with health and energy, and banish negativity. They might not appreciate it for the same reasons, but it was one of her favorite parts of this kitchen too.

Lola wandered over and looked at the sink and the stove, then turned to face Charlie. "I'd just about give my right arm to have a space like this to cook in at home. My place is so small in comparison. Only one person can fit comfortably in there. Although Mario doesn't cook much, so I guess that's not really a problem."

"You're making me feel guilty." Charlie laughed self-consciously. "I don't cook for myself much. I mostly use this space for, um...soaps and lotions and...stuff like that." Charlie wanted to kick herself for sounding like such an idiot. But soaps and lotions didn't sound as strange as magical healing salves and potions. And, in fact, she made most of those in her potions room.

A silence fell between them and stretched. Charlie asked desperately, "Can I get you anything while we're here? I have herbal tea and filtered water."

"No, I'm good," Lola told her, and held up a bottle of water.

Lola fidgeted with the bottle, looking uncomfortable. Charlie bit back a curse and said quickly, "You still haven't seen the garden. I think you'll like it."

"Oh, right. Lead the way."

Charlie exited the kitchen, aware of Lola following behind her again. She hurried to the family room where a sliding door opened onto the garden. And realized that the house no longer felt so empty. Lola's energy filled the void her grandparents had left, pushing it back. What would it be like to have that presence fill this space more often? Something bubbled under her skin; this time it felt like anticipation rather than nerves. And Charlie decided she was going to let Lola know she was interested before Lola left here today.

Charlie opened the sliding door, walked across the patio and stepped into the garden through the small gate on the other side. "Here it is," she said brightly. She started to turn back to Lola, but Sammy shot out the door, barking at a robin perched on an elderberry bush. Charlie shook her head in amazement. How could just the sight of a bird make Sammy forget he was developing arthritis in his knees?

At least the bird didn't have anything to fear from him. It flew off with a sharp flap of wings, but the yard still rang with birdsong and the hum of bees. The sun had risen higher now, chasing away the last bit of dew from the ground. Behind her, Charlie heard Lola breathe out an amazed sigh.

"You said you had a garden, but this is more than just a garden. This is magical."

Charlie shot her a startled glance. Had she sensed the magic here?

"It's like every secret, magic garden I've ever read about," Lola continued. "I swear I hear bells ringing, but I don't see any."

Charlie felt as if her knees had suddenly come loose. Only members of the coven had mentioned hearing bells. "It is pretty amazing," she said carefully. "My grandmother planted it decades ago, when she first married my grandfather, and she kept adding to it. She invited the cov...community to enjoy it, too."

Lola walked past her. "Your selection is amazing!" She began pointing in appreciation as she wandered away from the house. "Rosemary, lavender, basil, parsley, thyme – several different varieties, sage, tarragon, chives. This whole section is filled with culinary herbs. They're beautiful."

"I can let you take some cuttings if you'd like," Charlie said, suddenly feeling better about Lola being here. This garden was filled with things a chef would be interested in. She had no reason to feel so ridiculously worried.

"That would be great!" Lola sounded even more enthusiastic about the garden than she had about the kitchen. So far, Lola had shown excitement about parkour, herbs and cooking. What else could get her excited?

She needed to think of something else before she embarrassed both of them. "I can run in and get some cutting shears and paper bags." Charlie didn't wait for Lola to respond. She headed back to the house, rummaged for everything she'd need in her potions room, then hurried back outside. And stopped.

Where was Lola?

Charlie rushed forward, her voice coming out too high and tight. "Lola?"

"I'm over here. I couldn't resist looking around."

Charlie's heart sped up and began to pound erratically. Lola sounded like she'd called from the back of the garden. The part that had been safely warded against outsiders. Was there something wrong with the wards?

"Lola?" she called again. "Where are you?"

"Back here."

No, the wards seemed to be intact. At least, there had been the slight but distinct difference to sounds that came from there, due to those magic wards. Or had she imagined that? She rushed forward, barely managing to hold onto the scissors when she nearly tripped in her haste. She did drop the bags and left them where they fell.

She was muttering a combination of curses and prayers as she rounded the last curve in the labyrinth. Then a bell chimed, and Charlie felt the slight prickle of the wards along her skin. They were definitely working. So how in the world had Lola found her way here past them?

Lola was staring at a small plot that contained several of the herbs typically used for magical purposes. Goddess. How was she going to explain this?

Lola pointed at an upright, many-branched plant, about two feet tall, with a few remaining star-shaped, small yellow flowers. "That tag says *Hypericum Perforatum*. I've seen that before, in my great-grandmother's recipe book. I've never seen it for sale fresh anywhere, so I've never been able to try her recipe."

"Your great-grandmother's recipe book?" Charlie's mouth felt stiff as she forced out the words. That plant, one of the herbs Esther thought could be used against vampires, was used often by the coven for teas and tinctures and healing salves, but not normally in food dishes. So what did Lola's great-grandmother use it for? "What was her name?" And why did she have a recipe with this herb?

Lola smiled, eyes filled with memories. "Maria Borja. Her book is filled with some crazy stuff. Most of it doesn't taste particularly good, so I'm not sure why she kept those recipes. I guess I don't really have a practical reason to keep it, but it's written by hand, her hand, and it feels like an heirloom, so..."

"Maria Borja's recipe book?" When Lola nodded, Charlie thought for a moment her knees would fail her. Had Lola had Maria Theresa Borja's missing book all this time?

"Did you know my great-grandmother?" Lola asked, then shook her head. "Sorry. You'd have been a little kid when she died."

Charlie might not have to answer that question, but still felt torn. After all, Lola's book might not have belonged to Maria *Theresa* Borja. Charlie would sound crazy if she started talking about the greatest witch of the past century, and it turned out to be a different person. And even it was, it might not be her spellbook. After all, Lola had referred to it as a recipe book, and spellbooks were normally called –

"She called it a Receipts book, actually," Lola said, as if she'd pulled the word straight out of Charlie's head. "Most of it is recipes, though she had little poems that she collected in there, as well as drawings of herbs. Stuff about animals and nature and the moon. It's kinda cool, even if I can't use most of it."

That answered the question about the book. But did that mean Charlie should share being a witch? Lola hadn't mentioned anything about that...

"We used to cook together every Sunday," Lola added wistfully. "I loved our time together; it's why I love being a chef, I think. Nonna always said I was the best cook in the family." She crossed her arms over her chest, then let them fall back to her sides, shaking her hands out as if she was uncomfortable. "I still miss her. I mean, it's been years; she died when I was seven. But she left me her recipe book. She told me I'd be the best one in the family to use it."

Charlie let out a quick breath. Perhaps it was more than just a coincidence that Lola had found her way to this spot. Could Lola have a sensitivity to magic? Did she realize it? If so, why had Lola been so surprised about Charlie's leg being healed? Why wasn't she using herbs and magic to care for her own parkour injuries?

And if she did know, it would certainly make the whole earth witch conversation much easier.

"So what's the recipe for? The one that uses this plant?" Charlie reached out a finger and gently touched a small green leaf. She moved it just enough so the sun shone through, making the tiny pinpricks – the perforations – obvious.

"It sounds like a pesto recipe. I'd like to try it. It's made with a mix of regular basil and holy basil. I've never used that before. Then it calls for the usual: olive oil, pine nuts, garlic, salt, and parmesan cheese. But it also contains *Hypericum Perforatum* and *Verbena Officinalis*. I have no idea if it would be any good, but..." She shrugged.

For a moment Charlie couldn't speak. Lola had just listed off so many of the ingredients the coven wanted to introduce to the people in Sacramento. Lola's recipe would not only protect against vampires, it could make people feel better – potentially a lot better – at the same time.

Charlie heard Betty's voice in her head, almost as if she were standing at Charlie's elbow. *'Promise me, sisters – give me your binding vow. We will take whatever actions we can to stop the evil spreading through our town. We do have the ability to stop them. Please, I need your word.'* And Charlie had sworn a binding vow, along with the others in the coven, that she would do whatever it took to stop the disappearances. To stop the vampires. Now she had a chance to fulfill her vow, practically dropped into her lap. This was no coincidence. But she'd have to use this woman, the one she wanted to get closer to, in order to do it.

"Excuse me a moment, Lola. I got the scissors, but I need to get some bags." Charlie hurried back toward the house, scooping up the fallen bags as she passed. She needed to be out of earshot before she called Betty. She yanked her phone from her pocket, dialing as she jogged, and sighed in relief when Betty answered. She told her about the receipts book Lola had described and who it had belonged to. Betty's enthusiasm overpowered Charlie's hesitation. "That's wonderful! You have to give Lola the herbs. You said she works in a restaurant downtown, right? Ask her to introduce the recipe there."

"But it doesn't seem right to involve her in this without telling her what we're doing." Charlie remembered the promise she'd made to herself a few days before – that she'd ask Lola before assuming something in the future. How could two such important promises, the one to the coven and the one to herself, be suddenly in conflict? And which one did she owe her true allegiance to? "I feel really uncomfortable about this, Betty. She should have a choice."

"It's not just about the two of you." Betty's voice was firm, though not unkind. "It's about every person in the Sacramento area. This may only be one small part, but they're in danger and you can protect them."

"I'm worried what Lola will think when she learns what the herbs do." She'd like to believe Lola already knew about magic, but the truth was she had only been talking about recipes. So Charlie really had no way to be sure that she knew the true significance of her great-grandmother's book. "When she finds out that we used her to fight vampires. And what if it puts her in danger?"

"I'm sure it will be fine, dear. You shouldn't borrow trouble. And as long as she doesn't know, she can't mention it to anyone." Betty's tone grew more serious. "Promise you won't tell Lola the truth. She might say something to the wrong person. That *could* put her in danger. And if word of what we are doing reaches the vampires, it could ruin everything. You owe this to the coven, Charlie. Promise."

Charlie was aware of time ticking away. She had to hurry or Lola would wonder what she was doing all this time. "I don't think–"

"You know very well that you willingly made a binding vow in the circle, Charlie. So why are you hesitating?"

She did owe it to her coven. But what if Lola found out? On the other hand, how bad could it be? Lola had all but asked to take some cuttings of those herbs. That wasn't on Charlie. And she'd penetrated Charlie's sanctum when she shouldn't have been able to. Like Lola was tuned to magic, or perhaps the goddess had let her in. In either case, how could Charlie refuse?

"All right, Betty. I'll do it. I've got to go now." Charlie hung up and hurried back into the garden. At the center of the labyrinth, she extended the scissors and paper bags to Lola, and managed to say, "Take as much as you'd like." She swallowed past the discomfort tightening her throat and added, "If the recipe works out, you should try it at *Sorelle.*"

"That's awesome. Thanks." Lola flashed her crooked smile, squeezing Charlie's heart. "I promise to call you if it's edible."

Chapter Fourteen: Lola

"Lola, are you still up?" Mario asked as he strolled into the kitchen while stretching his arms over his head. He glanced at the clock on the microwave. "It's four o'clock in the morning."

I double checked the time but then went right back to chopping up my new herbs. "How can I sleep knowing my Nonna's recipe is within my grasp? I'm so close."

Various bottles of cooking oils, pine nuts, basil, garlic, and the cuttings I got from Charlie's garden filled every inch of counter space. Mario picked up a branch of the *Hypericum Perforatum* and peered at the small oval leaves, one eyebrow raised. Then he picked up a couple other cuttings laying on the counter. "Where did you get this?"

I wiped sweat from the side of my face with my arm and then continued chopping. "From Charlie." The corners of my mouth pulled into a smile that I couldn't relax. That afternoon with the woman lingered in my mind all night. "She has a ton of this stuff in her garden and gave me some to experiment with. I'm trying to recreate Nonna's pesto recipe."

Mario dipped his finger into one of the bowls in the sink that still had remnants of the first few trials and scooped up a sample to taste. His face pinched and he immediately spit it out. "That's awful!"

I nodded as I continued to chiffonade the basil. "No kidding. Why do you think it's in the sink?" I pointed to an old pickle jar filled with olive oil and plant sprigs. "I decided to try to infuse the oil with the *Hypericum Perforatum* to see if that makes the dish more palatable."

Mario wiped his tongue with a kitchen towel and then tossed it across the counter. "Maybe this recipe isn't supposed to be eaten. It could be an old healing tonic or salve for burns or something. You know how people were in the old days before drug stores were on every corner." He turned on the faucet and ran hot water into the sink. "When I was a kid and got a cold, my grandma would strap onions to my feet at night to pull out the sickness while I slept."

"My mom insisted on pouring bottles of cough syrup into us at the first sign of a cold," I said. "That stuff was disgusting. I think I might have preferred the onions."

"It did stink but I always felt better the next day. I think some of these herbal remedies are legit. One of my clients is really into herbs and has been teaching me all about them."

"Mhmm." I racked my brain to remember if he ever mentioned his new fascination with plants before but came up blank. "Are you turning into a hippie on me? Should I be worried you're going to move to a farming commune and change your name to Moonbeam?"

Mario washed the dirty dishes in the sink. "Moonbeam? Psh! I think Thunderbolt suits me better." He lifted his soapy arms into a bodybuilder pose, water dripping on the floor. "So," Mario said, returning to the dirty dishes."Charlie did pretty well at the course the other day."

"Yeah, she did," I admitted, a warmth growing in my chest at the memory of watching the ballerina leaping from platform to platform. "She surprised me. I don't really know why, though, considering how strong she was in that Pilates class I took with her." The way she held some of those positions had been remarkable. I had struggled to keep up with a couple of those moves. I almost dropped my knife at the memory of Charlie's hand on my thigh when she was helping me on one of the poses.

"When are you going to see her again?" Mario asked, glancing over his shoulder while his hands remained in the soapy water.

I shrugged. "I don't know. I said I'd call her when I was able to make something edible with this stuff." At the rate I was going, though, it might be days until I had something to offer.

"You could always call her to simply say hi," he offered.

I stopped prepping and gazed at the back of his head. "Why are you so interested in whether or not I call this woman?"

He turned around, his face void of humor, which was rare for Mario. "You haven't really been involved with anyone for a while and I think Charlie would be good for you. I saw the way she looks at you and the way you look at her when you don't think anyone will notice."

I frowned, letting my gaze drop to a loose leaf that had fallen to the floor. "I don't know if I'm ready for anything serious right now. What if I let her into my life and she bails? I don't want to go through that again. Besides, I like my life just the way it is." That wasn't 100% true. I did get lonely from time to time, but he didn't have to be so pushy.

"Then take it slow," he said. "Just give her a chance."

I hadn't seen this side of Mario very often and wasn't sure what it was about Charlie that he liked so much, but I wasn't going to push it.

I put the jar of oil and herbs in the cupboard and the rest of the prepped ingredients into the fridge. Mario had put the last of the dirty dishes into the dishwasher. "I think we should get a few hours of sleep before the sun comes up."

Mario yawned as he left the kitchen. "Sounds like a plan. We're going to need all the energy we can get to watch little Isabel tomorrow. Or, I mean later today."

I stopped dead in my tracks. I must've heard him wrong. "What are you talking about? I never agreed to babysit anybody." Especially a toddler or whatever age my niece was.

"Didn't I tell you?" Mario asked. "I told Stella we'd watch Isabel so she could take Tony and the baby to doctor appointments. She really needed some help."

I didn't want to sound petty so I gritted my teeth as I said, "Fine." He was going to pay for this later.

THE NEXT MORNING, I ran around the apartment, cleaning up and hiding anything that wasn't kid appropriate. All my knick-knacks got moved to the higher shelves to keep little fingers from playing with them. I never realized how dangerous our living room was until then. "What are we going to do with the coffee table?"

"What about it?"

"It's glass and has sharp corners. She could hit her head on it, break the glass and cut her face all up. My sister will kill me if that happens." My heart raced thinking of the scenario. I ran to the kitchen drawer and pulled out the brand-new roll of silver duct tape. I taped up the edges of the table until I ran out. There was at least an inch of thick padding.

"If it will make you feel better, we could always encase Isabel in a roll of bubble wrap. She wouldn't be able to move but at least she couldn't get hurt," Mario said.

"Ooh! Good idea. I have some in my closet." I thought it might be overkill but anything to keep the kid safe. I would never hear the end of it if anything happened to her.

"I was joking," Mario clarified.

"So was I." Only half true.

A knock on the front door nearly had me jumping out of my skin. I was a badass athlete, strong and capable. Why was I so afraid of spending an hour with a five-year-old? Mario opened the door and let Stella and the kids in. She carried the baby in a car seat carrier. Little Isabel, dressed in a sparkly pink dress, clung to the back of her leg. Little Tony stood behind his sister.

"Thank you so much, you guys. You have no idea how much I appreciate this." Stella slipped a small *Frozen* backpack from her shoulder and handed it to Mario. "Everything you need for her is inside. Her favorite sippie cup, her blankie, and a change of clothes in case of an accident."

"That won't be a problem," I chimed up. "I have bubble wrap so no accidents will be happening here." The blank stares the two of them gave me had me concerned.

"We'll be fine," Mario assured Stella before kneeling to Isabel's eye level. "Hey, princess, are you ready to have some fun today?"

Isabel glanced back and forth between Mario and me before finally releasing her mom's leg and nodding. She hadn't said a word yet, which gave me hope that she was actually a quiet child in unfamiliar places. This might not be so bad after all.

Stella picked up the carrier and headed to the front door. "I'll be back in a couple hours to pick up Isabel. You–"

"A couple hours?" I accidentally blurted out. "How long does a baby check-up take?"

"Well, our pediatrician is very popular," Stella said defensively. "She came highly recommended and sometimes we have to wait a bit before being seen.

And we have two appointments to get through." She switched the carrier to the other hand. "I'm sure you can handle this, Lola."

My spine stiffened as I faced my sister. "I know, I just didn't realize how long this would take." I tried to ignore the fact that I sounded like a baby. "We're going to have a great time, aren't we, Isabel?" When the kid didn't say anything, I added, "What would you like to do?"

Isabel's little eyes widened. "Can we have a tea party?" The excitement on her face was contagious.

"Of course," I said excitedly, even though I had no tea, no fancy teacups, or anything required for a little girl's tea party. But she seemed happy to be spending time with me and I didn't want to destroy that with reality.

Stella left with the other two, leaving us alone with the kid. I stared at her, not knowing where to start creating a tea party. Thank goodness, Mario was here to help entertain her. He loved kids.

His phone rang. "Yeah," he said to whoever was on the other end. "I'm a little busy at the moment," he added, glancing sideways at me. I glared at him, giving the 'don't you dare leave me alone with her' stare. "I'll be right over."

"You better call them back and tell them you're a liar," I said before he could open his mouth to attempt an explanation on why he was leaving me alone with Isabel. "You aren't going anywhere."

"Sorry, but it's important. It'll be so quick you won't even know I'm gone," he said, grabbing his keys out of the bowl by the front door. "You'll be fine."

"Where are you even going? There is no such thing as a personal trainer emergency." I couldn't believe he was abandoning me. Abandoning us. "What about little Isabel? She's going to be so upset if you leave."

Isabel sat on the couch, a neutral expression on her face as she glanced between us.

"My friend is super paranoid about the Disappeared and needs me to escort her home."

"Her?" Was he actually leaving to go to some chick's house? My jaw clenched. "I swear to god, Mario, if you're leaving us for a..." I mouthed *booty call* so little ears wouldn't hear. "I will make a eunuch out of you."

"I'll be right back, I promise." The door clicked shut behind him, leaving me alone with Isabel.

Nerves rumbled in my gut, my confidence slipping away. I think I'd be more prepared to encounter a mountain lion than this five-year-old. "So, what shall we do first?" I asked. "I might be able to find some silly cat videos for you." I pulled my phone out and searched for an age appropriate video Jackie had sent me weeks ago. Kids loved cats.

"You said we could have a tea party," her little voice squeaked.

"That's right, I did." I racked my brain to figure out what I had on hand for a tea party. I didn't participate in such things as a kid. That was Stella. Though I did contribute a few mud pies to her parties. Her teddy bears loved them. "Shall we make some finger sandwiches for our tea party?"

I thought her head might fall off by how fast and hard she shook her head. "I don't want to eat fingers!"

"No, no," I said, desperate to keep the tears welling up in her eyes from falling. "There are no fingers in these sandwiches. They are just sandwiches so small you eat them with your fingers. We can put some cream cheese and cucumber or watercress in them."

Isabel crinkled her nose. "I don't want water sandwiches."

"Okay," I opened up the pantry to see what else I could make to appease Isabel. There was a half-empty bag of chocolate chips in the back. Cookies were easy enough to make and I had never met a kid who didn't love them. "Do you want to make chocolate chip cookies?"

"Yeah!" Isabel jumped up from the couch. "Chocca chip!"

"All right," I said as I pulled the ingredients from the cupboard and set everything on the counter. Relief washed over me because the kid seemed happy. I had worried about babysitting for nothing.

The scraping of the dining room chair over the linoleum floor startled me. Isabel pushed the chair into the kitchen. "I wanna help."

I scooted over to make room for the chair. I unwrapped a stick of butter but before I could dump it in the bowl, Isabel said, "I wanna do it!" I handed her the opened stick of butter and watched her tip it into the bowl.

Next, I measured out the sugar. But before I could add it to the butter, Isabel once again insisted on dumping it into the bowl. This went on with each ingredient, including the eggs, which had me fishing out bits of egg shell.

"Aunt Lola," Isabel said as she dipped a finger into the batter while I filled the baking sheets with dough. "Why do you have a boy's haircut?"

"Girls can have short hair, too. Not just boys," I said a little more defensively than warranted. She was just a little kid, after all. I slid the first batch of cookies into the oven and then wiped my hands on a kitchen towel. "I keep my hair short because I am a chef, and I don't want hair falling into my food." I ran my finger through the side of my stubbly cut. "Don't you like it?"

Isabel nodded. "You look like a warrior."

"Thanks," I said, pleased that this little girl approved of my look.

"Do you have a boyfriend?" she asked. And before I could explain that I prefer women, she asked another question. "How come you never bring anyone to Sunday dinner?"

"Have you been talking to Grammy?" Had my mom been coaching this innocent child? This was a new low.

Then the onslaught began. She asked every question under the sun from why do elephants have long noses to have I ever met a mermaid. She even slipped in a question about how do babies get inside mommy's tummies. I distracted her with a fresh cookie to avoid answering that one.

"I need some tea to eat my cookie," Isabel instructed.

I didn't have any traditional teacups, but I did have coffee mugs. The ones that were clean had sayings that weren't appropriate for young eyes. "Can you read yet?" I asked.

"I know A is for apple," she smiled. "But that's it." She was still in kindergarten.

I handed her the mug. "That'll work." I looked in the fridge. "I don't have tea, but I have milk. Will that do?"

"Yes, please."

I filled two mugs with milk and put some fresh baked cookies on a little plate. We sat at the table and had our tea party. Or... milk party. It didn't take too long before she crashed from the sugar high. When Mario finally showed back up, an hour later, he found us fast asleep on the couch, a princess and her warrior.

Chapter Fifteen: Charlie

Charlie took a deep breath, trying to calm the butterflies in her stomach as she stood outside the dance studio Monday morning. She'd been practicing hard. She'd been in plenty of try-outs before. She was *ready* for the Nutcracker try-outs today. So why did the butterflies seem to be transforming into bats?

"You good for this?" Nathan asked, glancing over from where he stood nearby.

Oh goddess, was it obvious how nervous she was? "Of course," she said aloud. "Let's go."

"It can't be harder than parkour last week, right?" Nathan joked, as they headed up the front steps of the studio.

The comment brought back a memory of Lola in that tight t-shirt, and brought a smile to Charlie's face. "So much easier than that."

Half the company was already gathered in the auditorium, and Charlie hurried to shed her t-shirt and sweatpants, practice outfit on underneath. Dancers were stretching and warming up all over the stage, everyone giving each other an unspoken space to move. Victoria, Charlie noted, already had a light sheen of sweat, evidently having been here for some time. It didn't make the butterfly-bats any smaller, but she tried to shrug that away. Whatever, it wasn't like she was late.

She claimed her own bubble of space, rolled her neck, shook out her shoulders, and began her favorite series of warm-up moves. Out of the corner of her eye, she could see Nathan doing something similar a little ways off. Usually there was a lot of chatter, greeting each other and exchanging pleasantries, but today was quiet, only the sound of breaths and the soft thud and swish of feet moving on the floor. Everyone seemed focused, driven, wrapped up in their own thoughts about the try-outs ahead.

They started precisely on time, pairs of dancers going through their routines one by one. Charlie and Nathan had drawn the third slot, so she watched nervously, bouncing slightly on her feet, as the first two went. Then, finally, they were called.

Charlie felt better as soon as they were dancing. It was always the anticipation that was the worst. Once she was on stage with the music playing, the magic started. The swirl of thoughts in her head quieted down and her body took over. She and Nathan moved through their carefully planned choreography, step by step, and it felt good. It was a solid routine, traditional in style since *Nutcracker* was traditional, and it showed off what they could do. But it was the end that really counted, the finisher. The music swelled up towards the finale as Charlie and Nathan came into position for the final lift. Nathan swept her up, lifting her above his head with his hands on her hips. Charlie shifted her weight to balance, spreading her arms in a dramatic gesture. She felt herself wobble, just a little, but they both adjusted almost at once – there, stable again, and they held the position until the last note of the music faded. Then gracefully down again to finish with bows.

There was polite applause, and then it was on to the next performers.

"Good work," Nathan said, giving her a light punch on the upper arm.

"Yeah, you too," Charlie said, but she bit her lip and wondered if that wobble at the end had been visible. Definitely it was more obvious to her than anyone else – but *less obvious* didn't mean it couldn't be seen at all. Too late now, and she'd just have to hope their best was enough. It *had* been good. Yeah. Definitely.

Charlie was so intent on watching the next dance that she didn't realize Kayla had approached her until the woman spoke right next to her. "That was really beautiful dancing," Kayla said softly.

Charlie jumped. "Oh – thank you. That's, um, nice of you to say." The two of them hadn't exchanged more than the most perfunctory of comments since their last date – when Charlie had told her at the end of the evening that this just wasn't going to work out. "It helps to have a good partner," she added quickly, nodding to Nathan on her other side.

This did not work to diffuse the awkwardness, as Kayla stayed fully focused on Charlie. "You always dance beautifully, of course," she said with a little smile.

"Well, I do my best," Charlie managed. "We all do."

Now that she'd met Lola, felt the unmistakable charge with someone else, she was more sure than ever that it had been right to end things with

Kayla, where there'd been no charge at all. But that didn't make moments like this easier.

"Maybe after they decide the casting, we could help each other with some extra practice?" There was a hopeful glow on Kayla's face that gave Charlie's stomach a twist.

The easy choice would be to say something noncommittal but vaguely affirmative – but that wasn't going to help anything in the long run. "I'm...actually really busy," Charlie said slowly. "It's tough to get to the studio for extra practice."

Kayla's face fell. "Oh. Right."

They both went back to watching the other dancers, standing together in a heavy silence. Victoria and her partner Dylan were just starting their dance. They were good enough to distract Charlie even from the supreme awkwardness of Kayla standing next to her. She tried not to lose all hope of being cast as the Sugar Plum Fairy as Victoria moved through the dance with the fluid grace Charlie had always envied. She'd been complimented on her own gracefulness often enough, but Victoria was next level when she danced.

Was the applause at the end of their dance a little warmer, more enthusiastic than it had been for others? Charlie scolded herself for being ridiculous. Victoria was good, yes, but so was she.

Victoria stalked over to her bag, and picked up her sweatshirt. "You were slow getting into position for the *penché*," she snapped at her partner, yanking the sweatshirt over her head. Her voice carried even across half the studio. "And is it too much to ask that you lift me to a reasonable height? I know you can do better than that!"

Dylan just shrugged. "Sorry, Victoria."

Nathan nudged Charlie, and said in a low voice, "I told you – that woman is *never* happy."

"She has high standards," Kayla remarked, cementing Charlie's belief that Victoria's dance really had been extraordinarily good.

Charlie's phone buzzed just as the last dancers were finishing up. Part of her wanted to check her phone immediately, but she took a breath and told herself that was silly. It could be from anyone. Just because she'd been hoping to hear from Lola didn't mean it *was* her. It hadn't been her for days. And anyway, it was only polite to wait for the applause to finish, for the announcements thanking everyone for their dances and saying they'd let them know about casting in a few days.

Then she grabbed her phone, and felt her heart lift to see Lola's name appear on the screen. She had begun to wonder if Lola would ever get in touch.

> **Hey Charlie! Thanks again for the herbs from your secret garden! Finally worked out the recipe – my boss loved it so much we're debuting it at the restaurant tonight. You should come try it. I did a vegan variety you can get if you ask ;)**

Charlie's thoughts raced as she read and reread the text. Lola had asked her to come by the restaurant! It wasn't a *date*, Lola would be working, but still! And she'd made a vegan variety – had she done that just for Charlie? Plus the herb was getting out into the world through the restaurant, the coven would be thrilled – but Lola didn't know that the herb would protect people from vampires, so could that cause a problem...but no, it would be fine. Of course it would be fine. Was the winking face at the end better than a smiling face? What did it all *mean*?

"Get a text from someone special?" Kayla asked, and Charlie nearly dropped her phone.

She'd forgotten that Kayla was still standing nearby. "Oh – just a...friend," she said, knowing it was a cliche before the words were even fully formed.

"Uh-huh," Kayla said, and even though she looked a little sad, her smile seemed to be real enough too. "I'm glad you have a friend you're happy about."

"Um, thank you," Charlie said, and part of her really did wish she could like Kayla the way the other woman wanted. She was *nice*.

"All right, who's in for lunch?" Nathan said, mercifully interrupting the moment. "Don't say no this time, Charlie." He slung a companionable arm around her shoulders. "We can go to that cafe down the street you like."

A half-dozen of the dancers drifted into the conversation and the plan, until a whole group was gathered to eat together. Kayla was coming too, but

Charlie resolved to sit at the other end of the table, and that couldn't be too terrible with so many people as buffers.

"Hey, Victoria," Dylan called as they were gathering up bags and heading for the door. "Sure you don't want to come for lunch with us?"

Victoria shook her head. "No, thank you. I was planning more practice this afternoon." She cast them a pointed glance. "Have fun at lunch." Something in her tone managed to convey that she felt all the rest of them ought to be making her choice too.

She was going to go practice directly after try-outs? That was like hitting the books immediately after a final exam. Charlie had just one moment of wondering if maybe, if she really wanted to compete, she ought to do the same. But she shook the thought away. A person needs to eat, after all. And sometimes you have to get out and see friends too.

Including...special friends. Before she headed out the door with the others, she tapped a quick text back to Lola, congratulating her on the recipe and assuring her she would definitely be in soon to try it out.

Chapter Sixteen: Lola

I nervously wrung a kitchen towel after prepping the latest batch of my new pesto sauce for the brunch rush. My pasta dish had debuted the day before but Charlie couldn't make it so she said she would come to try it out today. I really hoped she liked the dish since she had donated a big ingredient for it. Thankfully, she had enough in her garden to spare for the restaurant. The infused olive oil was what really made the dish special, giving it that extra oomph that set it apart from traditional pesto.

About a dozen dishes had gone out and none had come back yet. That was a good sign. The number of orders had already doubled from yesterday and there were still hours left until the menu changed for dinner.

"What do you need me to do?" one of the sous chefs asked as he stepped over to my station. The dish was quickly out-selling what they had anticipated, and I was on the verge of drowning in orders.

I pointed to the bag of basil. "You prep that while I get some pasta going."

"Lola!" someone had called out. "Someone's here to see you."

My stomach flipped in hopes that Charlie had arrived and asked to see me, but I quickly tamped it down. My dishes were becoming popular and other people were requesting to compliment the chef lately.

I wiped my hands on the hips of my chef's coat and then straightened my hat. The urge to almost preen had come out of nowhere lately and I wasn't sure how I felt about it. I had even put some old lip gloss on before leaving the apartment this morning. I was going crazy.

Taking a deep breath before pushing through the kitchen doors, I walked into the dining area. As usual, every table was filled with chattering customers. I delighted at the sight of many empty plates smeared with pesto.

A waving arm caught my attention. Charlie's bright smile practically overwhelmed the room. I strolled to her table where her dancer friend, Nathan, sat across from her. "I see you ordered my dish. What do you think?"

"It's amazing!" Charlie gushed, making my heart pound. "I knew you'd be able to make your Nonna's recipe special."

"It's really good," Nathan said, though I couldn't tear my gaze away from Charlie to look at him when he spoke.

"Thanks, I'm glad you liked it," I said and was a little amazed at how true that statement was when it came to Charlie. Why this woman's approval was so important was still a mystery.

Charlie reached out and placed her hand on my forearm, sending a tingle along my skin. She gave a squeeze. "It truly is a masterpiece." Her hand lingered for many heartbeats. I was in no hurry to move away.

At last I said, "Um, I should probably head back to the kitchen." The manager had noticed me in the dining room, and I didn't want to get in trouble for visiting a friend.

"Of course," Charlie said as she removed her hand from my arm, leaving a noticeable absence in its place. "How are you doing on your supplies? Maybe you should come by my place this weekend to stock up?" There was a pleasing hint of hopefulness in her voice.

"Oh, uh, I work this weekend, but I might be able to stop by Friday night." I mentally crossed my fingers that Charlie wouldn't be on a date with some other woman.

"Oh," Charlie said, her smiling fading. That wasn't a good sign. "I have a performance Friday."

"No problem," I said in a rush. "I'll call you some time and make arrangements to stop by." I needed to get away before I did something to totally embarrass myself in front of this woman.

Before I could get away, Nathan said. "You should come to the performance. Charlie has an amazing part. It's a very sensual piece." His tone more than anything piqued my curiosity.

Charlie's cheeks flushed a lovely shade of pink. "Please, don't come if you don't want to. Ballet isn't for everyone." Nathan jumped in his seat as if he had just been kicked in the shin.

"Thanks for the invite," I said. "I'll see what I can do." I probably wouldn't go. Sensual was the last word I would use to describe ballet, no matter how hot the ballet dancer. Jumping up and down in tutus really did nothing for me.

I nodded goodbye and high-tailed it back to the kitchen and my station before the manager could say anything. But for the rest of my shift, the image of Charlie in her tights as she moved and danced on stage wouldn't leave me alone. Maybe a trip to the ballet was what I needed.

"WHY ARE YOU DRAGGING me to the ballet?" Mario asked as I paid for two tickets for Friday evening's performance. I had dressed up as well as I could with my best, and only, dress slacks and pink button-down shirt. I even put some gel in my hair when I styled it.

"You're the one who said I should give this woman a chance. I figured it's only fair since she tried her hand at parkour. I could at least watch her perform."

"That doesn't exactly explain why I'm here," Mario said as he pulled on the collar of his shirt.

"I need someone to keep me awake during the boring parts," I said. We followed the line of elegantly dressed people through the doors leading inside. The scent of expensive perfumes mingling in the air tickled my nose. I was already uncomfortable and had thought about bailing a few times but wouldn't let myself. Charlie had made the effort to not only visit my restaurant on more than one occasion but had accepted the parkour challenge and did better than anyone had expected. The woman kept surprising me, pleasantly. I wanted to do the same in return.

As we found our seats and the lights dimmed, I kept nervously rubbing my palms against the top of my thighs. Why was I getting butterflies? I wasn't the one dancing in front of hundreds of strangers.

As the performance started and dancer after dancer floated onto the stage, I wasn't sure if I would be able to spot Charlie. The women were all wearing identical black shift dresses – which was not exactly what I'd expected from the ballet, though the men in old-style suits were even less ballet-ish. Maybe I should have read up on this production.

Then a tall blonde came on stage, and I straightened up. There was no mistaking Charlie. Something about the way she moved rang familiar. I couldn't take my attention away from her no matter who else was center stage.

There was plenty else to stare at too. I had pictured a lot of women in tutus mincing around to boring classical music. Instead, dancers of both genders strutted and flitted across the stage to much more modern-sounding songs. I even recognized the second or third piece – wasn't that the Rolling Stones? Since when was ballet done to the Rolling Stones?

I glanced at Mario, who was watching intently too. "*This* is ballet?" I murmured.

"Who knew, right?" he muttered back.

It wasn't quite as shocking anymore that Charlie had been able to keep up in parkour. The movements were different, but the leaps and twists and even rolls they were performing on stage – damn, that was some hard work they were doing up there.

One scene in particular captivated me. Eight dancers were on stage, but Charlie's dance set her apart from the rest, on the fringe of the group as the others formed pairs, broke apart and came together again, dancing out a story about cliques and friendship, keeping Charlie's character out of the circle. It was incredible how clear the story was in just dance – and even more incredible how lively and fluid Charlie's movements were, skipping and turning and twisting.

Charlie moved so gracefully that I fully understood why Nathan would describe her dancing as sensual. Watching the woman move made my entire body respond, growing warm and sensitive. Was I sweating?

The song wound to a close with Charlie crouched alone in centerstage. One of the male dancers approached in a bound, lifted her over his shoulder in one movement, and carried her away into the wings.

"Holy crap, that was hot," Mario whispered.

I frowned at the thought that Mario would think that way about my Charlie. *My* Charlie? Where had that come from? I had to purposely loosen my fingers that had unknowingly tensed up into fists.

After the final curtain came down, I was the first to stand and clap as the company came out for their bows. I had never seen anything like that. And I still couldn't tear my gaze away from Charlie as she smiled and curtsied. As Charlie gazed out at the crowd while the lights grew brighter, she seemed to stop when she saw me. Her smile widened. I clapped even harder, ignoring the stinging to my palms. So many emotions were building inside me that clapping seemed the only way to relieve the pressure before I blew.

The curtain closed shut for the final time. Now what was I going to do? I really wanted to see Charlie and tell her how much I enjoyed her performance. But where should I go? Were people allowed backstage to see their friends? Would Charlie want to see me right after her performance?

"That was interesting," Mario said as he led us out of the row of seats to the nearest aisle. "Totally *not* boring. Maybe I should've been a dancer."

We wandered over to where a small group of people lingered by a set of doors. Were they waiting for their dancer friends? I wasn't ready to leave yet, so I figured I'd wait with the others.

"What are we doing now?" Mario asked.

I shrugged. "I just wanted to let Charlie know that we came and tell her how nice it was."

The doors opened and a few of the performers stepped into the lobby to mingle with their fans. I stood on my tiptoes, searching for any sign of Charlie among them.

"Lola!" a man's voice said. Nathan waved over the throng of heads. He motioned to follow him.

I weaved between bodies toward the front until I caught up with him.

"You want to say hi to Charlie?" he asked.

"Um, sure," I said, not wanting to sound too eager.

"I'll wait out front," Mario said, eyeing a beautiful patron by the cash bar.

Butterflies wrestled in my gut as I followed Nathan toward what I could only assume was backstage with all the ropes, wires and boxes everywhere.

Nathan rapped on a door but then turned the knob and opened it before anyone could answer. He peeked his head through. "I found someone who wanted to say hello."

He stepped back and pulled the door almost shut. "She'll just be a minute." Did we catch her in the middle of changing? Was she half naked on the other side of the door? Did the heater just kick on?

He swung the door open wide and motioned for me to come inside. Charlie sat in front of a make-up table with a large, well-lit mirror in what was essentially a large closet. She held a small towel in her hands that she used to delicately dab her face and neck. Her normally light skin on the back of her neck and shoulders was flushed pink and glistening with sweat.

A soft click of the door shutting indicated that Nathan had left us alone.

"Lola! What a surprise," Charlie said, watching me through the mirror's reflection. She spun around in her seat to talk face to face. "I didn't expect you to come. Like I said, ballet isn't for everybody."

I shrugged. "Yeah, well, I didn't have anything else to do tonight." Charlie's smile deflated a fraction though she managed to hold it in place. I wanted to kick myself for shoving my foot so far down my throat. "I mean, I was free tonight and after Nathan mentioned your performance, I was curious to see what you could do."

Charlie's face brightened, easing my anxiety of insulting the woman. "And what did you think?"

Images of Charlie moving gracefully on the stage flooded my brain. My pulse quickened and my mouth ran dry. I had to lick my lips in order to reply. "That was amazing. You were...amazing." Words escaped my grasp as I tried to adequately describe how moved and totally turned on I was by her performance.

Charlie laughed and simultaneously blushed as she gazed at the floor. "Thank you," she said softly. She lifted her head and met my gaze. "That means a lot. I'm glad you were able to come."

I couldn't look away from her. And not just because she was so beautiful, with little wisps of hair escaping the perfect bun, or the tiny smudge of lipstick below her perfectly, pouty bottom lip. Or even the bead of sweat trickling along her hairline and down her long, slender neck. But because of the fire burning in her bright blue eyes.

I fought the urge to grab her and kiss her. Thoroughly. Mario's comment about how Charlie was into me wasn't enough to make me that brave, though. She was too far out of my league, and I would only make a fool of myself if I had totally read the situation all wrong.

So I breathed in deep and took a small step back to put some much-needed space between us. "Well, thank you for inviting me to see you dance. I had a great time."

Charlie stood and stepped toward me with arms open wide. "Thank you again for coming," she said again as she came in for a hug.

I froze for half a second, not sure what to do. But when Charlie's arms wrapped around me, common sense finally caught up and I hugged her back. I was surprised at how strong and solid Charlie was, like hugging steel. The aroma of gardenias mingled with sweat made me a little dizzy. It quickly became my new favorite scent. I wasn't willing to release Charlie yet, wanting to commit this moment to memory to live off of for as long as I needed to.

My chest ached when Charlie pulled away. As my lips passed her face, the thought to kiss her cheek flashed in my mind, but I lost my nerve too soon and the opportunity fled. I was then gazing into her eyes. Before I could take my next breath, Charlie pushed against my shoulders until I bumped into the door. I swallowed a gasp when Charlie pressed her mouth against mine.

The shock of what was happening lasted only seconds, then instincts took over. I kissed Charlie back. All the tension that had built up from trying to repress my growing attraction to her melted into a frenzied need; the need to taste her, touch her, hear her moan.

The dam had burst, and I was helpless to stop it.

Chapter Seventeen: Charlie

Every time Charlie thought she'd learned to control her impulses, she discovered she was wrong. She shouldn't have jumped Lola, but goddess, the woman had felt so good to embrace, had even smelled good, like basil and spice. And she didn't have long to regret the choice, considering how quickly and thoroughly Lola started kissing her back.

Okay, maybe sometimes there was nothing wrong with a little impulsivity.

When they finally came up for air – and it wasn't soon – Charlie realized she had no idea what to say. "So..."

"Yeah," Lola said with a laugh. "So."

Charlie laughed too, sank back onto the seat in front of her dressing table. Too bad it was a tiny chair not big enough for two. They'd probably knock it over and wind up on the floor – which was also not big enough for two. "So." Say something, crack a joke. "Is Mario going to ask me my intentions?"

Lola bristled, and it was so *her* that Charlie loved it. "Mario doesn't have any say in who I date."

"I was just kidding," Charlie said, even though she figured Lola probably knew that.

"Yeah. Of course." Then Lola's gaze, defiant for a moment, dropped awkwardly as she kicked one heel back against the door. "Anyway," she mumbled, "Mario likes you. I mean, likes you for me. I mean..."

"Do you want to, I don't know, grab some drinks?" Charlie suggested. Ugh, so cliché – but she didn't know what else to suggest, she just knew she didn't want this, whatever this was, to end. Not yet for the night, and probably not for a long time. And saying 'hey baby, come back to my place,' seemed like pushing it a little after one kiss. One...very thorough kiss, but still.

Lola hesitated. "Oh man, aren't you tired after that performance?"

Charlie shook her head. "No, it takes me a while to come down after dancing on stage. I won't be able to sleep for hours."

A smile brightened Lola's face. "Yeah, that'd be great then – Mario and I were going to hit a bar down the street. That is...I mean, we could ditch him..."

It wasn't that date-like to go out with Lola's roommate. But could she say that? Was it rude or demanding to say they should get rid of Mario?

Before Charlie had figured out how to respond, Lola continued, gaze awkwardly dropped again, "I don't usually bring the women I date to hang with my friends. But, you know, we could. If that's not too weird."

This put a different light on it. Like maybe Mario wasn't so much a chaperone, he represented a part of Lola's life she was willing to bring Charlie into. "Let's go for drinks with Mario," Charlie agreed, feeling a grin tugging at the corners of her mouth. "That sounds awesome."

THE BAR WAS LOUD AND crowded in a good way, and had amazing vegan jalapeño poppers. Charlie liked Mario more when he wasn't flirting with her, and she liked even better the way Lola smiled when Mario teased her. She'd like to make Lola smile that way.

They'd been chatting for a companionable hour when Lola remarked to Mario, "I'm surprised you're hanging out with us for this long. Don't you want to score a date for the night?"

Mario grinned and shook his head. "You think I'd leave you two alone to be Disappeared? What kind of bodyguard would that make me?"

Charlie's thoughts flew to vampires, a dark image invading the pleasant evening. She knew he was kidding – but she'd have to make sure none of them ended up walking home alone.

"Hey, Charlie and I don't need guarding!" Lola protested. "You'd just better hope *we* decide to protect *you* if some crazy cult leader tries to snatch us. Am I right, Charlie?"

"So right," Charlie agreed, and Lola's smile did a lot to dispel the chill that the thought of vampires had given her.

Mario shrugged. "Well, then maybe I figure I'm already hanging out with the two cutest girls in the bar."

Lola rolled her eyes. "What have I told you about calling me cute?"

She was, though – she was so cute. Charlie took another sip of her beer and hoped she wasn't blushing.

"Let me think," Mario said, "were you going to murder me in my sleep, or put poison in my oatmeal?"

"Neither, and you should know it's against my principles as a chef to use poison. I was going to spread that story about Halloween when we were six years old and–"

"Okay, okay, point made!" Mario said quickly, with some frantic handwaving. "You're not even a little bit cute."

So cute. *So* cute. Charlie took another sip.

"Anyway, you must have noticed that redhead down at the end of the bar," Lola said, nodding that way. So *Lola* had noticed the redhead; Charlie tried not to be bothered by that. It was ridiculous to be jealous of a woman that Lola was throwing her roommate at.

Mario glanced that way. "Oh yeah – she's pretty hot."

Lola snorted, and gave his shoulder a shove. "Go on, buy her a drink. You know she's exactly your type."

"It's like you're trying to get rid of me," Mario protested, which put an intriguing new angle on the exchange.

Lola shrugged. "Stay if you want. I'm just looking out for you. Hasn't it been a couple weeks since – you know."

Not that hard of a code to crack.

"All right, all right," Mario said, and slid down from his seat. "Wish me luck. Not that I need it." He swaggered off across the room.

"Bet you another beer he's back in either sixty seconds or not at all," Lola said, watching Mario go.

"No, thanks, I'm sure you'd win," Charlie said. "Besides, I've had enough – I still have to drive home."

"Oh yeah. Thanks for coming out after your performance. Do you need to get home soon for Sammy?"

"No, I texted Betty to go over and check on him. He's basically her adopted grand-dog, so she doesn't mind helping out sometimes." Maybe she wouldn't mention that Betty had also texted back a strongly-worded approval of Charlie's choice to finally go out and have some fun. Or the follow-up admonishment to be careful, stay away from dark alleys, and look out for vampires. "Sammy's set for the night. Probably already sound asleep."

Lola smiled, a variation on the crooked smile Charlie already knew. "So...you pretty much have all night?"

Charlie felt her own mouth tug into a smile. "Pretty much."

Lola glanced across the bar towards Mario again. "Looks like he won't be back for *hours*. Maybe you could give me a ride home?"

Huh. Maybe she could have gone with, baby, come back to my place. Charlie's smile widened. "I'd love to."

LOLA'S APARTMENT WAS nice, if kind of plain. Charlie knew that her own home, still so much to her grandparents' taste, was not exactly typical for people her age. Lola and Mario had mostly bare walls, an old couch, and a lot of IKEA furniture, which was probably normal. The kitchen, however, seemed unusually large for a small apartment, especially since she remembered Lola complaining about how small it was.

"I guess it's not too bad for an apartment," Lola said when Charlie commented on the kitchen. "I still wish I had more room though, like yours. You wouldn't believe how Mario gets underfoot. Or the amount of counter space he can take up just getting a bowl of cereal."

The kitchen also had the most prominent decoration – a big poster stuck to the fridge with a half dozen mismatched magnets. "Isn't that Robbie Day?" Charlie said, studying the man in the chef's coat on the poster. "From that show – *Outcook Me?*"

"That's there to inspire me," Lola said, studying the poster too, a fierce gleam in her eye. "Someday, I'm going to be on his show and I am *so* going to outcook him. Maybe then my mom will finally get off my back about always working the Sunday brunch shift and missing her dinner; like maybe she'll finally get what I'm working towards."

"To outcook Robbie Day?"

Lola waved a hand. "To be the *best* at what I do. Outcooking him would just prove it."

Charlie nodded. "Like dancing the Sugar Plum Fairy. I get that."

Lola looked away from the poster, turned to Charlie with a gaze that was just as intense, but so very different. Her lips curled into a smile. "Maybe I could make you some sugar plums."

It was so silly, but sounded so sexy the way Lola said it. Charlie tried to play into it, putting a flirtatious tone on her words as she said, "Is that what you're going to cook for Robbie Day?"

Lola shrugged, a languid movement, as she stepped in closer to Charlie. "Haven't decided that yet. Maybe I'll cook my Nonna's pesto. That's been so popular at the restaurant – I really owe you one for giving me that herb."

Charlie wished Lola hadn't put it that way, hadn't brought the subject up at this moment. "You really don't."

Lola's eyes shone, and she was standing very close now. "Are you sure you can't think of something I could do for you? I mean, it's like magic the way people respond to that dish. Maybe I could...serve up something magical for you too."

Charlie *knew* Lola was flirting, that she didn't mean *magic* in the way that people in Charlie's life usually did. But now that the word was in the conversation, as much as Charlie wanted to just lean into this and let the night go wherever it might, it was hard to ignore the little itch at the back of her mind. There was *so much* she wasn't telling to Lola.

"You know," she said carefully, "I don't usually tell people this so early, but there's something you should know. Something sort of – unusual about me."

Lola frowned. "Do you have a food allergy? That's not that unusual, and you should know I take them super seriously – but also, I wasn't actually thinking of serving *food*, so..."

Again the temptation to just brush confessions away and go where Lola was leading. But no, surely it would be better to get this out in the open before they went any further. Surely she could make Lola understand.

Charlie took a deep breath. "What you were saying about magic – well, I'm a witch."

Lola blinked, a confused expression crossing her face like Charlie had just stepped wrong in this dance they were doing. "You're...a witch. Wait – is this some kind of fantasy role play? I mean, I can go for that, but you have to tell me the rules."

Charlie felt her cheeks going hot. "This isn't a game. I *am* a witch. I'm a member of a coven."

"I guess...I've heard of that?" Lola said doubtfully. "So you, I don't know, gather herbs at midnight and go chant at Stonehenge?"

"Kind of," Charlie said carefully, stomach sinking. If that was Lola's idea of a witch – she really didn't know *anything* of the truth. She hadn't thought she did, not really, but maybe some small part of her had still hoped – she *was* Maria Theresa Borja's great-grandaughter after all. She might have known something about magic. But apparently they were starting at zero here. "It's more than that. There are certain herbs with magical properties. I have magic in my blood. Magic calls to magic, and I can make...well, potions, and cast spells."

Lola frowned. "I don't judge anyone's religion, but you're seriously saying you can *cast spells*? So you're a witch like the ones in *Hocus Pocus*, who brew potions and eat babies?"

"Of course not, I'm vegan!" Charlie protested, shocked that Lola would really compare her to such ridiculous movie villains.

Lola stared at her for a second, then snorted. "Yeah, okay, in *that* case..."

Charlie took in a deep breath, trying to figure out how to explain. "Witches like the ones in *Hocus-Pocus* are just perpetuating terrible stereotypes. Real witches are more like – we're connected to nature, and we work with herbs and – we're just ordinary people, really." She could see it on Lola's face, that she was losing her. That this all seemed too strange, too different. It wasn't the first time Charlie had tried to explain all this to someone, and Lola wouldn't be the first person she'd lost because they couldn't understand. But the thought of losing anyone else – of losing all this possibility with Lola – felt too terrible. In sudden desperation, she said, "We're really just like your great-grandmother."

"Wait a second, your beliefs are your business," Lola said, frowning deeper now, "but what the hell does my Nonna have to do with–"

This might have been a miscalculation, but Charlie couldn't see anywhere to go but forward now. "Your great-grandmother was one of the most powerful local witches of the past two hundred years. Some of the older members of my coven remember her. You have her recipe book – you really didn't know that it's full of spells?"

"You're calling my Nonna a *witch*? Like you know anything about her or her recipe book?" Lola folded her arms, everything about her body language suddenly radiating the message to keep back. "Come on, Charlie, you can't just waltz in here and pretend you know secret things about my family. Because that is seriously boundary-crossing."

"I'm sorry, I never meant to – I just wanted to share this part of myself, all the amazing opportunities. Like...there are herbs you could use in parkour that would–"

"Hey, I don't need supplements!" Lola snapped, bristling. "I work hard and do it the right way!"

"No, of course not, I meant things like healing salves when you injure yourself. There are so many herbs with special properties–"

"What kind of *herbs* are you using?" Lola spat. "Because clearly they're giving you a really weird trip."

"I'm not on any drugs," Charlie said, cheeks getting even hotter. "I just – I'm sorry, I'm not saying any of this right–"

"You think? Because so far you've insulted my great-grandmother, suggested I should use supplements in parkour and, I don't know, are you going to claim people only like my pesto because of your magic herbs?"

And that was the heart of it, wasn't it? The reason she'd started this discussion, because she hated keeping the special properties of this dish secret from Lola. What would the other woman say if she blurted out right now that the recipe provided special protection against vampires? Charlie hesitated, the words there on the tip of her tongue.

Except she'd promised Betty, sworn to her coven leader that she wouldn't reveal this secret.

And Lola already thought she was crazy talking about witchcraft. How would she react to *vampires*?

"The herbs I gave you," Charlie said slowly, "they *do* have a special power to draw people in." That was the least of what they did, but how could she say more? "They sort of invigorate the people who eat your dish–"

"Oh good, you *are* saying it's your nutty herbs, not my actual cooking skill that made my most popular dish ever!"

"No, your cooking is amazing, but..." Charlie tried to get a grip on herself. This conversation had spiraled so far out of her control. "I'm explaining this badly. I'm sure it's all difficult to understand if you don't realize there's magic in the world."

"Yeah, because this is *my* fault for not *understanding*," Lola said with heavy sarcasm. "You know what, I really liked you, Charlie, but you clearly need to talk to someone about these delusions you're having. Call me when you've figured out the crazy. Or, you know, *don't*."

Charlie gritted her teeth, leaned back against the counter for whatever stability it could offer. "Please, just let me explain–"

"Don't sit on my countertop," Lola said coldly. "It's not sanitary."

It was the coldness that did it. Charlie sagged, stepped away from the counter. "I'm sorry. I wasn't trying to offend you. I just assumed you'd be open to hearing about new ideas–"

"Don't you dare try to make this about *me* being closed-minded. I'm *setting boundaries*, okay? And I don't date people who are on drugs, or people who insult my family or my cooking." Lola shook her head. "You know what, I think you'd better go."

Charlie thought of making one more appeal, but what was the point? She crossed the kitchen to the door, only to have it open just before she got there. The doorway framed Mario, with the redhead from the bar draped against him.

"Ladies," Mario said with a deep nod, "sorry to interrupt, we're just passing through..."

"Nothing to interrupt," Charlie muttered, stepping around him.

"Wait..." Mario said, confusion entering his tone. "What happened?"

"Don't ask," Lola snapped, and a moment later a door slammed, probably her bedroom.

"This isn't our fault, is it?" the redhead asked, what sounded like genuine concern tinging her voice.

"No," Charlie said flatly, "I just told her I was a witch. It didn't go well. Nice knowing you both."

Mario's eyes widened, then turned thoughtful surprisingly fast – but it didn't really matter what he thought of this development, because she wasn't likely to see either Mario or Lola again. She turned away, headed down the hallway towards the stairs.

She'd go home to Sammy. Sammy loved her. Sammy made sense.

CHARLIE OVERSLEPT THE next day, and yet Saturday morning still came too early, to the strains of "The Dance of the Sugar Plum Fairy." She had updated her ringtone a few days ago in a fit of optimism, and now she lifted her head and reached groggily for her phone on her bedside table. The events of the night before slammed back into her memory before her fingers had properly grasped the device, and she inhaled sharply. Maybe Lola was calling. Maybe she had calmed down, and thought things through, and –

She squinted at the screen. Oh. Nathan. Charlie sighed and pressed the green button to accept the call. "H'llo?"

"Hey, Charlie!" He sounded annoyingly awake. "I'm at the studio – came early for some extra practice – and they posted Nutcracker roles!"

"They did?" Charlie sat up in bed, heart beating harder. "What's the news?"

"Okay, brace yourself," Nathan said, and Charlie already knew it wasn't going to be what she wanted to hear. He *might* have said those words for good news, but the tone was all wrong.

"I'm braced," she said tightly. Just tell her and get it over with.

"So, they gave you the Snow Queen." He tried to sound enthusiastic about it.

He did a little better than Charlie did, when she said, "Oh. Wow. Great."

"You know that's a really good part, right?" Nathan said, and the sympathy in his voice made her wince.

"Yeah. Yeah, I know." It really was, and if this had been a question of the dance in itself, in isolation, she'd have nothing to complain about. It was only – it was the number two role. Again. She took a deep breath. "Well. We'll just have to rock that dance. It'll be good."

"Yeah..." Nathan said slowly. "They cast me as the Sugar Plum Fairy's Cavalier."

"Oh," Charlie said again. Then she took a breath. This wasn't how a good friend should respond! "That's awesome, Nathan, really. You deserve it."

"But now I have to dance with *Victoria*." Charlie could hear his eye roll in his voice. "She's going to be sniping at me every time we practice for the next three months."

"She snipes at everyone. It won't be that bad."

He made a noise of general disbelief, then in softer tones said, "I really would rather dance the Snow King with you, you know."

"Don't say that. The Cavalier is the best male role. You should aim for the best."

They passed a few more remarks, and then Charlie said she'd better get going if she was going to make it to the studio for the day's practice session. After they hung up, she flopped back onto her pillows, stared at the ceiling, and tried to concentrate on ballet. That was at least a little less depressing than thinking about Lola. Though not by much. She had started the week so hopeful – about *Nutcracker*, about Lola. And now here she was, *everything* fallen apart.

She sighed, and picked up her phone again. She really needed to change her ringtone.

Chapter Eighteen: Lola

I had tried to petition Madeline for us to stop making the pesto dish immediately. But we had enough infused oil to last a few weeks, and the dish had increased patronage so much – apparently it had been featured on the local news – that she had almost laughed in my face.

"Look, I understand having a fight with your girlfriend is rough, but that isn't a good enough reason to drop such a popular item from our menu," Madeline had said. Of course she was right (even if Charlie hadn't been my girlfriend), and I'd just have to swallow my pride until we changed the menu at its usual time at the end of the season.

"We can have the other chefs prepare it if you'd like," she had offered, but I'd told her I'd be fine.

However, I was not fine. I couldn't shake the bitter feeling coating me while I prepped for the Saturday dinner. Even the aroma of cooking garlic and butter couldn't lighten my mood. Finally the ingredients were ready and the dinner hours began, and as predicted, the pesto dish orders came in.

"It's because Nonna's recipe is good and I'm a great cook," I muttered to myself, as I plated the first batch. "How dare Charlie say otherwise. What was wrong with her?"

"Chin up, Lola! You got this," Madeline crowed, and I huffed out a breath and turned away to wash my hands. I didn't want her positivity right now.

About an hour into dinner service, one of the bartenders tapped my shoulder. I almost bristled, but maintained my cool just enough to turn toward him with a smile.

"I think one of your sisters is here; she wants to say hi."

Oh my god. I tried not to grimace. I was absolutely one hundred percent not in the mood to deal with one of my siblings on top of everything else.

I exited the kitchen and there was Bianca, smiling at me from the bar counter. Though I noticed the soda she had, instead of her usual cocktail. I leaned on the counter in front of her, and stared at her hard.

"What are you doing here? Were you running or something? You're flushed."

"God, Lola, you can be a little nicer to your little sis, you know. And... no, not flushed! Glowing!" She swished her soda, and batted her eyelashes at me.

Yeah, I put two and two together. She was pregnant. "Momma must be thrilled."

"I'm telling her at tomorrow's dinner!" Bianca practically squealed. "I just hit nine weeks along, and wouldn't you know, I haven't been nauseous at all? And they said pregnancy was going to be hard."

Somehow, I knew pregnancy wouldn't be sunshine and rainbows the whole time. I just raised an eyebrow at her, and clapped silently. "Congrats on being Momma's next favorite child!"

"Oh, come on, sis. You're doing great things too! Your dish was on the news! Didn't you see the clip? Why didn't they interview you for it? Mom just sent a youtube link to everyone she knows this morning. The hubby and I are here to try it."

Yet Momma hadn't even texted me. Or had she? How long had my phone been off today?

"Well, uh, thanks. I hope you enjoy it."

"Oh, I know I will. See you on Sunday?"

And witness Momma's explosion of baby excitement? Not on my life. I pushed away from the bar counter. "Not sure yet. Bye, Bee."

I returned to my station, and started on a new batch of orders. Bianca was pregnant, huh? Even with *Sorelle* being featured on the news, something always had to happen to overshadow my achievements. Like Momma's favorite thing – babies.

Later in the evening, I noticed the waitstaff whispering to each other and peering out the kitchen door. You don't have to be in the restaurant life for long to recognize the signs of agitation – to know there was someone undesired out on the floor. After sending out one of my last sets of pesto for the evening, I approached the remaining waiters and nodded at Keegan, while crossing my arms.

"Someone you need me to mess up out there?" I asked. It would suit my mood.

Keegan smiled, giving me a little shove. "Girl, maybe. There's this party of eight over on table twenty. They've ordered a single pesto dish and a round of black coffee."

The hair on the back of my neck stood up, and I willed my ruffled feathers to calm. "That's not the weirdest thing for a party to order."

"No, but look at them."

I took his place by the edge of the door, and stole as long of a glance as I dared at the back of the restaurant. Six of the patrons were intimidating – tall or broad, clad all in black with hair slicked back. The last two were an older couple dressed quite nice, including a necklace on the woman adorned with rocks I could make out from across the room. This wasn't necessarily unusual either, as this could have been a rich family with hired protection. The couple were sickly pale, like they'd be blown over by a light breeze. But the way they moved said otherwise. Swift decisive movements, heads held high in confidence. Like they were important.

The woman pointed a long, thin finger at my pesto dish, while talking to the man, who had his hand curled underneath his chin. The woman reminded me of an aging Morticia from the Addams Family, with long, straight, black-highlighted-silver hair, and high, prominent cheekbones. The thought of the Addams family coming to my restaurant dressed to the nines in spooky attire got me internally laughing enough to disengage from the wall and regard Keegan again.

"Okay, I see what you mean. Just let me know if you want me to take care of anything."

Another hour went by, and the floor slowly cleared. As orders halted for the night, the cooks and I focused on cleaning our areas, putting leftover ingredients in the fridges or packing up leftover prepared food to take home. Still, two of the waitstaff lingered at the door.

"They still there?" I called.

Keegan nodded. "Yeah. Madeline has already walked out there and introduced herself as the manager."

Suddenly she was by our side, lacking her usual peppy spirit. "They give me the heebie-jeebies. I don't know who they are, either. Usually I'm alerted when someone influential books."

"Did they ask about my pesto?" My voice cracked. I had no reason to be nervous about this, and again I tried to shake off my uneasy feeling.

"Yes, they asked what was in it. I said it was a family secret."

I frowned, and resumed cleaning. Another half hour later, the party of eight was all that was left, and most of the cooks and servers had left for the evening. Me, Madeline, and Keegan remained. Both Madeline and I watched from the kitchen as Keegan walked out there to ask the party to leave.

"Thank you so much for your patronage," he said loudly enough for us to hear.

The reply was too quiet, but three of the "bodyguards" stood.

Keegan followed that with, "I'm sorry, the chef has already left for the night. Perhaps you can come back another time and speak with her about the dish."

I grimaced, and side-eyed Madeline. Her arms were crossed and she had an expression as sharp as daggers, aimed out on the floor. I assumed she had gotten the same weird feeling I had; that even though this group had done nothing wrong, everything would be better if they left.

"Just one moment, please," Keegan called clearly, before he almost sprinted back to us. Yet still he managed to let the door shut gently behind him.

"They want to speak to someone about the dish, but they're freaking me out."

"I'll go back out there," Madeline said. But I held up my hand.

"No, I'll go. They want to speak to the chef. Let's let them speak to the chef."

"We're going together. Keegan, call the cops if you see anything wrong."

He nodded, and together Madeline and I walked out there. I put on a smile, took off my chef's cap and smoothed my hair back as well as I could. As we stopped in front of the group, I made sure to cross my arms in such a way to emphasize their muscle.

The three goons who had stood were in similar poses a few feet away from the table in three directions. The remaining three sat with their hands clasped on the table. The couple were somehow more foreboding close up. Silver hair clocked them as in their 70's to me, and their clothing was crisp, old-fashioned, and expensive. The woman's black dress glittered like it was covered in crystals, and the giant gemstones on her necklace also caught the light. Her make-up was dark, elegant, and perfect. The man wore a suit with a vest and jacket, expertly tailored for him. His mustache was meticulously trimmed into a thin handlebar shape, which I would have found ridiculous in a less tense environment.

"Lady and gentlemen," Madeline began, "I do hope you have continued to have a good evening."

"Yes, of course," the man said with a posh voice somewhere between New York and British. "Enhanced by your gracious service."

He smiled and it made my skin crawl.

Madeline gave a bow of her head. "I'd like to introduce to you one of our most popular chefs; this is Lola Morelli and she'll be happy to tell you more about the pesto dish."

This close to the table, I noticed that though the pasta dish looked picked over, it didn't look eaten. At all. Goosebumps erupted down my back again.

"It's a pleasure to meet you, Lola. Your manager said the recipe is a family secret. From your family?" the woman said, with a similar high-brow accent.

I nodded. "From my great-grandmother. Pesto was one of the many things she cooked. And she was the best cook I have ever known."

The man cleared his throat. "Could you tell us more about the ingredients?"

I hesitated, only for a moment. "It has all the typical pesto ingredients like pine nuts, basil, olive oil, garlic, and parmesan cheese. But it also has some additional herbs, like holy basil, which really elevates the flavor."

I wasn't sure why I left off the *Hypericum Perforatum* Charlie had given me. I hadn't believed her claims at all. But I still wasn't going to tell these people about it. The couple exchanged glances, then gave us what was probably supposed to be a pleasant smile.

"Ah, I understand it's a family secret," the woman said, her voice level. "But we can tell it has some, what do you call it, hypericum in it, yes?"

Instead of being intimidated, all the fear I had been feeling turned into anger. "Yes, it does. Are you going to tell me it's magic too?"

Madeline shot me a look, inhaling sharply. The goons tensed, and the couple lost what slight pleasant demeanor they had had. The woman practically scowled.

"Young lady, you are messing with things you do not understand at all. You are to halt making this dish immediately."

I scoffed. Madeline entered the conversation with, "My apologies, but we are not going to stop making this dish–"

"Did Charlie put you up to this? Were you paid to humiliate me?" I hissed. And the woman didn't even flinch. She smiled at the man, and regarded me again.

"If Charlie's your supplier of the hypericum, we'll pay you handsomely to tell us where this person is." She smiled, but her lips remained a tightly pressed line.

And despite the continued high tension in the room and my boss right next to me, I started laughing.

"I can't believe Charlie's done this! You all can drop the act, this has gone too far."

Suddenly, two of the goons were at my side, gripping my arms, and the third had Madeline in his grasp. With more effort than I was expecting to use, I yanked free, and held up my fists.

"Get your hands off me and leave my restaurant immediately!" Madeline yelled. "We've already called the cops." She tried to shake out of her own captor's hold but couldn't.

"The police won't do anything that we don't want them to," the man said coldly. "And I'd hate to have this amazing restaurant shut down because you won't comply."

I no longer believed that this was a prank from Charlie. It wouldn't have been this elaborate. It wouldn't have gone this far. But these people were clearly dangerous and delusional.

"You don't have that kind of power," I challenged, trying not to let the tension get to me. I approached the man holding Madeline and got right up in his face. "Let go of her, now."

"Boys, recapture her, and let's take them with us," the woman said, standing from the table. The rest of the goons stood, and I took the second it was going to take them to approach me to punch Madeline's captor in the gut, and pull her from him.

"Run with me," I breathed, grasping her hand. We stumbled around tables as we sprinted for the back room.

When we burst through the kitchen doors, Keegan was right there and ready, a broom in his hands. He wedged it through the doors' handles. Barely after he finished, a loud thud sounded, the door buckling. We heard arguments, and then another thud. I didn't think that broomstick would hold them for long, but at least it was something.

"Cops were called five minutes ago," he said, breathing hard. "And I've already locked the front door from the outside."

"You two get out of here," Madeline said. "Go out the back door. I'll stay to talk to the cops."

"You sure?" I asked.

She nodded, gestured at the kitchen with its assortment of knives. "Don't worry, I'm armed."

I laughed, a thin, anxious and exhausted sound, and motioned for Keegan to follow me. "Think they're smart enough to come around the back–"

I opened the back door and came face to face with one of the goons. So I did the only sensible thing: I shoulder-rushed him into a nearby wall.

In his panic, Keegan retreated back into the restaurant. He motioned through the door's tiny reinforced glass window for me to leave. He knew I could outrun and outjump any of these guys, and I assumed he'd locked the door. So I turned, and there were three more black clad muscles.

Outrun it was. I took off down the alley in the other direction, the scrapes of their footfalls echoing on the cement behind me. There was a chain-link fence at the end of this alley, which I leapt onto and climbed handily.

But so did they.

Down the next block, I kept my eyes out for those cop cars. It was almost midnight, but thanks to the weekend I had to run past more than a few groups of giggling drunk girls in wobbly heels. Only one of those groups hollered at me as I passed. Off to the left side of the street was new construction, and I climbed another chainlink and huffed up a large gravel hill. Two of the men were on my tail, just jumping down off the fence now, but the third was lagging behind. I continued on, jumping down cement floors of a new building, which led me downhill and back onto the street at the other side of the construction zone.

The fact that the men were keeping up unnerved me. They either knew how to navigate terrain like this, or were very fit. The whole evening was sinking into my chest – how weird the people were, how easily they put their hands on me and Madeline, how they were talking like we didn't matter. What the hell was going on?

I pivoted into an alley, hoping I had enough distance between me and my pursuers that they'd miss my turn. Hopping over a third fence though, I caught my arm terribly on a jagged piece of metal as I was trying to swing myself over. I swallowed a scream as my skin tore, and pushed my arm into my chest as I continued on.

I was out of breath at this point, blood soaking into my shirt and white hot panic edging my vision. I was too scared to even look over my shoulder to see if they were still following me. I just kept running.

Over a mile later, exhausted and breathing hard, I made it past the edge of downtown to some of the nicer, oldest houses in Sacramento. I chanced slowing to a walk; I hadn't heard the men chasing me in some time.

"That was impossible," I groaned. The world spun for a moment, and I ducked between a pair of shrubs to catch my breath and wait for my head to settle.

It was quiet around me, just the occasional car passing by or a barking dog.

The yip of one of the dogs reminded me of Sammy.

"Maybe... Charlie can help me." I was still mad at her. But not mad like I had been when I thought those weird people were tricking me. I wanted to have answers for their behavior. And what they wanted. Something about herbs? Maybe Charlie wasn't crazy. Maybe when I told her what had happened, she'd help this all make sense.

It was either that or call Mario to pick me up, and he'd freak out and take me to a hospital, and I couldn't face the embarrassment of explaining to him what had happened, or the huge deductible I'd pay for going to the hospital, or how to explain to *them* what had happened either.

So I dialed Charlie.

"Uh, hello?" came her soft voice.

It felt almost like a miracle that she answered.

"Charlie, something really weird happened, and I need help. Can you pick me up?"

"I'll be right there. I'm actually just leaving the studio. Send me a dropped pin of your location."

No questions asked, no poking fun at me for calling her crazy, just immediate help. After what I assumed was a performance, no less. It practically brought me to tears.

As I waited, I sent Madeline a quick update text.

She responded quickly. **I'm so glad you're safe. We are too. Unfortunately our guests escaped before the cops got here.**

That was not surprising. **Damn, too bad.**

Charlie arrived just as the night had started overcoming the day's heat. She stopped and got out of her car. I tried to apologize, but she held up a hand.

"I deserved everything you said. Let's move past that. Tell me what happened."

I nodded, and she pulled open her passenger door, gasping when I passed by her to get in.

"You didn't say you were hurt!" The concern in her voice messed up my insides.

"I'm fine."

"You're *not* fine. But... you gotta fill me in. Start at the beginning."

In the time it took Charlie to bring me back to her place, sit me down in her kitchen, and fix me a cup of tea while coaxing me out of my bloody work clothes and into a spare bathrobe, I had her caught up on the situation. She had stayed quiet, nodding and gasping where I'd expect, only interrupting to ask for more details on what the people looked like.

Her hair was pulled into a messy bun, she wore old sweats and a tank top, and she was just as beautiful as she had always been. I didn't want to still feel this attraction for her. But there it was as she listened to my story and cared for me.

"And your manager and coworker were safe in the restaurant when you left?" she asked as we sat at her kitchen table, where she'd pulled a chair up next to mine as she cleaned my arm.

"Yeah." I winced as she dabbed the wound with a wet cloth, coaxing the half-dried blood off my skin. "I'm going to have to go get a tetanus shot, huh?"

Charlie gazed at my arm, biting her lip just enough for me to notice. "Lola, do you trust me?"

It was a loaded question. Because after our earlier conversation, I clearly didn't. But I had just gone through something so unusual I didn't know what to believe anymore.

"Uh... yeah. I think... Yes."

She nodded and stood, returning with a jar of a green-tinged salve. Scooping some up with a clean cloth, she spread the ointment down the length of my gash.

I gasped as the sharp pain from the wound stopped after a burst of ticklish tingles, and then a wave of relief spread through me. I put my head down in the crook of my uninjured arm on the table. Charlie rubbed the ointment in, the soothing relief and her gentle touch enough to scrub away most of my panic and anxiety.

"I'm so glad you had some numbing stuff," I said into my elbow. "It's good. I'm assuming medical grade."

"Um, not quite," Charlie said hesitantly. I raised my head, then looked at my arm.

My wound was almost entirely gone.

"What? How?" I stood, ran my fingers down where the gash had been, where now only a thin red line of healing skin remained. I could try to believe it hadn't been as bad as I thought, but my bloody chef jacket was still on the chair next to me. The black undershirt I still wore had been soaked through.

"How?" I breathed.

Charlie held up the jar. "I told you, I'm a witch. This salve healed your wound."

I gaped at her. Didn't want to believe her. Remembered her parkour injury, how it had healed so fast too. "Like your leg from your fall?"

She nodded. "And your pesto might be more than just pesto." She sounded embarrassed. "It may be poisonous... to supernatural persons."

My stomach dropped. "If my pesto is poisonous, how could it be safe to serve?"

"Oh, no, no. It's just St. John's Wort. But some uh...supernatural persons react, um, negatively."

"Were..." I couldn't believe I was saying this. "Were those people in the restaurant... supernatural?"

Charlie nodded. "The older couple at least. The others, maybe not. You wouldn't have been able to escape them so... relatively unharmed."

My brain was working so hard to understand all this that my exhaustion was winning. "How were they able to be so close to the dish?"

Charlie scrunched up her nose. Maybe she didn't want to tell me. So I gave her my best impression of my mom's death stare until she squirmed and relented.

"The scent had to have caused them pain... But I think their curiosity and fear was stronger. And it would only cause serious damage if they ate it."

"How does it... no, no. What kind of supernatural... no." My head was pounding, and my chest felt tight like all of this was giving me an anxiety attack. "You know what, this is too much right now."

She nodded, but her gaze remained down.

"Are we in danger here?" I finally asked.

"No. This neighborhood is invisible to them."

Dozens more questions surfaced in my mind, about her witchcraft, about my great-grandmother, about those scary people. But I couldn't focus. Too many things had happened and the adrenaline was fading from my system. My eyelids drooped, and I sat back in the chair.

"I gotta get home."

"Please spend the night," Charlie said. "I want to make sure you stay safe and heal well."

In light of everything that had happened, that sounded like a good idea. I nodded, and pulled my phone out of my pants pocket. Sent Mario a quick text that Charlie and I had made up and I was at her place. He responded quickly with way too many inappropriate emojis. I'd have to explain all this at some point, but that was a problem for future-me. All present-me wanted to do was sleep.

"Do you have, like, a spare bed?"

Charlie stood. "Right down this way."

She led me to a small bedroom with a floral print on the double bed and a different floral print on the drapes. Old photographs hung in small frames covering one wall. I'd have to get a better look at those later. I sat on the bed, and looked up at Charlie, who hesitated by the doorframe and gave me the smallest of grins.

I patted the bed next to me. When she sat, and brushed stray blonde strands behind her ears, warmth spread to my cheeks. I clasped my hands in my lap. "Thank you for helping me. For... healing me."

"Oh, it's the least I can do."

"I'm sorry I didn't believe you. About being a..." It was hard to say.

"A witch?"

I rubbed my palms on my legs. "Yeah. It'll be something incredible for me to ask questions about – if you're willing to answer. But right now..."

"Right now, get some sleep," she finished.

I nodded. Took a deep breath. Then ran my fingers around the back of Charlie's shoulders, and pulled her into a kiss. She sighed contentedly and kissed me back, her fingertips caressing my cheek. It was warm, and probably would have been invigorating if I wasn't already so exhausted. We pulled apart, and I studied her deep blue eyes.

"Okay. Now I can sleep," I said.

Charlie laughed, and stood. "Goodnight, Lola."

"Goodnight."

Chapter Nineteen: Charlie

Charlie woke early with her stomach roiling and her nerves on edge. She wanted to believe it was just her concern for Lola, but knew there was more. It took time to sort out the cause, but finally she admitted she was angry with her coven. Giving those herbs to Lola, and encouraging her to use them at work had put Lola in danger.

And that anger mixed uncomfortably with her own guilt. She was the one who'd told the coven about Lola and her great-grandmother's book. Yes, she and everyone else in the Singing River Coven had vowed to do whatever it took to protect people from the vampires. But that applied to Lola, too. And Betty, the head of her coven, had made her promise not to tell Lola the whole story. And it was that promise that placed Lola in danger. So, at least some of this guilt was on Betty's head. But Charlie knew she should never have allowed either herself or Lola to be placed in this position.

She was determined to make Lola feel comfortable that morning, and after letting Sammy outside, she fussed in her kitchen, hoping to put together something Lola would like for breakfast. She worried that nothing she did would be good enough; what the heck did you fix for a chef? And Lola wasn't vegan. She might prefer eggs and bacon, which of course Charlie didn't have. She scanned her pantry and refrigerator, keeping an eye on the clock. It would spoil things to still be dithering when Lola woke up. Finally, she settled on a few of her favorite foods, got down her grandmother's china, and arranged everything on a tray. She'd watched enough cooking shows to know presentation was important to a chef.

Sammy scratched at the door, and started to follow her to the guest room, but Charlie told him to stay. She wanted to make sure Lola wasn't too confused, or too angry, or too, well, anything, after the night she'd had.

She knocked gently on the guest room door, heart beating too fast. Things had seemed better between them last night, but she wasn't sure how Lola would feel now. Being forced to confront the existence of magic – and "supernatural persons" – would be hard on anyone.

It might be extra hard for Lola to accept that her beloved Nonna was actually a witch.

When she heard Lola stir in the other room, she said, "I have some breakfast for you."

"Breakfast?" Lola's voice came out in a dry croak.

Charlie smiled; she had the perfect remedy for that. "Can I come in?"

"Um, yeah, I guess."

Charlie pushed open the door in time to see Lola frantically running her hands through her short sleep-tousled hair. Her very sexy, sleep-tousled hair.

"Sit back against the pillows," Charlie told her, then placed the tray carefully on her lap. "I wasn't sure what you liked to eat..."

"We meet early for parkour several days a week, so I don't have much time to make myself a big breakfast," Lola said.

Charlie bit her lip. "Um...well, there's something savory." She waved her hand at the everything bagel with vegan cream cheese on the left side of the tray. "Or something sweet." She indicated the croissant with powdered sugar and a bowl of strawberries on the right. "But of course you could have both. If you'd like. And there's a mimosa to wash it all down." She clamped her teeth together before she could start babbling.

Lola regarded the tray with the pretty china, and the bud vase with fragrant lavender and rosemary and lemon verbena, then she looked at Charlie and smiled. Her crooked smile. The one that always made Charlie's heart stutter.

"Join me," Lola said, and patted the bed next to her. Charlie swallowed hard. She was trying to feed Lola and make her comfortable, but all she really wanted was to throw down the tray and make her...hot.

Charlie forced herself to sit with a few inches between them.

Lola handed her half the bagel. "I like both sweet and savory, actually." She gave Charlie a suggestive grin, and added, "I like things that are complementary. Like a graceful ballet dancer showing moves of such strength and beauty it takes my breath away."

Charlie's mouth went dry and her hands began to shake. She wanted to reach out and stroke Lola's face.

Then Lola said, "Why don't we share with each other?"

Was there anything sexier than feeding strawberries and a mimosa to the woman you wanted to get in bed with? Well, other than actually getting in bed with her?

Finally, when most of the food was gone, Charlie couldn't bear to wait any longer. She picked up the tray and placed it on the floor. Then she turned and ran her finger along Lola's full bottom lip. "I wasn't sure what to fix for a chef. I hope you liked it."

Lola cleared her throat before saying, "It was perfect. I..."

Charlie leaned forward slowly, giving Lola enough time to pull back if she wanted. But Lola didn't pull away. Instead she moved into the kiss. Their lips met and clung, then their arms wound tight around each other.

They tumbled back across the rumpled blankets, hands struggling to push away annoyingly obstructive clothes. Passion and urgency made them both clumsy, but without any of those awkward first moments between new lovers. Finally naked, Charlie threw her leg over Lola's hips, straddling her, both covered in a light sheen of sweat. Both breathing hard. Charlie gazed down and grinned wickedly. "What do you like? Should I touch you like this?"

She reached down and let her fingers brush over Lola's breast. When Lola's breath caught, Charlie let her smile grow wider. "Ah... You like that."

Lola's answer was more moan than words. "I do." She leaned forward and kissed Charlie thoroughly. Now it was Charlie's turn to moan. Their eyes met, and Lola asked, voice low and rough, "What else do I like?"

Her voice seemed to rasp along Charlie's nerve endings. She gently pushed Lola flat on the bed, a smile playing on her lips. "Let's find out, shall we?"

LAYING SIDE BY SIDE in the tangled sheets, chest heaving, Charlie waited for her heart to settle into its normal rhythm. It had been a long time since she'd indulged herself like this – she hoped Lola didn't think she fell into bed with people she hadn't known long on a regular basis. Was that something she should say, or would it sound foolish?

Her thoughts – and her heart rate – kept scattering as Lola brushed her hand lazily up and down Charlie's thigh. It wasn't meant to be a seduction, it was comfort. A desire to keep connected physically.

It was, Charlie thought, a seduction of her emotions. And her thoughts suddenly coalesced into something she hadn't expected. She'd been lonely so long. Lonely for family. When her grandparents died, she'd felt a hole open inside her. She didn't belong to anyone anymore. She had the coven – they'd all crowded around, assuring her she wasn't alone – but it wasn't the same. There was still that hole inside her.

Why did it feel as if this woman lying next to her, idly running her fingers over Charlie's skin, could fill that hole?

LATER, AFTER THEY'D indulged in a long, steamy shower that almost sent them back to bed, Lola sat Charlie down in the kitchen. "I think I need more information about...uh...witches. And those supernatural – what, people? Beings? Escapees from Creepsville?" She swallowed and shook her head. "I've never imagined asking to have a rational discussion about either of those things." She looked at her arm, where there was only a thin, pink scar from the injury the night before. "I never imagined such things really existed."

"I can tell you about it, but it might be best coming from my grandmother's friend, Betty." That way Charlie wasn't betraying her promise, and Betty would have to deal with the results. "You saw her at the restaurant the first time we met. She's been the head of our coven for years, and knew your Nonna."

Lola gave a sly smile. "So it *is* like *Hocus-Pocus*?"

This time, Charlie was able to laugh at the comparison. "Well, not exactly. Coven is just the name for a group of witches that work together. Try to think of it like a...knitting club. A lot of our members do knit, actually."

"Only, you don't just knit sweaters. You make magic concoctions."

"Well, you make concoctions all the time at the restaurant. A combination of herbs, mixed together in the correct proportions, mixed into a base. Your base is tomatoes and basil. Ours is beeswax and sweet almond oil. Really, the only tangible difference is the bit of magic we add, to increase the desired effect."

"Really? You're going to compare making potions to cooking food?"

"Absolutely." Charlie grinned. "Now come and meet Betty. She can explain it better than I can." At least, she had better!

Charlie gave Betty a quick call, explaining about Lola's questions, and Betty said to bring her over as soon as possible. After feeding Sammy and telling him they'd be back soon, the two of them headed down the block together, shoulders bumping, fingers intertwined.

Charlie sniffed appreciatively. The air was filled with scents from the garden. They mingled together and she wondered if anyone else could have picked them all out. Lavender and rosemary. Thyme and mint. Cedar and basil. Sage and lemon balm. It was no wonder the air hummed with the sounds of contented bees.

Esther's husband Douglas was trimming overblown blooms from his prized rose bushes as they walked by. Charlie raised her hand, the one not clasping Lola's, and waved at him. Douglas smiled and waved back. "Blessed day, Charlie," he called as they walked past him.

"Blessed day, Douglas," she called back, knowing Esther must be at Betty's. Otherwise she'd be sitting on the porch with a glass of iced tea as he worked. That made Charlie wonder who else might be at Betty's. Hopefully, she wouldn't invite half the coven; that would be a bit much to subject Lola to. At least, on her first visit.

Charlie felt suddenly, uncomfortably hot. She wanted to blame it on the summer heat, but it wasn't actually that hot this early in the day; in the mid-seventies, with a slight breeze stirring the air. Thank the goddess for the Delta breeze. No, it was her discomfort at the thought of introducing Lola to the eleven other women who meant so much to her, so early in this...relationship?

The walk suddenly seemed too short to Charlie, only a few minutes from her door to Betty's. She wanted to keep walking, fingers tangled with Lola's. To keep walking, to keep enjoying the sun and the sound of the birds and bees. To ignore the reason she was out here to begin with.

"Your grandmother's friend lives right down the street from you?" Lola asked when Charlie tugged her toward the light blue house with the purple door.

"Yes." Charlie sighed, afraid Lola would find this very odd. "In fact, the entire coven lives within a couple blocks. They like living near the garden, and they all moved here together decades ago, when the neighborhood was new."

Lola raised an eyebrow, one corner of her mouth quirking up. "Oooo-kay." She looked around, then over her shoulder, back toward Charlie's house. "You said it's a community garden, right? Your grandmother dedicated it to the local community?"

Charlie nodded quickly, relieved at the change of subject. "Yes, all the coven members are allowed to use it freely, of course. There are wards to discourage others from entering the magical sections." She smiled at Lola, but worry had begun gnawing on her confidence. What was it about this woman that made her second guess herself so often? Did Lola think Charlie was inviting her over to 'meet family' too soon? When all Charlie intended was for Lola to understand the truth. All of it. Before things went any further between them.

They hadn't told Lola about the effects of the perforatum in her Nonna's recipe and that had nearly gotten her killed. Would Lola blame her when she found out?

What about Betty? Would she allow Charlie to tell Lola more about what was going on? Would Betty think Charlie was trying to force her hand by bringing Lola over like this?

And what would Betty tell Lola? Would she make it sound like they'd used her? For the good of the town, of course. To save people from murderous vampires. Would Lola believe it when they told her the strange disappearances being reported on the news were caused by the same creatures that had attacked her? Although from what Lola said, the ones that attacked her must have been human servants, otherwise Lola wouldn't be walking right next to her.

Charlie tightened her fingers around Lola's as that thought rolled through her, weakening her knees. She could have lost Lola last night. Before she ever knew how much she could care about her.

Charlie bit her lip – she had run out of time. They were stepping onto Betty's porch. She could only hope things went well, because she desperately wanted this relationship with Lola to work.

It might be new, but it felt intense and strong, and so very right.

Chapter Twenty: Lola

My limbs were trembling as we approached the picturesque blue house. With its white picket fence and rows of neat flowers, and purple shutters to match the purple door, the house looked straight out of an old sitcom.

"Like *Bewitched*..." I mumbled to myself, remembering the old Nick at Night favorite.

"Hmm?" Charlie said, her fist outstretched to knock on the door.

"Oh, nothing," I said, my cheeks growing red. "Let's do this. Let's..." meet another witch? Was I *in* a sitcom now?

A smiling older woman, with wavy silver hair and a checkered blouse answered the door. It took me a moment longer to realize this was the same woman who had been at the restaurant with Charlie the first time I met her.

"Charlie, thank you for coming so quickly. Lola, it's so good to see you again."

I could hear the soft murmuring of many people over Betty's shoulder, and I wasn't sure if a TV was on or not. She ushered us into the house, and Charlie stopped so quickly I bumped into her.

In front of us was a living room filled with overstuffed furniture and doilies and crystals, and, surprisingly, almost a dozen older women taking up the couch and a few dining table chairs that had been brought into the room. They chatted to each other, and several of them were knitting, their needles looking impossibly long in their aging hands. If I hadn't known better this really would have looked like a book club or gathering of old friends to play Bingo or whatever.

There were two vacant chairs wedged next to the couch, and we awkwardly shuffled toward them.

"You called the full coven?" Charlie asked, gesturing at the women with her eyebrows arched high as she took her seat. The full coven? Was that bad?

"Yes, everyone was interested to hear what had happened," Betty said. She sounded so sweet and gentle, but I sensed the authority in it. She regarded me, then gestured at a woman in a yellow sunflower dress.

"Samantha is our best herbalist. She is here in case there are questions about the herbs used in Maria Theresa Borja's Book of Shadows."

A "witch" named Samantha right after I'd thought about *Bewitched*? How on the nose could these ladies get?

"I don't know anything about some shadow book," I admitted, my throat tight. "She called it a Receipts book."

Charlie seemed troubled, and I gave her the most subtle wince I could muster. I was terrified I was going to inadvertently cause a mess.

Samantha nodded, her smile emphasizing the wrinkles around her eyes. "That makes perfect sense. My grandmother did the same thing. I'd love to see it at some point." She practically bounced in her seat. "Everyone knows about your great-grandmother. She really knew how to cook up a potion."

I just stared at the woman with wide eyes. Charlie squeezed my hand.

Betty continued introductions, gesturing at two women, the oldest of the group, sharing a loveseat, their expressions eager but gentle. One of them had bright red hair, which reminded me of my Nonna very much, as she had worn bright red wigs as she'd gotten older. "Esther and Catherine are here because they knew Maria well. I thought they should be here in case Lola has any questions that they can answer."

This was where I had to cut in. "You say you knew my Nonna, but no one in our family has ever said anything about her being a witch. I'm afraid you must have the wrong person."

Betty's smile faltered. "I'm not surprised that you don't know. Your grandmother, Maria's daughter, was a strongly religious individual, I believe."

"Do you mean she was Catholic? Is that against... all this?" I asked, searching both Betty's face and Charlie's for some direction.

"It's not as simple as that," Betty said gently. "But what I remember was that your grandmother didn't think witchcraft and her beliefs mixed. So she must not have allowed younger members of the family to know about your great-grandmother's practices."

"Well." I didn't know how to handle this, or if I could trust these women about the secret lives of my family. "I admit we only saw Nonna a few times a year. She passed away shortly after my eighth birthday. But I remember that she always liked to cook things, and she loved when I helped her in the kitchen."

Esther leaned forward as if she were trying to bow in her seat. "We loved Maria. She really was an excellent cook. But she was also a very powerful and respected witch."

Betty sighed, nodding. "She was head of one of the other covens in town. It was mostly because of her that we had such good relations for so long," she said. "She made sure our members worked together often. When she died, we wondered what happened to her Book of...her receipts. Her coven said they didn't have it, and we feared it was lost forever; years of carefully gathered spells and potions gone. I'm so glad you have it safe."

For a moment I wondered if the whole reason they had wanted to see me and talk to me was because of that book. But I didn't think Charlie was like that, and I wanted to trust her that these people weren't like that either. "Yes, well, her pesto recipe is fantastic, at least once I got it right. I–"

"Do people like it?" Betty leaned forward, her gaze intense.

I flustered at her interruption. "Yes, it's a favorite in the restaurant where I work. We sell out–"

"That's wonderful, dear." Betty sat back, and her voice was surprisingly joyful. "I'm so glad to hear it."

I hoped I wasn't scowling, but boy oh boy this old lady was acting like she didn't really care about what I had to say at all.

"We're getting off topic," Charlie said quickly. "We need to talk about what happened to Lola last night." She stared at Betty, eyes narrowed, and emphasized, "She was attacked by *supernatural persons*."

The mood in the room chilled. Betty demanded, "Are you hurt, child?"

"I was," I said and held out my healed arm. "Charlie... did some magic to it."

Betty sucked in her breath and turned a narrow gaze to Charlie. "And we are just hearing about all this now?"

Charlie clasped her hands and held her head high. "We had some things to take care of. So yes."

Betty turned back to me and asked, "Where were you attacked?"

"At the restaurant. This strange couple came in, surrounded by bodyguards. They stayed until the restaurant was closing, and then their bodyguards attacked us."

Catherine squeaked, "Us?"

"My manager and another server were still there with me. The server locked the doors of the restaurant and called the police. Then he barred himself and our manager inside the kitchen while I escaped. Everyone is okay, but the creeps got away before the police got there."

Betty pursed her lips, and murmured with some of the other members of the coven. Charlie still clasped her hands together, though her knuckles had turned stark white. After a conversation I couldn't overhear, Betty turned back to me.

"We're glad everyone is okay. Do you think your restaurant is going to reopen soon?"

I blinked, thrown off by the question. "My manager has no choice but to continue business as usual."

Samantha had come over while we were speaking and inspected my arm. She gestured at Charlie and said, "You did a great job, but there's definitely magic in her blood for her to heal this fast."

"Magic in my blood?" I couldn't hide the skepticism from my voice.

"Yes, your magic worked together with Charlie's," Catherine said as if speaking to a child. "Like called to like."

I frowned deeply, and had no idea how to respond. As the women around us started a soft chatter, Betty sighed. "We'll need to talk about this new attack at length soon. Perhaps–"

Charlie spoke. "With the utmost respect, Betty, there is something we do need to talk about now, with Lola. Specifically these *supernatural persons*."

After a tense moment, as many of the coven members exchanged glances, Betty sighed. "Charlie, you are unfortunately quite right." She settled back in her chair and said, "Lola, our world has been plagued by evil supernatural forces for centuries. Witches like Charlie, like all the incredible ladies in this coven and beyond, are the best line of defense against these forces wreaking havoc on humankind. We have sworn to protect everyone. I'm so sorry to hear of these creatures evading our protective measures last night."

"So what were they?" I asked, skeptical about the vague language Betty was using. "Werewolves? Vampires? Zombies? Oh, a rival witch clan?"

"Rival in a sense, yes..." Betty said, and beside me, Charlie coughed. Yeah, I also got the sense it was a flimsy answer. I met Betty's eyes for some time, but she stared right back at me resolutely. After a few moments I gave in to this battle of wills, and nodded like I was accepting what she said.

"They're terrible and manipulative," Betty continued. "Did they speak to you, Lola?"

"Yes. They asked about the pesto recipe. Even mentioned the perforatum herb by name. They wanted to know who gave it to me."

Betty straightened in her chair, and I noticed her give one of the other women a sideways glance. "What happened next?"

I held up my palms. "I gotta be honest, I didn't believe them at all at first. Accused them of conspiring with Charlie against me." I couldn't meet anyone's eyes as I said that. I just stared at my lap and hoped Charlie didn't hate me.

"You said her name to them?" Betty asked, with a harsh edge to her tone.

"Yeah, but there was no context. Just, 'Did Charlie put you up to this.' And they asked if Charlie had given me the herb, but I don't think I responded."

To my utter relief, Charlie reached for my hands and squeezed them gently.

"I'm sorry," I whispered to her. "I was just so mad. I didn't know what was going on."

"I understand, Lola. It's okay."

"Thank you for your honesty, Lola," Betty said. "We all understand that this was a scary situation. But rest assured we are very capable women, and we will not take this threat to an ally such as yourself lightly. We are here if you need us, for anything."

One of the women perked up. "We could do a blessing on the restaurant to help protect it."

"Thank you," I said, giving the woman a nod, though I still couldn't bring myself to believe that would actually do anything.

"I'll help organize the blessing," Charlie offered, and the woman gave an appreciative bow.

Betty clasped her hands together, and stood. "Thank you, Catherine and Charlie. That is the perfect start to our help. Now, all of this gives us much to discuss." She smiled, and I knew I was supposed to find it to be sweet, but it felt shockingly cold. The other women had started whispering to each other, but they kept fake-feeling smiles on their faces as well. This was not the kind of homely group of old ladies I had been expecting.

"There's one more thing," Charlie interjected, and Betty's face flashed with a look of surprise, maybe even annoyance. "I told you Lola wanted to know about witches and magic. I hoped you could answer some of her questions."

Betty sat down again, her expression softer. She gestured toward us.

"Okay," I started, heat in my cheeks. I felt more like getting out of here than asking questions. I'd rather ask Charlie more questions later, just the two of us. "I guess I wanted to understand better what you do? What your magic is?"

"Ladies, what do we do?" Betty asked, regarding the women around us with a gentle smile.

"Commune with nature," one said.

"Strengthen our bonds with each other and our families and communities," said another.

"Keep the people of Sacramento safe," said a third.

"Don't forget to pass down our knowledge to the younger generations so they can keep this all alive and strong," Betty finished, smiling widely at Charlie.

"That last one's a little more obvious when you see the make-up of the other Sacramento coven," Charlie laughed. "But these women have many years yet to share their knowledge."

Soft chuckles filled the air. I got the gist, but I also understood they weren't telling me everything because I wasn't a proper member. They told me the what, but not the how.

"Well, I think it's really special that you all have such tight bonds with each other," I said. "I gotta admit I'm a little jealous that you got to have this sort of bond with my Nonna."

"I'm sure you had a bond as well," Betty said. "Do you think it was your great-grandmother's influence that led you to become a chef? Working with her in the kitchen, I mean."

I hesitated, not sure I really wanted to share. "Food is family. I cooked with my mom, with my grandmother, all the time. Big pots of home-made spaghetti sauce. Fresh bread. Traditional polenta. Mixes of seasonings that

I had been told had been passed down since long before Nonna and our family immigrated from Italy. Whenever Nonna visited, we'd all be together, cooking in the kitchen. When I cook, I feel like I'm with my family. Like I'm expressing our history and culture through the ingredients I use."

The women around me smiled, and some even held hands. Apparently that had resonated with them, and these smiles felt more genuine. I thought again about the one who had claimed I had magic in my blood. But... none of this could be real magic, like shooting lightning from your hands. It was just lotions and herbal teas and reciting poetic "spells," right? Magic didn't really exist. But then what had Charlie done to my arm? I resisted believing. Could anyone blame me? It was so outside of everything I'd grown up with. My internal logic wasn't ready to give in yet.

Charlie spoke, interrupting my thoughts. "Lola, that was beautiful. I can't wait for us to explore your Nonna's history further when we have more time."

"Indeed," Betty said, smiling. "But right now, especially given what happened last night, I think we need to have an extended meeting about this, immediately. Can you all stay?"

The women nodded. Betty turned to Charlie.

"You too, I hope. But..." She cast a glance at me. I understood immediately.

"I'll get an Uber," I said. "Escort a lady out?" I added to Charlie.

"Betty, I'll be right back," Charlie said, and the two of us left in what I was afraid was an awkward silence. But as soon as we got out of range of the coven, Charlie slipped an arm around me. Overwhelmed, I brought her into a tight embrace.

"I'm sorry the whole coven was there, and that Betty would hardly let you speak before asking another question. That's not how I wanted this to go," Charlie said into the crook of my neck.

I squeezed her more, and gave her a chaste kiss. "It's okay. I need to process this. And I've got work again tonight."

Charlie met my eyes. "Are you going in?"

I shrugged. "Not sure what choice I have. I can't just leave my coworkers to deal with this alone. It'll be okay. They won't come back once you put up your blessing or whatever, right?"

"It'll encourage them to think better of it," Charlie murmured.

"And then I have a few days off. I'll text you, okay?"

She nodded. "Okay."

I watched her bounce effortlessly up the brick steps back into Betty's house, and sighed.

Chapter Twenty-One: Charlie

Charlie clicked the door shut behind Lola. In some ways it was a relief that she was gone; Charlie didn't know how much longer she could have kept quiet! She took a deep breath, and marched back into Betty's living room.

"We have to tell Lola the truth," she announced from the doorway. "*All* of it. We can't keep lying to her like this."

Every head turned her direction, the quiet murmur of serious conversation dying away. In the two minutes she had been out of the room, the mood had changed. It happened every time the coven was alone instead of in front of an outsider. Backs were straighter, heads lifted higher, sweet smiles replaced by something more confident and more genuine. Usually it was a relief and a little funny to see her friends give up their 'sweet old ladies' camouflage, but today it only made her angrier that they had kept up the deception in front of Lola. And it reminded her that they weren't going to be soft and easy to convince.

"Why don't you sit down, dear?" Betty said, gesturing to the chair Charlie had vacated to walk Lola to the door. "Have some tea and we'll talk this through, and–"

"I don't want *tea*," Charlie snapped. She curled her hands into fists at her sides. She wasn't going to be brushed aside like this. "I want to tell Lola the whole truth – about that herb, and the vampires, and the way we're putting her in danger. You just kept giving her vague answers that didn't actually mean anything!"

"*Sit down* and we'll talk about it," Betty repeated, and this time the steel glint was in her eyes, the one that belonged to a powerful witch leading a coven, and was so at odds with the sweet exterior she generally presented.

Charlie sat. But she still wasn't happy.

"Now then," Betty said, folding her hands in her lap. "While you were seeing Lola to the door, Helen has found some very interesting information on the socials."

They were going to just move straight into a different topic? "I want to talk about what we told Lola–"

"And we will," Betty said firmly. "But first – Helen?"

Helen cast Charlie an apologetic smile, and lifted the phone she had been tapping on throughout the meeting. "When you told us about the vampires at Lola's restaurant, I started searching around to see if there was any hint online about why they'd be there. I thought I'd have to search more, but – well, there's a post that's starting to be shared a lot. A young man is saying he barely escaped being one of the Disappeared. Apparently he was mugged a couple of days ago, he says by some sort of psycho who bit him, and then staggered away ill. And apparently it was all only a block from *Sorelle*."

"I think we can reasonably theorize this was a vampire attack," Betty said. "It seems likely the young man in question ate the pesto at the restaurant, based on the vampire's reaction after biting him. That may have been enough for the vampires to make the connection to the restaurant and the special recipe."

This fresh proof that vampires were targeting Lola specifically only fueled Charlie's fears and anger. "You said the pesto dish would only be one small weapon against the vampires. This isn't a small reaction! Lola needs to know what's really going on here."

"And what if that ultimately puts her at greater risk?" Betty asked. "I think we can all agree that Lola seems to be a lovely young woman, and of course we're very glad you've met someone you like. But you understand as well as any of us why we must preserve our secrets. Breaking our code of secrecy risks so much. It could damage our protections hiding this neighborhood, making us all more vulnerable. And it could also put Lola at greater risk if she starts telling people about vampires and brings more attention on herself. Suppose she wants to make a viral social media post herself. She may decide to stop making her pesto – which puts everyone in town in greater danger if we lose that weapon against the vampires."

It was all so reasonable – but it still felt so wrong! "But we could invite Lola into the secret," Charlie countered. "Swear her to secrecy too, and give her the chance to help, while actually *knowing* what she's doing."

Heads were starting to shake around the room. "But Charlie," Esther said, "you hardly know her. Perhaps you young people move fast these days, but you still only met her recently. To trust her with all of that..."

Were she and Lola 'moving fast?' She thought of the morning and felt her cheeks warm. Hopefully no one saw that – because as close as Charlie was to these women, they didn't need to know exactly how fast! "But it's not just about me knowing her." She appealed to Samantha. "*You* said she has magic in her blood. And she's the great-granddaughter of one of the greatest witches ever. That has to count for something!"

"Certainly," Betty put in. "It makes it all the more important that she continue making her pesto. It's undoubtedly more powerful than if someone without magic was making it. But as for Lola herself – her family has been away from magic for generations. We can't be certain what her attitudes and loyalties are. It's too risky–"

"And what about when she figures this out for herself?" Charlie demanded. That, she suddenly realized, was as scary as anything else. That this *wasn't* going to stay a secret, and that it was going to come out in the worst possible way.

Betty frowned slightly. "There is no reason she should ever–"

"She has so many pieces already! She knows strange people were interested in her pesto and she knows I gave her the herb. She's not going to be satisfied forever with that vague talk about rivals and supernatural persons. She's going to figure out that we deliberately set her at odds with vampires, and she's never going to forgive me for not telling her the truth!"

And that? That was terrifying.

No one else in the room seemed to think so. There were several grandmotherly murmurs that of course that wouldn't happen, and it would be Lola's loss anyway, and any girl would be lucky to date Charlie. As if it was that easy.

"Of course we all hope that won't happen," Betty said firmly, "but we have to be mindful of priorities. We have the chance to save many lives by weakening the vampires."

"What if Lola finds out the truth and refuses to keep making her pesto because she's angry that we lied to her?" Charlie demanded, because maybe *that* would matter to them.

Betty's lips pressed into a thin line. "Not lied, dear. Merely...withheld information, to protect her and others. The mere fact that you believe she might react in such an explosive way is an argument against entrusting her with the secret."

How had that backfired so neatly? "No, I didn't mean–"

"The ultimate point, Charlie, is that we can't put people in danger merely because something might be troubling to a young woman you're casually dating."

Charlie sagged back in her chair, defeated by that final phrase: *casually dating*. Of course that's what this would look like to Betty, who had been married to Herbert for forty years. And *was* it more than casual dating? Or would it become more? She and Lola hadn't talked about putting labels on their relationship, hadn't even discussed exclusivity.

It just *felt* like more. The way it hadn't in a long, long time.

"It's not as though we're leaving Lola defenseless," Betty went serenely on. "We'll put every protective guard we can around the restaurant. I think at least a few of us should be there tonight as well. And I have to say, after experiencing their brunch, I think we can all look forward to trying the dinner menu."

There was a gentle ripple of laughter, easing the tension in the other women in the circle, letting them all focus more calmly on the tasks at hand. Charlie knew that was exactly what that remark was supposed to do. She had been watching Betty and the rest of the Singing River Coven all her life.

Too bad it wasn't working on her. Not today. Today she sat back in her corner of the room, let the swirl of conversation rush past her, and stewed in her own frustration. None of them understood. None of them even *wanted* to understand. It was so much simpler to just sweep sweet little Charlie's relationship concerns aside and focus on *important* things.

She tried to let their plans be reassuring at least, tried to believe that, at a minimum, they'd protect Lola. There was discussion of the special blessing they'd do on the restaurant building, the protective potion they'd discreetly sprinkle across the doorways, the rotating schedule to ensure someone was keeping an eye on the restaurant all the time. They talked about how they'd step up their communication contacts around town and with the other local witches, Mystic Oak Coven, and keep a closer eye on the vampires; every woman had a complicated network of friends and former coworkers and nieces and grandsons and so on, spinning out into a web all throughout

Sacramento. If something happened, they *should* know about it. But they hadn't known about the vampire attack on the restaurant, a hole in their efforts they discussed resolving at length.

They were trying. They really were trying, and Charlie knew that. But by the time they adjourned the meeting and she was walking back home, it still didn't feel like enough.

She kept hoping she'd find a way to make peace with the coven's decision to keep the truth from Lola. But if anything, she became more concerned with every step she took. Except it was more than that. Concern wouldn't have her nails biting into her palms. No, she was frustrated as hell, and she didn't even believe in hell.

She hated being forced to choose between Betty and Lola.

Betty had been her grandmother's best friend. The woman who had been Charlie's rock after her grandparents died. Betty was also her coven leader. The coven she had sworn her allegiance to. Not some easily broken promise, but a serious ritual oath that had real consequences.

She hated that her coven was on one side, and Lola on the other. It should be clear where her loyalties would lie. But there was something about Lola. Something about who Charlie was when she was with Lola. And because of that, none of this was clear to her.

And no matter what Charlie said, Betty refused to see it. The entire coven refused to see it. But the coven was wrong, she was sure of it. For all the good that did.

What she needed was to think about something else for a while. Before she drove herself crazy.

When she got home, she let Sammy run out in the garden for a few minutes, wishing the sight of him barking at the birds and squirrels would lift her spirits. Then she called him in and went to her potion room, determined to do something constructive. Something that could do some actual good. Everyone in the coven seemed so sure they could protect Lola and the restaurant. That they were a match for the vampires. But Charlie didn't believe it would be that easy. If the vampires initiated a coordinated attack, they would all be in danger.

Charlie sank heavily onto her stool. What she was thinking of sounded like a war. A war between witches and vampires. Just what Betty had said could happen, weeks before. And if there was any possibility of a war, they would need weapons. The coven had taken a vow not to use magic to cause serious harm to others. Besides, she didn't know any potions that would actually kill vampires. But there were still a few battle potions she could create. Something that would emit full spectrum light – like a sunshine firecracker. That could drive the vampires back into the shadows, at least temporarily.

And perhaps something that would create a thick vapor. One comprised of perforatum and holy basil, garlic and verbena. That would be a severe irritant for any of the undead. While neither of those weapons would kill a vampire, they could certainly slow down an attack.

Thinking about a battle, Charlie felt her heart squeeze in her chest. Maybe instead of fighting so hard to tell Lola the truth, she should be hoping Lola would get angry and turn her back on Charlie. Maybe that would keep Lola safe if the vampires did attack the coven.

She couldn't do anything about Lola right now. What she *could* do was concentrate on making the strongest defensive potions possible. She grabbed several of Sammy's toys and placed them in the living room where they would keep him busy and safely out of harm's way while she was experimenting with various concoctions. Then she squared her shoulders and returned to the potions room, shutting the door carefully behind her. She breathed in the rich scents of the drying plants hanging under each cabinet. Then she forced herself to push aside her concerns as she gathered and prepared the ingredients. To concentrate on using each in the perfect proportions. To infuse everything with protective and strengthening spells. To ensure there were no mistakes like that last potion she'd experimented with. And for several hours she managed to exist only in the present, without worrying about what had already happened. Without fearing what might happen in the future.

But when those preparations did finally come to an end, her concerns came rushing back. And they brought others that were new. Worrying about a vampire war against a strong, prepared coven of witches was bad enough. What if the vampires evaded the coven and attacked Lola again? She would never forgive herself if something happened to Lola because her coven...Charlie...had dragged Lola into this without even explaining the potential dangers.

If something bad happened to Lola, it would be Charlie's fault. She was the one who'd given the perforatum to Lola. She was the one who'd encouraged Lola to make the pesto. Yes, it had been the entire coven's plan, but Charlie had agreed with them. And *she* was the one who had actually done it. Without giving Lola the slightest hint of what she might be getting into. Charlie had never given Lola a choice. The one thing she'd promised herself she wouldn't do, after that first time, when she'd all but forced Lola to go to lunch with her.

All the potions were in their various states of brewing, simmering, and steeping with no strange reactions. No bubbling or explosions. They should all work as designed. Charlie tried to shake the tension from her shoulders, but they were uncomfortably tight. She left the potions simmering, and went into her practice room

It had been her grandmother's craft room years before, filled with yarns and paints and pretty patterned papers. Now, the room had only one piece of furniture; a small table in the corner, with a good sound system and a place to charge her phone. The remainder of the room was empty except for the wall of mirrors and the long ballet barre.

She carefully stretched her muscles from neck to toes. Feeling the tension and stress stored in her body. Once she limbered up, she stood at the barre and began her normal warm-up routine, sliding her feet and arms through each of the positions, moving into a *plié*, then a *grande plié*. Switching to a *relevé*, then arching her back and lifting her leg behind her, up, up, straining into a high *arabesque*. Holding it until her muscles quivered in protest. She finished with a series of *sautées* that carried her across the floor, until she allowed herself to collapse, smiling with pleasure at the feel of loose, well-oiled muscles.

All the tension in her shoulders was gone.

Her phone buzzed – a text from Nathan. She felt a brief flash of guilt as she realized she'd been so busy worrying about Lola and betrayals and Betty and vampires, that she'd hardly spoken to Nathan since he'd told her about the results of the trials. He must be wondering how she was taking it. She sat on the floor, leaning back against the mirrors, and returned his text.

And spent a pleasurable fifteen minutes immersed in ballet company gossip, commiserating again about the parts they'd been assigned. Nathan reminded her, again, how much he hated doing lifts with Victoria.

Charlie didn't even need to hear his voice. His feelings were obvious.

N: Any more "constructive feedback" & I'll lose it. V picks @ EVERYTHING.

C: Ignore her. You're great – you got Cavalier!

N: Seriously better with you! V needs to ease up.

C: Next year will be better. Maybe V will go to SF. She's threatened to 4ever.

N: Yeah, V says I should go too. Says SF is "serious." Like I need a whole company like V!

C: And we'd really miss you! :)

They signed off soon after, and Charlie let herself slump back against the wall, her stomach feeling strangely hollow. Nathan in San Francisco? The ballet wouldn't feel the same if he left. But it would be such a good move for him. Somehow, she had to find sufficient enthusiasm. He'd earned his shot; she couldn't let it matter that she'd miss him. Besides, he didn't sound excited about the idea. Maybe it would never happen.

And he'd acted as if her part in the ballet was her largest concern and she had no way to explain that it just...wasn't. She only wished it could be, like it had been only a few weeks before. How had everything become so...complicated?

Maybe what she should do was reach out to Lola. And pray to the goddess that she wouldn't ask any questions Charlie couldn't answer.

Chapter Twenty-Two: Lola

"Here," Mario said as he handed me a pair of 30-pound dumbbells. This gym had the nicest sets of weights we'd found. We were meeting our friends Jackie and Andrea for a personal training session with Mario.

"Why do I need dumbbells? It's leg day." I took them anyway and did a few bicep curls.

"You need the extra weight for squats." He stood next to me and watched as I lowered into a squat. "Watch your knees. Don't let them go over your toes."

I concentrated on my form, relishing in the burn running through my thighs and glutes. I could almost feel my muscles getting stronger with every motion. My mind immediately brought up Charlie's strong legs. The image of my ballerina dipping into a deep *plié* taunted me as I dipped into my squats. Every time I went down, I pictured Charlie trying to outdo me by going into a deeper *plié*. "I wonder if I could out-squat Charlie," I mumbled to myself.

"Charlie?" Mario asked.

Apparently, I spoke too loudly. I needed to remember to keep certain thoughts in my head. I ignored him, continuing my exercises and hoping he'd drop it.

"So, you two worked everything out, huh? Did you have the wild make-up sex?" He rubbed his hands over his chest and said, "Oh Lola! You're sooooo strong!"

"Shhhh!" People were starting to watch. I set the weights on the floor after my last dip. "You're a pervert." I grabbed my towel and wiped the sweat from my face. "A lady doesn't kiss and tell."

"I know. That's why I'm asking you and not Charlie." He laughed and ducked when I snapped my towel at him. "Okay, okay. I guess I don't get the details. But everything is good with you two?"

I couldn't stop the grin spreading over my face as I thought of Charlie. "We're good." Being in a relationship with Charlie had been more exciting than I ever expected. So much better than the quick one-nighters I thought would be my life before I met her.

"Hey, guys," Andrea said as she walked up to us, a full water bottle in her hand. "Sorry I'm late."

"No problem," Mario said. "We're still waiting for Jackie to show up."

Andrea frowned as she sat on the floor to do her pre-workout stretches. "She's not here yet? Isn't the whole reason we go to this gym because it's only a block away from her building?" She pulled out her phone and checked her messages. "She hasn't texted me in over a week."

I drank from my water bottle, trying to recall the last time I got a text from our friend. "Maybe she's hung up on a big work project and is running late." That wasn't unusual for Jackie, but not texting to let us know was. Mario and I both checked our phones to see if we had missed any messages but came up empty. I typed in a quick query. **Where u at?**

"I'm sure she'll be here soon. She never misses a leg day." Andrea stood, grabbed a pair of dumbbells and joined in with us working on squats.

After squats came lunges. I eyed the machine Mario wanted me to use next. Someone else was using it but I planned to grab it as soon as it was free. Mario was busy helping Andrea improve her form. But I couldn't keep my mind from wandering to Charlie and her coven. More directly, the concept that magic was real and a part of my family. Did I really believe that? It would explain those people at the restaurant the other night. But I wasn't sure I was totally on board with what they said about my Nonna. She would've told me she was a witch, right?

The machine was finally available, but as soon as I reached it, a big burly guy got there at the same time. "Sorry, sweetheart. But you'll have to wait your turn. I'm next."

My fingers gripped the back of the padded seat as I forced a smile on my face. "Sorry, *sweetheart*, but I got here first." There was no way I was backing down from this neanderthal. I'd done enough running from goons lately. Besides, no man but my dad called me sweetheart.

The man's brows narrowed to a glare. "That's cute. I don't have time to argue with you so run along. Go jump on a treadmill or whatever machine you gals use." He stepped closer to the machine as if the argument was over.

But I still needed to work my inner thighs and I wasn't going to wait on him. I swung around the back of the machine and set my knee on the seat right before he could sit down. He cursed as he ran into me. "What are you doing?" he barked as he straightened up. He loomed over me, at least a foot and a hundred pounds bigger.

I stood my ground, pressing my knee more firmly into the padding. "It's leg day," I said through gritted teeth. "And this is my last thing to do so why don't you do some squats while I finish this."

Mario broke away from helping Andrea and placed his hand on my shoulder. "Lola, let the nice giant have the machine. It's not that important." His fingers pressed into my skin as he tried to gently tug me away. Did he forget who he was dealing with?

"Yeah, Lola. Listen to your friend and move," the neanderthal said.

My hand balled into a fist at my side as I imagined throat punching the guy. But he was pure muscle, and I really had no desire to break my hand, so I came up with a better solution. "You are going to have to drag my dead body away to get this machine before me," I said with all the determination I could muster. My heart thrashed against my chest when he took a step toward me. Would he really fight me?

He stopped and glanced around at the small crowd of onlookers our argument had attracted. But he didn't back away. "I'm not giving up my claim to the machine." He reached over and pulled the pin that held the weights so that it would be useless. He held up the pin and smiled. "Now what are you going to do?"

I glared at the guy. He was going to make us late for lunch and I was getting hungry. My eyes shifted over his beefy shoulder to the pull-up bars. "How about we compete for the machine?"

His eyebrow arched high. "What kind of competition? I will mop the floor with you in everything."

"So, you have nothing to lose then."

He smiled. "You're right. What do you want to lose in?"

"Pull-ups. Whoever can do the most, wins."

His gaze traveled up and down my body before he shrugged. "All right. This will be quick."

"Yep," I said as I strolled over to the bars. I turned to Andrea. "Watch the machine and make sure nobody else tries to steal it." She nodded and sat on the seat to save it for the winner.

"Ladies first," the guy said.

"All right. Go ahead."

If looks could kill, his glare would be considered a lethal weapon. I rubbed my palms against my shorts to wipe off any perspiration. I drew in a couple deep, cleansing breaths before I jumped up to the bar. I hung for a moment, readjusting my grip until I was comfortable. The group of onlookers counted off each time my chin reached the top.

I had to rein in the show-off part of me that wanted to do some one-handed, or pull myself up higher so that my waist hit the bar. I just needed to beat the guy by doing as many as I possibly could. At the forty mark, whispers questioning my humanity started swirling around me so I decided I should probably stop. I did an extra one for good measure and then released my hold and fell to the floor.

"That's 44 for Lola," Mario said. "You're next."

The smile had disappeared from the guy's face as he stepped up to the bar. He didn't need to jump up like I did. He simply lifted himself up with his tiptoes to reach. I knew I had the competition in the bag when he started struggling by the time he got to 15.

Laughter erupted when he quit before he got to 20. Guilt almost got me, but quickly faded when he said. "You win, sweetheart. Enjoy your workout." He sulked away, rubbing his arms.

"Good job," Andrea said as she got off the machine so I could use it. "I've never seen anyone do that many pull-ups before."

"Yeah," Mario said, his brow wrinkled as he stared at me. "And you looked like you could've done more."

I set the pin in the right place and then sat down on the seat. "I guess it was just my day." As I worked on my inner thigh reps, the conversation with Charlie's coven swirled in my mind. The implication that I had some magic in my family line wouldn't leave me. Was I really part witch? Is that why I was really good at sports? Did I have some sort of magical advantage?

My thighs burned as I pushed myself to do more reps. This was hard work. I worked very hard to get into such physical shape. No, I was able to do what I did because I worked for it. I didn't need any magic in my blood for that.

"I'M GOING TO BE SORE tomorrow," Andrea said as she rubbed the side of her thigh. After our workout we decided to get lunch by walking to the new café that opened a few blocks away. I loved checking out new places.

"No pain, no gain," Mario said. When we got to the place, he held open the door like a gentleman. He must be practicing. Thankfully, our timing worked out well and we arrived right after the main lunch crowd had left. The bus boy had just cleaned up a table for us to snag.

"This looks nice," Andrea commented as she sat down, gaze floating around the dining area at all the plants and artsy pictures on the brightly colored walls. It gave off a New Age hippie vibe.

I focused my attention on the lunch menu. The restaurant claimed to only use locally grown produce, which isn't really that difficult in California. The items were pretty basic with a few artisan twists. They even had a decent offering of vegetarian and vegan options. I made a mental note to bring Charlie here someday if the food was good. I smiled at the warmth filling my chest at the thought of more dates with Charlie. Who knew monogamy could feel so good?

We placed our orders and received our complementary glasses of water when my sister Stella and two of her brood came through the door. "Oh, hey!" She waved with the hand not holding a baby and headed straight for our table. "Funny seeing you here."

"You too," I said as she set the portable car seat on the empty chair next to me. "Don't you have a job or something?" I leaned over the table to get a better look at my nephew Tony who was hiding behind my sister. Little Isabel must still be in school.

"Yes, I have a job but there was an issue at daycare, so I had to pick these two up early. I'm just picking up my lunch order to take home. Did you hear the big news?"

I glanced over to Mario and Andrea across the table to see if they knew what Stella was talking about. Their blank expressions told me they had no clue either. "Um, no."

"Robbie Day is coming to San Francisco in a few weeks and plans to hit some other cities while he's in the area. Sacramento is bound to be one of them. You might get your chance to meet him." She practically bounced on her feet as her eyes lit up. You'd think she was the one with the chance to be on his show. When I wasn't matching her energy, she frowned and asked, "Aren't you excited?"

The butterflies in my gut were in a frenzy though I tried to keep my face neutral. "Yeah, no, this is great. I've been waiting for this chance to beat him." My lack of enthusiasm was getting to her, which made it harder to keep the smile off my face. I loved tormenting my sister.

"Not just beat him," Mario said as he slammed his fists on the table, making the ice in our water jump. "But pummel him down to a pulpy mess of loser!"

I nodded. "Yeah, like that."

The cashier called Stella's name to pick up her order. Stella rolled her eyes as she grabbed the baby carrier. "Well, good luck if you get the opportunity to cook against him. Let me know, okay?"

"Will do." We all waved goodbye as she and the kids left.

"Robbie Day, huh?" Andrea said. "That's exciting."

My leg started bouncing, unable to keep my emotions in check. "I know! I'm going to have to get another haircut soon. I want to look my best on national TV."

"Don't you want to practice your cooking too?" Andrea asked. The waiter arrived and set our plates in front of us.

The aroma of my patty melt hit my stomach, making it growl in anticipation. I popped a French fry in my mouth and talked around the too hot morsel. "I got that covered." I gulped some water to keep my tongue from burning.

My phone buzzed in my pocket. Gino texted. **Important question for u.**

I assumed he wanted to discuss parkour because that was all he ever talked to me about anyway. **What up?**

When u bringing Charlie to Sunday dinner?

I flipped my phone over, not wanting to discuss my love life with my brother. Why was he assuming that Charlie and I were serious enough to bring her to dinner? Were we at that place yet? Would Charlie want to meet my family? I took another bite of my sandwich, chewing harder than before, when my phone buzzed again. He must really want to know. Was he with my mom right now? I was sure she was putting him up to it.

I glanced to see what he said when I noticed that the text was from Jackie. I quickly swallowed and unlocked my phone. **Sorry I've been MIA. I'm fine. Had to leave to get my head together.** I held up my phone to show the others what she sent me, but they were already reading a text from her too.

"Do you know what this is about?" I asked them.

Andrea shrugged as she shut off her phone and set it on the table next to her plate. "No, but she's been working really hard at work. I'm sure she just has an important project."

"I guess." Being an up and coming executive wasn't easy and Jackie had a dream of making partner one day. It didn't surprise me that she was overworking herself and needed some time to decompress. I typed back: **Take care. Let me know if I can help.**

Mario didn't say anything but the crease in his forehead told me he was deep in thought as he finished his lunch.

"You okay?" I asked.

He blinked a few times before focusing on me. "What? Yeah. I was just thinking about my date tonight."

"A date? Who with?" Planning that far ahead wasn't his usual MO, so I was surprised.

"With Britney. You met her."

I didn't usually bother remembering the names of the women Mario brought home, so I had to think hard – wait, wasn't Britney that redhead from the bar the other night? "Another date? With a *Britney*? Wow, this must be serious," I said teasingly but was surprised when he simply shrugged.

"I like her." He wiped his mouth with a napkin, no sign of humor or deception.

"So, do you want to order Out-the-Door-Oatmeal for the morning?"

He smiled as he stood to leave. "Nope."

I sat frozen in my seat for a moment wondering what happened to my friend. He wasn't the commitment type and two dates was a big commitment for him. Andrea and I both stood to leave when we caught gazes. I wondered if the same look of amazement filled my face too. The world was really flipping upside down if both Mario and I were getting serious about a special someone. Maybe there was something in the water.

Chapter Twenty-Three: Charlie

Charlie had to smile as she watched Lola whirl around the kitchen, moving seamlessly from the four pots on the stove to the five bowls on the counters to the fridge for more ingredients and then back again. It was Lola's particular kind of dance, and it felt special to watch and even more special to have it happen here, in Charlie's own kitchen. After two weeks of dating, their schedules had finally aligned to make dinner at Charlie's house work.

"You seem to be enjoying yourself," Charlie observed, confining her own movements to the small space on the kitchen island where her cutting board rested, a growing pile of chopped, fragrant herbs in front of her. You never wanted to get in the way of someone else's choreography.

"Can't lie, I *have* been lusting after your kitchen ever since the first time I visited," Lola admitted, dipping a spoon into a steaming sauce on the stove.

"Hmm. I think that's the first time someone's ever been interested in me just for my kitchen," Charlie laughed.

"Not *just* for your kitchen," Lola said, and shot her a crooked smile. "You're really sexy doing parkour too."

Charlie felt butterflies in her stomach and looked down at her cutting board again hoping to hide a blush. Two weeks in, and the butterflies were still in full force. "You too," she managed, because it was true – but if she said anything more, about muscles and coiled strength and – great, just *thinking* about it was probably making her blush worse.

Luckily, Lola seemed to have focused in on the cutting board too. "Hey, nice job chopping those herbs," she said, sounding faintly surprised.

"Gee, thanks," Charlie said dryly. She was pretty sure Lola had given her the simplest task in the recipe.

"No, I really meant it – not everyone knows how to handle herbs correctly. I wasn't trying to be patronizing." Lola sighed. "Sometimes I open my mouth and my mother's voice comes out. It's very disconcerting."

"She's patronizing about chopping herbs?"

"Well – she taught me to cook and is sure everything I know was learned from her. And sometimes when we cook together, she forgets I'm not eight years old anymore."

Charlie found herself nodding. "Betty and the rest of the coven are that way sometimes. They all taught me so much – like how to chop herbs – and I love them dearly, but sometimes they think I'm still a cute little kid who's being precocious if I do something clever."

"*Exactly*," Lola said with a flourish of her spoon. "It's like Mama's proud of me, but still can't see the things I do as real, adult things. Like the way my pesto dish has been such a hit at the restaurant. She's proud, but still doesn't understand why my job is a reason to miss Sunday dinner with the family."

Charlie felt a new uneasiness in her stomach at the mention of Lola's pesto dish, and this one *wasn't* happy butterflies. For the past two weeks, no one had seen any vampires, no one suspicious had come to Lola's restaurant while the coven kept careful watch, and no new names had been added to the list of the Disappeared. It would be nice to think the effects of the pesto, and the special blessings protecting the restaurant, were enough to make the vampires leave – but no one in the coven really dared trust that. It felt more like they were just waiting, somewhere in the shadows. That was making everyone nervous.

Charlie didn't want all those thoughts intruding on the evening, but couldn't help asking, "So you're still serving a lot of your pesto dish?"

"Oh yeah, it's flying out of the kitchen every night." Lola grinned and winked. "I might have been after your kitchen, but you know you wanted me for my recipes."

Joking though the comment was, it cut even closer to the things Charlie *didn't* want to think about. She and Lola had talked about all kinds of things when they were together, but not much about witchcraft and supernatural enemies. Lola hadn't asked many questions, and Charlie told herself that maybe Lola had decided it was all too overwhelming, she needed time to process, and she didn't actually want to know more right now.

She was telling herself a lot of things – that Lola was safer not knowing, that Charlie had promised Betty and the coven to keep the secret, that the vampires couldn't attack the restaurant anymore so Lola didn't need to know. It might all have been easier if she'd actually believed herself.

And in her discomfort from pushing all that down yet again, all she could produce was a weak laugh that didn't sound at all convincing. In desperation, she made a mad conversational flail she wouldn't have made if she'd been thinking clearly. "Do you always cook special recipes for your girlfriends?"

And there was a sudden pause in the conversation, long enough for Charlie to fully process that she'd used the g-word, after – what? Two weeks of dating? She froze. So much worse than an awkward laugh! Should she take it back, should she say something light and dismissive –

"Not usually," Lola said slowly, gaze fixed on the steaming pots and pans on the stove. "Not for a long time." She half-smiled. "Lately it's been nothing more complicated than oatmeal that Mario helps me throw together in the morning. But – I guess this is pretty special."

And now the butterflies, the good ones, were back. "Yeah," Charlie said, smile tugging at her lips. "I guess so too." But she'd still dropped that *word*... "I didn't really mean – I know it's early still, we don't have to label anything..."

She wouldn't actually have minded if Lola had disagreed with that. But the other woman was nodding and saying, "Yeah, it would make us such stereotypes, right? The lesbians who commit after only a couple of dates?"

More than a couple, but – not many, sure. Charlie managed a laugh. "Sure, right. Of course."

"But..." Lola's mouth twisted, and her spoon started stirring more vigorously. "Even if we don't *label* it exactly – we could – I mean, if you want, we could agree to be exclusive?"

This – sort of implied there was a whole host of women Charlie would have to regretfully turn away if she committed to Lola, which was very much not the case – but she didn't quite like to admit that. Especially if Lola *had* been, well, making oatmeal for a lot of women recently. "Yes," she said, nodding, "I would like that."

"Well – good," Lola said, crooked smile appearing again. "Me too."

There was a new charge between them as they smiled at each other, and Charlie almost leaned into it, almost suggested to Lola that they abandon the dinner after all – but that was probably insulting Lola as a chef, which was definitely the last thing she wanted to do. So she made a joke instead. "Does this mean I get to use your super special knives?" she asked, gesturing to the leather packet Lola had unrolled across one counterspace, knives neatly stowed in pockets within.

"Oh, now *that's* a real commitment," Lola protested, laughing. "Nobody touches my knives!"

"Good thing the Uber driver didn't know you were carrying those."

"Definitely would have made me late to dinner."

"And we can't have that," Charlie murmured. She was looking forward too much to this meal – and everything she wanted to do after it.

THE EVENING WAS EVERYTHING Charlie could have hoped, and if she had any regret it was only that she had to get up early for a practice ballet session the next morning. At least she and Lola had that in common though, as she was off to an opening shift at the restaurant. They drove downtown together, and by the time most people were arriving at offices, Charlie was already deep into running choreography with Dylan, this year's Snow King.

Taking a breather, she wiped her face with a towel, and remarked, "That felt pretty good." She dropped the towel and tugged her hair to tighten her ponytail. "What did you think?"

"Not bad for a start," Dylan agreed. "Thanks for coming early to get some extra practice in before the full session later."

"No problem." Charlie stretched and looked around the empty practice room, doubled in size by the mirror covering one wall. Soon it would be full of dancers and instructors.

A knock at the open door of the practice room announced the first of those arrivals. "Um, hi, guys," Kayla said, awkward smile on her face as she stood in the doorway.

"Hey, Kayla," Dylan said easily, with probably none of the tension suddenly tightening Charlie's shoulders. "Here for the practice session?"

"Yeah…" Kayla said, and her smile widened, even as she looked at Charlie with some worry still in her eyes. "And they just let me know this morning – they want me to be the Snow Queen's understudy!"

"Hey, congratulations!" Dylan said with apparently unfeigned enthusiasm.

"Congratulations," Charlie echoed, with more complicated emotions. She was genuinely glad for Kayla, but she couldn't shake these awkward feelings, being around someone she had dumped.

"Let me show you what we're doing with the choreography," Dylan offered, extending a hand to Kayla. "It's not super different from last year, but we wanted to put our own signature on it, you know?"

"Yeah, that would be great," Kayla said, then glanced at Charlie again, as though for permission.

"You two go ahead," Charlie said, and gestured vaguely at the door. "I'm gonna go refill my water bottle." She made her escape, half-filled bottle in hand.

Charlie headed down the hall toward the drinking fountain, trying to shake the tension out of her shoulders. Maybe it would be *good* having Kayla as her understudy. They'd have to work together, so they'd have to get to a new place, right? Professional friends. Kayla knew Charlie was dating Lola now, Charlie could show she still thought well of Kayla and wanted to be friendly – yeah, this could be good.

Farther down the hall, Charlie heard the strains of "The Dance of the Sugar Plum Fairy" coming from another practice room. Nathan and Victoria must be practicing too. She drifted that way, to pause in the doorway and watch as they finished a run-through of their dance.

They were amazing together. They were only practicing, but Victoria's movements were perfect, flowing from one step into another, perfectly in time, perfectly in position. Victoria *was* the Sugar Plum Fairy, regal and elegant and magical, even dancing in a leotard, hair in a bun, sweat glistening on her forehead.

And Nathan – he was even better than Charlie had realized. They'd been right to cast him as the Cavalier.

And, though it made her gut clench to admit it, they'd been right to cast Victoria too.

The music and the dance came to an end, and Charlie spontaneously applauded. It was the kind of dance that deserved applause. Nathan glanced her way, grinned, and sketched a bow.

Victoria merely sniffed, head in the air. "This was a *private* practice session. I prefer not to be watched while my partner is still learning."

"Oh come on, Victoria," Nathan said, making an exaggerated grimace at Charlie from behind Victoria, "the door was open."

Victoria did not deign to respond, merely picked up her water bottle and duffle bag. "I'm going to the auditorium – they're supposed to make an announcement soon about the production schedule. Nathan, we'll discuss how we can improve that final sequence later."

Nathan rolled his eyes at her retreating back. "Sure, Victoria."

She stepped past Charlie and strode off down the hall.

Charlie shook her head, then turned to Nathan. "You two looked *amazing*. I knew you were good, but wow!"

He rubbed the back of his neck, grin looking a little sheepish. "Yeah, well. We've been putting in a lot of extra practice. Victoria is, um, kind of serious about dancing. You might have noticed."

Charlie sighed. "They made the right choice casting her. I'm *never* going to be that good."

"Hey, don't say that," Nathan said, coming closer and giving her shoulder a nudge. "You don't need to dance like Victoria. You dance like *you*. You put a lot more passion in, and that counts for more than being perfectly precise. And yeah, Victoria's really good – but dancing isn't everything anyway. She's that good because she doesn't care about anything else. That's not you, Charlie – and that's a compliment."

"Sure," Charlie said, only half-listening. She should really talk to Dylan about getting more practices scheduled. If she was going to be truly serious about her dancing, if she was going to compete with Victoria and get to number one in the dance world, she'd have to put more time in. Lola and the coven would understand...

The thought made her pause. Did she really want to spend less time with Lola? And the coven was still trying to keep an eye on the vampires, figure out what they were plotting and of course keep Lola's restaurant safe...

She'd figure it out. There had to be a way she could balance everything.

"So you really thought we looked good?" Nathan said, drawing her back to the moment.

"You looked awesome. I can see why Victoria was saying you could audition in San Francisco," Charlie said, remembering their text exchange on the subject.

"Yeah, she keeps mentioning that," Nathan admitted, and didn't immediately laugh off the idea like Charlie might have expected.

Was he actually thinking about it? Her stomach went hollow again at the thought of Nathan leaving town. But wasn't that being selfish? "You know," Charlie said slowly, "you really *could* go audition in San Francisco You're good enough."

He grinned. "Nah, I like where I am. Why leave the pond where you're already the biggest fish? How much else is really out there anyway? Now come on – let's get over to the auditorium and see about this big announcement they've been promising. Think they're doing something different with the production schedule?"

Charlie shrugged, covering her relief. It was easier to move on to his new topic. "How different can you make the schedule for a holiday show? Maybe they're starting earlier than usual."

"Because nothing says Halloween like *The Nutcracker*," Nathan said, slinging an arm around Charlie's shoulders as they headed down the hallway.

The announcement proved more interesting and unusual than an early start date to performances – though in one sense, it was a *very* early start. In two weeks, they would put on a special workshop performance, showing some of the principle numbers from *The Nutcracker* for an audience, while the numbers were still being created.

"But the public will see us dancing when we're not ready for that yet," Victoria objected from the listening crowd of dancers. "The dances won't be polished – we'll still be working on them!"

The company manager had her patient look on. "Yeah, that's the whole idea. People love behind the scenes stuff. We're calling it a special view into the process of creating the show. We'll do a couple interviews with people working on costumes and sets, we'll do partial performances of a few of the dances – it'll be really relaxed, very engaging."

Charlie thought it sounded like a lot of fun. A different spin on *The Nutcracker* and a new way to engage audiences. She started thinking how much of the Snow Queen dance they might want to do – probably not all of it, so which portions could she and Dylan best prepare?

"But we can't dance if we haven't prepared the dances yet," Victoria persisted.

"We have enough to show them something," the manager countered. "This is *The Nutcracker*. We have three-quarters of it before we even start. And besides, we're doing the whole thing for charity. Proceeds will go to one of the homeless shelters nearby. You probably all heard about the homeless who were disappearing over the summer."

A murmur ran through the crowd, indicating they had. Charlie's attention suddenly focused more sharply on the discussion. It wasn't likely anyone was about to make a vampire reference, but...

"There's a lot of good that can be done in the homeless community, plus the special event will be great advance marketing for *The Nutcracker*. We know the event's not too far away, but we'll all buckle down, sort out what we're showing off, and put on a great show. We're doing a social media blitz to help get people in the door, and an email is going out to our season ticket holders tomorrow. *The Bee* has already promised to do an article about the event, and you can all tell your friends to come. Any questions?"

There were questions, not just from Victoria, but Charlie's mind wandered off on her own thoughts again. This would be a lot of work in the next couple of weeks, which was a challenge with everything else she had going on – but maybe it was the perfect opportunity, a chance for something really substantial to focus on connected to her dancing. Maybe the pesto had worked and the vampires really were quieting down, and Lola would understand about being passionate about her career. She'd find a way to balance it all. If she was going to be as good as Victoria, she had to be dedicated.

Chapter Twenty-Four: Lola

"**A**re you ready to go?" I asked Mario as I knocked on the bathroom door. We were meeting the others for an early morning parkour run. Sacramento had been hit with an October heat wave, so we had moved our training to the coolest part of the day.

Mario trudged out of the bathroom, yawning and stretching his arms overhead. "It's too early. The sun isn't even up yet."

I rolled my eyes as I laced up my shoes. "That's the point. Unless you want to collapse from heat stroke…" I grabbed my gym bag and headed to the door. "C'mon already. Charlie is meeting us at the park, and I want to get there before Gino has a chance to interrogate her."

"I'm hurrying. Chill." He didn't kick his movements into a higher gear like I'd hoped as he casually filled his water bottle at the kitchen sink.

"Don't tell me to chill," I mumbled to myself, leaning against the door, patiently waiting for him to gather his things. I glared at him as he purposely took his sweet time. "Maybe I'll just meet you there."

He finally picked up his pace and shoved his stuff into his bag. I was about to leave without him when he rushed to the door. "What are you waiting for?" he asked. "Let's go."

As we walked down the stairs he asked, "So, you and Charlie are still good?"

I smiled at the memories floating through my head. The way her fingers grazed down my body, setting my skin on fire. And how sweet she tasted when I kissed every inch of her. Heat washed over me as I let those visions replay over and over. I was on the verge of sweating.

"Are you okay?" Mario asked, scrutinizing my face. "You look flushed."

I pushed him away, annoyed that he'd noticed. "I'm fine." Then I remembered he had asked a question about me and Charlie. "We're fine." I drew in a deep breath as I gazed up at the stars, hoping the early morning air would cool me down.

I glanced over at Mario as we walked down the street to the Light Rail station. "What about you? I've noticed Britney over quite a bit lately. Are you twitterpated?" I asked teasingly.

Even in the dark, I could see Mario's cheeks darken with a blush. He shrugged. "I think maybe I am. She's, like, the coolest woman I know." After my offended gasp he amended his statement. "After you, of course."

As we seated ourselves on the train, a man sitting a few rows down caught my eye. Something about him reminded me of the goons that chased me that night at the restaurant, making my stomach clench. I didn't know if it was his pale complexion or his stiff posture or maybe the almost dead look in his vacant stare but he gave me the creeps. I kept him in my peripheral as the train sped along the tracks.

The meeting I had with Charlie's coven came to mind. I still wasn't sure if I believed everything they said. The whole line about a supernatural rival clan sounded too vague. What exactly did that mean?

And what that one lady said as she checked out the cut on my arm kept popping up in my mind. Over and over. She'd said I had magic in my blood. *Like calls to like* she'd said. My stomach flipped as the implications were clear. She thought that I was a witch, too. Like Charlie. Supposedly like my Nonna.

Maybe I needed to ask Charlie more questions. I'd been afraid to open that can of worms and ruin the good vibes we had going lately. But it could be time to get some clarification on a few things.

A low ache squeezed my brain and I leaned over to rest my head in my hands. There was too much to take in. The train stopped at another station, knocking me into Mario.

Should I tell him about those supernatural beings? Would he think I'd lost my mind? Would the others? I should probably keep that to myself, but I also wanted them to know what was really terrorizing the city.

I glanced over to Mario. "Do you believe in supernatural stuff?"

His body stiffened. "What do you mean? Like angels and demons?"

I shrugged as I sat up straight. "I don't know, like magic. Do you think there are real witches in the world? And evil supernatural creatures?"

He stared at me for a second before saying, "Like vampires...or, uh, werewolves? I think there is a kernel of truth to all of these legends, don't you? Why do you ask? Is this something you and Charlie talked about?"

Why would he bring up Charlie? "I was just thinking about those creeps that attacked the restaurant. They were stronger than most people and they sa – the thought that there was something supernatural about them crossed my mind. That's all."

"When you leave work tonight, do me a favor?" he asked with all seriousness. I nodded. "Call me or one of the guys to walk you home."

"Seriously?" I asked. "I can take care of myself. I got away from them last time."

"Maybe you just got lucky. Maybe next time they'll bring more friends with them. Don't be stupid, Lola. Don't go anywhere at night without backup."

"Okay," I said, mostly to ease his mind. "The whole city seems to have calmed down anyway. There haven't been any new reports of Disappeared for a while." I'd never seen him so serious before. I regretted bringing the whole thing up.

GINO AND THE OTHERS were already at the park under a streetlight. Andrea was talking to Allen. Charlie hadn't shown up yet.

"It's about time you got here," Gino said, walking up and shaking hands with Mario, then capturing my neck with his arm and giving me a noogie. I hated when he did that, so I stomped on his foot to get him to release me.

"Stop messing up my hair." I tried to fix it, though there really wasn't much to fix, before Charlie saw it. But the others saw this as a challenge and made it their mission to keep it messy. Sometimes I fucking hated these guys.

"Hey," Charlie said from behind as she walked over. She kissed me on the lips to the oohs and awws of the others. I kissed her back, refusing to let their teasing embarrass me.

"Glad you made it," I said, my cheeks straining with the smile on my face. I tried to tone it down, but my mouth wasn't having it. "Oh, and I can't wait to see you dance the Snow Queen. I definitely want to come to your workshop performance tomorrow night." Charlie had texted me about it last night but my phone died before I could respond.

Charlie smiled, making my heart swell. "That would be great." She squeezed my hand and I never wanted to let her go. The desire to support her, not just in her career but in life, came over me. I liked the feeling.

"Are you ready to lose?" Allen interrupted as he high-fived Gino.

"Talking to yourself again?" I asked. I glanced around and noticed that not everyone had shown up. "Still no Jackie?"

"I'm sure she'll be back when she's ready," Andrea said.

I pulled out my phone to see when I last heard from Jackie and noticed I hadn't received any amusing videos from her in a while. That was our thing. What was going on with her?

"All right, all right." Mario clapped loudly, getting all our attention. "The sun will be up soon and bringing the heat, so let's get started. The first team back to the basketball courts is the winner. We all know the route by now, except maybe Charlie. Just stay with Lola and you'll be fine."

"What about you?" Charlie asked Mario. "Aren't you on our team?"

"Yeah, but I'll be so far ahead that you won't see me until the end. I'll be the one sound asleep at half court."

I rolled my eyes. Mario and his trash talk. Charlie and I stretched, intentionally bumping into the other or "accidently" brushing our hands over the other's body. I could've stretched like this all day.

"Are you two done yet?" Gino said impatiently.

Charlie and I both smiled as we got into position to start. I didn't really care about winning. I wanted to stay with Charlie and make sure she made it through. She pulled out her phone and leaned in close to take a selfie of the both of us.

"Go!" Mario yelled and we all took off. The route wasn't too long but it had many challenging climbs and leaps. Running this circuit while most of the city still slept would make it easier to get through without having to dodge people and cars.

Not too surprisingly, Charlie kept up well. I wasn't going full throttle, but I wasn't jogging either. She hopped over the first low chain link fence with little effort. I waited for her before I jumped up to grab the fire escape ladder and pull it down. I let her climb up first.

The morning sun's light had already begun to chase away the stars, leaving the sky a lighter blue. We ducked into the abandoned warehouse through a busted door. It was one giant room with large boarded up windows on one wall and offices on the upper story on the opposite side. When we got to the stairs leading to the main floor, I showed off by sliding down the handrail, surfer style.

"Impressive," she said while jumping down the steps, skipping every other one. Our foot falls echoed off the cement walls as we ran across the dimly lit room.

The exit door was already open, most likely thanks to Mario trying to shave a few seconds off our time. But just as we were about to run through, the door slammed shut and a strange giant of a man stepped in front of it. The steely-eyed glare this guy was giving us sent a shiver up my spine. He was looking for trouble.

I instinctively threw my arm in front of Charlie to stop her, only to see that she did the same for me.

Charlie gasped. "We need to get out of here." She pulled me back to go the other way,

Only there was another man a couple of yards behind us. Both men were dressed in thick, black cloaks, clean shaven with perfectly styled short hair. The man in front of us smiled wide, exposing long, sharp fangs. Freaking fangs!

"What the hell?" I whispered, my mind racing. Were those so-called supernatural beings vampires? "Blood sucking vampires?" I thought Betty meant they were rival witches, not the undead.

The man cocked his head in my direction but spoke to his buddy. "Is this the one?"

"That's her." He sniffed the air a couple times and added. "The stench of *Hypericum* is still on her. But this one..." He inhaled deeply through his nose, and then followed that up with a creepy, satisfied sigh. "She's a witch."

The first behemoth directed his full attention on Charlie. "We need to talk."

"I have nothing to discuss with you," Charlie said. I could feel her nervous energy pulsating as she stood beside me, and that protective nature kicked in.

I took her hand and pulled her away, intending to walk around him. "Let's go."

In a blur, he was inches away from me, our noses practically touching. He snarled. "You're not going anywhere until I talk to your mate."

A little thrill lit up inside me when he referred to Charlie as my mate, but I shoved it aside to analyze later. We needed to get out of danger first. "She doesn't want to talk to you, so beat it."

My gut twisted at the narrowing of his eyes. That couldn't be good. "Anthony, please detain this one while I speak to the witch."

I glanced over my shoulder to see the vampire that had been blocking the door walk toward me, a malicious smile spreading over his face.

Turning to Charlie, I asked, "Can't you knock them out with a spell or something?"

"It doesn't work like that," she said. "I'm not that kind of witch." Then she turned back to the vampire in front of us. "If you hurt her, I'm not telling you anything."

"We'll see about that," he said just before he nodded to his friend.

A split second later, pain exploded at my sides. I screamed as pressure clamped down against my ribs, making breathing nearly impossible. The vampire, Anthony, had wrapped his arms around my chest from behind and was crushing me. He was freakishly strong. He put the super in supernatural. I tried kicking against his legs, but it had no effect. He lifted me off the ground, rendering me defenseless.

"Let her go!" Charlie tried to pull Anthony's arms away, but it only made him chuckle and squeeze harder. Stars flashed in my vision, and I could hear my ribs cracking. My brain was getting light-headed, and the room seemed to be getting darker.

"Let the sunshine in!" Mario's voice sang out in the room. I tried to twist my head to where it came from but couldn't move.

Anthony's body stiffened though he didn't let up his hold on me. Not until bright light filled the room, stinging my eyes. Then I could breathe again, the vampire's arms no longer around me. Charlie caught me before I hit the floor. Bits of ash swirled in the beams of sunlight, settling to the floor into a small pile.

"Oh, my goddess. We need to get you out of here." Slowly she helped me to the door.

"What happened?" I rasped. One second, we were up to our eyeballs in vampire trouble, and the next they were gone.

"Mario," she said, her voice straining. "He pulled the boards off the windows, letting the sunlight in."

"You're welcome," Mario said as he took my other side, taking some of my weight off Charlie as he helped me get out of the warehouse. Once we were outside and on the curb, he said to Charlie, "Do you have something that will help her? If you know what I mean?"

"Yes. I have just the thing at home."

"Okay," he said with a nod. "Go get your car. I got her."

"I'll be right back." She ran, faster than I had ever seen her run, back toward the park.

I still couldn't take a deep breath and my ribs were killing me, so I let Mario keep me propped up. I trusted him. "Where did you come from? How did you know we were in trouble?"

He shrugged. "I was waiting for you outside so we could finish together. When you hadn't come out after a while, I went back in to make sure one of you wasn't hurt. That's when I saw those goons, so I went around to the fire escape and snuck in."

He must have heard me yell about vampires – lucky he believed me! "But how did you know the sunlight would kill them?"

"Everybody knows that vampires hate sunlight. I figured they would either take off, die, or sparkle."

I started to laugh but a sharp pain shut me up. A moment later, Charlie's car screeched to a stop right in front of us. Mario helped me sit in the front seat. "I'll let the others know what happened."

"You can leave some parts out," I whispered, hoping he understood which parts I meant.

"Don't worry. I'll tell them you were showing off in front of your girlfriend and fell. They'll believe that." He shut the door before I could argue, and Charlie pulled into traffic.

Charlie sat stiff in her seat; eyes locked on the road in front of us. "It's going to be okay," she said. "I've got something at home that can heal you or would you rather I take you to a hospital?"

"No hospital. They smell weird."

"Then potion it is." She stole her gaze away from the road to look at me. "You trust me, right?"

How could she even ask that? She healed my arm before. "Yes," I said faintly. "But..." A wave of pain hit me. My breathing was fast and shallow because it cost me the least pain, but I couldn't speak very loudly.

She reached over and squeezed my hand. "Don't talk. You need to save your energy."

I couldn't relax with everything that had just happened swirling in my head. "Holy shit! They were vampires! Actual fucking vampires." I drew in a couple breaths through my nose. "Did you see their..." I motioned to my mouth since talking was becoming harder. "And the one guy just..." He combusted into a pile of ash or dust or... "He just poofed!"

Charlie removed her hand from mine and gripped the steering wheel. "We'll talk about that later. First, I need to meet with my coven. Something will be done."

I smiled at the determination in her voice. The slight tremor in her body told me she was shaken by the incident but was putting on a brave front. For me. And I loved her for that.

Love? Yeah... maybe.

CHARLIE HELPED ME OUT of the car and into her house. A couple of her neighbors were already outside in their gardens and looked on. I could practically hear the gossip mill turning.

"Lie down while I fix the poultice," she said, easing me onto the same bed I had used before. I hissed in pain as I tried to get comfortable. She kissed me lightly on the lips. I wanted to kiss her more thoroughly, but the pain was too much, so I let her pull away without protest.

The incident with the vampires, or whatever we were calling them, ran through my head over and over again. At first, I thought they were after me, like at the restaurant, but the guy wanted to talk to Charlie. I was just in the way. Did he find out that she gave me the *Hypericum Perforatum*?

A knock on the front door caused me to flinch. Betty's voice eased my nerves. Why was I so jumpy? Vampires can't come out during the day, right? Wrong. They definitely weren't sleeping in a coffin when they attacked. But they weren't in the direct sunlight, were they? Not until Mario showed up. As long as the curtains were open, allowing the sun to shine through, we were safe. I hoped. At least until sundown.

"Are you all right, Charlie?" Betty's voice drifted down the hall easily.

Charlie didn't answer right away. After a moment she said, "I'm okay but Lola's hurt." Sounds of rustling utensils and bowls almost obscured her voice. "We were attacked by a couple vampires so I'm making a healing potion for her. I think she might have a few broken ribs."

"I hope you have enough ingredients to make a double batch. Vampires attacked Helen early this morning," Betty said. "That's another reason I came over, to get some herbs from the garden, but if you're already brewing the potion, I can help."

"How badly was she hurt?" Charlie asked. I could hear the concern in her voice.

"She's a tough old bird. Nothing too serious, but she does have a lot of bruises and is sore. She had gone to her gym to use the pool before anyone else and on her drive home she was run off the road. It was a vampire. The sun hadn't come up yet. She said he was covered from head to toe in a dark material and was about to break her side window when a patrol car stopped to see if she was okay. The vampire didn't stick around. The policeman drove her home and I'm getting Herbert to pick her car up this morning."

"That's terrible," Charlie said.

Shoes scuffed along the floor as Betty continued. "Those vampires must've found out that you gave Lola the *Hypericum Perforatum* as a weapon to use against them. We all need to be on alert."

I hissed at the pain that shot through my sides when I tensed. What did I just hear? Charlie gave me the plant to use in my recipe *because* she knew the effect it would have on vampires? Is that why they attacked the restaurant? But they didn't even eat my pesto. And why didn't she tell me, especially if it would put the entire restaurant staff in danger?

All the heat drained from my body. Was Charlie only with me because I worked at the restaurant? Or because of Nonna's receipts book? Was I simply a means to an end? My stomach lurched. I didn't know which hurt more; the vampire crushing me or Charlie's betrayal.

I tried to listen to Charlie and Betty discuss the vampires and coven business, but they lowered their voices. That and the clanking of metal and sounds of chopping made it near impossible to make out what they were discussing. Without words to focus on, even my anger wasn't enough to distract me from the pain and exhaustion pulling me toward sleep.

Chapter Twenty-Five: Charlie

Charlie sat next to Lola, watching her sleep and trying to match her breathing to the slow, steady rise and fall of Lola's chest. As though it might calm her, might relieve some of the tension vibrating through her every muscle.

It wasn't working, and eventually she gave up. She slipped out of the guest bedroom as silently as she could and went to her practice room, to go through a punishing series of ballet moves. She did her usual home exercises, and when she got to the end she started at the beginning again, until every muscle ached and shook with the strain. It didn't hurt worse than her guilt, or drive the events of the morning out of her mind.

First there had been the vampires, appearing out of nowhere. It had been terrifying when that vampire had grabbed Lola, squeezing until her ribs cracked and her face twisted in agony.

And there had been nothing Charlie could do but watch, vampire stories racing pell-mell through her brain, knowing that as bad as this was, it could get so much worse. She would have given anything in that moment to have a spell she could use to fight vampires. What was the point of being a witch if she was going to be so helpless?

It only made it worse knowing the whole thing was *her fault*, that the vampires never would have gone near Lola if she, Charlie, hadn't deliberately given her that herb, essentially set up a beacon for vampires to lead them to Lola and her restaurant.

If Mario hadn't come to the rescue with the sunlight, Lola would have died. And that would have been Charlie's fault too.

After her exercise, Charlie dragged herself into her workroom. She called in sick to the day's ballet practice, ignoring Nathan's multiple texts asking what was going on. He knew she wasn't sick – she had texted him a goofy selfie of herself and Lola that morning, posing for parkour, before everything had gone to hell. But she could not deal with explanations right now.

Instead, she threw herself into making protective potions and healing salves that she refused to use on her own sore muscles. She stopped frequently to check on Lola, who had settled into a deep sleep. She changed the poultice twice without waking her. Even with the magic helping, it took a lot of energy for the body to heal the way Lola's was doing.

Her phone buzzed throughout the day with texts from the coven, texts Charlie also ignored. They were analyzing the attack at the warehouse, trying to figure out how vampires had been there after daybreak, talking about Helen's accident, strategizing next steps, and Charlie just couldn't face any of it right now. Lola was safe here. For now, that was enough.

By mid-afternoon, Charlie had a long row of newly bottled potions standing on her worktable, and when she paused long enough to take stock, her legs nearly buckled with exhaustion. She took a breath, feeling it go just a little deeper than she'd been able to manage that morning. She knew she needed to rest, even if she didn't feel like she deserved to. But if she collapsed, wrung out from tension and exercise and potion-brewing, she'd be no use to anyone.

Afternoon naps were often a necessity when she'd had a long morning practice, with an evening performance still ahead. And this morning had been way harder than any practice ever was.

She started towards her bedroom, but hesitated in the doorway of the guest bedroom where Lola was still sound asleep. Maybe it would be better if she was nearby, if Lola needed anything. And maybe she'd sleep without nightmares, if she had the reassurance of Lola being right there, alive and safe.

Charlie tiptoed into the room and curled up next to Lola's sleeping body, careful of her healing ribs. The closeness didn't banish her fears.

She could have lost Lola today. Just like her parents. Just like her grandparents.

She was so fucking tired of loving people and losing them.

How could she have been so reckless, putting Lola in danger, not even warning her the danger was there? They hadn't been as close at the time, Lola wouldn't have believed her, she had made a promise to Betty...but none of those things felt like a good enough excuse.

She should tell Lola every bit of the truth. And then Lola would hate her, rip her head off and storm out. Charlie would probably never see her again. She'd never hear her laugh or watch her do parkour or see her crooked smile again.

And maybe that would be better, safer, for both of them.

She wanted to reach out and wrap her arms around Lola, bury her face against the other woman's shoulder and inhale her scent, citrus shampoo and, lately, just a hint of pesto.

But she didn't want to wake Lola, or hurt her ribs. And the scent of pesto would only remind her right now of her betrayal, that she shouldn't have the right to touch Lola, not with all her secrets.

She heard Sammy's familiar snuffling as he came into the room. He stopped by the bed and she reached down to lift him up before he could bark and wake Lola. She settled down again and waited for him to do his usual ritual of turning around and curling against her back. Instead, as though the little dog could sense the tumult of emotions inside her, he padded up near her head and gave her cheek a lick.

Charlie rolled over, away from Lola toward Sammy, and put her arms around her dog as he whumped down onto the blanket. She pressed her face against him, tears trickling into his soft fur as she cried for what she had lost, what she had done, and what she still had to lose.

IT WAS A LONG TIME before Charlie finally fell asleep, and she woke up late and disoriented. The morning felt like a bad dream, even harder to believe in when she found herself alone in the bed. She drew her breath in sharply, looking at the dented pillow next to her. Lola. She had been injured so badly, she shouldn't be moving...

Charlie rolled out of bed – no sign of Sammy either – and pushed open the closed bedroom door. She shuffled out into the hallway, squinting in the brighter light. Her instinctive panic subsided when she heard Lola's voice from the direction of the kitchen.

"There you go, buddy. Nice vegetarian dog food for you. I probably don't want to know what's in it, but if it makes you happy, I guess it's all good."

Charlie smoothed her hands over her wrinkled workout clothes. She hadn't bothered changing for her nap, but now she felt gross and uncomfortable.

Or maybe being uncomfortable didn't really have that much to do with her clothes. She had to talk to Lola, tell her the truth about what had happened, what she and the coven had done. She ran a nervous hand over her hair, and didn't feel better encountering her ponytail, now hopelessly rumpled. She tugged the hairband out, letting her curls fall to her shoulders and slipping the band automatically over her wrist. Then with a deep breath, she headed into the kitchen.

Sammy was face-deep in his food bowl, tail happily wagging as he snuffled at his supper. Nothing complicated there.

Charlie forced her gaze up to look at the woman rinsing out the empty can from Sammy's meal. She felt her heart squeeze looking at Lola, at the evening light filtering in through the window and lying golden on her face. She hadn't realized until this moment that some part of her, maybe a big part, had expected Lola to be gone, as though vampires could somehow have come and taken her away.

"Hey," she said, but her voice came out croaky. She cleared her throat and tried again. "Hey. How do you feel?"

Lola didn't look away from the sink, carefully setting the rinsed can down by the edge. "I'm all right."

Charlie wanted to move closer. She wanted to go wrap her arms around Lola – gently – and kiss her and tell her she was so, so sorry for everything that had happened and everything she had done. But Lola still wasn't looking at her, and something about the tension in the other woman's back seemed like more than just the stiffness of healing ribs. "You should take it easy," she said carefully. "That poultice I made you is good, but that was a serious injury and–"

"I'm *all right*," Lola said again, reaching for a dish towel and meticulously wiping down around the sink. "A little sore but – yeah, that was a really good poultice." Her voice was noticeably less warm than it had been talking to Sammy. She turned to face Charlie, but her gaze didn't lift to meet hers.

Lola had seen the vampires at the warehouse and knew what they were. How much had she put together on her own?

Charlie found herself twisting uncomfortably at the hairband on her wrist, her own gaze drifting to what she'd noticed but not wanted to take in. Lola's gym bag was sitting on top of the kitchen table, where it hadn't been earlier, visibly ready to go. "You should sit down," she offered anyway, as though somehow the idea might actually defuse the tension in the room. As though they could sit and talk things through and Charlie could explain everything and...what? What was even the best-case scenario here?

Lola looked up then, and it didn't feel better to see how cold her eyes were. "Thanks for the healing. Maybe you owed me that one, though. Since you gave me an herb that was going to bring vampires running, and didn't even bother to warn me. Or tell me the truth once they showed up."

Charlie's chest tightened. "I was...going to explain..." Too late, it was way, way too late.

Lola frowned, crossing her arms. "So it really is true? I overheard you talking to Betty when you thought I was asleep – I *was* half-asleep so I thought maybe I got it wrong – did you know what would happen when you gave me your herbs?"

Charlie searched frantically for the right words. If Lola wasn't sure what she had heard, maybe she could still smooth this over, still make it okay...by lying again? Not even a lie of omission, but an actual direct lie? She couldn't do that. Lola would be right to never trust her again if she did that. "I...didn't know the vampires would find you," she said carefully. "I never meant to put you in danger–"

"But you *did* know about vampires? And when they showed up at my restaurant, you knew what they were? And you took me to that coven meeting and you *all* knew and you just – danced around my questions? You told me a lot of nonsense about *supernatural persons* instead of telling me there were freaking *vampires* after me?"

Charlie swallowed hard. "Yes," she said faintly, because it was all far too true.

Lola's eyes narrowed. "Yeah. All right then. I think I'd better go."

No, it couldn't end like this! "We should talk about this–"

"You *used* me, Charlie." The words were biting, hard. "You put me at risk – my coworkers and my friends at risk – and you didn't even give me a choice about it. Instead you *lied* to me, you and all your witchy friends."

"I'm so sorry," Charlie said, knowing it wasn't enough. Would it do any good to say they'd only withheld information? But what difference did it make? "I tried to get Betty and the others to tell you – after you left the coven meeting–"

"You should have told me yourself, Charlie. You've had weeks to tell me. And just this morning – I asked you about the vampires and you said we'd *talk about it later*. Were we ever going to get to *later*?"

"You were injured, in shock – I *was* going to tell you though! When I came in here I was going to tell you everything!"

Lola snorted. "And why should I have any reason to believe that? I *trusted* you. You should have told me the truth a long time ago."

"I couldn't," Charlie whispered. She had been so conflicted, so torn about what the right thing to do was. She still didn't know what would have been right – but clearly this wasn't. "I made a promise to my coven leader–"

"Oh, that's convenient," Lola snapped, "you were just following orders, huh? It's not like you had any ethical obligation here, you were just following orders!"

"I didn't mean–"

"In fact," Lola said, eyes narrowing, "how long have you been following orders? How long have you and your friends been planning this? Is this why you wanted to meet me to begin with, way back when you tasted my vegan dish?"

"No," Charlie protested. "It wasn't like that at all – I didn't even think about the herb when I met you."

"When you started stalking me, you mean? Following me to Pilates class, showing up at my restaurant again." Lola shook her head. "I can't believe I thought it was just because you liked me."

"It *was* because I liked you – I do like you!" Charlie said, heart hammering hard in her chest. "None of that was about the herb."

"How can I believe anything you tell me? You've been lying to me all along." Lola let out a loud, angry breath. "It was bad enough when you had this secret life as a witch. But to drag me into your craziness and not even tell me the truth? To use me and put me at risk?"

Charlie struggled for words, but no matter what she said, it just seemed to be making everything worse. She still wanted to argue, to explain, to try to make Lola understand...what? Because even if Lola was wrong about how far back Charlie's plans had gone, she was right about far too much. She sank down onto a kitchen chair, rested her head on her hand. "I'm sorry. I'm really sorry."

Lola's phone, resting on top of her bag, gave a loud buzz right over Charlie's last word. "Good, Mario must be here," Lola said, scooping up her phone. "I called him for a ride."

"Were you planning to wake me up before you left?" Charlie asked in a low voice.

Lola didn't look up from the message she was reading on her phone. "I should have waited outside, but I didn't want to get snatched by a freaking vampire. Plus Sammy was giving me those big sad eyes, and then I couldn't leave empty cans all over your kitchen, so..." She grimaced, shoved her phone into her pocket and picked up her bag. She looked at Charlie again, eyes even colder than before. "You know the part of your master plan I don't understand? I don't see how sleeping with me helped you fight vampires."

Charlie's stomach dropped. Lola couldn't believe that! "That was *never* part of–"

"You know what, whatever," Lola said, waving her free hand dismissively and heading for the door. "It doesn't even matter. I have meaningless sex all the time."

Charlie was still trying to catch her breath from that when the door clicked shut behind Lola.

"It wasn't meaningless," she said into the empty kitchen, chest tight and words painful. "Not to me."

And surely, *surely* it hadn't been to Lola. It hadn't felt like it was, anyway. What Charlie had felt between them, when they talked and touched and laughed, none of that had been meaningless. It had to count for something, something important, and if Lola could just see that – if Charlie could finally find the right words to say, surely she could change something. Maybe they'd have a shot at getting past this. If she ran after Lola right now...

She actually tensed to stand, started to push against the table to rise to her feet. Then she stopped. Because then what? Lola had almost *died*. Could still die, if she continued to be part of Charlie's *craziness*.

Charlie couldn't do that to her. And she couldn't do that to herself either.

It was better if it really had been meaningless. It couldn't hurt as much, to lose something meaningless.

She looked down at Sammy, who had left his food bowl to sit next to her, tail thumping against the floor. "You and me, Samwise," she said softly. "That's all I need, right? Here at the end of all things."

Chapter Twenty-Six: Lola

Nothing felt right after Mario brought me home from Charlie's. It was almost dark but I had slept so much of the day that I was antsy. I paced through the living room and kitchen, and Mario watched me from the couch with an uncomfortably concerned expression.

"Do you want to go out or anything?" he asked, and I shot him a look. "What? I don't know what's got your panties in such a bunch. I thought you and Charlie were doing okay."

I had stayed real quiet during the drive home, and wasn't sure I could keep him in the dark forever. "We... yeah... uh."

Mario nodded knowingly. "Let's get out then. Go somewhere fun."

My thoughts flashed from Charlie's betrayal to vampires in the shadows. "No! Uh, no." I winced at my outburst and the resulting surprised expression Mario held. "How about we go to the gym?"

"Sure, I wouldn't mind going back for you."

It was inevitable that I'd be spilling my heart out and I wouldn't be able to say everything I wanted to say at the bigger gym Mario worked at. Not with other people there. "How about the one downstairs?"

Mario frowned, but only for a moment. "Well, I'm doing arms so I claim whatever ancient dumbbell set they have down there."

"Works for me." I threw some protein powder in a tumbler, changed into my gym shorts, and together we went to the apartment gym.

I hadn't gone to this gym in a long time. The apartment complex had a little community center with some tables and couches, and old games and books on a painted bookcase. To the side of this main room was a side room that held a stationary bike, a mediocre treadmill, a set of dumbbells next to a worn out bench, and one bowflex-type machine. Not much, but these would do the job.

"I should write to the apartment owner about some upgrades..." Mario mused as he hefted a dumbbell.

I chugged half the shake and started stretching out, shocked at how the severe injury I had suffered – that still made me flinch to remember – was nothing but passing soreness today. It was impossible.

Given everything that had happened, perhaps Charlie's healing magic was the only thing that I was truly thankful about.

Beside me, Mario completed some basic overhead press sets, his eyes darting away from me whenever I met his gaze in the wall mirror.

"So..." he started hesitantly.

Just a word, but it was enough to break the dam. "She used me, Mario."

"Go on."

So I did, as I completed dozens of squats and lunges, using every moment between sets to continue the story of her garden, the pesto, the attack at the restaurant, the coven, and what happened after the attack at the warehouse. He was mostly silent, the wideness of his eyes not really telling me if he believed me or if he was preparing to call a psych ward.

"And why couldn't she tell you what was going on?" he asked quietly from the bench, heavy weights poised on his chest.

"Something about vowing to her coven leader. Ridiculous, right?"

"Well, maybe that's really important." He pushed the weights up and I scoffed as I stepped onto the treadmill.

"You're gonna side with her?" I accused him. "Promising some old lady she wouldn't tell me anything was more important than my safety?"

Mario's cheeks were red as he pushed the weights up again, and I set the treadmill and got it started before he finished his set and sat up to look at me.

"You're right, it's not. But maybe, for her, it was more complicated than that."

Surprisingly astute coming from this himbo.

"I don't know how the hell you aren't yelling that I'm crazy for talking about witches and vampires," I admitted, walking at a brisk pace on the treadmill. "I hardly believe it and I lived through it. I have the bruises to prove it, and yet."

Marco just shrugged, putting down his weights, and stepping onto the foam mat squares in front of the mirror. "I dunno, man, maybe I respect you enough to believe you."

I was touched by his words, a well of emotion threatening me. So I spammed the increase speed button on the treadmill, and managed a "harrumph" before the treadmill got up to speed. It was smaller than the commercial gym variety, and shook a bit, but I got used to the shaking after a few minutes. I tried to focus on my breathing, and the rhythmic soreness that my stride and breathing caused my still-healing chest. But instead, my thoughts kept drifting back to what I had told Mario.

Charlie and her coven had used me. Had used my history, my family, my skill. Had used my work, had put my coworkers in danger.

And I had been so, so mad that I hadn't let her say a word. In the heat of the moment, she hadn't deserved to say anything. But that left me here today with still no context as to what, if any, thought was behind their actions. Mario's ambivalence on the situation annoyed me but also cast it in a different light.

Was I being unfair to her, to not let her explain? We'd been dating for almost a month. Maybe not that long, but longer than I had dated any girl in a long, long time. That had to mean... something.

But I didn't like the thought of giving her a chance to explain. I didn't want to hear excuses, and I didn't want to be in danger purely through association with the witches.

Though it might be too late to avoid that. I was still in danger, even here, even now. So was my work, and all my coworkers, and the restaurant's patrons. So was Mario, for knowing it all now.

"I'm sorry," I got out between breaths, and Mario looked up from the scuffed mat and his set of crunches.

"For what?"

"For getting you involved."

"What makes you think I'm involved? Maybe I'll forget all this by the morning."

Well, at least he could claim plausible deniability. But it still angered me that Charlie and her coven had let this all happen. There had to have been something else they could have done, that wouldn't have put so many innocent people in harm's way. Why would they have chosen such a reckless path?

I tried to keep wondering about what else the coven could have done that didn't involve ruining my life, but the running had caught up to me and I was getting winded, my chest's soreness flaring back into pain. I slowed down, came to a stop, and wiped my forehead with a towel.

"That's enough for now," I said, and Mario hopped to his feet, and nodded.

"I'm always here if you need to talk about anything, you know that."

"I know, ya big lug," I said, gently punching his arm.

"And..." he hesitated, his gaze serious enough to wipe the smile from my face. "I'm here for you. No matter what's coming after you, supernatural or not. I'm no Buffy, okay? But I'll try my best."

I cracked a smile. "Let's go watch some trashy movie."

"It's a date." Things were easier with Mario. He'd be my friend through any witchy business that could still come.

Chapter Twenty-Seven: Charlie

Charlie couldn't sit at the kitchen table forever. She had to let Sammy outside, and by the time he had finished his business and returned, she thought that as long as she was standing up she should probably eat something. She opened her fridge, saw leftovers from her most recent dinner date with Lola, and felt nauseous. Ice cream. This was definitely an ice-cream-for-dinner kind of day.

She downed an entire pint of Haagen-Dazs' vegan Chocolate Salted Fudge Truffle, lying on the couch watching her extended edition *Lord of the Rings*, trying and mostly failing not to check her phone every two minutes for a message from Lola that never materialized.

Even her favorite escapism let her down though. After *all* the times she'd seen this movie, she had never been struck so deeply, so intensely, when Saruman betrayed Gandalf. Saruman was evil, a monster, betraying and lying to his friend, working with another group behind his back for his own ends. The movie was so clear how horrible it was.

She had always thought she was one of the good guys, that she and the coven were on the right side. But surely Lola saw her as the villain in the story now, and maybe she wasn't wrong.

There was a slightly masochistic pleasure in continuing to watch. Sammy curled up by her feet, and she fell asleep somewhere during the Dead Marshes, waking up just enough, some time late in the night, to stumble off to bed.

It might have been nice in the morning to wake up to at least a few blissful moments of forgetfulness. But no. She remembered everything as soon as her eyes opened. Charlie lay in bed, staring up at the ceiling, acutely aware that both the other side of the bed and the guest bedroom were completely, painfully empty of any cute, buff chef, and that they always would be, and that it was completely her own fault.

She grabbed her phone from the bedside table, checked for any texts from Lola while she'd been asleep – no, nothing.

So yeah, they were going to be empty forever.

She was also acutely aware that she still hadn't changed out of yesterday's workout clothes, now slept in twice, that her hair was super tangled, and that she had a smear of dried ice cream on her shirt front.

A shower. She could fix none of the really important things, but she could at least take a shower.

The hot water did nothing to take away the ache she was feeling inside, but it did make her skin feel less gross. She couldn't stop herself checking her phone yet again when she got out of the steamy bathroom, felt a momentary lifting when she saw she had a new text.

Not Lola. It was from Betty.

Coven meeting ASAP, my place. Need to plan for vampires. Hope you and lovely Lola OK <3 See you soon!

Charlie gritted her teeth. The coven. The Disappeared. That was what she needed to focus on right now: her coven, the vampires, and saving the freaking world. That was obviously the priority. Wasn't it why she had lost Lola, because preventing people from dying was the most important thing?

"Okay, Charlie," she said into the mirror, rolling her shoulders and starting a few basic stretches. "Get your head together, or people are going to die. Maybe you don't get the princess at the end of the story. So what? You have a *job* to do."

She clipped Sammy's leash onto his collar, grabbed a soy protein bar, and headed down the street. Betty let her in, greeting her with a warm smile.

"How are you feeling, dear? Everyone's already gathered in the living room, you and Sammy just come right this way – and how is that sweet Lola of yours? Is she feeling better?"

"She's fine," Charlie muttered, because she didn't want to talk about Lola, or what had happened last night. She was focusing on the job.

It would be easy to be angry with Betty, who had insisted on secrecy about the herb. But that was the rule, and Betty hadn't been trying to cause trouble – she had been focused on the job too, on protecting people. That was what was truly important. The reason for everything.

Betty's living room was crowded, full of the coven members, a sea of graying hair and the smiles they always summoned for Charlie, even now, despite the unusual solemnity hanging over the room.

And one person who didn't belong here *at all*. Charlie squinted at the dark-haired young man perched awkwardly on Betty's embroidered ottoman. "*Mario?*" She couldn't help a quick glance around – but no, of course Lola wasn't with him.

"Hey, Charlie," Mario said, lifting a bright yellow *World's Best Grandma* mug in a kind of salute.

Charlie sank down into the empty spot on the floor near the fireplace, Sammy climbing happily into her lap, and stared at Mario. "What – why...?"

"Oh, have you two met?" Betty said, bustling back in from the kitchen with a fresh pot of coffee. "This charming young man was sent over by the Mystic Oak Coven. We really must get together more often for inter-coven socializing, you know we've been saying that for years. But anyway, they've been keeping an eye on the vampires in their neighborhood, and have some very concerning intelligence. Go on, dear," she concluded with a nod at Mario.

Mario...was part of Mystic Oak Coven? Charlie had *so* many questions. Though it did explain why he hadn't been more shocked by vampires. She'd assumed he was just distracted by Lola's injury.

What Mario had to say drove most questions right out of Charlie's mind. "So, my coven has been trying to dig into the vampires' movements. We think they infiltrated our parkour group online, and that's how they knew we'd be at the warehouse. They must have been keeping track of Lola since the incident at her restaurant."

Charlie's gut clenched at the thought of vampires paying that much attention to Lola, and she could see on Mario's face that he didn't like it either.

"Even worse," he continued, "we got a tip that the vampires tracked Charlie driving home from the warehouse yesterday."

"This neighborhood is warded to be invisible to vampires," Charlie protested, fighting the renewed jolt of fear rushing through her.

"Yeah, that's why they aren't here *yet*. But we think they've been trying to track you for a while. They've been narrowing it down, and yesterday they got a better idea of where you went off their radar. Our sources say they spent last night circling, trying to pin it down exactly. And the way they were gathering, the whispers we're getting – everything is pointing to vampires attacking this neighborhood. Tonight."

Chapter Twenty-Eight: Lola

Dreams came in fits and false starts, waking me many times throughout the night. I gave up by early in the morning, and snacked on pork rinds while women in fancy dresses and ill-fitted corsets complained about an ungentlemanly gentleman on my computer screen. With a late shift tonight, I was going to try my damnedest to take these few hours to relax.

But every time my memory floated to Charlie it was a little zap of pain in my still-healing chest. That I had either been used, or deemed too unimportant to be kept in the know, broke something far too fragile in me. Or even worse, that Charlie and her coven hadn't trusted me with the information.

Yes, we hadn't been together long, but it had meant so much to me. Why had I let myself get so invested in a girl? How many years had I resisted connection? How many perfect women had I made go home without my number? All to prevent the pain I was feeling now.

"It's not fair," I grumbled, hardly focusing on the computer screen anymore. I pushed my laptop shut, the drama no longer distracting me from the terrible dejection in my heart.

"Mario, did you have lunch yet?" I called.

Had Charlie cared about me at all? Had her smile, her tenderness, meant anything? Or had it all been a ploy to keep me feeding the city's well-to-do members a vampire vaccine? Obviously I'd pull Nonna's pesto from the fridges as soon as I got to work tonight and trash them, and make regular pesto for tonight's service. Charlie's coven wasn't going to use me anymore for their personal vampire deterrent.

"Mario?" I called again. Still no response. Muttering loud enough that he'd hear me, I pushed myself to my feet and shuffled out of my room. The rest of the apartment appeared to be empty. "Mario, where'd you go?" I asked the warm, quiet rooms.

I checked my phone as I threw together a quick salad with leftover chicken from the restaurant, and surprisingly, there was a text from Mario an hour ago saying he'd be back late tonight.

"Whatever, man," I said.

I felt a little better after a meal and a shower, but I paused at the foggy bathroom mirror, shocked to see what looked like multi-day-old bruises on my sides. An injury that had hardly occurred more than 24 hours ago, that should have put me in the hospital, was now well on its way to full recovery.

"Gotta admit that's a miracle," I said to my reflection. But unfortunately, the amazement soured into sadness. It was kind of Charlie to heal me.

And I had apparently been a fool to think we could be anything special.

With still over an hour before I had to report to work, I settled on the couch to kill time on my phone, when Mario returned.

"This isn't 'late tonight,'" I challenged. "Lost your confidence already?"

And then I looked up.

Mario looked off, though I couldn't put my finger on it. He looked shaken. He dismissed my words with a wave of his hand and jogged past me into his room. He was also on the phone, and from the pet words he was throwing into the conversation I assumed it was with his new girlfriend. But what else he was saying caught my attention.

"Yeah, I'm sorry, babe, I won't be there tonight. No, it's something super important. No, not my dad. My family's fine. It's... other stuff. *You know.* I just... I want you to know I love you, okay?"

What? He loves her now? When did that happen? Even though I never had romantic feelings toward this practically-brother, my heart still did a little squeeze. *I thought I was the only girl you loved.*

Then the rest of what he said caught up to me. Why was he talking so seriously? And what... other stuff? I pulled myself to my feet, my ribcage tight and painful in the rising worry from his tone.

I stopped at his doorframe, as he was still talking on the phone.

"Yes, tonight. Exactly what we feared. No. No, I don't want you there. If you got hurt..."

"What is going on?" I asked, loudly.

He held out a finger at me. "I gotta go, okay, Britney? I'll call you back in a few. Please, don't worry about me. I know how to take care of myself."

Mario shoved his phone in his pocket and threw some clothes into a backpack, purposefully not looking up at me. "Nothing's going on. Everything's fine."

I bristled at his tone. "You are *lying* to me, and it's not okay."

Finally, he looked up at me. "I don't think you need to have any more burdens on your shoulders than what you already have right now."

How dare he say that? I sucked in a breath, shocked and hurt.

"You don't get to decide that for me, Mario. I do. You're my friend and I'm worried about you. I'm always here for *you* and what's coming after *you* too, got it?" I said, echoing his own words from yesterday back to him.

Mario groaned, and ran his fingers through his hair. "I hate that you're right. Okay, then."

Mario had always had an antique cupboard in the back corner of his room; a family heirloom, he'd called it. He had said he kept old paperwork and clothing and the like in there, nothing useful, but didn't want to part with the carved, wooden furniture in the hopes one day he'd own a house to put it in.

Now, he opened up the double doors of the cupboard and revealed shelves that housed some sort of altar and an organized collection of dried herbs, vials of oils, and beautiful faceted crystals. A week ago, I would have thought some of the herbs were weed and the rest of this was hippie bullshit. Now I knew better. I'd seen Charlie's workroom.

"You're... you're a witch?" I breathed, fully in shock. "Wait, a wizard? A warlock? You're... you're one of *them?*"

Mario grimaced, as he turned back to me, showing his palms in defeat. "Uh, surprise?"

It was like a kick to my sore ribs. "Why didn't you tell me yesterday?"

"Man, Lola, I wasn't ready to tell you, and I didn't want to turn the focus on me. Yesterday we were working through your situation."

I groaned, mad that he actually made sense, my mind still reeling from this news. "I don't understand how you're a witch. I just got my heart broken yesterday and I can't get it broken again today because I find out my best friend in the world is also a part of this reckless magic bullshit. I thought I met Charlie's whole coven, and I didn't see you in there with all the gray-haired ladies!"

Mario looked defeated as he ran a finger along the edge of the cupboard shelf. "I'm not in Charlie's coven. I'm in a different one. Mystic Oak Coven's a bit younger than Charlie's Singing River Coven. A bit more... co-ed. And it's not warlock, it's witch. I'm... a witch."

"This is wild," I muttered, pressing my palms over my eyes like if I didn't see Mario's cupboard I could keep pretending he was just the normal gym guy I'd known for years. "How? Why?"

Mario scanned the shelves and started plucking jars and bundled herbs to put in his backpack. "I joined it a while ago... I had felt so lost, you know? Like I didn't know what I was doing with my life and I wanted to be part of something more important." He shook his head, and finally met my eyes again. "Man, now that I'm saying it out loud it sure sounds like I'm in a cult."

"With the way they treat innocent people, maybe it is one," I bit out.

"I'm sorry," Mario said. "I don't think any of us thought things would get bad enough for this."

"The vampires attacking me?" I asked. "Or the coven using me to drug Sacramento elite? Do your and Charlie's covens work together? Did *you* know they were lying to me?"

"No, I didn't know you were involved, and I didn't know about the pesto. Our covens usually don't work together. But if Charlie's coven leader vowed her to secrecy, she can't break that. It's, like, a magical thing. She literally couldn't tell you what was going on."

My body wanted to recoil at that but I held steady because I was too *mad*. "Why are you trying to back up the woman who lied to me? You're supposed to be *my* friend."

Mario reached for a high shelf in the cupboard, needing to go on tip-toe to grab more bottles of... whatever. It really bugged me that he was still packing his backpack the whole time we were talking.

"I'm just trying to give you some context," he finally said.

I rubbed my temples. I didn't want context. I just wanted my life to go back to the way it was before I knew my best friend was a witch and my girlfriend was a witch and we were all under imminent threat of *supernatural persons*. "So why can *you* openly talk to me about stuff?"

"Because *I* didn't vow secrecy for something her coven did. And it's way bigger than that now." Mario brushed his sweaty hair off his forehead, and met my eyes. "The vampires are going to attack Charlie's coven."

My chest went tight, and I sucked in a breath through the soreness. Something deep inside me instantly ached for Charlie, fearing for her safety. I shook the feelings down. "How do you know this?"

"Because my coven's been tracking them."

I pinched the bridge of my nose, and breathed deeply. "Of course you have. So you've been a witch spy?"

"Not me personally. Our members have been watching them for weeks. There've been so many more vampires than there used to be, and they've been on the move so often that all our alarm bells were going off, you follow me? I think they've been turning people, not just killing them. And last night, we're pretty sure they figured out Charlie's neighborhood is the source of the Singing River Coven. Charlie and her witches are a lot more active against the vampire groups, so it makes sense that they'd get targeted first. With this threat of attack, the Mystic Oak Coven is joining them. To help protect them."

I took a shuddering breath. "To protect the whole city."

Mario zipped up his backpack. "Basically."

His next words hung unspoken in the air. I knew exactly what they were going to be before he said them. And I didn't want to hear it. I wanted to push all of this away, go to work, keep living my life. But if he uttered his next words, my whole future would change. I could feel it.

"Lola, I know you can help us, if you're willing to."

Charlie's betrayal was still fresh in my mind, and my heart couldn't let that go so quickly. I wanted to say no so, so badly. I wanted to tell Mario he was crazy and then turn around and go back to my room. But I knew he wasn't crazy. My healed body – twice healed now – was proof he wasn't. And if he wasn't crazy, that meant everything he said was true. Which meant this was a real, true danger, and real, true magic to fight it.

Magic that I had. Somehow. *Like calls to like.* Maybe… maybe I could actually make a difference. With this being bigger than Charlie and the witches who betrayed me… with this involving one of my best friends directly, and possibly so many more, how could I say no?

I ran my hands through my hair, still conflicted. "I don't know if I want to help them that much after what Charlie did to me."

Mario hefted his backpack, glancing at the doorway behind me. I turned and walked out, and in the front of the apartment, he stopped again. "What Charlie did doesn't feel right. I get it. But maybe you need to step back and look at the bigger picture. You know what's going on now. You know you can help."

I let out a breath. "I'm out of my league trying to help you guys in a vampire battle. What the hell would that even look like?"

"I don't think you would be." He chuckled. "You'd probably love it."

I still wanted to say no. But now that familial guilt was creeping in on me. "Damn it, Mario. Fine, I'll give you this much. I'll call Charlie. See if she even wants me there."

He sighed with relief. It surprised me to see him so invested in my decision.

I pulled out my phone, and my fingers started to shake as I placed the call. My heart hammered as it rang. And rang. And went to voicemail.

I hung up without leaving a message. She wouldn't want me there. And even if Mario did, what was I doing? I had work in half an hour. I couldn't abandon my shift, and my coworkers. Not the way Charlie abandoned me.

"Mario... you know what... I can't. I have work tonight. Someone should be there that knows what's really going on, in case something happens there too. You know they've already attacked the restaurant once. At least I'd have a chance helping people get out, or something."

Mario nodded, his shoulders slumping. "I understand. I'm going to Betty's house, you know where that is?"

I nodded.

"If you change your mind, head there, okay?"

I nodded again, my heart still hammering and my gut twisted up in a knot. "Please stay safe."

He grinned, giving me a salute. "Nope, gonna go get bitten by a vampire tonight. I'll make sure you're my first victim."

"Fucking asshole," I smiled.

After Mario left, I changed into my work clothes, and spent a few minutes packing an extra bag with a change of clothes, a first aid kit, and some water.

"Just in case," I whispered, lifting the bag onto my shoulder.

It felt wrong not to be going with Mario. He was as much family to me as Gino and everyone at my childhood home. But thinking of Charlie still made my gut clench, which made my chest pain flare, and reminded me how mad I still was at her.

I had a duty to my restaurant, and my current life, first. It wasn't like they needed my help saving the city anyway.

Chapter Twenty-Nine: Charlie

"Really, Mrs. Johnson, you don't want to miss the performance tonight," Charlie said into her cell phone, keeping her voice bright and chirpy and happy, just as though she wasn't less than a day from a wrenching break-up, just as though there weren't vampires planning to storm her neighborhood at sundown.

"I don't know, dear," Mrs. Johnson said doubtfully, "it just doesn't seem like the right time of year for *The Nutcracker*..."

"But it's a special early workshopping performance," Charlie persisted. "The proper show won't run for several more weeks. This is a kind of sneak peek. Lots of the neighbors are going tonight. It should be really fun – and it supports a good cause!"

And it was way better than staying home to be collateral damage in a fight between the Singing River Coven and the vampires. She crossed her fingers while Mrs. Johnson continued a monologue of internal debates. So far she had convinced almost every non-coven family in the neighborhood – fortunately, only a handful – to go out to the show tonight. This was her assigned task by her coven leader, protecting the non-witch neighbors. And if Mrs. Johnson would just agree, then Charlie could go help with the thousand other tasks that the coven was doing to prepare.

"I told you I'm dancing tonight, right?" Charlie put in when she got a word in between Mrs. Johnson's rambles. At least – she was *supposed* to dance tonight. "I think you'll really love it." She paced back and forth in Betty's backyard, gaze on the edge of the garden she could see from here. Samantha and Esther were sprinkling protection potion along the border, strengthening the many layers of spells already wrapped around the garden, and Charlie itched to go help.

"Ooh, how lovely, dear! Did they finally cast you as the Sugar Plum Fairy?"

Charlie suppressed a wince. "Ah, no. The Snow Queen. But that's a really good part – I have a really complex dance..."

"Oh, what a pity they didn't give you the lead," Mrs. Johnson said, voice sympathetic. It was only worse because Charlie knew she meant it kindly.

"Well, I think Jim and I would just love to come see you as the Snow Fairy instead."

"Queen," Charlie corrected automatically. All right, so this was super patronizing, but whatever, as long as it got the Johnsons out of harm's way. "I'm arranging tickets, so just give your name to the box office and–"

Her phone gave a sudden, sharp vibration in her hand, startling her enough to almost drop it. What – oh, an incoming call. She looked down at the screen, just in case it was one of the coven members with an urgent update – and nearly dropped her phone again.

Lola. Lola was calling her. There was her name, stark white against the black screen, with the stupid little <3 Charlie had added to her contact when she was feeling gooey a couple weeks ago.

Why was Lola calling? What did she want? Was she still angry?

Stupid question, *of course* she was still angry, how could she not still be angry?

She was probably calling to yell some more, or maybe to tell Charlie to leave Mario out of her craziness, or to arrange a time to meet up so Lola could throw a plate of pesto at her. Or something.

But maybe she did want to talk things out after all. Maybe she had calmed down enough to realize how torn Charlie's loyalties were, that it was a really tough situation. Of course it hadn't been okay to mislead her, Charlie knew that, but maybe Lola wanted to at least...try to figure things out? And what, come fight the vampires? Risk her life trying to help Charlie and her friends?

Charlie remembered the vampires grabbing Lola, the hideous crunch when they broke her ribs, and shuddered.

If Lola was calling to make up, to offer to help, that was even worse. That was the *last* thing Charlie should want.

She took a deep breath, carefully and deliberately pressed the red "Ignore Call" button, and brought her phone back to her ear. Mrs. Johnson did not appear to have noticed her brief distraction. "So, we're all set then?" she said, voice surprising her with its steadiness. But ballet did call for a certain amount of acting ability.

Another minute or two and she hung up with Mrs. Johnson. That was the last of the neighbors, all taken care of and arranged to be out of the way. Good. That was good.

Her phone buzzed again, her heart jumping into her throat. A voicemail? Maybe Lola had left – no, it was a text message. From Nathan.

Sure, take my 3 comp'd tickets. Your neighbors will love it! You owe me – like an explanation for why you played hooky yesterday? And you're gonna rock Snow Queen tonight! :)

Charlie let out a breath, tried to refocus. So, three tickets from Nathan, plus her own tickets, plus the ones she'd begged off of Madison and Dominique – that would be enough for everyone. Done. Settled.

Charlie headed back into Betty's house to figure out whatever came next. Inside it was noisy, crowded and chaotic, exactly why Charlie had gone outside to call the neighbors to begin with. She dodged Samantha rushing by with an armful of sharpened white ash sticks, and walked past the coffee table in the living room, covered with bottles of potions. Esther was stirring a steaming vat of additional protection potion at the fireplace, with Helen sitting next to her and offering advice. Helen was moving a little stiffly after her car "accident," but had insisted on coming to help anyway. Charlie paused, watching Helen and hoping she really was well enough to be here, when a heated argument suddenly erupted from the laundry room between Margaret and Amelia.

"Why did we just waste an entire load on polyester shirts?" Margaret demanded, pulling damp clothes out of the washer. "You know the protection potion only adheres to natural fibers!"

"But it's a polyester *blend*!" Amelia protested.

"The magic doesn't care!"

Charlie remembered her original goal and hurried on into the kitchen, where Betty was bottling more vials of sunshine potion. "Everyone's agreed to go to the performance," she announced, not wasting words on preliminary pleasantries. "They should all be okay tonight." Assuming the coven could protect the neighborhood, so there'd still *be* a neighborhood for everyone to come back to.

"Excellent, dear!" Betty said, without looking up from her careful pouring. "We must remember to write some nice thank you notes to your friends who gave up their complimentary tickets. Later, obviously."

"Right," Charlie said with a quick nod. As if any of them were expecting that! "So what can I do next? What do you need?"

Betty hesitated, and that was not a good sign. "Hadn't you better get off to the dance studio? Isn't there, you know, warming up or something?"

Charlie frowned. "No, it's still early. How can I help?"

"Really, dear, I think it's best if you go over now. We have things all under control."

With the hurried footsteps sounding around the house, the view out the kitchen window of witches rushing between yards with armfuls of wooden stakes or bottles of potion, and the shriek from Margaret in the laundry room of "What do you *mean* we've already used all the cotton shirts?" things were obviously not *all under control.*

Charlie took a deep breath. She hadn't expected to have this argument for another couple of hours, but sure, why not now? "Actually, I don't think I should go to the performance. It's much more important that I be here." And she *knew*, without a shadow of doubt, that the coven had only pushed her to go dance tonight because they wanted to keep her safe. Sometimes it really was annoying being the youngest in the group by thirty years.

"But you told all the neighbors you'd be dancing tonight," Betty said, using her even more annoying 'patient tone.' "That's why they're going, to see you dance."

"Yeah, but that was to get them out of the neighborhood. They won't realize I'm not there until they're already in their seats at the theater. They're not going to get up and walk out *then*." And okay, she had lied to them, one more lie to add to her list, but it was way more important to save lives.

Which was the same logic she'd used about misleading Lola.

But this was obviously different; it was no deep betrayal to trick someone into attending a ballet performance.

"My dear, I really think it's important that you be there for your ballet company and—"

"*Stop* dear-ing me, and it's important for me to be here for the *coven*," Charlie snapped. "No one's going to die if the understudy dances the Snow

Queen at the workshop performance." In fact, it would be a great opportunity for Kayla, who deserved something good happening to her; that felt like a small silver lining in this horrible day. "You know you need me here." They needed every member of the coven. That was why Helen was here, even though she was still recovering. That was why all of them were here, and why Charlie had to be here too.

Betty's lips pressed into a thin line. "Charlie Ryan, we will handle this situation—"

"Freaking vampires are coming to kill us all and torch the garden and you *need* me! I get that you didn't want to call your extended family for reinforcements and put them at risk, but we need more people and *I'm* a coven member. I get to make this choice!"

She didn't really think it would work. Betty had been running things for so long, had been kindly and cheerfully directing the Singing River Coven and especially Charlie for so many years, that it was very hard to override her view on anything.

Betty looked at her for a long, long moment. Then she sighed and said, "Your grandmother would have insisted you go somewhere safe. But you're right. You are a coven member. And you are not a child anymore, even if the rest of us don't always remember that."

Charlie felt a sudden, unexpected heat in her eyes. It was all too much, all at once. But bursting into tears would really, really undercut the ground she had just gained. So she took a deep breath, and carefully said, "Good. Now what can I do?"

Charlie spent the rest of the afternoon at her house, preparing battle potions, leaving them to simmer. Then she went back to Betty's to help pass out magically-protected clothing (after Margaret and Amelia finished infusing the non-polyester clothes), giving Sammy a bath in the special warding potion, and greeting the members of Mario's Mystic Oak Coven as they began to trickle in.

She ignored two calls from Nathan, which only led to a text message.

Charlie, where are you??? You're not sick – what's going on? Do I have to hunt you down?

She finally relented and replied. **Sorry – taking care of something important.**

His reply was almost instantaneous. **More important than the performance? Are you OK?**

Charlie's stomach twisted guiltily. Victoria probably wouldn't have missed the performance for anything, wouldn't have made this choice. But it wasn't really a choice, was it? **Helping some friends – can't explain. Don't worry.**

That always means I should worry! ARE YOU IN TROUBLE?

Charlie was too keyed up, too overwhelmed by *everything*, to deal with this right now. Without pausing to decide if it was a good idea, she tapped out a fast response and hit send. **I'm defending my neighborhood from a crazed vampire horde, OK? Kinda busy – gotta go.**

He called again. She ignored it. He'd have to stop soon – he'd need to get ready for the performance, and in the meantime, she didn't have to pick up.

And it was really just the same thing, not picking up a few minutes later when Lola called a second time.

That definitely wasn't harder to resist. Not harder at all.

Chapter Thirty: Lola

My heart leapt when Charlie's voice came over my phone but then quickly settled once I realized it was only her voicemail. Again. Why wasn't she picking up? She was the one who had lied. Not me. I should be avoiding *her* calls. How did this get so totally twisted? "Ugh!" I slammed my thumb against the red button on the phone screen, refusing to leave a message as I stomped through the back door of the restaurant.

I tried to shove thoughts of Charlie, Mario, and vampires to the back of my mind as I slipped on my chef's jacket, trying to get my head into the cooking game. I was failing miserably.

"Do you think he'll come here?" Keegan asked as he stepped in front of me, making me halt before I slammed into him. I really needed to pay better attention.

"Who?" I asked, doing my best to focus on him. Only then did I notice the heightened excitement buzzing through the kitchen.

"Robbie Day!" he said, as if it were common knowledge. "He's already been by Cactus Jack's Barbeque this afternoon. From what I heard he usually stops by at least three restaurants in whatever city he visits. He could totally come here. I think he will. What do you think?" He was so excited he didn't even take a breath between sentences.

It took a moment for his words to sink into my brain in any coherent fashion. "Robbie Day? He's in Sacramento?" Stella had mentioned that he'd be in the area. My stomach flipped at the implications. This might be my chance to meet him and impress him with my cooking. Different recipes flipped through my head as I headed to my station. Should I make him a tried-and-true favorite or something more daring? He was most known for grilling but he'd already been to a barbecue house today. Maybe he would be looking for something different.

"If he comes here," Keegan said, following right behind me, "are you going to serve him your pesto dish?"

It felt like cold water rushing over me at the mention of my pesto. For a second, I had forgotten all about it and Charlie and vampires. I couldn't serve him that dish now. It might have helped people who lived around here, which Robbie Day didn't, but it was tainted with betrayal and monsters. Knowing that there was some form of magic involved in the recipe felt like cheating. I would not cheat to win a once in a lifetime opportunity. Would I?

No. Of course I wouldn't. Maybe if I tweaked the recipe, left out the special herb and used traditional basil, it would still be as appealing as it was now. Just thinking of the pesto made me nauseous, knowing how I'd been used. I didn't want anything to do with it anymore. Supposedly helpful or not, it had to go. In the cupboard were a few bottles left of the oil infused with Charlie's herb. There would be just enough time to dump this stuff and whip up a new batch of untainted pesto for tonight's service.

"What are you doing?" Madeline asked as she snatched the bottles of infused oil from my arms right before I dumped them into the garbage. "Robbie Day is coming. Here. He's probably heard all about your famous pesto and you want to throw out the main ingredient?" She set the bottles on my station and then turned to me, ignoring the frown pulling down my face.

I wanted to tell her that I refused to use it because it was infused with magic to ward off vampires, but knowing her, she would think that was a great angle to attract the Geek Chic crowd. "*If* he comes here, I doubt he'll want a meatless dish. He's a grill guy. All of his competitors are known for their meat dishes. So, I was thinking about offering to cook him my Beef Wellington or maybe my spicy meatballs."

She rolled her eyes which immediately put me on edge. "We don't have time for your Beef Wellington. Besides, stick to what's hot, and right now it's your pesto." The hostess called her over. "Get it ready," she ordered before she headed to the front to see what was needed.

I leaned against my station, scowling at the countertop. Just the sight of the oil stung my eyes. How could I make the pesto when it now reeked of betrayal and lies? Sure, Mario said she physically couldn't tell me because of some magical vow and Charlie insisted that she wanted to tell me everything. They, she, tricked me in order to protect people from vampires. To keep as many people as possible from becoming the Disappeared.

I sucked in a deep breath and my side ached. A reminder of what a vampire had done to me. And suddenly the overall picture cleared in my head. There were vampires in the city. Vampires that were going to attack my girlfr – whatever-Charlie-was-to-me-anymore's coven tonight. Mario and his coven were going over to help. How could I just sit here and do nothing? Maybe the part I needed to play was to protect as many citizens as I could by feeding them my Anti-Vampire Pesto. Not that I would actually tell people that side effect, but I could inoculate as many people as possible. Keep them safe from the blood suckers. I wasn't going to let them take anymore people. Not today, Satan!

I hadn't forgiven Charlie for not telling me the truth, but I could still do my part. I pulled out my Nonna's book and flipped right to the page I needed. "Let's do this!" I shouted as I pulled a large bowl out and set it in front of me. There was already so much excited chatter going on in the kitchen that my outburst went unnoticed. Either that or my outbursts were so commonplace that my colleagues had learned to ignore them. Either way, I was fired up.

"He's here! He's here!" Keegan shouted as he came hustling up to me. A hush fell over the kitchen.

My heart pounded as he said, "He wants a bowl of your pesto! The vegan version. I didn't even have to suggest it. He came in here knowing all about it and wanting to try it. Oh my gosh, I think I'm going to puke!"

Suddenly, I felt the same way. I placed my hand on Keegan's shoulder and looked him in the eyes. "No puking," I said to the both of us. I drew in a few deep breaths and was pleased to see him following my lead. "Okay, go get him whatever appetizers he wants while I whip up a fresh batch of the pesto."

With a nod, Keegan zoomed over to the appetizer station and gave them his order. I went straight into cooking mode, determined not to be distracted by drama or anything else. I put a pot of water on to boil for the pasta. Check. I grabbed a fresh bunch of basil from the fridge. Check.

"He's here," Madeline told me as she stopped by my station.

"I know," I said as I chopped up the herb. I wanted to tell her to go away before she became a distraction, but I knew it would only make her want to stay and "help."

She stood next to me wringing her hands. "You should probably – Oh, you're making a fresh batch. Good, good. Don't forget to – The water is already on. All right."

I paused my chopping and turned to her and said as calmly as I could, "I got this. Trust me. Why don't you go charm him while I make the best damn pesto I can? By the end of the night, this will be his favorite restaurant in Sac."

Her hands stilled and she stood straighter. "You're right. You don't need me getting in your way. I'll make sure everything else is taken care of." She marched off, leaving me in peace.

With all the ingredients prepped, I read through my Nonna's recipe, reciting the rhymes I had already etched into my brain, but this time I said them with more purpose than before. Now that I knew it was more or less a potion I was creating, a greater sense of responsibility came over me. It was like I let a bit of Charlie rub off on me, recalling how she sounded when she made the healing potion she gave me.

My chest hurt thinking of Charlie. Was she in danger? Had the vampires arrived yet? Charlie was a strong woman but was she a match for a group of vampires coming to kill her and her coven? A bunch of old ladies? And what about Mario and his coven? They were at risk of getting hurt, or worse, too. A chill ran down my spine at the thought of one of my oldest and dearest friends getting eaten by a bloodsucker. A part of me felt impotent being so far away from the danger, and from her. I kept reminding myself that I had to stay and protect as many patrons as I could. But I still felt like I should be doing more.

"Is it ready?" Madeline appeared suddenly at my elbow, startling me. Her eyes were wide with excitement.

I swiped the edge of the bowl clean with a damp towel and then added a sprig of parsley as garnish. It was the most beautiful bowl of pesto I had ever created. I gently set it on her serving tray. "Wish me luck."

I ignored the other orders of pesto that came to me as I headed to the door to the dining room so I could peek out to see Robbie Day's reaction to my dish. I bit my lip as I watched Keegan set the bowl down in front of him. He was sitting at Charlie's table. Was that a good thing or a bad thing? Was she doing all right? Was she in danger?

A jab to my sore side made me hiss. My manager pointed out of the little window in the door. "I think he likes it."

I refocused on Robbie Day, pushing Charlie out of my mind, or at least to the edges. He chewed on that first bite slowly, letting the tastes linger on his tongue like all good critics do. He seemed to take forever as I waited for him to swallow.

He smiled and took a second bite. My heart leapt. I hadn't even noticed that Keegan was still standing next to Robbie Day until he said something to him, and gave a thumbs up. Keegan practically sprinted to the kitchen. I barely missed being clobbered by the door as he rushed inside. "He likes it!"

He clamped down on my arms and jumped up and down in excitement which caused me to do the same. I barely noticed the ache in my ribs. A second later and my manager joined us. If only Charlie was here. She would be so excited for me. My excitement waned as worry took over again.

Another waitress walked into the kitchen and said, "He wants a word with the chef."

Suddenly, my feet felt like they'd grown roots and attached to the floor. Panic rushed over me, drying out my throat and taking all my words away. Keegan pushed me through the doors. "Go talk to him."

I stumbled out of the kitchen, about to go meet my hero. I wiped my damp palms along the side of my jacket as I trudged to the table. Charlie's voice rang in my head. *How lucky he is to be meeting Lola Morelli, the greatest chef in California.*

A surge of confidence came out of nowhere, alleviating the heaviness of my steps. I was the badass chef that made the dish. The dish that had the entire city singing its praises. I stopped at his table and smiled. "Hello, Chef. I hope the pesto was to your liking."

"Yes, I must say that your dish has exceeded my expectations." He leaned back in his chair, a broad smile across his face.

His words made me feel weightless. I had to glance down to make sure I was still connected to the floor. "Thank you, Chef. It's an old family recipe."

"And it's vegan, right? That surprises me because there is so much depth of flavor inside. What do you use to replace the cheese?"

"Did I mention it's a *secret* family recipe? I'd tell you but then I'd have to kill you." I laughed as his eyes widened, letting him know I was joking. He laughed along. "But maybe you'll find out when you put me on your show."

"Well," he said, nodding. "My producers and I have been discussing having a vegan episode. That way of eating seems to be on the rise, and we could probably attract more viewers. I would love to discuss you being a possible competitor."

"That would be awesome!" I blurted out before I could stop myself. Then I composed my cool and said, "I would love to kick your ass on TV. Just let me know when."

Out of the corner of my eye, a woman with long blonde hair sat at a table in the corner. Her hair was the same shade as Charlie's. My gut clenched. What was I doing here? I was schmoozing with a big time chef about being on his TV show while Charlie, Mario, and their covens were fighting vampires, putting themselves in mortal danger. Fighting not only to protect themselves, but to protect all the people inside this restaurant. All the people of Sacramento. The air seemed to thin because I suddenly couldn't breathe.

"Um, I have to go." The walls seemed to be closing in on me, chasing me out of the restaurant.

"But don't you want to discuss being on my show?" He seemed puzzled as he watched me back away. I couldn't blame him. I was acting like a crazy person. I had dreamed of being on his show for so long but right now, I couldn't care less. There was somewhere more important I needed to be. Someone more important I needed to be with.

"I would love to be on your show. Leave your number with my manager and I'll contact you tomorrow." Without waiting to hear what he said next, I spun around and ran to the kitchen.

"What are you doing?" Madeline practically screamed at me as I grabbed my car keys. "You just can't leave Robbie Day hanging like that. And what about the rest of your shift? We're running a restaurant here."

"I'm sorry, but I've got somewhere else I gotta be." I ran out the back door and practically flew to my car. The sun hadn't finished setting yet so there was still time. There was a vampire rumble I needed to get to where my friends needed my help.

Chapter Thirty-One: Charlie

Charlie pulled on her hoodie. She'd put that off until now; it had been soaked in vampire repellent earlier that day, and was still uncomfortably damp. *That* she could ignore. Harder to ignore was the scent that surrounded her. The scent so intensely reminiscent of Lola's pesto.

Before stepping out into the cul-de-sac, she glanced at her phone one last time. There were a number of increasingly worried texts from Nathan, but a big, blank nothing from Lola. Not that she'd expected anything. But there was that small, stupid hope she hadn't been able to stop. Which was ridiculous, because Charlie had decided it was for the best that Lola not contact her. Right? That's why she'd deliberately not answered Lola's calls earlier.

She roughly shoved her phone back in her pocket, then lifted her arm and sniffed. Yes, the scent was nearly identical to Lola's pesto. Tears pricked behind her eyes and she blinked them back furiously, torn between the desire to rip the hoodie off – risk of vampires be damned – and the sudden need to wallow in the reminder of Lola. Of lying beside her. Of the feel of Lola's skin against her fingers. Of seeing her crooked smile. That thought made her heart squeeze even tighter. Would everything remind her of Lola?

Charlie chided herself to get her head in the game. Because she was about to fight vampires, and her coven was depending on her. She needed to get out there and get to work.

She grabbed the boxes of potions she'd come for and hurried out the front door.

It was obvious as soon as she stepped outside that the coven had been busy. The first glow of sunset washed the scene in pinks and golds, illuminating the two motorhomes that had been moved nearly end to end to block access to the cul-de-sac and the coven's garden.

Those two motorhomes were their main line of defense. The RVs covered most of the round end of the cul-de-sac though there was a nearly seven-foot gap between them. The Singing River coven had spent most of the day filling that gap with branches from the Ash tree in the garden, after soaking them in vampire repellent potions. It should be difficult for vampires to climb over those branches, but the coven wasn't willing to bet their lives on it. So Dorothy's husband Steven had volunteered to risk his beloved truck to help fill that gap. Seventeen feet of heavy-duty truck, he'd assured them. Repeatedly.

It was parked across the narrow part of the street about ten feet in front of the RVs, but even those seventeen feet of truck couldn't completely block access to Charlie's end of the street. Behind the RV barrier, nearly thirty feet closer to her house, three cars parked end to end made up their final defense, parked at the very edge of the garden's protective shield. A shudder shook Charlie at the thought of vampires getting that far. Because after that, the members of her coven would be all that was left to keep them from the garden, and they'd have no protection at all. They'd be standing alone against the vampires and each of them would be at risk. And if her coven failed, those protections would also fail.

Charlie shot a quick glance at the sky. In another thirty minutes or so, it would be dark. Vampire time. Charlie shut the door behind her and hurried toward several of her coven members. She cast out a quick prayer as she reached them. "Great Goddess, let our preparations be enough."

Amelia looked up and gave Charlie a smile that looked only a little strained. "Think positive thoughts. We've done everything we can."

Charlie glanced around, counting those present. There would eventually be all twelve members of her coven, even Helen, plus a few others from the Mystic Oak Coven. Hopefully they could expect more of them to show up. But even if every one of them came, there would only be twenty-five coven members. Twenty-five against a hoard of strong, fast, lethal vampires.

And even if spouses or family came, even with more than twenty-five, not all would be prepared for a fight. She glanced around, already seeing a few people hiding in the trees and perched on the surrounding rooftops. And in front of her, Amelia's husband and someone she didn't recognize were climbing up on the RVs.

Charlie passed one of the potion boxes she carried to the tall, thin woman on her right. "You should have a good view up there," Charlie said. "Hopefully the height will keep you safe."

The woman grinned and flexed her arm. "All-star pitcher here. I'll make each of these count."

Charlie grinned back, glad she didn't need to ask if they were coven members. She'd formulated the potions so anyone could use them, magic not required. That part had been tricky, but she'd managed it. Magic had been required to create them, but anyone could use them.

Esther's husband, Douglas, was perched in the tree in front of their house. Instead of watching the street like the other non-combatants, he was staring in the direction of Betty's front door. Esther must still be at Betty's, finishing the rest of their defensive measures.

Would Charlie ever find someone who would love her like that? She'd hoped for a while that person could be Lola, but she had pretty much destroyed any chance of that happening. Looking around at all the preparations, she decided it was probably a good thing at the moment. At least Lola wasn't here. The vampires had already hurt her enough.

The members of her Singing River Coven were standing behind the RVs. The motorhomes provided safety, but had them all blind to what was happening at the other end of the street. Two watchers in the surrounding trees were acting as lookouts and would warn the coven when anyone approached.

Especially any vampires.

Charlie's heart squeezed as she looked at her coven. Amelia, Margaret and Helen clutching their long, wooden knitting needles. Frances – her cap of brown hair, normally so smooth, now sticking up at wild angles. Elaine – for once not wearing one of her favored long skirts – barely recognizable in loose, faded blue jeans. And the others, all nearly her grandmother's age. They should be relaxing, enjoying their golden years, not preparing to fight vampires. None of them were indestructible, just like her grandparents.

How had it come to this?

Her phone pinged with an incoming text. She pulled it out, half aware that others in the cul de sac were doing the same.

She found seven pictures labeled with members of the Mystic Oak Coven. Something tight in Charlie loosened. Most of the other coven had come, though not Mario.

She shoved her phone in her pocket, then jumped as it began to ring. Lola? For just an instant, that earlier stupid hope rose up and nearly choked her. She couldn't lie to herself, not any more. She couldn't pretend she didn't want a chance to talk to Lola one more time. Because as she'd thought moments before, none of them was indestructible. Including her.

She didn't even look at the screen, merely answered breathlessly, "Hello?"

Her foolish hope shriveled as Mario answered. Her sudden stab of disappointment was so strong it took a moment to pay attention. "...most should already be there. I'll be there soon. I'm getting the holy water now."

Charlie cast her eye at the rapidly darkening sky. He would be cutting it close. "Hurry, you don't want to get here after the vampires arrive."

Mario laughed. "I ain't afraid of no vamps."

Charlie rolled her eyes. "This isn't a movie, Mario. This is real. Please be careful."

"Don't worry. I know how to take care of myself."

Charlie bit her tongue, trying to hold back the words crowding into her throat, but they came blurting out. "Have you heard from Lola?"

Silence. Her ears nearly rang from the intensity of that silence. Then Mario groaned. "No. Absolutely not. I'm not doing this, Charlie. I'm not getting involved."

And Charlie was left with the phone in her hand, connection broken. Mario had sounded so...so...final. She looked around again, and this time didn't feel that same sense of accomplishment. Now the street merely felt cluttered with people and vehicles. She put her phone back in her pocket, feeling a prickle of tears, and let her shoulders slump.

Douglas called, "Don't you worry, Charlie. Those vamps don't stand a chance of reaching the garden. Not with my Esther helping."

He'd been too far away to hear the call, but must have noticed her defeated posture. She forced a smile to her lips. "Thanks, Douglas. I'm sure you're right."

THE NEW MEMBERS OF the Mystic Oak Coven kept trickling in, and had started taking up positions behind the motorhomes and up in the trees. The dying light made them hard for Charlie to see. Hopefully the vampires wouldn't think to look up.

Thank the goddess they'd all come. Meeting once a year at the solstice wasn't enough. They needed to get together more often, like in Maria Theresa's time. As a start, they should plan a large All Hallow's Eve celebration after this. If there were enough of them left to celebrate.

This end of the street was filling with people, but she had no idea how many vampires they were likely to face. With all the disappearances, she'd bet there had to be at least twenty, maybe more. More than twenty preternaturally fast, strong monsters. How could so few humans fight them? Even if most of those waiting had magic.

They definitely needed that holy water.

Her hands began to shake as she remembered Mario's last words on that call. "I'm not getting involved." She'd assumed he meant not getting involved between her and Lola. But what if her question had bothered him more than she'd realized? After all, Lola was his roommate and his parkour buddy. Maybe he'd meant he wasn't going to get involved with Charlie and her coven.

She wrapped trembling fingers around the bandolier she'd strapped on her chest earlier. They'd all put a lot of care into making these weapons, but they were merely defensive and wore off after a distressingly short time. That's why Mario's part was so important. Holy water could permanently destroy vampire glamour, marking them forever as a monster.

Charlie's phone pinged with another text. This time the picture sent by their lookouts had a question mark. But Charlie didn't need it labeled; she knew exactly who it was.

Her stomach twisted like it was tying itself into knots as she texted for someone to help Nathan get past the RVs. She strode over to meet him, grateful she didn't know any seriously nasty spells, like turning him into a toad. Though it *would* serve him right.

His eyes were wide and startled as he looked at their preparations. He turned as she drew near, mouth opening to say hello. Or maybe he planned to ask 'what the hell?'

She beat him to it. "What the hell are you doing here?" Nathan was *not* supposed to be here. He was supposed to be safe at the ballet, putting on a performance for her non-magical neighbors. A chill chased down her back. Had the performance been canceled? Were her neighbors on their way back?

"Did you really think I was going to ignore this?" Nathan grinned at her, then looked around, eyes still too wide, and muttered, "Whatever this is." He focused on her face and Charlie struggled to think of something to say other than 'get the fuck out of here.'

Nathan shrugged. "Besides, I couldn't stay at the ballet tonight. I told you I didn't want to lift Victoria."

There was no good way to explain all this. No way to shrug it off or joke her way out of it. So instead, she opted for the truth. "You can't stay here. It's dangerous."

"Yeah, about that. When you didn't show up for the performance and refused to explain, I knew something had to be wrong. Kayla was excited about filling in, but it got me thinking. You've been acting strange for days. I was pretty sure you were going crazy or involved in something dangerous. So I decided I had to be here for you, either way. It's what friends do."

Charlie felt a stab of terror. Nathan had no idea monsters were real. This wasn't a rumble like *West Side Story*, where all the moves were choreographed and the worst thing you had to worry about were knives. Fake knives. "You don't understand what we're up against. And you didn't believe me when I told you."

"Stop joking around. I'm here now. Try me." His grin said he wasn't worried.

Charlie had to make him leave. It was bad enough her coven was in danger. "Like I said," she bit out. "Vampires. We're fighting vampires."

"Vampires." Nathan shook his head, a flash of disappointment in his eyes. "If you don't want to tell me, just say so." He held his hand up and worked a smile back onto his face. "But no matter what you say, I'm not leaving."

Charlie sighed and gave up. "Park yourself up on something high." She threw her hand in front of him when he opened his mouth to argue, and added, "I know you don't like heights, and it won't keep you safe forever, but it could help keep you alive."

She looked around and fought the impulse to stick close to him. She had other places she had to be, damn it, and Nathan was too big a distraction. She couldn't allow herself to spend the rest of the night trying to protect him.

There were so many she needed to protect today.

Charlie's phone pinged. Three more members of Mario's Mystic Oak Coven had arrived, along with someone else. She studied their photos, wanting to be sure she'd recognize them in the dark. The someone else caught Charlie's eye. She looked so familiar. Red-hair. A picture of Mario sauntering across the bar towards...what was her name? Bridget? Bailey? No, wait. Britney. Lola said Mario had started dating Britney. What was she doing here?

She looked at the other pictures again. No Mario. What was Britney doing here without Mario? Then her phone pinged again, distracting her from the red-head who shouldn't be here. Then it pinged again. And again.

Texts were coming from several people, and their panic was obvious.

Heads up!

They're coming

Battle stations. Now!

They're early!

The sun's not down

How?

Cloaks. Hoods. Protected from UV?

We're not ready

Ready or not, they're here

Charlie shot a glance at the sky. It was nowhere near fully dark! She flattened herself along the back of an RV. It was bordered by a tall hedge, and she peered through the small space between them cautiously. Betty was hurrying out of her house, phone in hand, with Esther on her heels. Charlie's view was restricted, but not so restricted that she couldn't see those last few Mystic Oak Coven members. They rushed toward the RVs, movements clumsy with panic, throwing hunted looks over their shoulders. Moving at a very fast, but very human pace.

Dread nearly stopped Charlie's breath as she stared at what was frightening them. Ten, twelve, no, even more shadowy figures followed close behind. Moving *faster* than humanly possible, though they weren't running.

Vampires.

Charlie squatted and duck-walked under the bumper of the RV. Betty's house was on the wrong side of the motorhomes, and she wanted to be close enough to help if Betty or Esther needed her. She called Betty's name, then had to raise her hand and wave. No one more than a couple feet away could have heard her. Not with that fear strangling her lungs. She was a ballerina, damn it; she knew how to control her breath.

Betty and Esther were by her side in seconds. "It's too early!" Esther said, a trace of panic in her voice. "The sun hasn't set."

Charlie shrugged and pointed to the far end of the street. There were even more vampires now, massing there. More than twenty. Waiting in a silent, deadly pack. She grabbed Betty's arm, and had to force words out past the tension in her throat. "We have to get behind the motorhomes before they get here."

Betty and Esther hesitated, eyeing the narrow space under the RV. Charlie realized they would have to crawl rather than squat like she had. Charlie threw a worried glance down the street, then wished she hadn't. Someone must have given a signal, because that silent horde started forward. They almost seemed to be floating, and Charlie realized each of them was wearing long, dark cloaks that skimmed the asphalt, with a deep hood that shadowed their faces.

Someone had been watching *Twilight*.

She wanted to laugh, but nothing about this was funny. No wonder the vampires had been able to come out before the sun was down. No wonder they'd been able to attack Helen's car, and ambush her and Lola in the warehouse. Still, they really must be desperate to ignore the danger of a breeze blowing back a hood or exposing a hand or wrist.

Why were they suddenly so reckless?

The faintest whiff of basil from her hoodie reminded her of exactly what had changed. Lola's pesto. So many people in Sacramento were making reservations to try it. And already at least one of the vampires had gotten sick from it. The rest must be getting hungry.

As they drew nearer, the sight of bloodthirsty grins twisting many of the shadowed faces nearly locked her knees with terror. Fortunately, the sight of them managed to get Esther and Betty moving. Charlie ducked down behind them and followed them to the other side of the RV, tension making it feel too slow. As she straightened in relief, she heard Nathan's bit off, "Holy sh–"

He wasn't safely up in a tree or on top of the RV. He was on the ground, not far away from her. Vampire bait.

Damn it.

Sudden murmurs spun her around to peek between the RV's. The vampires had stopped a few feet beyond Steven's truck where it blocked the street. An older woman, who appeared to be in her 60s or 70s, wearing an old-fashioned black dress only partly obscured by her cloak, moved forward. At her side, a man looking around the same age, wearing an expertly tailored suit, moved with her, then both of them paused – their stillness eerily unnatural. His cloak looked more like a cape, though it too had a hood.

She would have guessed who they were from Lola's description, but the man's meticulously trimmed handlebar mustache made identification certain. These were the vampires who had orchestrated the attack on Lola in the restaurant.

Anger flooded through Charlie and she clenched her hands in tight fists. These two had likely been preying on humans for decades, and Lola had been their most recent victim.

"Who dresses like that?" Nathan asked from behind her shoulder.

Charlie closed her eyes and sighed. It was too late to get him somewhere safe. The best thing would be to keep him as far out of sight as possible.

"That's Edwardian," Esther answered him. "You can tell by the broad bosom and narrow waist. It's most likely made of silk, and you can see the light catching the beading around the neckline and waist. Those are probably made of jet."

Charlie, Betty, and Nathan turned to stare at Esther.

"What?" She shrugged, and added, "I took History of Fashion in college."

"Of course you did," Betty said. "When was the Edwardian style in use?"

"Around 1900. If that's *her* dress, not a reproduction, she's well over a hundred and twenty."

Charlie knew vampires could be decades or centuries older than they looked, and they'd been preying on humans all that time.

Rotten, stinking vampires.

Anger broke through her terror. She was furious with Mario for being MIA, and frustrated with Nathan for showing up here. The only thing to be grateful for was that Lola was home safe. Lola had already fought those vile things twice, and the memory of her bloodstained clothes and the sound of her ribs cracking made Charlie's hands shake. Yes, Lola had already done more than enough fighting with vampires.

Now it was Charlie's turn.

That strangely still tableau had shifted while Charlie allowed her thoughts to distract her. The female vampire had taken a short step forward. Her voice was low, oddly accented, and had an unpleasant grating quality as she stated, "This truck is in our way. Move it now."

From around Charlie, members of both covens muttered denials. The female vampire merely smiled. She motioned sharply with one gloved hand, and said again, "Move it *now*."

Four vampires moved to the side of the pick-up, reached down and grabbed the bottom of the truck frame, then flipped the truck with one quick movement. Steven moaned from somewhere behind Charlie as it flew over the curb, metal screeching as it rolled twice, before finally coming to a stop on the front yard of a neighbor who was, fortunately, at the ballet.

The silence when it stopped was profound.

One of their barricades had been destroyed by just four vampires. The coven still had the RVs and the potion-soaked Ash branches which would provide some protection. But Charlie no longer felt confident that the line of cars – their last resort – would even slow the vampires, let alone stop them. Not after what happened to the truck.

The female vampire motioned the four back behind her and spoke again. "Let the leader of the witches come forward, and let her pathetic followers acknowledge our presence."

Betty moved to the edge of the gap between the motor homes, eluding Charlie's instinctive attempt to stop her. Betty paused next to the barricade of branches, head high as she stared challengingly at the vampire. "I'm here. And all of us are aware that you are present."

"You may call me Madame Durand. And what should I call you?"

"Betty."

There was a moment as Madame Durand waited for her last name. When Betty didn't offer it, a brief flash of annoyance marred the vampire's impassive face. Then she pasted on a stiff smile. It looked unnatural, as if she hadn't smiled in a long time.

"Fine, *Betty*. We intend to reach your garden with or without your cooperation. It will go much better, for you, if you let us pass unmolested. We are willing to ignore what you have done to harm us with your poisonous food, and will merely do what is necessary to ensure it does not happen again."

Charlie stiffened at the threat. She wanted to move closer to Betty but was afraid any movement now would cause the vampires to attack. She had to stay by the RV with Esther and Nathan, and hope Betty could handle this creature as she threatened the coven and their garden.

"You lie," Betty challenged. "Our food does no harm to those who eat it."

The woman pulled back her hood and Charlie realized the sun had dropped fully below the horizon, leaving only the barest hint of light in the west. She'd been so focused on the confrontation, she hadn't noticed the streetlights come on.

The vampire's expression was icy as she snapped, "You well know that your poisonous concoction causes my vampires to become ill or die if they feed on someone who has ingested it."

Betty smiled grimly. "As I said, our food harms no one who eats it. It would cause your...followers... no harm if they refrained from draining the blood from humans. A life for a life seems fair."

A deep, vicious growl forced its way between the woman's lips. "We will not allow this to continue. Move now, or die."

Betty raised her voice so everyone could hear. "I've lived in this neighborhood fifty-three years. I've spent my life guarding and caring for our garden and the people of Sacramento. You will not scare me away."

Before her voice died away, the vampires surged forward, heading for the barricade between the motorhomes. Betty backed away quickly as the first of them began to grab the Ash branches which the coven had soaked in herbal solutions for this very purpose.

Charlie snapped at Nathan, "Stay back here and stay safe." She didn't wait to hear his response. She rushed toward the attacking vampires, pulling two potions off her bandolier. As much as it made her skin crawl, she had to be close enough to make sure she hit what she aimed at.

As long, white vampire fingers grasped the wood, guttural screams reverberated around the cul-de-sac, reminding Charlie that these were vampires. Not human. No human could make a sound like that. Many of them shoved back from the barricade, fingers reddened with burns, skin raw and blistered. That wouldn't stop them long, but it gave Charlie and others a chance to throw a barrage of potions. Some hit with blinding flashes of full spectrum light. The sunlight vials would burn the vampire's skin and temporarily blind them, hopefully forcing them to back away.

Those flashes of light were partially obscured by the other potion – vampire repellent. Green vapor came swirling out when the vials broke. The potion could actually kill vampires, but only if they were foolish enough to drink it. But the vapor would spread, making vampire eyes swell shut, mouths blister, and throats close. It should terrify them, and perhaps even make biting anyone too painful, for about fifteen seconds.

Damn it. She hadn't been able to make the effect last longer, and fifteen seconds was over in a blink of an eye.

The vampires closed in on the barricade again. Mario's contribution of holy water could really turn the tide right now. So where in Hades was he?

The coven members on top of the RVs kept low and flung potions at the advancing vampires. Those potions had seemed so clever when they'd discussed them. But now Charlie felt a spurt of terror. They were such puny things against this deadly onslaught. How could they possibly hold back beings so much stronger and faster?

The potions, Charlie knew, couldn't stop this attack. The holy water Mario was supposed to bring could. It wouldn't only destroy vampire glamour, it would weaken their terrifying strength, and slow their speed. And not just for a measly fifteen seconds. Forever.

It was probably the *only* thing that could stop them.

She plucked two more potions off her bandolier and flung them at the closest vampire. It growled, fangs glinting in the streetlights. Then her vision was obscured as her potions hit, bright flashes erupting as the sunshine vials splintered against its face. Around her, other coven members threw theirs. As they crashed against vampires or the pavement, glass shattering, they lit the scene in strange, strobe-like explosions of light, highlighting snarling faces. Long sharp fangs. Long fingers with dagger-like nails.

For now, the potions were keeping the majority of the vampires away from the motorhomes and the barricade. Nathan was suddenly next to her, hand resting heavily on her shoulder. "Those are vampires," he gasped. Then repeated with more volume, "*Vampires!*"

Charlie smiled wanly. "Next time maybe you'll believe me."

A vampire reached across the top of the barricade, snarling. Charlie grabbed Nathan's arm and pulled him back a few steps. "Now will you *please* find somewhere safe?"

When he nodded, she turned back to the chaos. She told herself not to relax, but allowed herself a moment to take in what was happening.

A group of vampires had peeled away from the others, heading to the spaces between the motor homes and the houses.

Then more movement caught her attention. Other vampires had stripped off their now unnecessary cloaks and flung them over the barricade between the motor homes. They were climbing over the Ash branches without being burned.

Exclamations of shock and horror buzzed in Charlie's ears as the first vampires landed on their side of the RVs. She sensed more than heard coven members backing away from the barricade.

Panic tightened her chest as she swung her gaze from one group of vampires to the next. She bit back a scream when one of the thick hedges blocking the end of the RVs, keeping the vampires out of the remainder of the cul-de-sac, went up in flames. Acrid smoke swirled about, tickling Charlie's throat, making her cough violently, bringing tears to her eyes.

Even without her blurred vision, the scene was surreal.

Vampires darting between streetlights, breaking them since they could see in the dark and the coven couldn't.

Howls of pain and rage.

Guttural screams from inhuman throats.

Swirling smoke, punctuated by green vapor and flashes of blinding light.

Shadowy shapes darting back and forth through the confusion.

Then a new sound, that carried strangely over the confusion. As if a large balloon had popped, followed by a brief hiss of escaping air. She didn't understand that sound, not at first. Then she saw one of the Mystic Oak Coven, cornered and desperate, strike a vampire with a sharpened piece of wood. And heard those same disturbing popping, hissing sounds before the vampire collapsed into a pile of ash.

She stood transfixed until movement to her left made her spin in that direction. She grabbed two more potions and flung them as a vampire loomed out of the murky dark, arms reaching for her, fangs extended. The potions forced it to turn away, and she was grateful she had something to defend herself with. But if she could reach the barricade safely, she was going to grab one of those Ash branches. Just in case.

The mass of vampires that remained on the other side of the barricade began to break apart as some were forced to pull back, blinded by sunlight explosions or pain from the vampire repellent. It lessened the number pushing forward temporarily, but not by enough.

Too much was happening. She couldn't keep track of it all. She was surrounded by people involved in desperate, life and death struggles. Sounds and smells assaulted her. She tasted ash on her tongue.

Then Charlie noticed Amelia's husband trying to get off the top of the closest RV. She hurried over and helped him down. He had a gash across his forehead, blood running into one eye. "I can't see to aim any of the potions up there," he panted. "Someone needs to get the rest of them down."

Charlie looked around, unsure who could help. She was getting dangerously low on potions herself, so she couldn't just abandon them up there. Then Nathan was at her elbow, eyes too wide in his pale face, but filled with determination. "What do you need?"

"I have to pull a box off the top of the RV." Charlie pointed up where the RV loomed ten feet high. "I can't reach it."

"I can lift you," he said. "Ready?"

Charlie stared at him a moment, then a smile curved the corners of her mouth. "Ready!"

They'd done this lift so many times when they were practicing for the Nutcracker try-outs. She didn't need to think about it; her body knew exactly what to do. He swept her up, lifting her over his head, hands on her hips, high enough to reach the potions box. She arched her back and grasped it firmly. "Got it!" He lowered her down and started to speak, but a shadowy shape was moving toward them. She thrust the box into his hands, grabbed two of the vials, and flung them at the approaching vampire.

It veered away and she turned back, quickly filling her bandolier with potions. There were a number left when she was done. "Keep these," she told Nathan. "You don't need to be a witch to use them."

"You're a *witch*?" Nathan's face went blank. "Vampires? Witches? Is there anything else you've been hiding from me?"

Well, damn. This was going to take some explaining, and now wasn't the time. "Just take them, Nathan. Use them if any vampires come after you." She started to turn away from him again, then turned back. "And thanks. You were perfect."

"I like lifting you, Charlie; you know how to balance your weight. So take care of yourself; I'll need you to dance the Sugar Plum Fairy next year."

Charlie turned away, a smile playing on her lips. Maybe Nathan being there wasn't so bad.

Then the smile died. More vampires were flooding past the motorhomes. The two covens had started retreating behind the row of cars. Their last line of defense. They had to hold that line or they would die, and the garden would die with them.

Without the magic-infused herbs for the pesto, the vampires would expand their killing spree, and even more people in Sacramento would join the Disappeared.

The covens had to hold on. Somehow. Until Mario got there with the holy water. She had to believe he would come; that he wasn't irrevocably upset with her question about Lola. Because without holy water, the fight was already lost.

Dorothy shouted for help, shaking Charlie from her darkening thoughts. She raced forward, yanking a repellent potion from her bandolier, using ballet-strengthened legs to reach Dorothy quickly, and ballet-strong arms to hurl the potion at the attacking vampire. Fortunately, she'd developed plenty of strength, holding her arms up, gracefully curved at shoulder height, for long periods of time.

She began to fling sunlight potions, one after another, at the flood of vampires. Several fell back, screaming in pain, unable to see, and Charlie grinned fiercely.

Several other coven members made their way over to her, each of them throwing potions. The air was filled with the unnatural screams – low and grating – of injured vampires, mixed with cries of pain and fear from the members of the covens. From her friends. There was blood and clouds of vapor and other less pleasant things all around. And overlaying everything, the nearly overwhelming smell of vampire ash, tainting the cleaner scents of lemon, garlic, basil, and roses.

Madame Durand remained where she'd been since the fight began, standing with her back ramrod straight, a smirk playing on her lips. That smirk, unlike her smile, looked completely natural.

Another volley of potions forced the attacking vampires back for a moment, giving the two covens time to regroup. They were all a mess, covered in potions, clothes torn and stained with soot, faces streaked with sweat from the still warm autumn night.

Charlie shook out her arms, aching with the effort to keep throwing so many potions. She allowed herself a moment to breathe. To cling to the belief that everything would work out.

Unfortunately, the vampires also used that time to regroup. Madame Durand, still looking pristine, damn her, stepped closer to the RV's. "We have penetrated your puny defenses. We will take your sanctuary next. Surrender now and you will not be harmed. But know, if you continue this useless, quixotic defense, you will all perish."

A wave of bitter resignation swept over Charlie. Mario hadn't come. Their defensive potions weren't enough. The vampire leader was right – they couldn't win.

Betty laughed, startling Charlie. "Is that a long-winded way of saying that resistance is futile? I must remind you that it's always darkest just before the dawn."

Several vampires glanced quickly to the east, as though the reminder of dawn frightened them. Charlie wished that thought could give her hope, but dawn was hours away. Still, Betty was right. Things weren't over until they were actually over. They weren't defeated yet.

Charlie felt her faltering nerve, on the edge of breaking, stiffen. This battle would not be done while one of them could still fight. As long as she could move and breathe, there was still something to fight for. Even if losing was obvious, she could still take down as many vampires as possible, leaving that many fewer to harm her town.

She glanced around, seeing the fear and despair on the faces of those cowering around her. Most looked pale and shaken. Others were exhausted, leaning on the cars as if they had no more strength. Betty's response hadn't been enough to put the heart back into all of them, and that *had* to happen before the vampires came at them again. They had to be ready to fight to the end, whatever that end might be.

The image of Aragorn before the Black Gates popped into her head. He'd known that their fight would be impossible – that they would all die – but their battle would give Sam and Frodo a chance to succeed. He'd given a rousing speech. She couldn't remember all of it exactly, but could remember how it made her feel. It was about saving friends from pain and death. Of ignoring fear. Of knowing that courage might fail someday, but not *this* day. Today, they would fight.

That's what they needed. A Black Gate speech to put the heart back into them. To keep them fighting.

She sucked in a deep breath and stepped forward.

Chapter Thirty-Two: Lola

My hands left streaks of sweat on the steering wheel as I sped toward Charlie's neighborhood. Thanks to evening traffic, this trip was stretching out forever. Every red traffic light shone as an omen of death. And the closer I got, the more I realized I was...

I was feeling something else too.

A weight in my chest, that I dismissed at first as a symptom of panic but soon realized was not on my body, or my rib cage. It was a weight on my soul.

Perhaps the magic around the coven, combined with all the vampires in the city potentially congregated in one area, made it strong enough that even I could feel it.

Honestly, it scared me as much as it thrilled me.

"I'm almost there, you guys," I whispered, just a few blocks away.

But as I got within a block of her cul-de-sac, a wave of wrongness pulsed over me. I couldn't get to her from this direction. There would be too many enemies in the way. So what else could I...

The garden. Of course!

I pulled hard on the steering wheel, my tires screaming as I swung the car around. Mario would be so proud of that drift! I sped in the opposite direction, and turned a few corners until I was at the empty land between this neighborhood and the river – which, if I followed the river upstream, would lead me right behind Charlie's garden.

After screeching to a halt, I jumped out of the car and started sprinting through the long, golden grass, past boulders and twisted trees, until I got to the rocky riverbank, a wide, flat expanse of shrubs and rocks before the slow river. It was dark, and the deep shadows between rocks were like little black holes – just one wrong step and I'd be down with a twisted ankle.

"Damn, I hope leaving Robbie Day in the middle of my restaurant was worth it," I mumbled, calculating and stepping, one rock at a time. Much slower than I wanted to be going.

The weight on my chest changed. I felt pulses of ... something... reaching out to me, almost welcoming me. I didn't have the vocabulary to describe it. But I guessed I was feeling the charms around the garden, and recognizing them for the first time. And the charms were friendly to my energy. I wanted to cherish this revelation, but this wasn't the time. I scrambled over a six-foot wooden fence, and was then surrounded by the fragrance and growth of the coven garden. Even in the darkening atmosphere, or possibly because of it, the place really did feel magical.

There was a rustle of something moving through the grass, and my heart leapt into my throat before I noticed a familiar terrier hurrying toward me. I breathed a deep sigh of relief, and Sammy and I exchanged a brief greeting.

"Where's your mama?" I asked him. He looked toward Charlie's house, so I rubbed his furry head, and continued on.

The back door was unlocked and inside the house was dark and messy, with empty cauldrons, bowls, and vials strewn across every surface. I panicked, thinking I was too late and the place had been ransacked. But then I heard commotion outside. Wanting to avoid the front door, I slipped through the garage and out the side door, just in time to see Charlie sprinting across the cul-de-sac, tossing potions as she went. She drove off a person – vampire, presumably – at Betty's back, before guiding another coven member to behind the cars. She then hurled herself back into the chaos.

She looked more in her element than I had ever seen her. Like she was made for this, even more than she was made for dancing.

I had come here, leaving Robbie Day, because I had to do the right thing. I had to help my friends – all of them – win against evil. But seeing Charlie like this brought all my adoration for her hurdling back. I was here to fight for the witches and humankind, yes. But I couldn't deny that I was also here for Charlie. If anything were to happen to her...

A shrieked howl pierced my thoughts, and I tracked the sound to the vampires I recognized, that immaculate older woman and her partner, who stood in a clearing right ahead of two motorhomes. The woman held out her hand in a command for respectful silence.

The woman spoke to the crowd, some crap about vampire history. In front of me, half a dozen older Singing River Coven members stood with baskets of vials, their arms ready to throw. Beyond the women, the more agile coven members were crouched behind three cars parked longways near the sidewalk.

The cul-de-sac itself was strewn with broken glass glittering in the few remaining street lights, with enough spilled liquid to make the street look like it had rained. A few people, vampires I hoped, lay strewn out among the glass, writhing or groaning.

Ominous figures crouched in front of the motor homes and idled in the bushes and lawns on either side, just past rows of pointed wood that the coven must have erected as barricades. The figures made my skin crawl, especially now that I recognized them for what they really were.

One of the figures caught my attention. They had their hood off, their hair bearing a striking resemblance to Jackie's. But from this distance, and the heavy cloak obscuring the outline of their body, I couldn't know for sure it was my missing friend. That... would definitely explain some things from the past few weeks. A swell of questions threatened to overwhelm and distract me – when, where, how, what would happen if I met her on the battlefield – but I pushed them all down. Right now, I had to focus on the fight.

I zeroed in on a piece of wooden post laying on the grass by a barricade. There was my weapon for the fighting that would break loose at any moment. As I started that way, as stealthily as I could manage, I heard Betty quip out in response to the vampire leader, "It's always darkest before dawn."

I could appreciate the resolve it must have taken for her to remain strong against these superhuman enemies. Within moments of her utterance, many of the vampires began to charge. I took that as my moment to sprint for the wooden post.

Just as Charlie took that moment to add her voice to the fray.

"We will never lay down and let you claim us or our power!" Charlie shouted, startling those around her, including a vampire not even a dozen paces away. "We are stronger than you realize. And we fight not just for ourselves. We fight for the innocent of this city!" she called, hurling a potion, and all of the coven cheered and threw a volley. Her potion hit the approaching vampire square in the face, and he screeched and fell, clawing at his eyes.

"We fight for the ones we've lost!" Another cheer, another volley.

"We fight for the ones we love!"

The wooden post now in my hand, I gripped it expertly. I was going to fight for the one I loved too. Wow, Charlie had really channeled her inner

Aragorn with that one. That would be exactly where the music would swell in a movie, with a drumming beat and thrum of guitar.

I could hear it now, even.

Wait.

I craned my head, noticing a flash of headlights past the motor homes. And a literal, actual swell of music. "Another One Bites the Dust," to be exact.

Then, light spilled onto the cul-de-sac from between the motor homes, and with a screech of tires, a car – a shockingly recognizable car – barreled between the larger vehicles, and straight over the two vampire leaders. Leaning out the side of an open-air Jeep was none other than Mario, with Andrea at the wheel, and Allen in the back seat.

"Mario!" I screeched, but there was too much going on for him to hear me. Andrea had literally run over several vampires, and the remaining vamps in the cul-de-sac were getting *blasted* by super soakers that Mario and Allen were holding.

And the vampires howled! At first I couldn't imagine why. Until a second car came skidding to a halt behind the first. A VW beetle with plastic eyelashes over the headlights.

My Mom's car. I stood there stunned, unable to process why she was there. It didn't make any sense.

And then the vampire closest to me turned away from an onslaught of water, and I saw his terrible, twisted face. He was gaunt and ashen and his eyes were like black holes of terror in this low light. He looked nothing like any vampire I had yet seen. And he stumbled toward me.

"It's holy water," I mouthed, things starting to fall into place. "There's holy water in the super soakers." That my mom must have taken from Our Sacred Lady Church and provided to Mario.

Still, the vampire approached, even if he wasn't paying attention to me. I held my wooden post tight and swung as hard as I could when he stumbled close enough. And he went flying.

"I... I guess I don't know my own strength?" I laughed to no one.

Around the cul-de-sac, there were cries of triumph. Everywhere, vampires were stumbling and crawling, and humans were advancing. But then, with their perfect outfits now in tatters hanging from their terrible forms, the vampires who had been run over by Mario's Jeep pulled themselves to their feet. And even from forty feet away, I could tell they were *mad.*

Another ear-piercing scream hit the air, and many of us humans ducked and covered our ears. By the time I could look up again, every vampire who could still move dashed or scrambled toward Mario. Including, to my dismay, the vampire from earlier who I thought might be Jackie. As she moved with that superhuman speed, her cloak fluttering behind her, I knew it was her.

But I couldn't mourn, not now.

"Hold on, buddy," I muttered, as I sprinted toward the fray, my impromptu weapon ready for more vampire baseball.

Right before the vampires reached Mario, several blinding flashes of light popped up around him. I blinked hard, trying not to stumble. What was that? Witch magic? The light forced the approaching vampires to pause, which allowed Mario and Allen to level their super soakers at them. As I reached Mario's side, several vampires had been knocked to their backs, and witches drove stakes – no, large knitting needles! – into their chests. And they *exploded into clouds of ash.*

"Fucking metal," I breathed, unsure if any of those had been our friend. I had lost track of her in the strobes.

That moment of awe was all I got, as a snarling vampire surprised me from the side. I sidestepped just in time, and swung the wooden post, catching the vampire on the shoulder. He fell back. But another growled in my face almost immediately. Before I could swing the post again, I heard a tinkling pop as a vial shattered on the vampire's chest. Ooh, that must have been a potion! The vampire let out a strangled groan, and dropped to its knees. I looked over my shoulder to see who had helped me, and there stood Charlie, hair plastered to her face with sweat, her eyes wide. She said something, and though in the commotion I couldn't hear, I could read it clear as day.

Why are you here?

My heart pounded in my chest, not just because of being in the middle of a damn vampire battle. But I couldn't dwell on it. Mario let out a yell, and our attention swung to him. One of the vampires had reached him, and he was holding their snarling form just an arm's length away. As I sprinted toward him, another vampire landed a massive blow from behind. Mario fell, and I saw red.

I laid out the first vampire with one hard swing of my post. I pulled it up to hit the other vampire, when he recoiled screaming from none other than a crucifix. Held out by Gino. Beside him, my mother was shoving her own, larger crucifix into the face of another vampire, her face twisted into the heated anger of a mother who is *done putting up with your bullshit*, and holy hell I was here for it.

I took this opportunity to check on Mario. His girlfriend Britney was by his side, helping him up. So she had convinced Mario to let her go after all. It was like everyone I'd ever known was here. Was my kindergarten teacher here?

"You okay, man?" I asked.

"Lola? You... decided to come?" He must have had the wind blown out of him, and he sucked in breaths as he spoke.

"Yeah, 'cause someone needs to save your sorry ass," I quipped. I thought, but didn't say, that I couldn't just leave it to Britney.

Faster than I thought possible, something slammed into me, and I suddenly lay prone, staring up into the terrifying face of a vampire. Reflexively, my arms went up to shield my face, and tearing claws clasped my arms and tried to pull them away.

Then with a shatter of glass, potion covered us. The vampire rolled off of me screaming, and I could hear a sizzle that I assumed was the vampire's burning skin. I sat up. Beside us stood one of the older coven members, her long, bright red hair partially knocked loose from a bun, and a mostly empty basket of potions in her arms. What was her name? Esther, I think. She smiled at me and I smiled back, feeling for the first time like a true part of all this, instead of being used.

Then, with whatever inhuman strength the vampire still possessed, it leaped at Esther, and she went down far too hard for someone her age. Something about the streetlight highlighting her red hair, messy across her fallen face, broke me. I shrieked, launching myself at the vamp. I had lost my wooden post somewhere, so it was just me and my bare hands, trying to pull this creature off the woman.

With the vampire's attention on me, I sprinted toward the center of the cul-de-sac, but then it reached me, grasping my clothes and sending us both stumbling to the ground. Before I could regain my senses, its strong hands were on my throat. Those terrible dark eyes focused on me, its lips curling into a disgusting snarl, revealing filthy, long fangs. At least I had succeeded in getting it away from Esther, though I didn't know if she was okay. But now I stared right into the eyes of death. Despite my panic, I still felt a prayer of strength as I resisted the advance of this beast, my muscles straining. I would not let this demon defeat me. I would not let –

A brilliant light burst into existence, a white light so powerful and bright this close that I had to squeeze my eyes shut. The grip on my neck loosened, and then someone grunted and pushed the vampire back.

I regained my senses in time to see none other than Charlie, her face twisted into a grimace, as she used all her strength to hammer a stake into the vampire's chest.

With a burst of ash, and the creature was gone.

She sat back, her task complete, and let out a breath. Our eyes locked, and I couldn't help but chuckle.

"So when were you going to tell me you're a complete badass?"

Chapter Thirty-Three: Charlie

"I'm a ballerina and a witch," Charlie said, pushing sweaty strands of hair off her face. "I thought being a badass was just assumed."

Lola laughed at her stupid, off the cuff remark, and in the middle of the hellscape of a vampire battle, it was the best sound in the world. And the worst, because why by the goddess had Lola charged into all this? Charlie had vampire ash on her shoes and everybody she cared about was in danger and more vampires would be coming at them any second. So it was also the worst, and the best, moment for Lola to grab her by the shirt and kiss her.

For one perfect, fleeting instant, the whole world went still and silent and nothing mattered but that Lola had come back, that Lola still wanted her after all, that there was still some good in this world worth fighting for because Lola was here, with Charlie...in the middle of a vampire battle. And with that thought, the world started up again, the shouts and the crashes and the screams, the flashes of light and the stench of burning vampire. A beach at sunrise it wasn't.

Charlie pulled back, drew in a shuddering breath. "You shouldn't be here – this is so dangerous–"

"Yeah. I know." Lola leaned in again, pressed her forehead against Charlie's, and in a low voice said, "Charlie, I just want to tell you...if we both survive this...I'll go to another Pilates class with you. I won't even complain about it."

Charlie blinked, eyes suddenly wet, and struggled to find the right words to respond.

Before she could say anything, Lola flashed her beautiful crooked smile and said, "Now come on, let's go take down some vamps."

Right, back to business – but it felt good to think of fighting *together*. Charlie swiped a hand across her eyes and got to her feet. She offered Lola a hand up that she probably didn't need. But it was a good excuse to feel their fingers entwine. Charlie looked around, trying to assess the state of the battle. Only seconds had passed, though it felt longer.

And apparently it had been long enough. Coven members were retreating again, back toward the houses, and the vampires were surging forward. Plenty of their number were on the ground, but there were just so *many* of them. In fact, the way the battle had shifted, she and Lola were at the front line now.

She tried to think where to go next, what was best to do – and her scanning gaze suddenly snagged on a body lying crumpled on the asphalt a dozen yards away, a fall of red hair bright even in the darkness. Esther. Charlie's stomach lurched and she wanted to run that way but she felt frozen, unable to move or think, because Esther was lying too still for too long, and something about her position seemed unnatural. No one alive would be lying like that, so that meant... Her mind flashed to her grandmother, skittered to frightened thoughts of the rest of the coven, came back to that still body. This was so *wrong*, Esther *couldn't* be...

A body slammed into her from behind, knocking her down onto the asphalt. She had no time for thought, only instinct from years of ballet causing her to bend her knees and elbows to spread the impact, turning her head to the side to protect her face. Though that did nothing to protect her neck from the vampire crouched on top of her, shoving its face toward her throat.

Oh goddess, it was going to bite her, even with all their protective potions she was going to get bitten, she was going to die, it was about to... It was *sniffing* her?

"This one smells like a witch," a raspy voice announced, way too close to Charlie's ear.

"Bring her," an imperious voice, the vampire leader, ordered. "Leave the useless human."

Charlie was yanked to her feet, given no chance to get her breath or her balance back before the vampire, grip tight around her arm, started dragging her away. She twisted her head desperately, looking for Lola, she had been *right there* – there, she was sprawled on the ground a few feet away, way too much like Esther – but no, she was *moving* at least, shaking her head groggily, but was she hurt...

The vampire hauled her relentlessly forward and Charlie stumbled after, two more cloaked vampires bringing up rearguard as they moved back through the neighborhood, back towards the garden. Madame Durand, the leader of the vampires, strode serenely ahead, as though unafraid of anything.

As though the battle was already over. It was only the tiniest of comforts that her ridiculous dress, so pristine at first, was muddy and disheveled now.

Words were starting to come clear in the general din – more distant vampires, ones on the fringes, shouting, "Burn the garden," over and over. The cluster surrounding Charlie were inhumanly silent. She didn't know which was worse.

They halted at last in front of the small wooden gate closing off the entrance of the garden. It was quaint, pastoral, and far less a barrier than the powerful enchantments woven over it.

Madame Durand turned to face Charlie, paced close enough that her eyes glittered in the streetlights. She reached out, traced one fingertip over Charlie's throat, and purred, "Invite us into your garden, little witch."

Charlie swallowed hard, tried to reach again for her image of Aragorn at the Black Gates. "Not today," she whispered.

The woman's face tightened. "I will kill each of your friends. One by one. Or you can let me into your garden, and this all ends. No one else gets hurt."

"My town gets hurt," Charlie said. The next victim could be Kayla, or one of her neighbors, or any other unsuspecting person who didn't deserve a vampire bite in a dark alley. And *no one* deserved that. "Besides, you're lying about not killing us anyway."

"It's like you think you still have a *choice* here," Madame Durand growled. "This is *over*. You have no way out. Do you think your friends are coming to save you?"

Maybe, if she held on long enough, if she could resist in the face of that achingly cold finger caressing right across her very vulnerable throat, if she could continue standing while flanked by vampires – maybe Betty would come up with a new strategy, maybe Lola would get back to her feet, maybe...

A movement caught Charlie's eye, from behind the vampire leader. Something very small, moving low to the ground just beyond the garden gate – Sammy. *Stay there, stay there*, she tried to think at him, but he was charging forward at a speed he hadn't managed in years, ducking right under the wooden gate and pelting this way.

"No one is coming to help you. No one is–" The vampire leader's words suddenly dissolved into a shriek as Sammy sank his teeth into her leg.

One shriek might have been caused by surprise, but Madame Durand kept on shrieking, loud and shrill. Her cronies fell back a pace, evidently at least as shocked as Charlie. Sammy's jaw wasn't that big, and his teeth weren't that sharp. When Sammy let go, the leader doubled over, clutching her leg, and when he made a move towards the next nearest vampire, they all jumped back.

Sammy dashed over to Charlie, twining around her ankles, and she caught a whiff of the potions she'd bathed him in earlier. Huh. Maybe that had had some unexpected effects, besides the protection she'd intended.

But this was her chance – if she could grab Sammy, get back to the rest of the coven –

Before she could move, the balance shifted again as Lola, Mario and two of their parkour buddies – wasn't that Lola's brother Gino? – came racing up, Mario spraying a jet of holy water from his super soaker as they ran. The vampire bodyguards, already spooked by Sammy, retreated farther. Madame Durand hissed, straightening up as though she meant to back away too.

"That one's the leader," Charlie said quickly, pointing to her.

The two parkour guys tackled her, and she went down with another shriek.

"How did you get past the other vampires?" Charlie asked, still trying to catch her breath from the suddenness of events.

"Parkour, baby," Mario said, cocking his supersoaker on his hip. "We know a lot of moves."

Then Lola was grabbing her arm, tightly, but so different from when the vampire had done it. "Are you all right? They didn't bite you or anything?"

"No, I'm okay," Charlie said, and reached up to squeeze Lola's hand. Her gaze was on the pinned vampire leader, twisting and cursing in the guys' grip. Even if she'd been weakened by Sammy's bite, how long could humans hold down a vampire? "We have to – do something. About her."

They all looked at each other. Because – now what?

It was always easy in the movies. Stake to the heart, finished. Charlie had done that, just a few minutes ago – but that vampire had been attacking Lola, it had all been in the heat and urgency of an active battle, over before she had any time to really think. And she didn't like thinking about that moment now, had a feeling she was never going to. This was even worse; this was deliberately marching up to someone who was being held helpless on the ground, and delivering a killing blow to – well, to what looked like an old woman. Like so many of her friends.

"We can't exactly report her to the authorities," Mario said, sounding doubtful.

"There's no prison for vampires?" Lola asked.

"Only in books," Charlie said. "Maybe the coven could hold her for a while..."

The conversation wasn't going unheard. Madame Durand glared at them, lips curled to show razor-sharp fangs. "You pathetic humans will never contain me. I have lived ten of your generations, and no one has ever stopped me. I have seen you live and I've made you die and you can no more stop me than you can stop your own pitiful mortal ends!"

"I don't generally take the word of a vampire," Betty's voice said, and Charlie turned her head to see the woman approaching, a thick wooden knitting needle gripped in one hand, "but I'm afraid this sounds very true."

She marched up to the prone vampire and calmly, methodically, drove the sharpened knitting needle straight into her chest. There was one final shriek, and then nothing but dust on the ground.

Betty rose to her feet again, brushing off her palms, while Charlie and everyone else stared at her. "Sometimes," Betty said, voice almost gentle, "we have to do what needs to be done, no matter how hard it is. Now, as to the rest of the battle..."

But as they looked around, the rest of the battle seemed to be coming to an end. Already the scene had grown far quieter – no more chanting, no pounding of footsteps, no shouted taunts or threats. Every vampire Charlie could see was in retreat, slinking away through the shadows.

"As I hoped," Betty said in tones of satisfaction. "Often a vampire leader of this much power is feeding strength to her followers. It gives them some advantages – until, of course, that source of strength is gone."

Coven members were beginning to emerge from wherever they had taken refuge, behind the overturned cars or off of porches. Realization that the battle was over seemed to be slowly filtering through the crowd, just as it was slowly filtering through Charlie's own mind. There were a few ragged cheers, though the mood seemed overall to be one of exhausted relief.

It was over, but not without a cost.

Charlie could still see Esther's body, lying near where she had run to help Lola. Douglas was already kneeling beside her, face stricken as he gently touched his wife's red hair. Some people were hurrying that way, while others were helping the wounded. Charlie ached for her friends, and knew she should help, she should *do*...something. But the adrenaline and the fear and the fury of it all were too much and she couldn't quite put together in her brain what she ought to be doing next, while events continued to swirl all around her.

"Mario, there you are!" The redhead from the bar – Charlie was really going to have to learn her name – came running up and threw herself on Mario. "You were so awesome, babe!"

"Didn't I always say that?" Mario said, and it sounded *almost* like his usual cocky self-assurance, but – there was something a little different in his voice when he talked to her, something special in the way he was hugging her. Yeah, it looked like Charlie would definitely need to learn her name.

She bent down to pick up Sammy, buried her face in his familiar soft fur, inhaled the herbal scent of protection potions. Beside her, she could hear Lola talking. "How about someone explain to me why *Mom* is here? How the hell did that happen?"

Mario's voice. "Not my fault! I want it on record it wasn't me that told her."

"Gino?" Lola said, a warning edge in her voice now.

"Hey, she sent me a jillion texts, and when I didn't reply she called just as I was going to help Mario. You know I had to pick up or she'd freak out."

"But you had to tell her about all of *this*?"

"You *know* I can't lie to Momma! She always sees through it. And then she insisted on coming – why do you think we were late, we had to go meet up with her so she wouldn't just come here by herself."

Sammy started to squirm in her hold, and Charlie lifted her head to look around again. She was just in time to see Nathan approaching. He was a lot more disheveled than when he'd arrived, but he was walking like he was tired, not injured.

"Hey, Charlie – you all right?" he asked, his gaze scanning over her as though he was making a similar assessment.

"Yeah," she said, letting out a slow breath. "You too? You found somewhere safe?"

He shrugged. "I climbed a tree like you said. Threw some potions at some vampires. You know. Ordinary evening."

Charlie smiled in spite of her exhaustion. "What happened to your fear of heights?"

"Turns out I have a worse fear of being bitten by vampires. People make enough assumptions about me already, being in ballet. Imagine if I sparkled too."

"That's not—"

"Yeah, I know," he said, and grinned. "Honestly, this whole evening was awful and incredible and – I just can't believe there's *so much more* in the world than I ever realized. I have so many questions."

The thought made Charlie feel tired all the way down to her bones. But she did owe Nathan some explanations. "I guess—"

"Hey, it can wait," he said, and squeezed her shoulder. "Catch your breath. I'm going to go help clean up."

He trotted off, joining a couple coven members with brooms. She should be doing something like that too. But maybe she'd just – sit down for a minute, before starting all of that.

Lola was still in heated discussion with her brother, so Charlie made her way over to the nearest front porch, sinking down on the wide steps. Sammy scrambled up into her lap, and she idly scratched his back. She could see the whole cul-de-sac from here, and the garden too. She looked out over the overturned truck and cars, the dented RVs and the splintered wooden posts, shattered potion bottles and damp splashes of – potions. Yeah. She'd assume that was spilled potion, not blood.

Part of her mind was adding up the work to be done to clean all this up, thinking about the best methods and where to start and how she was going to rope Mario and his friends into helping, while stopping the oldest members of her coven from trying to do too much. Another part of her just marveled that her neighborhood, her garden, her town, were safe again. Somehow, against the odds, it was going to be all right.

A brief shadow fell over her, and then Lola was sitting next to her, close enough that their hips and shoulders touched. "Hey," Lola said quietly. "You okay?"

"Yes," Charlie said automatically, then actually thought about it, more than she had when Nathan had asked. "No, probably not. But I will be."

"Yeah," Lola said with a nod, as though that made perfect sense. She reached over and rubbed Sammy's head. "And you're quite the little hero, aren't you, Samwise?"

"I'd never get through Mordor without him." Without everyone, really. Maybe Frodo had made it with just Sam, but it was definitely better to have an entire Fellowship. Especially Lola. "I'm glad you're here," Charlie said, because this was no time to beat around the bush. Whatever was between them still felt fragile – but that was better than when she'd thought it was all over. "You *shouldn't* be here. But I'm still glad you are." Here, at what was, after all, not the end of all things, but maybe just the beginning.

Lola smiled. "Me too." She let out a long breath. "There'll be hell to pay at the restaurant, but – oh hey, guess who came in tonight? Robbie Day."

This was a breath of good news from a different world, and it took a second for Charlie to blink and assimilate the words. "From the TV show? Really? That's – wow, that's amazing."

Lola ducked her head, a grin creeping across her face. "Yeah. He liked our pesto."

"Lola!" Charlie gave her arm a nudge. "That's *great*!"

"At least, he said he did, right before I ran out on him. But hey, maybe he'll find that intriguing."

"You *left* the restaurant while Robbie Day was there? *Robbie Day*?"

Lola shrugged. "I had somewhere more important to be." Then she shifted position, leaning over to rest her head on Charlie's shoulder.

Charlie tipped her own head to rest her cheek against Lola's hair and took a deep breath. The smell of smoke and spilled potion, but under that – citrusy shampoo and a hint of pesto. Perfect. "Just so you know, I'm holding you to that promise to attend a Pilates class."

Lola groaned. "Are promises made in the heat of battle really binding?"

"Hell yes," Charlie said with a smile.

Terrible things had happened tonight, and there was so much work still to do – but just for right now, she was going to savor this one, perfect moment.

Chapter Thirty-Four: Lola

A wet tongue licking my cheek woke me from a deep slumber. Instead of being drained by the vampire looming over me, suddenly my dream morphed into Charlie, straddling me on the pavement and trailing her mouth along my cheekbone. I smiled and creaked open my eyes. "Good morning to you, too, Char – Sammy." I patted the dog on the head and gently guided him away from my face. Dog breath.

I sat up from the couch I had crashed on early this morning, wiping off my cheek with the back of my hand. The scent of something burning got me out of my seat. "G'morning. What's cooking?" I asked Charlie when I stepped into the kitchen.

My breath caught at the sight of her; hair pulled back into a messy bun and the beginning of dark circles under her eyes. She smiled as she held out a plate with a toasted bagel. "It's actually afternoon but I'm too tired to do anything more than heat up some bread."

"Thanks." I took the plate and leaned against the counter to eat. Every flat surface was still cluttered with the remains of her potion preparations from the day before. We had stayed up until dawn clearing away any evidence that we rumbled with vampires out on the street. Mario's coven took care of removing the truck and RVs. Piles of broken glass and vampire dust had covered the cul-de- sac. There had been a small army of us sucking up the mess with vacuums and Dust Busters. I used Betty's Kirby with many extension cords. We'd emptied the dust into the garden's compost bin when we were done. Apparently, vampires make great fertilizer.

"So, Lola," Charlie said, leaning against the counter right next to me. Her tired eyes welled up as she said, "I am so, so sorry about–"

"Stop." I knew what she was going to say and I decided last night, in the middle of battle when I thought that vampire leader was going to kill her, that I didn't need to hear it. I understood why she lied, though I still didn't like it. "I'm here. I'm here and I don't plan on going anywhere. Let's make a pact right now that there will be no more lies between us. Okay?"

Charlie sniffed as a tear spilled past her lashes. She swiped it away as she cleared her throat. "Absolutely," her voice rasped.

Seeing her looking so vulnerable pierced my heart and I immediately wrapped her in my arms. This amazing woman had been carrying the weight of the world on her shoulders for too long. I needed to let her know that I was her safe place to land. I squeezed a little tighter.

"Ow," she said and then immediately squeezed her arms around me, too.

"Ow." Most of my body hurt from going full force on adrenaline and falling on pavement but I didn't want to let go. We stood in her kitchen, holding each other while tolerating the pain.

After a few moments I loosened my hold and leaned back to see her face. "So, what's the plan for today?"

Charlie stepped back, rubbing her face with her hands.. "Betty is having a coven meeting in about thirty minutes." She glanced at the floor as she asked, "Did you want to come with me?"

"Am I allowed? I'm not a part of the coven."

"True, but we wouldn't have made it through the night without your help. And..." Her cheeks flushed with the prettiest shade of pink. "I don't want you to leave."

There was no way I was saying no to that. I stood straighter. "I'm all yours."

"Really?" Charlie asked with a flirtatious tone. "All mine, huh?"

I shrugged. "If you'll have me."

Charlie reached out and took my hands in hers. "Now I get Arwen when she said, 'I would rather share one lifetime with you than face all the ages of this world alone.'"

I tried to resist, knowing that once I tasted her lips, I wouldn't be able to let her go for the rest of the day but hearing those words and looking into her eyes, I broke. I pulled her in and kissed her, slowly. I wanted to savor this moment, express to her how much she meant to me. I wasn't as good with words but I could certainly show her.

So many emotions filled my heart I thought my chest might burst open. We stood in that kitchen, tangled in each other's embrace for what felt like mere seconds until Charlie pulled away just far enough to break the kiss.

"We need to get going," she said breathlessly.

"Go where?" I asked as I leaned in to recapture her lips. I liked the way the world disappeared when we kissed.

She giggled. "The coven meeting. We're going to be late."

"Late? You said we had a half an hour." I glanced around her kitchen, looking for a clock. Surely, we hadn't been making out for that long. "Oh. Time flies when you're having fun, I guess." I gave her one last kiss before untangling myself from her hold. The air around me suddenly chilled my skin when she stepped away to grab her keys.

I slipped my sunglasses on as we stepped outside. The bright sun reminded me of those flash bomb potions the witches used last night. My chest swelled with pride knowing that Charlie had a hand in making those.

As we walked past the damaged RVs still parked on the street, a neighbor lady gawked at the scene. "Oh, Charlie. Can you believe this?" she said, motioning to one of the campers with a giant dent on the side. "This has got to be the most unusual accident that has ever happened in our little neighborhood."

I had to bite my lip to keep from laughing. Charlie nodded her head and with a straight face said, "No kidding. It took forever to get them moved and by that time I was already too late for the show. I'm sorry you didn't get to see me perform, Mrs. Johnson."

The lady gave Charlie a sympathetic head tilt. "There will be other performances."

Charlie said her goodbyes and we continued to the meeting. On the way, we passed by a house that captured Charlie's attention. Her eyes filled with tears as she gazed at the property. "What's wrong?" I asked.

"Esther," she choked out.

I had barely known the woman, but she saved my life. I wanted to say something to comfort Charlie, but I couldn't get any words past the lump of emotion forming in my throat. So I held her hand instead, sending her all my strength and love. She tightened her grip as we made it past the white picket fence.

Charlie didn't knock on Betty's door when we arrived but walked right in. The rest of the coven was already seated in the living room, quietly chatting. A somber mood hung in the air. No one was laughing or smiling. There was one chair left unoccupied in the corner. I was about to go claim it when Charlie's grip on my arm stopped me. The look in her eyes told me all I needed to know. That was Esther's spot.

The house seemed more crowded than the last time I had come to a coven meeting. And younger. Were they from other covens in Sacramento? Everyone looked exhausted and battered, covered with scrapes and bruises.

I found a spot along the wall to lean on while Charlie made her rounds to make sure everyone was okay. The thud of the screen door caught my attention, and I was shocked to see my mom and sister follow Mario through the front door.

"What are you doing here?" I asked as I reached them. Stella glanced everywhere, as if trying to take everything in. There was an excited gleam in her eyes.

"Last night was an eye opener for me," momma said. "That there are real monsters lurking in my city is unforgettable and unacceptable. I need to know that there will be precautions in place to keep last night's events from happening again."

"That's exactly what we will discuss," Betty said with a kind smile as she placed a comforting hand on my mom's shoulder. It was weird seeing such a gentle demeanor after watching this woman stake a vampire to death only hours earlier. "I'm glad you were able to make it. Please take a seat while we get the meeting started."

Charlie had found some folding chairs and set them out for the extra guests. She led my mom and Stella to them and then came and stood next to me. She stood close enough that our arms brushed against each other, bringing me a comfort I didn't realize I needed at that moment. Just having her close by lifted a weight off my shoulders.

Mario sat next to my mom and sister, turning the folding chair around so he could rest his arms on the back.

Betty opened the meeting with a kind of prayer to their goddess. I didn't know the words, so I just watched the room, or more specifically my mom. Witchcraft and magic were against what she had been taught by my grandmother so I was curious how she would react. She sat stiff in her chair but otherwise did nothing. Not that I thought she would stand up and condemn the room for blasphemy, but I was relieved she kept quiet.

After the prayer, Betty stood. "Thank you all for coming. I know you are exhausted and probably sore from last night's battle with the undead but we need to discuss how to keep our city safe from these vampires going forward."

She paused, clearing her throat before continuing. "Last night was difficult, to say the least. But the show of dedication and determination I saw from all of you will forever encourage me to persevere in my darkest moments. I am awed by your strengths." Her gaze drifted to the empty chair in the corner. Her eyes glistened. "We lost one of our most devoted coven members last night. Esther might have been one of our daintiest witches, but she was fierce. She was one of my closest friends from childhood and she will live forever in my heart."

Betty glanced to the ceiling, blinking her eyes rapidly to keep the waterworks from running amok. I swiped away a runaway tear before it could trail down my cheek. Sounds of sniffles came from every corner and tissue boxes passed around the room. Even my mom dabbed the corner of her eyes.

Betty drew in a deep breath and continued. "We will have a proper memorial for Esther and if you would like to help out, see Gloria after the meeting. She will be coordinating the arrangements and putting together a care package of sorts or meal train for Esther's Douglas. He is a priority for our coven, and we will make sure he gets through this difficult time."

I appreciated that even though Douglas wasn't in the coven, they were rallying around him as one of their own. It reminded me of momma's congregation and how they would flock around the family of a lost member at their time of need. In some respects, their beliefs weren't so different. They were each different forms of family and seeing my mom here made me realize how much I appreciated my own.

"Last night's events might have been the first, but it won't be the last unless we make some changes," Betty's voice cut through the sorrow that had settled in the room. "I have invited members of the Davis and Bay Area covens to help us come up with a game plan to protect us all. We can share strategies to not only improve our communities, but ourselves as well. For example, our coven has been attending special Senior Ballet classes at Charlie's studio to keep our strength and agility in top form for situations like last night. Working together is the only way to prevent another uprising of this magnitude."

A vampire uprising. My thoughts drifted to Jackie and the shock of seeing her as a vampire soured my stomach. When was she attacked and transformed into a bloodsucker? What do I do about her now? Should we have a funeral for her if she technically still walking around? Was she really dead? Or undead. I'd have to talk to Charlie later to figure out what to do. What would Mario think?

For the rest of the afternoon, a strategy was created. Each coven had a part to play to keep the region vampire-free. Even I had a part to play, or at least my pesto dish did. That was about as involved as I wanted to be at the moment.

"Are you sure you don't want to join our Singing River Coven?" Charlie asked me away from anyone else. I could see the excitement glistening in her eyes at the thought of being coven sisters as well as lovers, but that was something I wasn't ready for.

I didn't want to kill her hope though. "Maybe someday," I compromised.

Stella, on the other hand... "I would love to learn more about my magical heritage," she told Betty after the meeting had officially adjourned. "Finding out that my great-grandmother was a witch has been mind-boggling. I would love to learn more and be a part of something that was important to her. And having a little grown-up time to myself will be a great bonus."

"We would love to have you with us," Betty said, a smile on her worn face. Even after delegating tasks among the different covens, the weight of the world still shown on her face through every wrinkle and gray hair.

Charlie stepped up next to Betty. "I've been thinking that maybe I could start hosting the coven meetings again. Like my grandmother did. I have a lot more room to accommodate everyone and..." She swallowed. "After everything that has happened, I'm ready to step up and do this for my coven."

Betty smiled, her eyes shining with unshed tears and pulled Charlie into a hug. "That would be lovely, dear. Your grandmother would be so proud of the witch you have become." After a few moments, Betty pulled away, her hands now on Charlie's shoulders. "Why don't you host the All Hallow's Eve gathering with all the covens?"

"I would love to."

I helped Charlie clean up as people began leaving, folding up the metal chairs and putting Betty's living room back to normal. A group had formed around Gloria to help with the memorial arrangements. Another pocket of witches was making plans to meet and get to know each other better.

"Thank you," Charlie whispered in my ear as she stepped up behind me while I put the last chair on the stack. Her breath sent a delicious tingle down my spine. I had to fight the urge to spin around and crush my mouth to hers, to taste the flavor of her that I had so quickly become addicted to.

Instead, I turned and smiled. It was easy, really. The sight of her face brought me so much joy that I couldn't help myself. Unable to keep from touching her, I pushed a strand of hair off her cheek, letting my fingertips graze her skin. "You know I would do anything for you, don't you?"

Her eyes lit up with her smile, nearly suffocating me with the affection I'd developed for this amazing woman. How did I get so lucky? At that moment, the fact that we were not alone couldn't stop me from pulling her closer and capturing her lips with mine. Nothing too scandalous but just enough to ease my craving.

"Ahem."

I opened my eyes to see who was trying to get our attention and immediately stepped back when my mother's eyes stared at me. "Hi, Mom." I was still wrapping my brain around the fact that not only was my mom at the coven meeting, but she had shown up last night to help fight against vampires. The woman was full of surprises.

My mom glanced at Charlie and back to me. When I didn't say anything, she held her hand out. "Since my daughter won't introduce us... My name is Sofia."

Charlie shook her hand. "I'm Charlie. It's so nice to meet you. Now I can see where Lola gets her gorgeous eyes."

My mom's shoulders relaxed as she smiled at Charlie's flattery. "You must be Lola's new girlfriend. It's nice to finally meet someone she's dating." She narrowed her eyes at me, only half serious as the corner of her mouth tipped up.

"Mom," I said as a warning. I didn't want to have a conversation about my dating life here, in front of Charlie.

Charlie glanced at me, as if asking permission to confirm my mother's assumption. The idea that this amazing, beautiful, badass woman was my girlfriend thrilled me to my toes. I wrapped my arm around her waist and squeezed. "Yes," she said with a sense of relief in her tone. "I am."

My mother glanced around the room, at the few people that were still hanging out and chatting. "You seem like good people. And if you make my daughter happy, then I am happy for you both. Maybe you can get her to come to dinner this Sunday."

Charlie laughed, the most wonderful sound to grace my ears in a long time. "I will do my best. I'm looking forward to getting to know her family."

My mom smiled, patted Charlie's cheek before pinching mine, and then headed out with Stella. I placed my hands on Charlie's hips as I gazed into her eyes. "You're going to regret saying that."

"Saying what?"

"That we'd come over for dinner. My family is crazy. And when we are all together, it's mayhem."

She smiled. "It sounds pretty perfect to me."

We leaned our foreheads together and just stood there, soaking up that perfect moment, not wanting it to end.

Epilogue

R*eturn of the King* played on Charlie's living room TV as I reclined on the couch and Charlie rested curled up next to me. It was a wonderfully lazy afternoon. Mario and Britney sat on the loveseat beside us, while Sammy scampered happily across the carpet by our feet, tailed closely by an energetic young terrier we'd rescued just a few weeks prior and named Frodo. We'd been able to have a lot more lazy afternoons lately, now that we were done saving the city.

A lazy afternoon felt even more warranted, after the wild rush of travelling to Robbie Day's studio in New York the week prior. Laurie had been understanding of my "family emergency," and she even helped half the restaurant staff come with me to New York. I cooked my butt off, and got to face off with Robbie Day with Momma's Lasagna. I couldn't wait until everyone could watch me beat him when the show aired.

Of course, this afternoon wouldn't stay lazy for long, given Momma was expecting us for dinner in an hour. And given we hadn't even gotten to the first fade-to-black false ending of this movie...We'd be cutting it close. That was okay though. After standing my ground against a bloodthirsty vampire, I could handle my irate mom.

Charlie, on the other hand...

"Are you sure you don't mind coming to dinner?" I asked quietly, under the tense music of all the people of Middle Earth coming together to defeat the enemy. "It's not too... hectic?"

Charlie twisted her head up to look at me, the smirk on her face and raised eyebrow looking eerily familiar. "Lola, it's not nearly as hectic as you think it is. Besides, I love all the noise and commotion."

I smiled, refocusing on the movie, feeling the swell in my heart of the uncertainty the characters felt, their hoping beyond hope it would all be okay – even when I already knew that it would be.

"I wouldn't miss dinner for the world," Charlie finally added, the confidence in her tone seeping relief into me.

"Speaking of not missing it," Mario said, "We have a few errands to run before dinner, so we better get going."

Britney agreed and stood, and I looked at them agape.

"And miss the end of the movie?" I cried.

"We've seen it a dozen times!" Mario tried, and I shot him a look that said, *how dare you.*

"See you both there!" Charlie's chipper voice rang out, and I rolled my eyes.

"Fine, just don't get attacked by vampires."

"Of course not," Mario said. "Now werewolves on the other hand..."

"Mario!" I screeched, Charlie laughing beside me. Sometimes I didn't know how I could stand him. The rest of the time, I didn't know how I could possibly live without him.

"No, no werewolves, and no vampires," Mario assured us. "Though if you want to tag along to be our bodyguard, I wouldn't say no."

I shook my head. "And miss the end of this movie? Not a chance. At any rate, Charlie's my ride."

CHARLIE BUMPED HER shoulder against Lola's and grinned at her, repeating one of Lola's favorite sayings, "Yeah, ride or die."

Mario laughed and saluted both of them. He slung his arm over Britney's shoulder, then the two of them left, heads close, whispering together, and Charlie heard Britney laugh as the door swung closed behind them.

Charlie started to turn back to the movie, but her phone pinged with an incoming text from Nathan.

N: Got to San Fran yesterday. Tryouts today. Cross your fingers...

C: Don't need to – you'll be great!

N: Victoria is here too. ◈

C: You knew she would be. Just ignore her.

N: Plenty of guys here – I won't be stuck lifting her all the time.

C: Perfect welcome to San Francisco. ◈

N: Gotta go – See you soon!!

Charlie turned back to the movie just in time to hear Frodo say, "I'm glad you're here with me. Here at the end of all things, Sam."

Charlie's stomach clenched. She remembered when she'd said that to Sammy, back when she'd thought Lola was walking out of her life, forever. When Charlie thought she didn't have the right to run after her and beg her to stay. Not after she'd already put Lola in so much danger.

She looked at the woman leaning comfortably against the couch by her side and felt a smile bloom from inside her chest and spread across her lips. So much had changed since that day, all for the better. She was no longer alone and lonely in the world. She had her coven back, she had Lola, and she was rapidly becoming part of Lola's large, exuberant family. She had everything in her life that she'd ever dreamed of.

She turned her body so she was facing Lola and said softly, "I'm so very glad you're here with me at the end of all things." Then held her breath, not sure Lola would understand how she meant that comment.

Lola turned to face her, their knees bumping together, and gave her the crooked smile Charlie loved so much. "Yeah, I love you too, babe."

Charlie felt her heart swell. How did her life get so beautifully full? "You shouldn't smile at me like that. We'll be late for dinner."

Lola reached over and ran her hand down Charlie's cheek. "Hell *yeah*, we are... Very, very late."

And somehow the two of them were flat on the couch, Lola's mouth on Charlie's, blocking out the movie and everything else.

And they were, in fact, very, very late to dinner.

About the Authors

KAT BLAKELY – Kat Blakely is a lover of coffee, cats, chocolate, and compelling fiction. She's been writing most of her life, but got serious about it in 2011. She writes romantic paranormal/urban fantasy, involving secrets, prophecies, and quests; mingled with adventure, mysteries, and suspense; searching for found family and true friends; sprinkled with darkness, danger, humor, and a cat or two.

Find her: Bluesky at kat-tales777.bsky.social, Instagram at karen.kat_tales, Threads at karen.kat_tales, and Facebook at K D Blakely. You can also visit her website at www.kat-tales.net.

R.A. GATES – R. A. is a single, working mom living in Sacramento, CA. But you can call her Ruth. She enjoys writing what she loves reading most which is young adult, urban fantasy. She loves writing about strong characters that may not realize just how strong they actually are. Humor is also part of her writing because she can't help it. She never matured past sixteen.

Go to Ruth's website, ragates.wordpress.com to find out more about me and what I'm currently writing.

KELLY HAWORTH - Kelly's day job may be in business, but at heart they are a writer. Kelly has been writing science fiction and fantasy since they were twelve. They love including characters and themes across the LGBTQ spectrum in their work, as we all deserve to see ourselves in the characters we read. Kelly lives in Sacramento, California with their husband, two kids, and four birds. Find Kelly on Instagram and Threads at @kells_creates or bluesky at @evensofaraway.

CHERYL MAHONEY - Cheryl Mahoney lives in California and dreams of other worlds. She is the author of the Guardian of the Opera trilogy, exploring the Phantom of the Opera story from a new perspective. She is currently writing The Thorns Saga, a romantic fantasy and court intrigue series about after Sleeping Beauty comes home. She also wrote the Beyond the Tales quartet, retelling familiar fairy tales, but subverting expectations with new twists to the tales.

Cheryl loves exploring new worlds in the past, the future or fairyland, and builds her stories around characters finding their way through those worlds—especially characters overlooked or underestimated by the people around them. She has been blogging since 2010 at Tales of the Marvelous (http://marveloustales.com), and has been a member of Stonehenge Writers since 2012.

About the Story

For over a decade, we've carved time out of our busy lives to have a yearly writer's retreat weekend. Some years had seven authors up in the Sierras, at a house on a hill that you only reached after a lengthy, windy road. Other years had only three authors in person with a 4th calling in, at a house less than ten minutes from where some of us lived. Our writers' retreats have always been a needed escape from reality, and a delightful weekend of writing exercises, movies, and home-cooked food.

In 2019, the four of us – Cheryl, Kat, Kelly, and Ruth – stayed at a beautiful house in the foothills that had the best pool we'd ever had the pleasure to use (complete with water slide and cave). But we resisted the temptation to spend the whole weekend in the pool, and one of our days featured a lengthy character-building exercise. We imagined up a personality and backstory for a woman named Lola, and within an hour she had her career as a chef, her skilled athleticism with parkour, and a strong love of big family gatherings and even bigger pots of food on the stove. We decided she was stubborn, compassionate, and had a secret love of period dramas and pork rinds.

We loved Lola so much during that brainstorming session we began to dream up a girl for her to fall in love with. Charlie was a skilled ballerina from the beginning, with a tragic backstory having lost her parents and then her grandparents. But she had her dog to keep her company, and... what's this? She's a witch in a coven? Suddenly, everything we had imagined for these characters turned on its head – there were secret witches fighting secret vampires, and Charlie was part of the coven fighting them? How could Lola tie into this?

Why, with a life-saving pesto recipe, of course.

We had almost the entire outline of *Pesto and Potions* dreamed up by the end of that first day. We decided we'd write the novel round-robin style, with Ruth and Kelly writing Lola's sections, and Kat and Cheryl writing Charlie's sections. We returned home after that weekend ready to begin.

But that was the easy part. What we didn't anticipate was how four authors writing this novel together would take us many years, including one pandemic, one baby, one heart attack, countless writing sessions at local restaurants and each other's houses, entire days of each year's retreats devoted to making our plot and characters stronger, drawing maps of the battle at the end, and scouring the internet for the perfect pair of clasped hands for the cover.

It's been an incredible ride, and we're so happy that we made it out the other side and are able to share this special story with all of you.

Acknowledgements

A huge thank you to our writer's group, Stonehenge. You all have helped us become the writers we are today, and we absolutely deserved getting our butts handed to us when you reviewed the first draft of our blurb.

And thank you to our beta readers: A.Y. Caluen, Mason, and Gillian. You all helped us make this story stronger and more engaging.

Finally, thank you to our family and friends for your support and encouragement while we worked on this seemingly never-ending project.

Also By These Authors

Works Featuring All Four Authors
Plot Twist, or Into the Pages (A Stonehenge Circle Writers Anthology)
The Servants and the Beast
After the Sparkles Settled

Kat Blakely:
Under K D Blakely
Secrets in the Dark
Secrets in the Deep
Secrets in the Dawn
Secrets in Disguise
Secrets End
Under Karen Blakely
Audrey Murphy
Under Kat Blakely *(Coming Fall/Winter of 2025)*
Once Bitten, Twice Shy
Rising from the Ashes
Very Nearly Unbearable

R. A. Gates:
Pucker Up
The Tenth Life of Mr. Whiskers
Fragments of Darkness
A Small Medium at Large

Kelly Haworth:
Y Negative
Gotta Catch Her

Cheryl Mahoney:

The Thorns Saga
The Princess Behind Thorns
The Princess Beyond the Thorns
The Lady Between Thorns (*Coming Soon*)
The Guardian of the Opera Trilogy
Nocturne
Accompaniment
Dawn Melody
Beyond the Tales Series
The Wanderers
The Storyteller and Her Sisters
The People the Fairies Forget
The Lioness and the Spellspinners